I0640345

This book is a work of fiction. All characters, names, locations, and events portrayed in this book are fictional or used in an imaginary manner to entertain. Any resemblance to real people, situations, or incidents is purely coincidental.



ISBN: 978-0-9996182-0-2 (Paperback)
ISBN: 978-0-9996182-1-9 (eBook)

Cover Design by Delaney-Designs. All Rights Reserved.
Cover photograph by Jill Wellington from pixabay.com

# Riches of a Lifetime

Enosh Sunny Lazarus

That, which is lived, is lost. That, which is yet to be lived, is a dream. But to regret the loss of yesterday or to shape the dreams of tomorrow, the present is usually diminished. The world rushes down a road that, with all its endless farrago, couldn't deliver them to their purpose. And that's as certain as the fact that the world is round and the road being traveled a loop, which meets no end. Our wisdom lies in our failures and our success begets arrogance. But in our pride and defeat, if there is a truth that's kept us alive, it is the truth of love. A life deprived of love is like an ocean deprived of waters. Both are barren and worthless without that which completes them. Just like water gives life, so does love. Water sustains life, love does it even better.

The world accelerates rapidly toward its aim, but somewhere in that hustle, life seems to be slipping away. In the market of time, life is traded for things in haste. It was never supposed to be a competition, it was never meant to be harsh. In all its simplicity, life was supposed to be lived. But in the rush of defeating the rest, we've rushed to rest in defeat. In the race of getting ahead, we've forgotten what was left behind.

Whenever there's a sound, emptiness echoes. But the lonesome quiet of a heart beating in solitude is incessant. The emptiness needs to be filled, filled with laughter, and loneliness with memories and people. To make a paradise out of desolation, seeds need to be sown. To grow a garden, the *greens must be watered. To relish a restful shadow, a tree with many branches needs to be rooted.*

*The inescapable reality of suffering will continue to haunt us even to our graves. We are all given our fair shares of hardships, but counting your own as the greatest of them is ignorance, and treating people unfairly out of such ignorance is evil. Our existence has a deeper meaning than self-indulgence and personal longings. Perhaps, to forsake the shadow of need and discover the light of giving. Love doesn't have to be confined, it is meant to be pervasive. It is in living that we remember our past, but in love that we shall build tomorrow.*

*Love one another, love all there is. A greater purpose awaits new souls.*

Jeff Saunderhurst, drowned in contemplation, rested a manuscript down before him, a conclusion of which he had indited some nights ago. He stretched recumbent on the couch, gazing at the sheaf of unkempt pages on the table. That prolonged stare stirred within him the will to tackle some other task.

He rose from the couch, goaded by an engaging thought that had just invaded his mind, and approached a small desk at the corner of the room and unfolded a writing pad. Hurriedly taking a seat on the chair kept at an arm's length away, he attempted composing a letter with keen enthusiasm.

But the spirit swiftly ebbed from his soul as more pressing realities took shape in his reasoning and he fell back into the chair tapping the thick ivory paper with the back of his pen, leaving slight but noticeable indentations on the formerly smooth surface. The clicking sound of a wall clock was a close semblance to hammer strokes in such profound silence and it trickled past eleven thirty, gradually leaving ages behind.

It was approximately two hours later when Jeff took a resounding sigh still hunched over the desk. His creased forehead deepened with earnestness for the content he was about to bleed into the letter. His dark, cryptic eyes squinted to garner the appropriate words. His chiseled face, mysteriously handsome in a way that conveyed equanimity and innocence yet strength and tenacity, expressed countless emotions. And a lean structure that impatiently waited the completion of the letter, displaying signs of restiveness with shaking of the feet or tapping the floor, or at times, cracking of the joints and rubbing of the hands. But the latter was an effect of the weather outside, which was quite unavoidable as the desk was placed near an open window and it was an early December afternoon.

Jeff resolved to end this weary endeavor and abandoned the thought of writing a letter altogether by tossing the pad and the pen back into the drawer. But suddenly his eyes were riveted by a diary that rested in a deep, forgotten crevice.

He rescued it from the disregard of time and opened it wide before himself, remembering. The last entry in the journal dated August 18th, 1999, but it had no memory scrawled under it. The page was untouched and so were the rest beyond as he flipped through the treasured possession of a nebulous past. It dimmed his eyes and he drifted into contemplation again which, after a while, somehow imbued in him some confidence and certainty that impelled him to pour a little more travail into his previously forsaken attempt and recover the writing pad for a final effort.

A salutation was swiftly penned followed by a beginning that was limited to health inquiries, but just coming past the third line, his right hand ceased gliding across the page. He was yet again at a loss for words.

Sinking back into his chair, he glanced out the window and his eyes met the street five floors below. A frigid, overcast day it was, but still not imposing enough to dull or dampen the spirits of an exuberant family that emerged from the corner of the block. Their two children, probably four and seven, Jeff hadn't had much practice as surmising kids' ages, pranced forward joyously and stood transfixed by the grandeur of a storefront, filling their sight with the most fantastic images they'd beheld this whole year. An abundance of toys, glistening and sparkling like a treasure, befitting a royal collection of the two desirous souls watching in arrant awe, separated merely by a glass wall which was yet an obstacle to reckon, thick enough to part them from the riches of a lifetime. But little did they know that a lifetime is a long span to be content with one such treasure.

They stood rubbing their noses against the glass and breathing vapor on it, having the merriest of all Christmases ever. The parents maintained their distance from the toy-store display, monitoring a greater obstacle commonly known as a budget, as they furtively spied the price tags dangling from the worthless, plastic miniatures. But all done with an array of smiles and gaiety, as it was in their hearts that they rejoiced and celebrated the intimacy of their family in this festive season and not their eyes that dealt with the realities of living.

Jeff smiled at this pleasing presentation of love and proximity of relations, arose from his chair, shaking off some somnolence that had crept into him, and headed to the kitchen to pour himself a drink of water, also some crackers to go with it.

Just about to leave with the eatables, the kitchen window suddenly loomed before him bringing an altogether different depiction of life to his sight.

A hazy view of the main avenue until it faded in a wafting thermal, connecting numerous silver facades of commercial structures through myriad bus routes and possibly a subway caved underground. The stare persisted as a wave of undulating heads, moving like streams from all ends of the city and amalgamating into one, panicked Jeff in a way. A headlong rush of a multitude. An absolute picture of compromised survival. Crowds and crowds of pedestrians skittering across crammed walkways, returning from lunch, coffee breaks, unsuccessful afternoon meetings. Busses, cabs, cars, a deathly overload of vehicles up and down the street, jammed to congestion. Bumper to bumper traffic with an inch wide space intervening between a ride back home and a call to 911 reporting an accident. Horns, blatant and vehement, screams and shouts equally boisterous. Heat steaming upward from all that commotion even in thirty-degree temperature and above that, a cloud of smoke and suffocation stifling earth.

Jeff returned to his desk and began his letter anew. Surprisingly, without a single distraction and an unmoving slouched posture for the next forty-five minutes. He finished it right till the end defeating the procrastination that had hindered him for days now. Triumphant, he shifted back on the chair and reviewed the letter with satisfaction. An enigmatic satisfaction that comprised contentment as well as uncertainty. A decisive nod followed and the letter was folded and placed in an envelope, which was then sealed and prepared for mailing.

He glimpsed out the window again, the gleeful family had departed. The street was empty again, except for a faint rumbling of the city sounds in the vicinity.

Early December days were naturally short in duration and were veiled by twilight as early as five. It was well after the typical New York City rush hour that Jeff decided to leave the convenience of home to seek a mailbox, which he could avail to place his letter in hopes of having the hands that raised him to touch the folds of his sentiments a few days later.

Coming out of a temporary winter vestibule erected at the entrance of his apartment building, Jeff added himself to the bobbing horde that had noticeably dwindled at this hour in failing daylight. Snow had just begun to waft as crystalline flakes floated in the air and a few tardily came to rest upon his forehead.

Jeff looked up at the gray, darkening skies and beamed gladly, his love for icy precipitation was evident. He stood motionless in the midst of the moving crowd taking a long moment to relish his affinity for snow. Then upon an abrupt awakening, he observed his surroundings with a fleeting visual scan. Nothing much had changed around or in life in the recent moments, but somehow an inexplicable bliss was triggered within him.

His sight swept all that flooded his view on the street upon which he stood, and he discovered nothing but people trapped in the banality of life. But he found his liberty and respite in the lights and trinkets that hung around every storefront and facade. He found happiness in the Christmas trees and the ornaments that embellished them and the flickering flashes of green and red taped to apartment windows. In those huge garlands that were suspended in successions, from one end of the street to the other, and the lighted star that adorned the center of each, swaying against the wind. He even derived joy out of those strands of clear lights that were displaced by gusts and now dangled precariously from that one strong clasp that prevented their demise. And all this materialized in companionship of faint but mellifluous sounds of Christmas carols seeping through open crevices of storefronts. The revelry of the forthcoming millennium was in full bloom and the year 2000 was at hand.

As he satiated himself in this visual delight, Jeff realized he had stood in the middle of the sidewalk for quite a while now and before the encompassing, pedestrian eyes could elevate to intrusion and suspicion, he took gradual steps to his destination, leaving the moment behind but taking its fulfilling memory along.

Jeff plodded further and found what he sought right at the end of the block. The mailbox squealed as its lip was parted and the letter was deposited inside. He stayed and meditated on his decision for a while, whether he was right or wrong, a span of half-a-day wasn't enough to determine that. With that uncertainty to accompany him, he started tracing his steps back to the comforts of his home.

Jeff found the wall clock ticking close to seven as he entered his apartment. He relieved himself of his keys at the entrance console table and hung his coat on the rack, continuing to the hall.

His home was a modest setting for a living. Though the place was purchased for a hefty amount that would have rattled a commoner's wallet to its creases, but Jeff refrained from any pretentious display of complacency. His style of existence was subtle and subdued. There was an outlandish despondency in this enclosure. The air inside was heavy and hushed and somehow Jeff did not find this peculiarity uninhabitable. He was living alone for a while now as it had become ordinary for him to care for himself and was quite customary for a man his age to do so. But sometimes such autonomy also accounts for loneliness whether it is acknowledged or not. Hence, conceding that fact, it was safe to admit that he wasn't just alone but lonely as well.

It took him a good half an hour to finish preparing his supper and when he had filled his plate, he headed off into another one of the rooms adjacent to the living.

His ingress was greeted by a warm smile that creased a seasoned face of an elderly. His grandfather looked back at him as he came close to the bed and sat down on a chair. Absorbing the tranquility that reflected from that face, it frequently rendered courage and fortitude to his weakened will. Due to a condition, his grandfather did not speak much, in fact, he didn't converse at all. All Jeff was left with were some of his grandfather's ancient words that he remembered and a trace of his voice that still lingered in his senses. There had been a plenitude of instances, times that had tested Jeff's courage and in such situations, he had always resorted to his grandfather's wisdom. As Jeff's recollection deepened, he found his strength in a discourse he once conducted with his grandfather and repeated the latter part of it in his mind.

*'The tasks of this world are complicated. From the most insignificant jobs to the most influential works. Your family is always going to be proud*

*of you, even if you accomplish the most little of things. From your first test grade to your graduation, from your sweet sixteen to your marriage and children. Your parents, your grandparents would never judge you. But what makes a person stand out from the rest? The moment when the works you have done proclaim to the world of your worth. Not the ones you love or the ones who love you, but the tasks you have performed. When your work declares unto the world that this is how I'm done, this is how I'm achieved, that will make you the proudest. And that worth goes a very long way.'*

Jeff closed his eyes with redolent satisfaction sweeping his visage. He opened them again and reciprocated his grandfather's smile, even when it came through the fragile glass of a photo frame that graced the bedside table. And the words that had held Jeff's composure for so long were out a personal diary that had interminably kept him company during long, trying nights of his life. Jeff opened the drawer of his bedside table and retrieved a diary, placing it before him on the bed. It was an old journal, withered, battered, yellowing, but precious. He was about to meet with his grandfather once more tonight, though, he had been dead for a very long time.

*I saw my grandson this blessed morning. I couldn't hold him for very long as he was quite heavy for a newborn, but I couldn't thank God enough for this blessing.*

As the first page of the diary was turned and the writings navigated, it was evidence enough for Jeff to realize that the beginning of his life was the origin of this journal as well. Jeff was comfortably nestled in his bed as he read through the scribbled content.

*All I wanted to do before leaving this good earth was to see his face. Now I have.*

Many more memories were scrawled in the pages that followed with photographs taped next to them, some black and white, some sepia-toned.

*My grandson took his first step today. As I sat on the porch this afternoon, he ran over to me from the stairs to my chair at the far end. It was a long walk to begin with, but wonderful to watch.*

Jeff treasured these jotted instances of his childhood that still invoked a smile across his face. He gazed at an old, deep color toned photograph that pictured a seven-year-old boy with a man who seemed to be in his early seventies. The boy was undeniably the former and shorter version of Jeff, while the elderly man was his grandfather, Anthony Saunderhurst, who bore the little mischief on his lap. There was a close resemblance between them both with their strong jawlines and creases across the forehead that had deepened on Anthony's face due to age, but were beginning to follow suit on Jeff's.

1972 was the year when a seven-year-old had assumed an adult responsibility, to plan his grandpa's seventy-first birthday with a trip to the carnival where this picture was taken and myriad rides were relished by one of the two. It was followed by a cheeseburger meal, which Jeff adored, with a side of fries and a shake at the diner and an ice-cream from the parlor at the end of the day for the journey home. Though, Anthony had very little enjoyment in the rides at the carnival, or the cheeseburger and ice cream due to his frail dental health, the felicity of spending a day with his grandson, defraying the cost of his every little want and watching him revel in these trivial pleasures was a significant triumph for the old man.

It was a time of peace and quiet when altruism was greatly appreciated and discourtesy instantly noted and remembered. The elderly regarded their tranquility as most vital and much of their excitement in life was related to their family's furtherance and the upbringing of their grandchildren. For the immature young who planned their grandparents' birthdays to their own likings, it was an age when their miseries were confined to limited school holidays that were only two months long, and anxieties were aimed at play, food, and clothes. Anything beyond that was beyond them.

Anthony was one of such elderly who enjoyed his lifestyle watching his four grandchildren develop in health as well as maturity as years passed. Though, Jeff knew very little about his grandpa's past, due to a dearth of time he had with him and lack of gravity in Jeff's character for that duration when he wouldn't even imagine in a dream to have discussed their family's history, he knew that Anthony had been a professor of English Literature for forty years, half of which time he spent itinerant teaching in many universities abroad. In the latter part of those years, he had been unemployed dealing with the aftermath of the Second World War which forced him to relocate to the United States in mid 1950s after the passing of his wife.

Martin Saunderhurst, his son, was in his early thirties and married to Lena when they both accompanied Anthony into the country with hopes of The American Dream effusive in their veins. Martin worked as an electrical engineer in a factory back home that closed due to the war and never opened since. The war induced unfathomed asperities on the family and after almost a decade of nomadic travel from city to city in central Europe in search of a decent living and employment, their haggard souls were propelled to migrate overseas.

The diary said very little about their experiences in USA, but it did have traces scattered throughout of how after three years of rigorous living in Boston they had found their refuge in a humble town in New York State, near the northern end of Hudson River, making a scarce but peaceful living. A friend who acquainted Anthony in Boston had helped them settle in their new home but died soon after leaving the Saunderhursts friendless and isolated in the developing surroundings.

The town back then was just as sparse and modest as a village and constructing a home in these areas was a personal toil as opposed to a contractual job. But the lands were sold for a bargain and Jeff's grandfather had invested all of his life savings to secure that piece of land so his future generations could never worry about a sheltering home. He had also secured a part-time job at a nearby school as a professor of English. But Anthony's work was limited in the States as his retirement swiftly approached and after his dormancy, it was Martin who took the responsibility of the house.

Never giving much prominence to wealth in life, they were content with what they had. Besides, substandard living wasn't an uncommon sight back in the day or rather considered so. The decades of 1960 and 1970 were intrinsically deficient and inferior to those that followed as the wants and earnings to defray the costs of those wants increased substantially in the subsequent years. The Saunderhurst home was comparable to any other in that insignificant town, but then again, every home does not cultivate aspirations as grand as some.

As Jeff progressed flipping the phases of their joint lives, his recollection flew him back to a bright mid-summer afternoon of 1974. It was the day when something extremely important was instilled into his understanding quite subtly which still hadn't dissolved after all these years; an attribute largely and inherently missing in a majority of people, self-belief.

"I hit that one, did you see grandpa?" Jeff squealed excitedly.

"Yes, yes, I saw it." Anthony lounged on his rocking chair under the comfort of the porch. His diary upon the armrest tucked under his hand, occasionally being availed to inscribe the thoughts springing in his leisured mind.

"I'm not going to miss another one now, ever."

Jeff's endeavor to master the sport of baseball was unwavering. Though, his interest and practice at playing the sport was novel. He continued tossing the ball up in the air and striking it with his bat which rarely swung on target.

It took Jeff a couple of attempts before admitting failure that dulled his face. Anthony noticed this vacillation that inched along and now completely imbued his grandson.

"I'll never be able to do this. I suck." Jeff abandoned his bat and ball, shuffled to the shade under the porch, collapsing at the steps sitting in sheer suffering. Anthony shook his head in disbelief at this exhibition of doubt and defeat.

"Come here, son. Come here closer to me, I did not expect such a grim attitude from my grandson."

Jeff deferentially walked over to his grandfather and folded himself right next to his legs that waved back and forth on the rocking chair.

"Don't you ever say you cannot do it! That glum perspective is for cowards and last I looked around the Saunderhurst house, I did not sight any. There's no one out there, and I mean no one, who's better than you are. What you have, no one does. Just believe in yourself. Whatever you do in life, do it with passion, with all your heart and you'll never be defeated. There's always a new dawn waiting and there's always one more game yet to be played."

"You think I can hit the ball?" Jeff questioned innocently, brows converged, mouth parted, but yet failing to grasp the philosophy showered upon him.

Anthony laughed, "I know you can hit the ball. Now, go and do what you have to and don't enter that home unless you're good at it. One day you'll remember me for telling you this."

Jeff kissed his grandpa's hand and in an explosion of exuberance, jumped up to his feet. "What do you keep writing in this, grandpa?"

"Things, things that might interest you one day."

"About baseball?"

"No," Anthony smiled. "It is something bit more valuable than that, or so I think."

"Can I see it?" Jeff stepped forward to take a quick glimpse.

"When time comes, you will." Anthony precluded the intrusion.

Jeff shrugged and rushed off with revived spirit to challenge his skills anew with bat and ball.

Such encouragements from his grandpa had sustained Jeff throughout his childhood. As for his father, he had a lot more matured responsibilities that kept him out and away from domestic obligations including a baseball match of his nine-year-old, while his mother had her hands buried deep in household duties taking care of the whole family. It was Jeff's grandfather who appeared to him like an anchor in moments of trouble or dejection. As time progressed, Anthony taught Jeff most of the things about life he needed to know. The rest came from a beautiful friend.

# Chapter Three

✵

A school playground was suddenly awakened from its slumber at the thunderous stampede of a group of nonchalant nine-year-olds, almost instantly after the bell for lunch. The grounds were swiftly swarmed as children, with an arrant disregard for their hunger, clustered around the swings and slides, and teeter-totters and ace flyers. Some of the young souls, too concerned with propriety, silently watched the clamorous horde from the benches afar with their lunch-boxes neatly stationed upon their laps, and in sober etiquette, nibbled on their sandwiches.

"Children, all of you will stay in sight. No wandering, all right?" A young third-grade teacher accompanied the intractable crowd to the school grounds.

The children, so accustomed to hearing that instruction every day of the school week, silently dismissed her with a louder commotion.

"Stay within sight." She repeated herself but knew her words were hardly heeded.

Jeff fidgeted amidst the group of unruly boys waiting his turn at the slides. Finding himself next in queue to impress the bystanders, he hastened up the steps, skimmed down the smooth silver sheet of metal and leapt to a landing. He acknowledged his precision with a nod to his fellow perpetrators and headed off to a massive log at the corner of the playground. He began balancing himself on the cylindrical piece of wood, tip-toeing from one edge to the other.

"You're going to fall, you know?"

As this remark interrupted his grueling maneuver, he glanced back at the origin of the voice. He sighted a girl staring back at him with clear folds of vexation across her face.

She was of similar age, in fact, came from the same classroom, held her lunch-box neatly between her crossed arms and pierced his gaze with her striking green eyes.

"No, I won't." Jeff wasn't going to accede so easily. But then he tripped, almost slipping down the length of the log.

"That's because you won't leave me alone. It's your fault," he countered, imputing it back to her.

She shook her head and settled on the log opening her lunch-box. "What did you get for lunch?"

"I don't know." Jeff continued tipping from one end of the log to the barricade that now sat in the middle with her lunch on her lap. "Would you just move already?"

"You don't want to eat, like always?" She carried herself with certain delicacy and poise, yet it wasn't perceived as pretentious in any way. She pretended to be a pontificating warden to this boy who blundered about her, but at the same time wished for his company.

"I'm not hungry." On the other hand, Jeff took this beautiful guardian for granted.

"Not hungry? You really need to be disciplined, you know that? You're never hungry when it's time to eat, but the minute we step back in the class you'll start making those faces as if you didn't use the powder room this morning. Not to mention the stomach growling that had the entire class staring at you suspiciously yesterday. If you wish to associate yourself with me, you have to stop doing that. I cannot have a smell passer for a friend. Now sit next to me and open your lunch." Her voice was peremptory and it was obeyed soon enough as Jeff perched next to her and began stuffing his jelly sandwich down his throat.

"That isn't even a word." Jeff protested on being labeled the aforementioned title.

"It sure is." She countered him this time.

"No, it isn't."

"Well, when you find a better word suited for a school playground, let me know. And stop forcing that sandwich down your throat, you're going to choke to death."

"It's my lunch. I always eat like that."

"For your information, that isn't called eating," she went incisive this time.

"Then what?"

"You wouldn't like the word I have in mind for it this time." She chuckled and trounced her competition to speechlessness.

End to another day at school resonated against the concrete walls in form of a final bell that sounded off to the relief of a thousand souls. The hallway was diffused with teeming cacophony and amongst the bobbing heads came two familiar ones jostling through other classmates, racing each other, absconding from the heinous institution of education to the exhilarating solitude of freedom.

Jeff led the charge as his green-eyed friend followed close behind and just as they departed the school gates, they were joined by another little rugrat who toiled to keep up with their pace managing her backpack as well as her eyeglasses that were as big as her cute little face.

"Wait for me." She called out from behind, pushing her glasses back up to the nose bridge that had bounced down the length of her nose to the verge.

Her entreaty vaguely impacted Jeff, but it did bring the second position runner to abate her galloping strides. The two girls now joined forces and ran together a couple of paces behind the male. As the two ladies eyed each other, not diminishing their gait even a little, they smiled.

"Hey Erica," the third saluted.

"How was school, Maggie?" The green-eyed custodian asked. "You didn't get into any trouble, did you?"

Their voices cracked as they ran, but the discourse was too important to be left out for later.

"Any trouble with that pudding head who keeps pestering you about your glasses?"

"Nope, he was all by himself today, didn't have much to say. I feel bad for him. We shouldn't have scared him off like that. He fell and broke his glasses. They still aren't fixed."

"Well, that's what you get for making fun of someone and calling them four eyes when you wear glasses yourself."

The trio nimbly but gracefully cut across and careened through a number of pedestrians as their haste was so haphazard yet cautious that wiser adults would glare at them irately, but these three young minds expressed indifference to every angered stare hurtled at them. All three driven with one headlong ambition to get to a destination which was equally and greatly desired.

They turned the corner and found themselves amongst a sea of houses separated by streets and sidewalks. The green-eyed friend parted from the other two and entered the environs of a house that sat silently at the end of the block surrounded by the lush green lawns. Jeff and the four-eyed abettor steered into the second last house on the street and neared a freshly painted porch.

Jeff collected his bicycle from the front-yard and cast aside the backpack like a sack of burden. The green-eyed friend appeared to be conducting a similar drill in the background.

"Hey grandpa, bye grandpa." Jeff and his four-eyed company both uttered in unison.

Anthony, still perched on his rocking chair at the far end of the porch, smiled and shook his head after receiving a kiss from both.

Jeff hurried down the sidewalk on his bicycle and his friend joined him from one house down. The third one completed the squad on a tricycle.

"Hey wait for me." The last repeated her usual plea.

All three flew down the street and off to another world of adventure.

Their travel was not an extended one as they rode swiftly across the end of the town and sighted a beam bridge approaching fast. The construction of the bridge was not very young, in fact quite frail with age and deterioration, but as scarce of traverse it saw from day to day, it was adequate for its purpose. The bridge was forbidden to trespassers as a crooked board registered dangling by a post that was concealed behind overgrown bushes, but obeying the warning was an adult obligation and an insult to the kid world of which these three intruders were the monarchs.

All, as part of their mischief, could be overlooked but for one little detail that might prove to be perilous if not addressed. The bridge was unrailed. The metal curbs had never been installed on either end of the bridge to make passing of oversized trucks into the forest, that loomed ahead, a possibility. But the stream that coursed under that bridge, which had an unknown origin and went off to the far end of the town, was fast and unfathomed.

Jeff, in his arrant insouciance to the danger that lurked near the edge of the bridge, propelled his bicycle extremely close to the brink deliberately, oblivious to the consequences a small misstep could impose. The two behind him followed suit. The tricycle rasped against the verge but passed onto safer land. The forest now welcomed the three adventurers into its womb of marvel.

The years of Jeff's childhood were comparable to any other kid in that town with some exceptions and dissimilarities. One of the biggest enviable benefits was the friendship he had with green-eyed

Erica Johnson, and his four-eyed younger sister, Maggie Saunderhurst. Maggie was two years younger than him and was the last of the four children in the family. She was sweet and compassionate at heart and believed in forgiveness, a virtue that was probably passed onto her by their mother. She was also a dreamer and one of those dreams was to find her perfect match in whom she would find her future life partner. An endeavor for which she would gather various cutouts of different parts of a masculine face from magazines and newspapers, shuffle them around, and structure a creation of her own from that farrago. She would construct these "faces" in her scrapbook and juxtapose for a thorough and elaborate comparison. As she would go on with her puerile mission to produce her future husband, Jeff and Erica would scamper over a couple of rocks and a length of a log and leap into a pool of crisp waters that collected right under a cascading fall.

"Hey!" Maggie quickly secured her work from splashing water.

It was an unfrequented area of the forest that might have been a discovery of this impish squad, or maybe a forgotten sanctuary of reprieve that was kept a secret by the people from the people, and eventually effaced from all memory. All in all, the place was a hide for these three souls as they would visit this haven for a duration of an hour or more every day after school.

The pool was surrounded by large rocks that were tall enough to barricade further flow of the falls which resulted in the formation of this body of water to gather in the space between the rocks. But every time the pool filled up to the fissures and creases in those rocks, the water seeped through, hence, never filling to the brim. The fall was scarce and short as it emanated from a larger current of water that streamed beyond the woods, but that was an area never mapped by either of the three. Encompassing the ablated rocks was a clearing that gave the trio a nice view of their environment and also some inimitable views of each season.

The springs brought along lushness of greens and fresh falls from melting snow, while the summers would bring warm daylight filtering through the thick cover of tall trees seen far above and beyond as well as warmth to the pool. Autumn was a mess to deal with as the wafting leaves draped earth and formed an arid coverlet over everything. And then the falls froze cold as ice as winters approached, the pool would turn into a rink and falling snow would find its path through dry sticks of trees. At times the clearing would be bright white and it would remain so for days until the sun would awaken. Jeff and his two associates would willingly risk injury by sliding upon the frozen pool just to lick the icicles, that hung from the branches, with the tip of their tongue.

Today was a warm day and everything was just as pleasant as one could wish for. The glade was imbued golden with daylight and coruscated off the pool surface.

"Look at this one!" Maggie had completed assembly of a face and displayed the finished product to her companions.

The water agitated as Erica emerged after spending a minute deep in its basin. She swam over to the rock where Maggie lounged, climbed right next to her and dabbled her feet in the pool.

"How is it?" Maggie questioned, though, not necessarily seeking an honest critique.

"I believe the previous one was much better. This one has a big nose. It's not balanced with the skinny face." Erica reviewed.

"I like it. Look at this Jeff." She held the scrapbook aloft for him to view.

"Go bother someone else, Maggie." Jeff retorted as he emerged from the pool and climbed up a sturdy branch that extended a couple feet above the rocks. He squirmed to the tapering tip of the barky branch and alighted at a vantage point.

"You never look at my pictures," Maggie remonstrated.

"I'll look at them again, and I have something for you-" Erica reached for her backpack and removed a magazine from it. "Here, this is for you."

"Thanks!" Maggie rejoiced.

Erica Johnson was just another girl in school who happened to share Jeff's age and classroom, and coincidentally, shared the same street for a home address as well. She had known Jeff as long as she'd known the world and it wouldn't be an exaggeration if confessed that their worlds revolved around each other. Though, the diurnal functioning of their world spun around the axis of play and school, they were in no rush to outgrow either one anytime soon. Erica had lost her mother to an accident at a very early stage in life. Reared by her father since the tender age of two, she hadn't even remotely sensed the comforting shelter of a mother or what having one actually meant. There were some misty sensations of delicate caresses, soft kisses and dulcet sounds of an unknown lullaby that remained with her as impressions of her mother's affection, but otherwise, her mother's memory in her mind was as incomplete as a sentence trailing off before reaching its most purposeful word. But being raised by a single male parent had instilled in her character some traits that were quite commendable for a girl so young. She had been tutored to survive with stern discipline in matters of demeanor and diction, and to abide by her word no matter the circumstance. A word as little as teaching the pesky boy in Maggie's class a lesson, to as serious as never touching ice-cream again in life after a severe throat infection when she was six. Erica preferred conformity to sobriety while in presence of her father and other elders but permitted herself some amusement in the company of her two closest companions.

Erica's perpetual amity with Jeff accounted for the part of their analogous nature which involved a lot of aimless running around, unwarranted bicycle excursions and a deranged proclivity for playing in precipitation, much against the admonition of Jeff's mother, be it summer rains or winter snowfalls. Apart from these eccentricities which made a mimic out of her, it was Jeff the other times who exhibited compliance with her demands. She wasn't tomboyish or masculine in her style at all, as that was one aspect in which Mr. Johnson had kept her inviolable and well acquainted with genteel panache and lady-like elegance. Out of that regard, she took great care of herself and especially her auburn hair which was her best feature in Maggie's opinion as she would spend hours on weekends tailoring Erica's hair into different setups and then boast about her deft abilities. But varying in that sense of concern, Erica was much attentive and caring toward the needs of others, Jeff being the special one of the few. Undoubtedly, she was a very close friend to Maggie, but the intimacy that transmutes close friendship into best friendship transpired only between her and Jeff. That care was obviously unrequited from Jeff's end as he had many other imperative matters at hand, like climbing a tree, than being appreciative of someone's solicitude.

When Jeff looked down at the two important distaff members of his life who now sat together and worked on Maggie's amusement, he realized he had never given Erica the due credit for her companionship back then. But now as he would think about the times of their proximity, all he could do is ask to relive those moments again to cherish her friendship.

As the sun paralleled to the ends of earth and cast tall, dispiriting shadows all across the lands, thoughts of returning home confronted their minds. The three would gather into their uniforms, which were tidily folded and kept aside in Maggie's bike basket, mount their transport and head back into the peripheries of their hometown. They would face separation yet again, but a reassuring thought of union after some hours of prevalent darkness would dwarf any distressing outlook on the matter.

At home, Jeff's evenings would be spent inside his grandfather's corner enclosure as that was one place most favored by him of all the seven rooms in the house. It might have been due to the fact that most of his childhood was spent there learning or listening to the wise elder and he had become accustomed to that dense, resolute air that filled the room along with an old, resolute soul.

The room was commodious, still lacked furniture. But it could have been Anthony's wish to accommodate only important and needful things to consume the space he had left, which was manifested by a single bed, one cabinet against the wall and a rocking chair to occupy the floor and nothing else. Jeff and Anthony would exchange places often as when Jeff took the bed for his homework, Anthony would keep a keen eye on him from his chair moving to and fro, and if grandpa would experience weariness straining him physically, Jeff would merrily surrender his location for the marvelous swinging chair that he rarely received a chance to relish.

The nights were quite mute in the Saunderhurst home. Martin would return home only after seven putting in extended hours at work almost every day of the week to ensure smooth financial functioning of the family. Upon his arrival, the table would be immediately served with dinner and Lena ascertained there wasn't any delay in his sleep schedule either. Martin was a disciplined man, strove to keep his timings consistent with his routine. The only obstacle that he allowed to manipulate his timetable was work. Family wasn't permitted to tamper with it. But he was never faulted for maintaining his discipline, not even by his wife, as they all knew he travailed for eleven hours a day and returned with strength barely enough for anything but dine and retire to bed. Martin worked a factory job in a local cannery that supplied a few towns in the vicinity. He'd been employed there since the time he accompanied Anthony into this town and considering those years of loyalty and experience he was promoted to site manager. The company was not expansive nor imposing in revenues, consequently, the earnings weren't grand either. The workforce received what was deemed sufficient as paychecks and the higher personnel enjoyed perquisites in addition to their pay, which were rare as well. But the populace of the town did not object to the low wages as they were grateful to be earning one, and it did not take much to get by either.

Martin wasn't the only member of the family employed at the cannery. He had harnessed his influence as the manager to admit his elder son into the labor force and for the past six months, Dave had accompanied his father to work for a complete eight-hour shift at the factory.

Dave Saunderhurst was the second born of the four children and eight years Jeff's senior. He had only recently completed his schooling and was instantly pledged into service, but never objected to such swift thrust into drudgery. He valued reticence over every emotion, a result of which he became quite judicious as well as reliable for the family as time evaporated. He was rarely aroused to emotions but loved everyone dearly. Following his father's footsteps, he was quite a handyman around the house and demonstrated great avidity towards mending things, whether they were damaged articles of furniture or dismantled family relationships. His ambitions were minimal, even throughout the years of adolescence his demands were scant, which made him a true family man. Although, he was far from the age of being referred to as a man, his circumspect character made a man out of him years earlier than the appropriate time.

The gathering at Saunderhurst dining was hushed and ingestion swift as Martin refrained from much talk except for some essential inquiries pertinent to home and family. Their table had remained incomplete for the past year since the oldest of the four left home for college.

Linda Saunderhurst was the family's first born and the expectations attached to her were tremendous. Since the time of her birth, she had seen her elders flock around in extreme guardianship and regard her with extraordinary care. But with such incomparable regard came immense obligations and anticipations. Being a year older than Dave, she was accorded the responsibility of the

Saunderhurst family pride in whichever aspect she could be held accountable. Whether it was being an honors student seven years in a row until graduation, or winning an academic excellence award for topping the boards in the final year and breaking the record for the highest cumulative GPA ever obtained in sixteen states. Whether it was having a personal salutation on a stenciled brass plate that graced the top shelf of a trophy cabinet or landing a scholarship to pursue further education at Brown University. She was the kind of person the townsfolk pointed at and proudly said "that girl hails from our hometown," and rather for those who knew her intimately, would applaud her and pompously promulgate to those around saying "she is a member of our family and was raised in our home." She had been away for more than a year and only visited after intervals of six months or during summer break.

Jeff and Maggie hadn't spent much time with Linda or even Dave as they both had been burdened with adult responsibilities quite early in life. Or at least they didn't gather many memories of their older siblings since they developed their recollection, maybe cradled once or twice back in the day when they were manageable but not much of it. This was mainly out of the considerable divide between the age of the elder duo and the youth of the younger two. But just as Linda and Dave treasured their affection towards each other, Jeff and Maggie equally celebrated their love as well.

Linda's absence was followed by another deduction from the table, but this time the oldest member of the family who now preferred his meals in the comfort of his bed. Lena had expressed extreme caution toward Anthony's wishes since his ailment began about a year ago or perhaps more.

Jeff was oblivious of his grandfather's dwindling health initially when his sickness commenced, but recently intuited his diminishing vitality as Anthony retired to his room and bed more often than usual and that gradual change altered into a permanent ill. There wasn't anything officially or medically wrong with Anthony, the effects of old age were beginning to take a toll on him. But he was a content man, content in the fact that his home was now established and his family could carry on adequately even without him. Content in the fact that he had seen all of his four grandchildren, two of which were almost on the verge of beginning their adult lives while the other two still had a bit more time to reach that stage. But this contentment was limited to him as the whole family was disheartened at the thought of his impending departure. As time passed, Jeff went on living with that melancholy imbedded in his heart, without the requisite liveliness commonly seen in children his age. He simply couldn't imagine this house or his life in his grandfather's absence because he simply hadn't known much of it without him.

# Chapter Four

It was just another ordinary Monday and the three sped to the falls on their bicycles. Jeff, in his recklessness, challenged the threat of riding too close to the edge of the bridge while Erica followed but stayed inward. Maggie was a junior mile behind them both as she came upon the bridge when Jeff and Erica had already crossed.

She dittoed her elder brother's maneuver to demonstrate her fearlessness and careened close to the edge. Her right training wheel slid off the side of the bridge and spun in the air. As Maggie attempted to get that wheel back on solid surface and her focus digressed to the rear of her bike for a glimpse, her front wheel bounced upon a piece of detached wood that was a part of debris strewn on the bridge after an inclement rainstorm that persisted for a few hours last night.

The bike lurched to its left and the left training wheel pushed the weight back while the right wheel dangled precariously in mid-air, failing to generate stability. Maggie slew right off the edge of the bridge and rode straight into the streaming river underneath.

She rigorously held onto the bike handles that prevented her from drowning immediately, but it was imminent. Strong thrusts of the water tossed her around and just as the bike began to sink, she was pulled along.

"Jeff! Help!" She screamed for her life and released her tightening grips around the bike handles. She was flailing and flapping her arms, squalling for attention.

Jeff and Erica heard the distress call and halted right at the end of the bridge. Turning to face the terror of the sight ahead, their hearts skipped a beat observing the peril that was about to claim a life, an invaluable one in their case. Jeff and Erica abandoned their bikes and rushed to the edge contemplating methods of a rescue. Their faces were creased with a frown of helplessness, and their limbs weakened with numbness. But Jeff gathered his strength by thrashing about his arms and reasoning to save his sister from her possible demise.

Fortunately, Maggie had clenched a hold of a boulder that protruded a foot above the stream, but the current was swaying her dangerously close to and against the rock.

Erica skimmed along and stretched out her young arms to help her friend, but her reach was short and apprehension was endless.

"Give me your waist belt," Erica demanded in a loud voice as she had just begun whimpering.

Jeff submissively removed his belt and grasped the idea. Maggie squealed again, but just as she did, her voice faded into the roiling torrent that shoved her against the rock. Her head struck the boulder and an open gash appeared oozing blood.

She went limp and began to drown, her blood vanishing in water and froth. Just as she was completely submerged, an arm wrapped around her shoulders and drew her back above the water. Jeff hauled Maggie with his right arm and held on to the belt with his left from one end as Erica labored at the other and towed twice her weight or strength. Her only ally was her seated posture that kept her from tumbling in.

She strained all the muscles in her body and pulled them closer to safety with every drag and every tug. Jeff reached the bridge and held onto the beams forcing Maggie up into Erica's embrace. Securing Maggie on the bridge, Jeff clambered up the beams panting and exhausted, but swiftly focused his attention on something more crucial.

His deepest fears surfaced as he knelt by the unconscious body of his younger sister who was as pallid as snow. Erica shuddered by his side and began shaking her friend, rummaging for that one sign of life within her. Jeff saw no light in this dark moment and receded away from the body, aghast and despairing.

"We need to take her to the clinic. Jeff..." Erica still held her composure in all this trepidation. "Jeff, she is not dead." She rushed over to him and rocked him out of his daze.

Jeff gazed at her, still perplexed and dreadfully crippled.

"You have to save her, Jeff. Take her now." Erica barked at him and Jeff regained his senses and nodded.

Jeff crouched over the limp body and lifted Maggie into his arms. They both were dripping wet, one breathless and the other lifeless. With nothing more important to him than the survival of what he held tightly against his pounding chest, he ran, ran faster than he'd ever run before. Ran faster than he ever rode. Ran a total of two and a half miles to the center of the town to a lone clinic which was the only medical facility in sixteen miles. With every galloping step, he remembered the past skirmishes or altercations he'd ever encountered with Maggie, be it what side of the room she wanted or a toy Jeff had to relinquish to her obduracy. With every breath he fetched, he remembered her galling habits and fatuous questions that he would now gladly accept as the only conversations in life. With every glimpse he shot down at her, he remembered her tinkling laughter that he might have neglected in the past but couldn't bear to accept them as her last. If that were to be an end to her life, it wasn't just going to be hers, there was one more that would follow her fate tonight.

Upon reaching the destination which he so ravenously sought, Jeff delivered Maggie to the care of some medical professionals. The clinic was run by a doctor who operated five similar offices in the neighboring towns and employed a couple of specialists in each who would visit the facilities on selected days of the week. Today, fortunately, was one of those days. A nurse and a laboratory assistant conveyed her from Jeff's arms to a gurney and engaged in some preliminary check-ups which were quite novel and alarming to him.

He stayed gazing at his sister, shivering in dismay as she was taken into one of the examination rooms ahead and a doctor crossed the hallway entering right after. Erica came close behind Jeff and kept a hand on his shoulder, a reassurance he unreservedly needed. Tears trickled down their eyes and hearts immersed in a sense of foreboding as Jeff slightly twisted to acknowledge the encouragement. But that glimpse back at Erica was disrupted by a view of a diminutive chamber at the end of the entrance hall with its door ajar and a towering wooden cross mounted on the wall inside. The door gently swayed against a draft of wind and incessantly concealed and revealed the sight of the cross. It also sported a tablet nailed in the center that bore an inscription. Jeff focused on the engraving that read, "Let not your hearts be troubled. You believe in God, believe also in me. - John 14:1"

Jeff had never felt the necessity of religion in life ever before, but today he waited, waited for a godly miracle to materialize.

Erica had provided the nurse with the contact number, after exerting her memory, of the house which was one of the few that owned a telephone in the town.

Lena was shaken out of ennui as she received a message from the neighbors informing her of a phone call from the clinic and the recent calamity that had occurred. Within a matter of minutes, Lena and Martin scampered into the facility with fearful anticipation. When Jeff espied his parents approaching, engrossed in terror and emotion, a deep feeling of regret and anxiety flooded his reasoning and he fled. Erica stood in ambivalence whether to accompany her escaping friend or stay and explicate the situation to his parents. She found wisdom in executing the latter.

Some hours had depleted since the event and finally, a doctor approached the parents and broke the news of their daughter's recuperation, briefing them about her present condition and advising them of the precautions that must be taken to ensure her recovery. Maggie had gained consciousness but was detained, against her pleasure, for some tests and examinations, while her parents aided the nurse in completing the needful procedure by alleviating their daughter's adamant request to return home and not be stung by a needle again. When Erica had witnessed Maggie's amusement after seeing her parents and friend, her disdain for a prolonged medical examination and her usual puckish demeanor to elude all of it, she was relieved of her responsibility towards her and was reminded of another toward someone a tad more dearer. She left the clinic in search of him.

The Saunderhurst home was wide open and unattended when Erica stepped inside and searched the deserted rooms for Jeff. She called out his name but perceived no sound in return. As she explored further, she heard a wispy voice calling out from somewhere indistinctly close. She navigated her way to Anthony's bedroom and gingerly pushed the door open. She peered inside and through a ponderous air of stillness, she saw an ailing, old man at the peak of his suffering. His voice was flimsy and hoarse and was produced with great difficulty.

"Is that you Jeff... who is that?" the effortful sound questioned.

"It is me, Mr. Saunderhurst. Erica." Erica answered, maintaining her distance from the bed out of respect.

"Erica? Oh... it is you. Have you seen Jeff?" He struggled for a glance at her, straining forward from his pillow.

"No, sir. Do you know where he is?" She asked with extreme courtesy.

"He must be hiding after what happened. Find him for me." He fell back flat on the bed again.

"No, Mr. Saunderhurst, it was not his fault." Erica erupted before Jeff could be implicated any further. "Maggie fell by the side of the bridge. He wasn't even there at the time."

"I know, my child. Accidents like these are hardly ever the fault of those involved. It's just a dark passing of time that entraps randomly at will. There is no escape. I will not blame that poor soul for something like this." He began coughing, but contained it to utter some more. "Go and find him, bring him to me."

Erica nodded dutifully and went on hunting again.

She stepped into the living room and looked through the window after sensing a car engine and doors being shut. It had started to drizzle as Martin hurried up to the house with Maggie tucked in his arms and enveloped in a blanket. Lena followed after thanking the ambulance driver for the lift. They brought in the convalescing seven-year-old and placed her tenderly on the couch. She was sedated now, but slightly flickered at intervals. Erica went closer and crouched by her side caressing Maggie's face. Her eyelids fluttered and she parted her mouth but no words came out.

Just as Lena returned with a hot water bottle to give her blanket the needed warmth, Jeff appeared in a doorway gazing back at his sister. His gaze was fixed and spoke volumes about guilt, regret, and joy to see her moving again. Lena refrained from interjecting that torrential regard, while Erica just waited for anyone in the room to disrupt that grim silence.

As Jeff remained in the doorway, a firm hand flew toward him abruptly and slapped him across the face. Erica was stunned at the impact of the sound it created. Lena looked away, fighting to quieten her verbal contempt for the act but also finding it reasonable to incorporate rebuke in early years of upbringing. Jeff held onto his cheek which was now crimson and possibly a partial print of Martin's hand across it.

"Don't you ever touch her again!" Martin's voice was elevated to such extent that it resonated throughout the house.

Jeff fled once again, slipping into his grandfather's room. Erica followed.

Jeff rushed across the floor and buried himself into the folds of his grandpa's coverlet, curled up aside Anthony's legs. His whimpering escalated into uncontrollable sobs as Anthony scrabbled his bedside to find and strengthen his grandson.

"What's the matter, my son?" He patted Jeff's head and comforted him.

"I didn't do it, grandpa. I didn't do anything." Jeff was hysterical by now and trembled as he slurred.

"I know, I know it wasn't your fault. Come here, come close to me." Anthony compelled and he twitched closer.

Erica watched from her place just inside the door, she was exuding empathy.

"Jeff, a father's anger is provoked not because his children did something wrong, but because they were subjected to something harmful. It is the deepest fear of a parent to have their children face an adversity. If he's hit you once it is not because he hates you, but because he wants you to keep yourself from such an event again in life. Your life is precious to both of them. They cannot bear to see you take it lightly. Look here, my child. Maggie loves you. It is a difficult word to define to a seven-year-old, but when she will be wise enough to know, she will realize that you once saved her life. And her love for you would only grow, never lessen. You will remember this one day." His words mollified Jeff to an extent, but his weeping continued for some more minutes as he wrapped his arm around his grandpa at the torso and stayed. Those gentle, comforting pats on Jeff's shoulder worked like a lullaby for him.

Erica was relieved a bit at her end.

# Chapter Five

The words Anthony had spoken to Jeff that night were the most precious words he could hear after being imputed the blame for the event that day. There was a certain glint of truth in those words as the very next day, while still recuperating, Maggie was back to her former inclination to pester Jeff to his wit's end. But it was not her badgering that aggrieved him, it was Martin's decision to limit Maggie's outdoor expeditions with Jeff and Erica. She was to return home right after school and stay indoors under supervision of her mother. He didn't entrust Jeff with her responsibility any longer. It was an ephemeral heartache as they both adapted to their new lifestyles, Maggie facing a greater change in hers, but Jeff continued his regimen with the exception of his sister by his side. But there was a greater grief approaching his life.

Anthony's condition had worsened in the past weeks, and it became apparent to Jeff as he wouldn't see him sit on the porch anymore when he returned from school. He wouldn't find him take a stroll every morning and late afternoon which were rarely skipped in the previous decade. He wouldn't see him participate in discussions or furnish his wisdom or opinions on vital matters of the house. Jeff's small world, which was once filled with his grandfather's presence, was now forlorn in his increasing absence.

Due to this grievous situation, he was beginning to lose interest in any other matter except his grandpa's health. Even the most rapturous hour of the day that he spent at the falls with Erica was gradually growing into silence and despondency. Perched upon the rocks, with their legs dangling and feet skimming the water, Jeff would sit in rumination and Erica would watch him crumble day by day.

"Jeff, what's the matter?" She would try to make him talk, hoping to divert his pensive contemplation onto something else.

"Nothing." He would shield himself away.

"I know there is something wrong, are you going to tell me or what?" She insisted.

"No, I'm all right." He would leave his place and go up a tree, distancing himself from the world.

Erica would look away in deep dejection.

She knew Jeff well enough to comprehend his troubles without having him to say a word. She could grasp his slightest unease with a single intrusive stare into his eyes. This time, unfortunately, his unease wasn't slight in any respect.

Jeff stepped into his grandfather's room hoping he could entice him to go on his long-forgotten evening stroll and if he could accompany him. His presence was wordless for a while as he went to his grandpa's rocking chair brushing the armrest with his fingers, watching Anthony breathing tardily with shallow inhales.

"Grandpa?" His whispering stirred the old man.

"Jeff? How is my brave little one?" He attempted a smile, which barely surfaced on his withered face.

"Okay, I guess." Jeff hid his pain.

"You guess? Now, you can do better than just guessing your circumstance, can't you?" He coughed, running out of breath.

"I don't know." He scratched the ruptured side of the old chair. "How are you, grandpa?"

"I'm perfectly fine, Jeff. What's the matter with me?" He concealed his suffering, but his guttural voice deceived him.

"You don't look too good," Jeff said innocently.

"I don't look too well? What makes you say that?" He went on with the conversation.

"You don't come out to sit at the porch anymore. We don't go out for a walk now. You never leave this room." He laid out his grievances.

"That is called old age, my son. The days of play are for the children, the years of amusement for the young. But old age knows only the time of anguish and loneliness. The only thing of substance to an old man, at this age, is that he'll have to leave his family. And that journey, no matter how old you are, always seems to have approached too soon." Anthony was eventually articulating his sentiments rather than answering Jeff.

"Yes, that's one complication that troubles us all." Anthony drew in a cold sigh. "But that's something not worthy of your concern, my lad. From now on, I would sit on the porch every day when you return from school. Go for a walk every afternoon, and come to the dining every supper. Are you happy?"

"Yes." Jeff nodded excitedly, "are you going for a walk now?"

"Hmm? Oh, I suppose I must. Now that I have made a promise." Anthony strained his decrepit structure up and to the side of his bed. His struggle was excruciating as well as prolonged, but observing the torturous effort, Jeff quickly came to his aid putting on his loafers for him. Anthony beamed acknowledging the offered succor as he held on to Jeff's arm and impelled himself up to his feet. His legs were rickety after days of stagnation but intentions were firm and resolute as ever. Jeff assisted him out the door and emulated his slow and dragging strides.

They both had reached the sidewalk and plodded further on the concrete. Anthony glimpsed at his neighborhood that he hadn't espied in a long time. A sea of identical constructions, almost as old as him, lined up and down the street, housing a thousand souls he knew, some of whom he hadn't met in a long time, and some who hadn't seen him ever.

Jeff walked in front of him proposing his sturdy form as a walking aid and just as Anthony gripped his shoulder to ambulate, Jeff's shoulders heightened with pride and stiffened to furnish more strength to his grandfather.

They had just walked past another neighboring house on the right, and Erica viewed this duo from the window that overlooked the street with delight glinting in her eyes. She hurriedly exited the house and came down the steps of her front porch and exchanged a tacit discourse with Jeff, which was triumphantly joyous from his end and rendered courage from hers.

She pantomimed a sign, an act of knocking on the door. Jeff answered with an inquisitive nod. She tapped her forehead again gesturing something arcane and they both laughed. It was wordless and mainly portrayed by the eyes, but it was wholly construed. She waved to him as he passed and he motioned in return and went on his way with his grandfather following close behind.

They had reached a dead-end which bordered the Johnson residence. Anthony reined his acceleration that he had gained in the past minute or so, rallied out of excitement derived from using his limbs again, and alighted on the lonesome, corner bench. Jeff took a seat right by and watched his grandfather alleviate his gasping lungs which took him quite an extended moment to achieve.

"Are you leaving grandpa?" Jeff's voice reflected a tinge of emotion.

Anthony turned and looked straight into Jeff's eyes and smiled. "We must, all of us."

Jeff was overcome with misery. He lowered his face and gazed into the stark nothingness of the concrete below.

"Look, Jeff, life is an immense voyage. We smile at the one who cries and then cry for the one who smiles back at us. It is the beginning and the end, and it will never cease to exist because where there's an end, there has to be a beginning and where there's a beginning, there has to be an end. That's life. We are meant to cherish our blessings and cope with our losses. But you have to promise me something, from one man to his grandfather."

Jeff pushed his hand upon Anthony's forearm and collected his shriveling skin into folds and released it as it did not retract. "A promise?" He asked looking up at Anthony.

"When I'm gone, you will not give up or surrender to life and the troubles it brings along. I know it will be hard, but you will fight. Give me your word that you will love everyone like you've loved your grandfather. You will take care of every member of your family, promise me that."

"I love them, grandpa. If you want I'll kiss them all tonight and tell them I love them." Jeff answered innocently.

"I know you will. But the kind of love I'm talking about is the one you don't need to tell."

"What kind of love is that?" It sparked the boy's curiosity.

"You will find out. Just remember this promise when you do. I may not be there to hold you to your word, but I can trust you on it."

"Why are you leaving?" Jeff's eyes dimmed. "Don't go, grandpa." Jeff threw himself at his grandfather and clung to him in an embrace, beginning to cry. Anthony held him in his quivering arms and pacified him.

"Tears are not something I wish to leave behind, but something much more valuable, your belief that I'll always watch over you. All you need to do is think of me once with all your heart and I'll be somewhere really close. You might not see me, but I surely will see you. That's my promise. Now, where's yours?" Anthony shook him gently for a response, but he stayed wrapped around his grandpa.

"Okay, I will do it. But I won't let you go." Jeff sobbed quite vehemently now.

"I wish, my son. I wish." Anthony looked up to the heavens, closing his eyes and clenching Jeff around the shoulders.

The sky was crimson with streaks of dawdling clouds, the breeze was mild and serene passing through trees as the branches swayed and the leaves rustled. The days were dismissed early and earlier as they progressed and a feeble daylight receded beyond the woods and homes, casting horizontal shadows across the town. Autumn had come.

About forty minutes later, Jeff guided Anthony back into his room and did the needful to prepare him for supper, but surprisingly, in the dining. It was after months of his absence from the table that Anthony agreed to dine with his family that night at Jeff's behest as he had taken full responsibility for his grandpa's comfort and provisions, and astounded even the adults of the house with his ardent commitment towards his obligation. As a warm smile spread across each face at the dining that night, it was a duty well performed.

When night prevailed, Jeff led his grandpa back to his enclosure and placed him upon his bed asking if he needed something else to outlast the night. Anthony patted his back and caressed his face, kissed him on the forehead and sent him away. Jeff reached the door, but just before leaving, he returned and faced Anthony again.

"I love you, grandpa."

"And you don't know how much I love you in return."

"If you're feeling all right and you go for a walk, can I come with tomorrow too?" Earnestness dripped from his words.

"You must, I wouldn't be able to go much farther without you."

"Good night, grandpa." Jeff was jubilant hearing that affirmation. "Tomorrow I'll wake you up myself with breakfast in bed," Jeff added to his exuberance with another offer.

Anthony chuckled, "all right." He emitted a deep sigh, "we'll meet at dawn then." He squeezed Jeff's tiny left hand within his cold, arid mitts and nodded his snow-capped summit, slowly releasing him.

With unfathomed trust in his grandfather's word, Jeff exited the room and went upstairs to his bed, sleeping soundly with hope tucked under the blanket next to his heart, clenched firmly within his furled palm.

# Chapter Six

Darkness had elapsed in tranquility, but by dawn, Jeff had heard some muffled sounds of a disturbance. Not bothered by them, he continued his dormancy for another hour or so thinking it might have been a common household errand gone wrong. But after a while, just as he descended the stairs after awakening to unusual silence on a Saturday morning and entered his grandfather's chamber, he witnessed an empty bed that was neatly made and tidied at all ends but no one on it to share the breakfast with.

It was eerily strange for him not to find his grandfather there early at dawn, especially when the integrity of his promise was in question. His senses were numbed momentarily as he stood wordless and bewildered at the vacuity of that room. Something about that enclosure appeared different, dissimilar. The dense air that once coursed the room profoundly had diminished into a fresh draft of morning breeze. Jeff glanced around and saw the source of this breeze that permeated the room. It wasn't novel for him to find the window slightly parted in the morning, he himself had delivered to the request at times, but that heavy air of inhabitance, which harbored the certainty of a living soul, never deserted the space between these four walls.

Jeff stepped out in his confounded condition and saw Lena whimpering at the dining table while Dave comforted her. He sighted Martin outside with the male nurse from the clinic and heard as they both spoke about some processes that would follow a nameless event. And then a rattling realization dawned upon him; Jeff Saunderhurst's grandfather had betrayed his trust.

Jeff was suddenly made impervious by that shock, as no feelings or emotions trickled his stern countenance. He had gone around the house conducting his daily chores but never actually substantiating the dreadful supposition. Whether it was fear of a loss being validated and shattering that last string of hope he had, or simply to give other family members time to cope with the news before another heart-rending inquiry, no one knew the truth behind his dissimulation. He maintained that visage with a glower, which hinted more of regret than grief, for much of the time that followed, and confronted only one thought that deluged his mind; if only he had inconvenienced his slumber earlier today, he might have caught the last glimpse of his grandpa still alive.

That impression was indelible in his mind as morning transmuted into noon and noon faded into evening. He had seen the preparations of the obsequies being concluded by nightfall.

The time was set for the following day and as the clinic did not have a facility of a morgue, consequently, Anthony's dead body was directly sent to a funeral home. Martin refrained from dining that night while Lena compelled the children to fuel their bellies at least enough to get past the night. It was a silent gathering at the table that evening, there was mourning in every exhale that warmed the air. But Jeff's reckoning was yet blatantly lambasted with one recurring thought. The one thought he took to bed that night, and it was the first time in life he had seen the short hand of a wall clock do a full round of the dial. It was all witnessed without a single blink of the eyes; if only he had awakened but a little earlier to see his grandfather for that one last time.

It was an overcast noon when the procession reached the graveyard. While the people waited in and outside their vehicles for the morticians to unload the hearse and prepare the grave for the lowering of the casket, Maggie viewed the long file of parked vehicles from the side-view mirror and attempted to count them. They were uncountable to an extent of appearing like specks in that mirror and eventually becoming invisible with distance. The whole town had come and it was quite customary for at least one member of a family to show up and pay their last respects to anyone who died. It was the kind of town that was built upon acquaintances. There were no strangers that lived here. Anthony Saunderhurst had dwelt here for a very long time, almost as long as the existence of this town itself. He had seen the foundations being laid and houses being built upon them. His own was one of many. He had seen families relocating and inhabiting those constructions to make them a home. He had seen countless families bid welcome and farewell to generations. His last rites were not going to be missed by more than a few.

When Maggie was soundly defeated in her attempts to count the cars, her attention now diverted to Jeff who sat alongside her at the rear seat. She extended her arm and tried to wiggle him out of his gloom. Jeff ignored her and shifted away closer to the window and retained his misery. After some time the crowd was addressed to follow the family of the deceased to the grave site. It wasn't conventional for children to attend interment in general unless it was family related occurrence, and this was an unprecedented experience for Jeff, Maggie, and Erica as neither was permitted to a goodbye ceremony before. But they kept each other company as they straggled after Dave and Linda, who had arrived from Rhode Island late last night, being led by Martin and Lena. As the people dispersed in a semicircle around the grave, the parish priest assumed his obligation and commenced the ceremony.

"Let us join our hands in prayers." The pastor announced while opening his holy book. The crowd responded in unison, bowing their heads and closing their eyes.

Erica, who now stood next to her father gripping his finger for stability on the uneven ground, had a gaze fixated on Jeff. He hadn't spoken to her in a very long time and the painful aspect about his reticence was that she couldn't apologize to make things better as it was no one's fault, or she would have done that to end their suffering, as her agony was equally disheartening in his silence. Jeff's sorrow couldn't be subdued with any material thing, she was aware of it. She had endured a greater loss in her life as well.

This riveting thought of bringing her friend back to life consumed her mind as she weighed in all possible actions or words she could harness to revive him, but none apparently availed her hopeless intentions. Just as she was ruminating on the matter, the words of the minister resonated through her soul.

"Blessed are those who mourn, for they shall be comforted. We have heard this beautiful verse from the book of Matthew..."

His voice faded once again into the overlapping fervor of her interminable pondering. How shall Jeff receive his comfort? Was it going to appear out of heaven as a miracle, or will it evolve over time with fading memories of a person departed? How could she help him be her ten-year-old friend again? What could she say that might allay his pain?

"Oh-" Erica bellowed her fervent despair out loud publicly. All eyes turned towards her. But acknowledging her distress, they all nodded and looked away in empathy allowing her time. She regathered her trembling stance and lowered her mortified face while Mr. Johnson tapped her shoulder and clenched her against himself. Lifting her eyes back up, she gazed at Jeff again and yearned for him to hold that gaze for some time. He did exactly that. In that protracted gaze, she questioned him about his troubles but intuited no answer in return.

Jeff averted his stare off of Erica and perused the faces he saw in the crowd, his eyes settled from one to the next. Amidst the sea of expressions, he distinguished grief from apathy and classified a larger part of the flock to the former of the two. He saw his father stand there in strange deliberation which was neither grief nor apathy, but rather a complication. He lacked the foresight to say where it led to, but recognized it well enough. He saw Dave being the firmest of all in display of emotions as he stood with a dispirited but unyielding countenance, rendering courage to all those around him. Lena and Linda were the ones most touched as each leaned onto Dave on his either side and wiped their eyes with tissues as the funeral progressed. Maggie went on to imitate the faces around her and stood stagnant with a sealed mouth and drifting eyes.

If only he had awakened earlier, he would have met his grandfather. That unrelenting view was instilled in his mind. He abruptly reverted to his guilt. No matter the number of worldly distractions he endeavored to divert his attention with, he could never escape the culpability he'd inflicted upon himself.

"A loss is never easy for the ones who're left mourning the departed. But it is in the word of God that we must place our trust and in his promise of eternal life after death."

Jeff tried to listen intently, but the vociferous thoughts of guilt blending with the words of the Reverend disarrayed his reasoning and perception.

"Anthony was a devoted father, a devoted grandfather to four grandchildren and a devout believer. I know what devotion to one's faith means, I have done it all my life. I've spent my entire adulthood working for the church. I'm saddened by the passing of our dear friend. I'm miserable. But I'm certain about one thing on this blessed day, his soul will be at rest tonight. I'm certain about it."

Jeff glanced up at the priest and wondered about the credibility of his words. Anthony hadn't been to the church in a while, and it was more than a month ago that father Thomas came to see him following recurrent requests from Lena for a couple of Sundays in a row after mass. Requests that were made in Jeff's presence as he always stood by his mother's side when father Thomas and Lena alluded to Anthony's health and she implored him to visit. Jeff never really understood the importance of a man given religious prominence by other men to actually furnish faith to the dying and desolate, as by their visits to the homes and places where loss is impending. He didn't understand why the wiser adults insisted on such folly, but decided not to follow suit. Faith isn't a boon exclusive to such men, or their belonging to give to whomever they wish. Faith is simply depending on those who carried you when you couldn't walk until the day you ran your first race. Faith is trusting the company of those who spent the blissful years of schooling with you from that first fearsome day to the last proud moment of graduation. Faith is relying on someone you've allowed to hold your hand and guide you through the rest of your life. Faith is sitting at the final days of your existence and looking back at the chapters of life and believing in something that made it all happen. If we can place our faith in the people around us, we can definitely place our faith in that which granted us those people to cherish.

"I had known him for years, and I'm proud that I had him as a part of my congregation. I remember the time I stood alone with a dream of a church in my heart. I was alone. But I worked hard and I accomplished my dream. I achieved what I strove to achieve." Father Thomas continued blabbering in his own laud.

Jeff remembered that grandpa had never been an ardent follower of father Thomas' doctrine for operating his church. His benevolence was more inclined toward the wealthier division in the pews as opposed to the poorer side. It was his way of pleasing the financial chieftains of this and neighboring towns to run the church according to their demands and penchants which created a rift between him and Anthony at times. Being an educator for most of his life, Anthony couldn't take the prejudice without dissent and he had always spoken about the asperities of the church in passing.

While Jeff was never exceedingly zealous about the church, he heard his grandpa utter praises for the minister that he was an entertainer. He loved to make a spectacle out of a hushed event and was proficient at distorting words with eloquence to gain renown. After all, it was out of that glib ability that he got to travel domestically to conventions and meetings with the aid of his affluent patrons and was one of the richest men in town.

"The times that were most difficult for him, I stood by his side. I was there." The pastor was almost as adept as an actor portraying the role with fervid interest and expressions. But his speech was at the verge of propelling people into ennui as there were a couple yawns here and there. "These are the kind of people who build a congregation. Those who stand by their church, no matter what adversity we must face."

"Finally something about the deceased," Jeff spoke within his mind, his lips remained sealed. The priest had possibly discerned the boredom on people's faces and quickly returned to the subject matter.

"For it is written, as the body apart from the spirit is dead, so also faith apart from works is dead. His faith was alive to the last day I met him." The pastor gained substance in his words now.

Grandpa's faith, Jeff thought, could never be suspected, as even in his final days the only things he possessed were his ailment, his compassion, and an old battered Holy Bible.

"He himself bore our sins in his body on the cross, so that we might die to sin and live for righteousness." The priest adjusted his satin stole and secured it around his neck against the progressive wind that now stirred the grey clouds above. "He was a man of his word, I could personally testify to that fact."

For the first time in life, Jeff had perceived differently than what others deemed about his grandfather. "He wasn't a man of his word." Jeff's sentiments now became audible and barricaded every other exterior noise from entering his senses. "If he were a man of his word, he would have waited to have breakfast with me yesterday morning. If he didn't want to keep his promise, why did he make it in the first place? The minister was lying." Jeff was enraged at the idea of being deceived.

"Whoever does not love does not know God, because God is love. And love is forgiveness. Anthony had an abundance of both." Erica was riveted by the pastor's allusions. She gazed at Jeff reflectively yet again.

"I'm sorry grandpa," he whispered to himself. "It was my fault. You were sick and you couldn't get up. I should have been there." Anger ebbed away bit by bit, as Jeff slowly receded into the shackles of guilt again. "It's all my fault."

"Neither death nor life, nor angels nor rulers, nor things present nor things to come, nor powers, nor height nor depth, nor anything else in all creation, will be able to separate us from the love of God in Christ Jesus our Lord." Pastor raised his arms aloft and closed his eyes. "And in that divine promise, let us lift his departed soul to the gates of heaven and eternal life therein, and let us elevate our faith for God's glory. May his soul rest in peace."

The crowd was directed to part with their flowers and bouquets as the family members tossed in a handful of earth onto the lowering casket. After another moment of mournful silence and a handshake with the elders of the house, people began to scatter and leave. The family stayed until the horde of guests had dwindled.

It was now well past two when the last of the mourners entered the Saunderhurst residence with eyes filled with empathy and hands with a casserole. The house was teeming with a throng in black as every window and door gave a view of the assemblage. But there were three souls that still lingered in the isolation of the front yard. Jeff sat under a massive oak tree that grew in the center of their yard while Maggie swayed on a tire-swing that hung freely from a low but sturdy branch. Erica had arrived with her father to join the grieving crowd inside the house but separated from him after leaving his hand at the threshold and approached her preferred company.

She began to give Maggie a push for her amusement, but her eyes were upon Jeff who sat muted in his plaintiveness.

"If I had made a bit of an effort, I wouldn't have missed seeing my grandpa for the last time." Jeff's guilt was as loud as a promulgation that flustered his soul.

Erica stepped closer to him in ambivalence, whether to speak or not. She tried to palliate the atmosphere and the people affected with light blather.

"Hey Jeff, I haven't seen you at the falls in a long time." She herself hadn't been to the falls in a long time, but it was a mutually relished subject to converse upon.

There was no verbal response from him, but his mind spoke nonetheless. "I should have woken up early at dawn. Grandpa said he'd see me at dawn. Dawn isn't nine thirty."

"Do you want to race me to the falls? On our bikes? I'd love to go!"

There was silence at his end, but it was limited to his lips, not his soul. "Weekend isn't an excuse to be lazy. He must have waited so long to see me there and I was busy sleeping!"

"Do you like my dress? I bought it just for today. I like your suit." Erica attempted to insinuate a comforting touch by brushing her fingers along his arm.

It did not stir him a bit.

"You really need to be disciplined, you know? A lady is trying to make a conversation here and you haven't even a word to share?" Erica raised her voice on him which at least elicited a glare from him. She had her chance to scrutinize his soul with an intrusive stare into his eyes. She sought to read his mind.

Thunder crackled at a distance and a deep rumbling followed initiating sporadic droplets to pelt the earth, which soon transformed into a downpour. People ran for shelter saving themselves from this sudden deluge. Erica and Maggie rushed toward the porch, but one of them stopped and came back under the ragged cover of the tree.

"Get up silly, it's raining. You're going to catch a cold. Come'on." Erica travailed to heave Jeff who was heavy as a boulder. Jeff abruptly gained his ground and shoved Erica away. She took a pratfall into the damp earth, her dress all wet and soiled.

Jeff ran to a distance, his thoughts ringing in his body now. "He must have waited for me. He must have waited so much. He must be hungry as well. He wouldn't have had breakfast without me. He must have called out my name, with his last breath, he must have called out to me." He sought as little as a fleck of fortitude but failed to attain it.

Maggie watched this from under the porch and hastened to aid Erica in getting up and tried to dust off her begrimed dress. It was futile now. Erica saw Jeff stop after a couple tired strides and collapse to his knees.

He plunged into the darkness of woe with that fall. The reason he imputed his grandfather's death to himself was still an enigma for Erica, but she couldn't allow it anymore.

"He waited, he called out to me, and I wasn't there. He must be so sad." Jeff's eyes swam in tears as his face and clothes were drenched in rain. Even the heavens wept for his loss. He was about to give up. "He must have hated me so much, he must have hated -"

"He loved you!" Those three words suddenly riveted him and absorbed his emotions as if all his burdens had been relieved with that one single exclamation. He looked at Erica who now stood beside him, gazing piercingly into his eyes, liberating him from all his shackles. She had shot an arrow in the dark, or perhaps it was her understanding of her friend who had wrestled the oppressive thoughts for two days and only she could extricate him. Maybe she was more than a friend to know his strife. Jeff's tears vanished, his suffering abated. Erica crouched by his side and embraced him. Maggie stood right behind the two. The rain continued to pour, aiming to relieve the earth of its swelter.

# Chapter Seven

New York City gave itself away partially to the view of a man who lay recumbent in a deep pensive state. A light drizzle flecked the glass and the asphalt jungle beyond appeared gleaming just as it typically did after a mix of sleet and snow. Traffic had eventually declined, and consequently the concurring dissonance as well, which was a divine blessing for the dwellers by nightfall. It was now sound to open the window that overlooked a formerly busy street, especially as the clock ticked close to 2 am. Jeff nestled in the folds of his bed with a nightcap half consumed on his bedside, but his mind hadn't returned with him from the events of the past. Rain was one of such events that were dearly treasured by his grandfather, an affinity that descended into his character as well. Just the way Anthony would perch upon his chair at the far left corner of the porch and watch nature exhibit its wonders for his amusement, Jeff imitated his grandpa's inclination and enjoyed the sight of precipitation from his room with a serene smile across his lips.

Deserting the confines of his bed, Jeff approached the window for a closer look outside and parted the pane. A cold draft of air washed upon him dotting his face with drizzle. Though, his view lacked an extensive grass-covered lawn, an ever-growing oak tree in the center, and two grandchildren who soaked themselves silly every time it poured, he was fairly content with what he felt rather than what he viewed. Glancing at the dark night sky above, searching for that one last sight of someone he loved, but couldn't find it up there. He knew the heavens should not be tempted for such a miracle every night, there was another route to fulfillment of his needs. A gentle knock on his chest where his heart resided and a memory would simply pop up and reveal itself gradually enough for him to relish for the rest of the night. Inspirited by the certainty of a copious reserve of such memories, he returned to bed, switched off the lights and drifted off to a peaceful sleep.

The next morning Jeff had awakened to a peculiar consolation that surprisingly revived him to an extent he hadn't sensed in a long time. His refreshment was continuous for the hours that followed after breakfast and he decided to spend the day in a blissful repose. He had actually enjoyed that leisure for some days now as he hadn't worked in more than a week. Though, his work wasn't very stressful or onerous to him, on the contrary, he enjoyed his line of work. He was a writer. A ghostwriter to be precise. Numerous of his works were published, yet he remained unrecognized. Many of his works were quite renowned in the public eye, yet he remained nameless. Being the composer of the works didn't necessarily mean for him to be identified as the owner of them. He was the faceless mind behind the celebrity of several names.

He sold his craft. He traded his brilliance in exchange for money and there wasn't a dearth of shoppers in the market. Some of them were established, who had just written a great deal and ran out of brains to spawn another idea, and some amateurs who dispensed handsomely from their deep vaults to exploit the service. This clandestine trade had brought him some lucrative deals if not many, but most of such deceitful transactions were dealt in high amounts of money. It was a distinctly profitable prospect in comparison to simply putting your work to be published under your given name.

At some instances, the rewards almost doubled. Jeff gave away a piece of his life for cash every time he signed a piece of an agreement. He was content, or rather bound, to see a stranger's name put up in front of his work and be praised for it, or at times, criticized, which was infrequent. He'd almost gotten too habitual about it with time. But it wasn't a voluntary measure when the first ordeal was induced. He had no intentions of giving away his precious works for something as insignificant as money. It was more than his life and soul that was put into all of them. But time and circumstances concurred in coercing that decision upon him and inundating his reasoning.

Due to a lack of means and technology, the writers had no other choice but to incur the favor of a publisher in order to get printed and because of that constraint, the publishers were quite imposing in their positions and captious unless a well-established name was attached to a manuscript. This situation was quite analogous to that of a novice who looks for work after education and isn't hired anywhere due to a lack of experience. Jeff searched for a similar opportunity to prove his capability and attach his name to it, but there was no one willing to attach their trust to his name.

To survive those trying times, he worked with a construction company to defray the costs of living, and his scuffle with rejection sustained for three years before he conceded, yielding to the inequitable demands of those in power. Selling his works for complete ownership did not take as long and it brought him some hefty amounts of money with which he rebuilt his life. An apartment followed after a couple of deals and moments of tranquility came along. He had left his job about two years ago and now enjoyed the splendor of relaxation at home. But the home he yearned for was far from here, where two old souls still nested in solitude but placidity. Where his siblings gathered for occasions and celebrations at least twice in a year, while he was the only one missing. Where the companionship of a true friend waited. The home he left five years ago, he desired to return to it once more. The reasons behind his departure were various, but the reason behind his return would be solitary. He had realized it was time for him to fulfill a part of his life that was left undone. Family. And to accomplish that want, he must go back. It had been a couple of days since he mailed that letter and hoping the recipients might have received it by now, he anticipated it would turn out to be a pleasant surprise for which they have waited quite long.

The rust and decay of two and a half decades had caught up with the Saunderhurst home now. The rooms that once endured the frolic of four grandchildren and exuberance of a complete family now housed the solitude of two aged souls. The porch that accommodated an obsolete chair that rocked a senescent elder from dawn all the way until Jeff and Maggie returned from school, now lay in deterioration of age and absence. It had always been the good ole' house, but now even time regarded it so.

But surprisingly, the same old chair, that once rocked the eldest of the house, had stayed its location and in progressive decay, swayed yet another man. Probably a dream, the image of a man on the chair. An illusion perhaps reminiscent of an antiquated memory. A gray cover for a head, a plaid shirt, which once tautly fitted, had loosened around the shoulders, and a withering hand that tapped the armrest in perpetual enervation.

It wasn't an illusion. It was time simply playing its trick or rather effectuating its purpose. The old had departed, the young had assumed their places and as the seasons elapsed, there was yet another change of shifts waiting to transpire.

Martin leaned back coolly in his chair with eyes closed and head tilted to the side. He was older now, about a quarter of a century older. And he looked his age with creases by the temples and eyes, and deep crevices around the mouth with folds under the chin. He had turned into a grandpa himself quite a while ago.

His languor was disrupted by a greeting that emerged from the right of the porch and was genially voiced by an approaching mailman.

"Takin' a nap, Mr. Saunderhurst?" The mailman shuffled through his bag as he ambled closer. "Better watch out for that snow headed this way. Quite cold to be outdoors, don't you think so?"

The mailman was a man in mid-30s called Henry. Must have been an old acquaintance as his demeanor and dialogue suggested.

"Then you shouldn't be out here, son, should you?" Martin responded nonchalantly.

"Nah, just had this letter to deliver. And one more house to go, your neighbor's on the right. Then I'm done for the day." He dispensed the letters.

Martin examined the mail apathetically. "How are the wife and kids?"

"Ahh, troublesome for a lack of a better word. And it's not the young ones I'm talkin' about. They just run you out of breath with their cute little ways, but them wives, they run you out of your wits, squeezin' your brains out of your skulls. Suddenly between takin' care of your kids to runnin' to the store to get a gallon of milk, bein' a housewife becomes borin'. I said I make enough to run the house, why do you need to press years out of your life with all that stress? You could turn a chargin' missile headed your way, but not a woman. It's the TV I tell ya. Them talk shows early in the mornin', eatin' away whatever they have up there for a brain. But I guess you know plenty about that." Henry scratched his head expecting commiseration.

"No, son. I'm afraid I don't. The women of our time were made to become wives. Now they're made to become anything they wish. Time changes people, it also changes their necessities. Family might not be one of them." Martin was incisive yet composed.

"Hmm, I guess you're right. Shouldn't marry a girl who completed high school when you didn't even get past junior high." He shrugged, Martin chuckled. "Those were the days, no school for boys, no sir. All of us lined up in that school playground, includin'

Jeff, no hopes for a future. Speakin' of him, is that what I think it is? If you don't mind my askin', where's that letter from?" His eyes went from his misfortune to the one Martin possessed.

"I don't know, you delivered it." Martin looked at the letter inquisitively, then back at him.

"Sorry for the intrusion, sir, but on my way here I happened to check where it was from. Just a regular handwritten address and I thought, who writes letters these days? It wasn't a bill or an invoice. So, I took the liberty and if I'm not mistaken that handwritin' belongs to Jeff."

Martin perused the letter with escalating concern. He inspected the address and found Henry's conjecture surprisingly accurate. He detached the flap swiftly yet so gently and retrieved the letter. His eyes darted from one end of the sentence to the other and his face illumined with a glint of hope and joy.

"Oh good heavens!" He exclaimed in utter excitement.

"It's him, isn't it?" Henry stood proudly after discovering the precision of his guess.

"Yes! He's coming back. Oh, I don't believe this. He is really coming back this Christmas. I have to tell her about this. Lena..."

Martin had already rushed inside the house as his voice echoed in the vacant rooms.

Henry saluted the old man, delighted by the news. Just as he intuited his solitude and his lonely laughter on the porch, he scratched his nose rubbing away the embarrassment. Along with it vanished the awkward gaiety. He stepped down the stairs and back into the tedium of his routine.

Martin scampered down the hallway laboring to make his strides rapid, but his decrepit body was taking its time, much to his dislike. He reached the kitchen at the end of the corridor and turned into the doorway panting. Lena eyed him rinsing a bowl of vegetables under the faucet.

"Slow down, dear. The blizzard is still a day or two away." She demanded solicitously.

"When have you seen a blizzard excite me like this before?" He gathered his breaths.

"Then what is it? The breakfast was just as usual." She said keeping the bowl aside and drying her hands on her apron.

Martin wrapped Lena into his arms kissing her on the cheek.

"Now hold on, dear. That is too much excitement indeed, your old age cannot take it. Please." Lena continued with her kitchen chores, placing a pan on the stove and pouring some oil into it. Martin spaced himself from her and prepared to deliver the surprise.

"Guess what this is?" He tapped the sheet of paper held in his hand.

"You certainly didn't win the lottery or that kiss wouldn't have landed on my cheek." She laughed at her own remark. "Is it a refund or a rebate, that's what usually gets your spirits high?"

"It is something greater than that. Something you've prayed for years." Martin stepped closer with a glimmer in his eyes.

"Something I've prayed for? Um... a dishwasher?" She answered questionably.

"A dishwasher?" Martin was bemused. "You've prayed for a dishwasher?"

"At times, yes I have. If your hands had crinkled like a dead corpse, you would know what it means to not have one. But I highly doubt it would be delivered in an envelope."

"If you want a dishwasher, I'll get you one." Martin seriously proclaimed.

"We'll see when that happens. For now, tell me what's that you're holding." Lena had heard too many of those promises.

"It is bigger than anything we can imagine."

"Now Martin, you're beginning to frighten me. You know how these surprises make me nervous. I'm too old for thumping heartbeats. Tell me or I'll faint." Her concern elevated.

"Okay, okay, don't collapse. Take a seat." Martin assisted her to a small dining table for five in the corner. "You seated?" She nodded, Martin resumed. "It is Jeff. He is coming home for Christmas."

Lena was devoid of an expression for a moment. Her mouth was partially open, her eyes darted from the letter to her gleeful husband and they suddenly filled with tears, releasing a stream down her cheeks. Her breathing heightened and shallowed. She pressed her heart through her chest and tried to alleviate the exhilaration that had flooded into her.

"Oh God..." She began whimpering as Martin handed her the letter. "He's is coming, isn't he?" Her inquiry was full of expectant yearning and Martin sublimely confirmed with a nod. She buried her face into his embrace and strengthened her failing emotions. She looked up at Martin. "Read it for me, please."

Martin took the letter and went over it.

"Dear ma and dad. I know it sounds a bit odd to be receiving letters in this world full of technology and other ways to communicate, but honestly, I wasn't certain if the two of you would be familiar with the new devices used as means to talk, message or write e-mails. I remember we had a home telephone, but I really wanted to write to you guys partly because I prefer this method and most importantly because you prefer it as well. Writing a letter has always seemed earnest to me. My request this time is earnest. I'm coming home for this Christmas. I don't know if this will be a burden or a boon, but I have also written to Linda, Dave, and Maggie and asked them to join us for one big family Christmas. Just like we once did. I wish for all of us to be together again. I'll be arriving on the fifteenth. It isn't too far away now, but every day in wait seems like a century to pass. I hope to see you just the way I left you all. Love you both. Your son, Jeff." Martin finished with his own eyes swimming in tears.

Lena took the letter and placed it next to her heart. "You didn't skip any lines in between, did you?"

Martin chortled, "Now, that's one grave mistake I couldn't make. I know the only thing you're going to do between now and until the time he comes is read that letter. I don't want to lose my two day's lunch or dinner."

Lena gently hit him on the shoulder and hugged him. "You're right. I can read this letter over and over again. And every time I will, it'll read like I just read it for the first time."

# Chapter Eight

✵

Jeff had emptied his bedside table of the most treasured possession he had -- the beloved picture of his grandfather. The frame had lodged in its resting place for so long that it left a discolored indentation in the mahogany when it was removed and escorted safely into a luggage. The object was gone, but the mark persisted.

A luggage lay open on the bed and clothes were neatly folded and arranged harmoniously with other items like the frame and some gifts. As the closet was evacuated, the luggage was loaded to the brim. It was zipped and locked, and wheeled to the corner of the living room, against the wall next to the entrance. As he passed through the rest of the house, the rooms appeared strangely bare. The belongings that once adorned this dwelling were largely boxed, and those too sizable to encase were vastly shrouded for preservation. He stepped out on the balcony and respired the brisk cold air of the city, a prolonged stare into the tumultuous chaos down below followed. He leaned onto the railings and reveled in the view. Then returned into the living and secured the door locking it from inside.

Jeff took a conclusive glance around the vacant room, a sigh followed, which vaguely hinted toward fatigue but rather towards a certain inadequacy. He had lived in this apartment for two years and the thought of abandoning it for the holidays was suddenly too oppressive upon him. As joyously as he had determined to visit his home and town this Christmas, he was unexpectedly deliberating to reverse his decision and cancel the trip. But it was quite too late for that. The family was about to gather after years of separation. Each must have planned myriad instances of celebrations in togetherness and deep affection. A termination to such innumerable moments of intimacy might result in a greater dejection and self-hatred. There was a feeling of plaintiveness descending onto him and it appeared as if he didn't want to leave. But leave he must.

He was already dressed for the trip and in those ultimate minutes of departing the apartment, Jeff yet again went around the living and kitchen. His fingers slid across the walls and furniture with a veiled unease and a fleeting glimpse at the emptiness around. It was an internal struggle and a fervent one. He finally collected his coat and luggage and exited home.

There was a taxi waiting for him outside the building vestibule and the trunk was loaded with two suitcases by the concierge aided by the driver.

"Off to a holiday getaway, sir?" The concierge approached Jeff on the sidewalk rubbing off the trunk dust from his gloves and adjusting his brass name badge that was pinned to the chest pocket and read Jacob T..

"Yes, you can say that. Going home after five years." Jeff nodded as he conceded that fact.

"Makes it even better, but quite a long time to be away. Must be a revelry for the folks back home?" He smiled and the remark emerged as a gesture intended to invest him with confidence and courage. Jeff accepted that.

"Hoping for that to be the case." Jeff nodded and proceeded toward the waiting cab, but halted halfway and returned.

Jacob anticipated some last minute instructions and began rummaging for his diary to jot it down.

Jeff deliberated his words as he spoke. "Some jobs are said to define the people who perform them. But then there are some people who define the services they're in. You don't meet such people every day of the week. But they deserve every bit of appreciation there is to show. I would like to offer you my honest gratitude. Thank you, Mr. Tanner, for being a man who defines his work. And I really mean it." Jeff offered his hand for a shake.

The concierge was utterly astounded to incur such a high regard from him and his eyes glinted with subtle dignity. His response to Jeff's hand was delayed but avid nonetheless. "Thank you, sir. I am honored."

Jeff tapped Jacob's arm and took leave of his benign personality. He entered the taxi and as it rolled further, adding to the frenzied traffic down the street.

Jacob stood in disbelief for an extended moment and marveled under his breath. "He knows my last name."

An exultant feeling diffused within him as he went back to his job, of manning the door, a prosperous man.

Jeff had boarded the 10:15 69 Adirondack at Penn Station and located his reserved window seat in the seventh aisle of the third car. The train wasn't congested with passengers which was quite uncommon, especially ten days before Christmas. But it was probably due to the fact that today was a Wednesday, and there was yet another weekend intervening before the holidays. People were favored with a couple more daybreaks to make an earning to compensate that additional extravagance right at the end of their splurge, which usually is that one long-fancied object for themselves out of a whole bunch of gifts for others.

Jeff parted the curtain from his window and eyed fleetingly the faces at the platform who were mostly boarding or simply there to see off their loved ones. Emotions pervaded those faces copiously that ranged from heartache of separation to elation of imminent union. He related to the latter himself and the feelings derived from the commencement of this travel evoked a subtle excitement within him. He meditated on the elusive emotions and situations that would arise and how the rest of the family would conduct itself and respond to his arrival.

He hoped for all his siblings to be there when he reached, as to face them individually after such a long estrangement and implore each for forgiveness might be too arduous for him. He was willing to accept the censures but wasn't strong enough to endure it multiple times.

As he speculated into his foresight, his face was infused with a sublime feeling of peace and contentment. The faces of his loved ones flipped through his memories, from his siblings to his parents. From the nurturing shelter of Lena's unconditional love, to the unyielding foundations of Martin's austerity. From those unremitting moments of pride and honor induced by the brilliance of Linda's unmatched capabilities, to the sturdy assurance of support from Dave's diligence and perseverance. And finally, the impish shenanigans orchestrated by an incorrigible mind belonging to Maggie. He just imagined the house with the complete family back together again. He fancied the long talks and accompanying laughter in the folds of comforters and coverlets upon over-populated beds. The ceaseless revelry and hopeless discussions outlasting the dark, snowy nights. He gradually turned nostalgic and drifted away, putting his eyes to rest. He hoped to live and make a memory out of every moment, for today will not dawn again.

The departure announcement resounded through the PA system and the train lurched into ambulation. The trip was almost 7 hours long providing Jeff enough time for the desired state of mind and body. Whether it'd be rest or reminiscence, that was one dilemma he was quite proficient at resolving.

Martin sat on the porch, his eyes ever watchful of the graveled road that extended both ways, awaiting a blessing long desired. His sight, perpetually laid out on the street, gradually gave way and fluttered to a close. He had just dozed off when a sudden tap of car horn roused him up.

He squinted to ward the plentiful white of snowfall in the background and shadowed his eyes for a better view. His view was blessed and face exultant as a Honda pulled into the driveway and a waving arm appeared beyond the greenish tint of the passenger window. The joy was equally beaming from that obscured face that shone with laughter. Even before the minivan could be parked, the door of the vehicle was opened and a woman stepped out in fervor of a union with arms aloft for an embrace.

"Lena, they're here." Martin floundered down the length of the porch.

The two met on the lawn and clung to each other for a long moment. They parted with a runnel of tears down their eyes. Martin held her face in his weakened, shivering hands and kissed her forehead. As the pair of big brown eyes opened to behold her father, they quickly darted toward another voice that called her name in pure delight.

"Maggie!" Lena opened the mesh screen door and stepped onto the porch.

"Ma..." Maggie rushed over and hugged her tightly.

Two children, six and four, led by a man, came into Martin's embrace as he knelt to match their stature.

"My babies." Martin attempted to lift them up in his arms, but was too old and feeble to accomplish that. "Oh kids, I wish I was young again." Martin noted his failing health and gaining age.

"Can't always have what we wish for, can we Martin?" The man came over for a vigorous handshake. Dressed in a signature jacket and neatly groomed, he appeared quite urbane and dignified.

"Welcome Edward," Martin nodded.

"Thanks for having us," Edward winked at him.

"Ron, Helen won't you say hello to nana?" Maggie drew the children to the porch as they ran to Lena and each landed a kiss on her cheek.

Lena retaliated with multiple on theirs and wiped away the droplets of jubilance under her eyes. "You two little devils, always have me cry."

"Yeah, I hope they step out of their malice and get a little older." Edward came with a peck on Lena's cheek.

"How are you, Edward?" Lena queried.

"Trying to make a living." Edward rejoined dryly. Maggie' s smile faded at that remark and was furtively discerned by her mother.

"Is everything all right, son?" Martin staggered closer and kept a comforting hand over Maggie's shoulder.

"The weather's gone bad to worse. It's good we made it out of Boston before the roads got undrivable." Edward's dissimulated response was enough for the old souls to intuit the gravity of their hardships.

"It's so wonderful to see all of you again," Lena quickly masked the situation. "Let's go inside, it's getting awfully cold out here. How about some hot cocoa, children?"

"Yeah!" They both bawled in unison.

She led the kids inside and Edward trailed with the luggage. Maggie delayed on the porch hiding away from her father's intrusive stare.

"What's the matter, Maggie? Is everything all right?"

"Everything is fine, dad. It's just been a little stressful for him for the past couple of months. That's all."

"Is that all?" Martin confirmed solicitously.

"Yes, that's all." Maggie laughed and threw away any possibility of continuation of the subject. She wrapped her arm around Martin's portly waist and placed her head upon his chest. "This isn't about us. Tell me what's stirring with Jeff? All of a sudden, he writes to me calling us here for Christmas, asks us to reach here exactly on the fifteenth? What's going on?"

"If I knew, I'd tell." Martin gave her his honesty.

"Did he write to you?"

"Oh yes, he wrote. But I guess I only have as much information as you at the moment." Martin shrugged and joined Maggie in her perplexity.

"He didn't tell you anything?" Her tone made more of a statement than a question. "That is so unlike him."

"Well, big cities change people."

She promptly looked up at him. Holding that gaze, Martin grasped the troubles that glinted in her eyes and she allowed him to extract as much as he needed in a wordless stare.

"Am I good blocking the sidewalk?" Barked a voice.

Maggie and Martin were both stirred out of their gaze and glanced at a Mercedes M-Class joining the queue almost barricading the sidewalk.

The voice was familiar, in fact too familiar that sparked a cheerful laughter across their faces. Martin and Maggie went on to welcome them. The eldest of the siblings stepped out of the driver's seat and hugged them both. Linda was accompanied by a sixteen-year-old and a man about a couple of years older than her.

"Father, you surprise me every year with your ability to stay young. And I thought you turned seventy two Christmases ago." Linda remarked teasingly with a wry smile.

"Really? Well, you get the child of the year award then. Your mother keeps complaining about this pot belly here. This seems to be going the wrong way each year." Martin retorted in equal frivolity.

"Then you should give up on your drinking preference, Martin. Try bourbon for a change. There's a reason it's called a beer gut." The man was attired in a charcoal three-piece suit, graying hair, a tremendous appeal of an erudite personality dripped from his mannerisms.

"James, please, don't start your counseling with him all over again. I think he had enough of it the last time." Linda objected and continued toward the house.

"I'm just trying to help. How are you, Martin?" He shook his hand.

"Trying to keep up with the recommendations from two years ago. And you?"

"Trying to keep up with your daughter. There she goes." James went after her.

Lena came to the group of coalescing relatives and kissed them one by one.

"Lena, beautiful as always. Now, you are a living specimen of age defiance. I must bring you along to our next convocation. My friends would be thrilled to see you." James commented after landing a kiss on her cheek.

"It's not the thrill of his friends that excites him, but the idea of having you by his side. He wouldn't give up on flirting no matter how many rejections he encounters." Linda raised her brows trying to convince Lena of the humor behind the affray.

"I don't keep a track of that, you may if you want to. It is in perseverance where lies the success of a human." James aggravated her even more.

"I'd love to see you die trying." Linda taunted him this time.

"At least I'll have a reason to die for." James was incisive.

Exasperated to the core, Linda wagged her head. "You can't defeat a flirt in their own expertise."

"You know it, don't you?" James chortled.

"Nancy, come along now." Linda gestured to the girl who was leaning against the car for all this time. The teenager had a typical aura of indifference encompassing her which also implicated traces of misanthropy. She finally moved rolling her eyes in annoyance.

"How is my big girl?" Martin uttered as he kissed Nancy. She managed a fake smile across her lips and proceeded into another dreadful embrace from Lena and one more from Maggie.

"Grandma, grandpa." The two coveted words came out perfunctorily from her mouth, and it was sealed after that. She had done them a huge favor by acknowledging them both.

"The table is served with brunch. Let's hurry inside." Lena clenched her granddaughter by both shoulders and aided her into the house.

"Sounds like a great idea. Only if your daughter could cook as well as you do." James nudged Linda marching past her onto the porch.

Linda again shook her head in disbelief. "Why don't you take some cooking classes yourself? At least we'll have a use for you." She entered door as their discourse was muffled beyond the walls.

Maggie reveled in their playful banter then tarried on the porch. Martin halted at the door and returned to her but didn't disrupt her pensive contemplation in which she saw the years of her childhood in every crevice and corner of the house. After a while, she smiled again.

"It is so nice to see you and the house, dad."

"I am very happy to have everyone here, especially you after three years." There was a tinge of complaint in Martin's voice, but it was forgotten instantly.

"I'm glad to be home." Maggie squeezed her father's arm.

"I know. And I can't say about the rest of the things he plans, but Jeff has succeeded in bringing us all together once again. Right?"

"Yes."

"Then let's go in and enjoy while it lasts. It isn't every day I get to see all my children at home together."

She laughed a little, then absorbed the memories of her past strewn around this home and in everything that surrounded it. She nodded decisively and entered the house with her father, hand in hand.

# Chapter Nine

✵

A ball went up soaring through the air, gaining substantial elevation right off the bat and landed beyond the fenced periphery of a junior baseball field. Homerun! The crowd bellowed in celebration, as the base was loaded and the batter had ju st scored a win for their school's team. The mates rushed out of the dugout, as the runners completed the circuit, and charged the batter, lifting him up on their shoulders and carrying him around the diamond. Jeff raised his cap in exuberance and waved to the spectators. It was a proud moment for him as all he could hear was applause and chants in praise of his name echoing throughout the grounds. But in that clamor, the sole voice of his grandpa still remained in his soul and the promise he had made had just materialized.

Suddenly, the festivity of a win was deluged by a bursting downpour. The day had been gray for long, it finally yielded to torrential rain. The crowd scattered in all directions and ran to shelter, as for some it was inside of a car and for the remaining, the looming building of the school behind the field. The storm had been forecasted by the weather authority for a week now. It was finally here and was planning to linger for quite some time.

This relentless precipitation had rattled the town for three days now and had altered between rain and sleet intermittently. The town school had closed its doors indefinitely until the capricious weather subsided. That unforeseen recess was a blessing for children, as most of them would gather at the school play-field and exhaust themselves to death by the end of daylight and return home begrimed and mud-soaked with no more strength than to curl up in their beds and sleep the night out to awake to another day of play. Jeff and Erica were a part of those draining recreations along with other thirteen-year-olds. But as the storm placated, it was obvious for the school to reopen, and when the households received an official notification from the principal's office of resumption of sessions, the children were nothing but dismal. The rain hadn't stopped altogether, but it was now feasible to roam the streets of town without any intimation of a hazard. But the aftermath of this rainstorm was aiming for a greater dealing with a lot of unsuspecting townsfolk.

Since the day the incident at the bridge transpired, almost claiming the precious life of the youngest of the Saunderhurst family, Maggie was never permitted to travel with Jeff alone. She was dropped and collected from school by one of the adults of the house and it happened to be an uncanny coincidence that it had never rained much in the morning in the past three years or so. Maggie was safely deposited in her school classroom, and if the weather turned inclement by the end of the day, there was always a family member waiting outside for her, with an umbrella tucked under the arm.

It was just another dawn as rain still pelted the town, but the schools were officially open and Lena wasn't exceedingly indulgent to grant another day off even after constant excuses proposed by Jeff that ranged from health issues to unavailability of school supplies, while Maggie just sat back and watched for the outcome. After about good fifteen minutes of venturing every way he could, nothing availed him, and he simply picked-up his backpack and headed for the door with Maggie right behind.

"Wait, both of you. The school's arranged for a bus to pick up children. They'll be here shortly." Lena wiped her hands and joined Jeff at the door keeping an eye on the road.

"Ma, do we have to take the bus? I'll ride to school, everybody else is." Jeff protested.

"Look outside, Jeff. You won't even get past one block and catch a cold. I'm not risking that this year. Besides, you've had enough days off." She pushed him away from the ajar door to save him from a cold draft.

"I already have a fever, look." Jeff tipped upwards for her to feel his forehead. She didn't bother. Jeff wailed falsely.

"Yes, I know you don't. But don't make it happen now. If I knew where you were going for the past three days to play, I would have given you something to cry about."

Jeff jolted to silence. "Why don't we have a car, ma?" he asked innocently.

"We don't have enough money to buy one." Lena glanced down at him, as he had gone into a trance of sadness. She patted his back and revived him. "Maybe we will one day. Besides, not many people in town have a car. Do your friends have a car?"

"Two of them do." Jeff tried to remember.

"See? Only two. When all of them would have one, you'll be one of them as well." Lena smiled reassuringly, Jeff reciprocated.

The bus horn sounded at the street.

"There you are." Lena checked her kids for the last minute swathing.

"Is that the bus?" Maggie was terrified at the sight of the vehicle.

The bus was an old model transport medium, bedraggled and dingy.

"That bus is lucky to be moving on those wheels." Lena concurred with her appraisal of the begrimed wreck. "Well, all you need to do is get to school. I hope it makes it there. Let's go." Lena took them by their hands and led both of them down the path under the umbrella.

As the kids boarded the dilapidated box, the metal creaked and sank at the weight.

"Does this move, sir?" Lena questioned the driver with concern in her eyes. "I mean this is safe, right? The bus is in a poor condition."

"I guess so." The guy drawled, closed the door shut and accelerated further picking Erica down the street.

Erica ascended the steps and just when she came past the driver's square, the unkempt man crouched to his left and slipped a copper flask from his breast-pocket. He removed the screw-top, took a large swig from it, concealed it right back where it came from and geared the bus to continue driving after maneuvering speedy a u-turn.

Erica walked past rows of classmates and found her best buddies at the rear, claiming a seat right next to Maggie.

"Mornin' Maggie. Jeff." Her amenity was halfly requited as Jeff remained hushed on the back seat.

He quietly eyed the trees in a rapid loss against the pacing vehicle and the light crackle of sleet against the window-glass. He also discovered the aftermath of the storm in the detritus that now littered the streets. Toppled mailboxes, dangling tree branches, aluminum roof panels that were blown off sheds and barns.

The scruffy driver prompted the switch for windshield wipers as the sleet had intensified and the tires bounced over debris. He leaned forward in his fuddled state and attempted to wipe away the steam from the glass, pushing into the horn and tapping it repeatedly. He fell back and maneuvered the bus upon the icy road nearing a bend, without any consideration toward slowing down or the children that packed the vehicle to capacity.

Just as the curve deceitfully narrowed requiring an essential deceleration, the inebriated driver was too foggy to lift his foot off the pedal.

The bus hastened forward and abruptly approached a looming obstacle. A fallen tree branch blockading the road partially and its tapered ends protruding menacingly in all directions.

The driver slammed on the brakes and spun the steering wheel completely to the right. The bus lurched sideways and careened. A pool of grease had dappled the road in the center as the front left tire slithered through it and the entire bus tipped sideways banking on two left tires.

The children in the rear were thrust to the side and those sitting at extreme left were shoved against the metal and glass. With the sudden increase in weight on one side, the bus overturned and crashed into the road as metal crumpled, screeched and sparked against the gravel. The glass imploded, shooting fragments all around the panicked, fragile young bodies. The slide slackened the grinding bus, but it hadn't reached a standstill. The grease and ice aided and the force of unchecked velocity dragged the bus to the edge of the road as it plummeted into a deep, gaping creek.

The drop wasn't too long in duration but monumental in suffering as the bus went on whirling for a good thirty feet, trampling undergrowth and tenuous forest of young evergreens, disintegrating its outer hull. The children were thrown around and hurled against gravity inside the cartwheeling cubicle.

It finally came to a stop and the shattered wreckage was an unnerving sight. The bus, now nothing more than remains, stayed motionless for a long moment with no indication of life inside or out.

It was a pandemonium at the clinic that noon. A traumatized throng of parents bustled in a desperate plea to find and subsequently tend to their ailing children. The doctors and the nurses were already devastated with the sudden adversity as their few numbers and a diminutive infirmary were inadequate to treat all those children at once, and the turmoil added to their agony. The gurneys were laden with two or three kids each, some of them unconscious and some groaning with affliction. The checkered tile floor was stained with blood, as people trudged right through marking red footprints all over the facility. Fearful family members rushed about with nurses and doctors with persistent inquiries, some unanswered, some insufficiently answered. There was an avalanche of tears staining every face, plenty of distraught creases on sweat-moist foreheads.

A dreadful calamity for all affected, and joining the sea of overwhelmed faces were Martin and Lena. They jostled through the disorderly commotion and checked the stretchers for their own heartbeats. They finally breathed in some relief locating Maggie on a corner bench with hers and Jeff's backpack by her feet.

"Maggie!" Lena screamed in thrill of the heartening view and wrapped the little one in her arms. "Are you hurt? Does it hurt anywhere?" Lena perused her for injuries.

Maggie pointed to some abrasions over both elbows and forearms, and a laceration on the right leg which was still bleeding and untreated.

"What the hell is wrong with these people, can I get someone to do their job? She is hurting right now." Martin was incensed to see his daughter's open wound. "Hey you, we need some immediate help here."

There was hardly a soul heedful to his demands as their own plights were enough to render them incautious of others.

Lena's fear was only partly abated, "where is your brother?"

"Jeff was on the bus?" Martin asked anxiously.

Lena looked back at him confirming his alarming dubiety. "They both went together. He didn't want to go, but I made him!"

"Oh..." Martin receded into the crowd once more scanning the helpless young faces to find the one he was most desirous to see.

After a while of harrowing search and inquiries, Martin found Jeff inside the infirmary. He was unconscious and severely wounded, as multiple bloodstained bandages manifested. Martin swallowed some courage into him as he was about to collapse into a poignant state of desolation. Lena joined him in the doorway and held onto his trembling hand for encouragement. Their journey to his bloodied gurney forced the most disconcerting steps they had ever taken in life. The nurse approached Jeff's limp body and checked for vitals.

"That's my son." Martin's voice became guttural. He cleared his throat. "That's my son, is he all right?"

The nurse turned toward them both. "He is unconscious. The injuries he's sustained are not lethal. He is all right, but it will be a while before he awakens." The nurse passed a subtle smile that assured them of their son's condition.

Martin pressed Lena's hand in his own and solaced each other. "Would you please take a look at my daughter, as well? Her lesions are still untreated." Martin requested in a dulcet tone.

"I will. Would you bring her in here, please?" The nurse prepared an examination table.

Martin gestured Lena to bring Maggie along. "Thank you." He took Jeff's hand into his and caressed it soothingly.

After a moment Lena walked in with Maggie and Erica. Surprisingly Erica was identically harmed as Maggie, bearing some scrapes and scratches around limbs and torso. The nurse helped Maggie on the examination table and placed her leg up on the cushion and dressed her laceration with betadine.

"This is nothing to worry about. Strong girls like you can take a gash like this with no problems, right?" The nurse eased Maggie's apprehension with her gentle words. "See, nothing even happened. Say, how did you two manage to get away with these small scratches when those big boys over there are fraidy-cats right now?"

Maggie took a moment to respond, then pointed toward her sleeping brother. "He saved us."

"He saved you? Wow, how did he manage to do that?" The nurse became exceedingly interested in the whole story.

"He put his arms around us and covered us both." Maggie went on nonchalantly. "When the bus would go upside down, we would hold on to him and he came between me and the bus from this side and then the other. He even hurt his arm when we squeezed into him."

The nurse, as well as the parents, were now equally curious.

"She means to say he pinned us both and cushioned us under the seat. We weren't tossed around because we were tucked under him. But when we went sideways, he'd turn himself over to save us from all that metal, putting himself between us and anything else, which hurt him on the back and arms. But it didn't hurt us except these scratches because of the floor." Erica completed the elucidation, leaving the adults in disbelief. "He knew what was going to happen, and he just shoved us both under the seat when the bus tilted. He did save us."

That was one instance when the adults were speechless against the composed recollection and calm words of the young. There was nothing more left to be said, it was all done and over with.

It was that fateful day when Jeff had realized the true intentions and power of time and how it affected a life. It was that day when Jeff and Maggie had taken a bus for the first time ever to school. It was that day when they both met with such an endangering catastrophe. And it was that very day when the Saunderhurst family realized the true value and extent of Jeff's love, especially for the two most special people; one with whom he shared the house and the other with whom he shared everything but the house.

That patch of narrow curve was notoriously prominent when disasters were debated in this town. Even though they were rare, but threatening nonetheless. Use of cars was not frequent amongst the townsfolk and there weren't many households who owned one, hence the streets initially built were not designed for vehicles. It had been ages since the thought of restructuring this town according to modern needs had entered the mind of the governing offices. And even if it did, this small place was not worthy of their forethought or any implementation in its regard. The kids had utilized other shorter and faster routes to get to the school as their bicycles allowed them to cut through backyards, alleys and vast unkempt lands, while vehicles would almost double the amount of time taken to reach the same destination using roads.

When the investigations into the case of the school bus accident progressed, it was divulged to the public of the town that the same patch of road underwent another mishap approximately an hour earlier to that incident. A shabby delivery truck carrying barrels of machinery lubricant had lost control at the bend and reeled, dropping a loosely clasped barrel and spilling the content on the road. The matter was negligible and unreported, but the mess that was left behind proved to fatal. That stain of grease on a rain-drenched street inflicted an inexorable trauma upon twenty-nine young souls, but before encountering that deadly misfortune, the bus seated thirty-eight.

Jeff had been confined to his room for a couple of days that followed as he rested and recuperated under extreme care and provisions. For the duration of each day, he was closely observed by Maggie and Lena as they both flickered about his room in errands hardly required of them, but their determination to comfort Jeff with any amenity demanded right from the convenience of his bed met with greater appreciation and gratitude from him. Erica would join this compassionate service at times wherever she would deem a possible discharge from her own chores.

A doctor would regularly visit to examine Jeff's injuries and briefed Lena on his way out about her son's swift recovery and the necessary changes to his routine for better healing. By nightfall, Jeff was tucked into his bed after a full nourishing meal which was mostly consumed in the company of the family as all would gather around his bed and narrate the day's happenings for his amusement. It was a joyous talk as long as it lasted and just when Jeff would begin to drift off with fluttering eyelids and a swagging head, they would quietly disperse to allow him a sound sleep. Jeff would not be awakened until daybreak when a soft, mellisonant voice belonging to her mother would ring in his senses while he'd still be gaining consciousness.

"Jeff... Jeff, wake up sweetheart. Wake up..."

"Wake up, Jeff... Jeff, wake up sweetheart." A familiar sound resonated in Jeff's dozing senses. He abruptly awakened from an unfathomed sleep. He looked straight ahead, but could not find her mother peering in from the door. He glanced around himself, but couldn't feel the comfort of four pillows bolstering his head and back, or a snug cover of his plush blanket enveloping him. He was on a reserved window seat of a coach, and the passing landscape hinted that he was about to reach his destination. It had begun to snow, and quite heavily.

The upcoming station was named in the announcement and Jeff experienced the shudder of anticipation as well as nervousness infiltrating his frigid hands and feet. It was just another twenty minutes to his destination, a duration which was soundly spent in contemplating the greeting he would propose to his family which would bear a tone of remorse, a tinge of plaintiveness and a whole lot of apology.

The train had come to a gradual halt as a few passengers alighted with their handbags and luggage, and marched in a rush to the exits.

Jeff found himself searching for a cab in the blinding snow as there was a dearth of taxis outside the station. He shielded his eyes against the burst of flakes and wind, and found one parked at the far end of the street. He swiftly trod toward it.

He approached and knocked on the passenger side window. It rolled down instantly and he leaned into it.

"Two Brooks. About an hour's drive west." The gusts were howling and the snow swirled suppressing any sounds emitted. Jeff had to elevate his voice to almost a shriek and also guard his mouth from being stuffed with flakes.

"No, no, no. That's too far. Won't be able to make it. Look at the weather." The driver seemed terrified at the thought of driving in the conditions. Snow blew into his car.

"I'll make it worth your while. How do three hundred dollars sound?" Jeff attempted to persuade him with a wad of bills.

"How far's it from here?" The driver was tempted.

"About an hour. More if we drive at a safe speed." Jeff had to shout at the limit of his lungs. "I would've taken the bus, but it doesn't leave until 6 pm."

The driver opened the passenger door and allowed him inside. Jeff quickly took the invite. He put his luggage in the back and jumped on the seat, closing the door. The snow gradually settled along with him.

"Now, let me hear what you sayin'?" The driver eyed the wallet that Jeff had flourished all the way entering the car. He could see the bills all right.

"An hour to get there--"

"So means about two in this weather. Three hundred dollars you said, right?" The driver reconfirmed.

"All here."

"A hundred and fifty an hour? Hmm... now that's a lot of money to give you second thoughts. Three figures an hour. You know, I always wanted to score like those big bankers and city lawyers always gloating about those numbers they make hourly. Finally get into their league." He had almost drifted into a fantastic world of dreams.

"We're good to go then?" Jeff enjoyed the glint of greed in the driver's eyes.

"Hell yeah, I'm never gonna have a ride agree to an outrageous fare like this ever in my life drivin' up and down this godforsaken place. I'm in." He geared the car and rolled forward.

"Outrageous situations call for outrageous measures." Jeff buckled up for a jarring ride.

The moving car jerked to a stop. "But that fare isn't fair to you."

"It doesn't have to be. A fair deal never fares well for both ends. In all fairness, one must emerge more satisfied with the deal than the other. Just a matter of who's willing to yield in a given circumstance. Besides, it's something I offered to give to you, not that you are trying to swindle an innocent passenger out of his life savings. So, doubting the fairness of a fare is really subjective."

The driver chortled and pressed the accelerator. "Are you a banker or a lawyer?"

"Neither. Writer."

"Ahh... now I know where you get your words from. That brain up there is good." He squinted to get a view of the road ahead in the snowstorm. "You're a wise man. The bankers and lawyers not too much. They speak all those big business words and talk about everything like they know it, but nothing out of that makes sense in life." He had a peculiar disposition of thrashing about his arms when talking, which amused Jeff in a way.

"You drive a lot of bankers and lawyers, don't you?"

"Everyday. But all the money they make, never give a dollar more than the fare, change here and there, but never a nice tip. Think about that."

"Yeah, that's frightening." Jeff agreed gladly and adjusted the heat toward his knees.

"But who cares about them! I'm an honest man and make an honest buck. But you're a crazy man yourself to be out in this weather. People out today are mostly regular riders up and down a station north or south. Not many out of them are town travelers. And believe me, if they didn't have a car parked outside this station, they would have found a place to lodge. Nobody is that eager to get home, you know what I mean. I know what I'm talking about."

"We are all lunatics, my friend. Most of us have a crazy reason behind it when by the end of the day, it isn't that crazy at all." Jeff tapped a picture of a young girl clipped to the dashboard. "Some travel miles knowing the possibility of never reaching their destination on time. Some wait in a blizzard the whole day knowing they might not find a rider at all. But when the hopes of two hopeless ends collide, the outcome seems to be hopeful."

The driver conceded a moment of silence. "That's my daughter, she's nine. Her mother right there. It is hard to feed a family at times when you don't have a paycheck mailed to you every week. You are my first customer today, probably the only I'll need. But I'll be a happy man when I return home tonight."

"So would I." Jeff yanked the lever and angled his seat to an incline. He pushed back and relaxed.

"Hey, I don't know the way, you gotta help me here."

"I'll show you the way. You just follow where I'm going."

The driver brayed, "I'll wake you up when we get to the highway. Take a nap if you want." He nudged Jeff teasingly. Jeff remained silent with his lips streaked with a wry smile, eyes closed.

A melodious Christmas song played soothingly on the CD changer. But there was hardly a person listening to the mellow tune, as all were engaged in conversations, in groups of twos and threes, around random areas of the house.

"Hey kids, watch out for table corners." Maggie checked the three children who were preoccupied with their puerile missions to save planet earth and destroy evil for its sustenance. "We don't want any pirates with an eye patch for the holidays."

Ron and Helen found their companion in Charlie who was about three years Ron's senior and abetted them both in mischief. Helen was somewhat left out of this faction as a four-year-old sister wasn't a significant ally to their team. But she availed her absence from the mission to grab a bite or two from her mother's plate, and Maggie was more than glad to find her eat something for a change. But just as soon as she would replenish her strength, she was back trailing her elder brothers around the house once again.

"I miss the taste of your hands, mom." Dave had just filled up his plate with cut slices of turkey and fried beans.

"You don't have to miss anything. You know you're always welcome here." Lena leaned into him and patted his cheek. "I'm just a couple minutes of drive away."

Dave had grown and it wasn't only evident in age but size as well, being heavier around the middle. He was unshaven, ungroomed, a pair of light blue denim and a green plaid shirt that adorned him. Overall, a typical laboring, small-town family man.

"I know." Dave passed the dining table and a group of gossiping women hushed as he went across.

Linda was held in a worrisome exchange by Gloria who was a perfect counterpart for a small-town family man, as she could trounce a competition between small-town ladies to win the title of an exemplary, ideal housewife and mother any day of the week.

"My concern isn't for our own lives, we're halfway down already. But I tell you in the presence of God, I'm worried about my child." Her voice resumed as Dave faded beyond hearing distance. "I have been married to your brother for fourteen years, and I tell you in the presence of God that I never asked him for anything. Any luxury, any comfort, I never forced him to exhaust himself for those sort of things. I'm happy with what we have, our home, our lives. But I now have a child, a child we both must worry about. His future, his education, the family he will have in some years. And in the presence of God--"

"I think we went on too far with that, Gloria. He has a lot of time until he gets married and begins a family." Linda had a subtle frown of confusion across her face which was veiled behind her solicitous eyes but lingered on there somewhere.

"Yes, but wouldn't you worry about your daughter? As parents, it is our duty to provide for our children and plan a better tomorrow. I'm sure you've started to make decisions about Nancy?" Gloria's sincere concern reflected in her eyes.

"Gloria, I understand what you're trying to say. And I believe, as a mother, you are very devoted toward Charlie which is a wonderful thing." Linda held onto Gloria's hand and her gaze.

"As his elder sister, I can only look up to you to change his mind. He wants to stay in this town for the rest of his life. Charlie is nine right now. He has about nine more years to begin college. I want to give him a valuable educational beginning."

Maggie had listened to all of this from her chair at the far end of the table. There was a concealed smile on her face which she shared with Lena as they both glimpsed each other. But that glimpse was so cursory, that no one noticed. Just as Gloria turned toward Maggie, she quickly pressed her lips back to an all solemn countenance.

"I have spoken to Maggie and she agrees with me. Isn't that right Maggie?"

Maggie nodded truthfully. "Yes, Gloria. Absolutely." But just as Gloria turned away, a laughter diffused across Maggie's face again.

"There is nothing we have here, the city offers so much more. Charlie's future will be so promising if we move." She was almost imploring by now.

"I know Gloria, but I think Dave might find it offensive if James and I speak to him about this. He's always wanted to live here. He's never left this town in his life." Linda presented her ambivalence for Gloria's consideration.

Lena averted from the stove and looked at the women. "Anything I should know about?"

Gloria faked a laugh. "No, Lena. It's just casual talk."

"All right." Lena moved over to grab a chair next to Maggie.

"I will try to speak to him. I will try." Linda assured Gloria which satisfied her greatly.

"I think the men would need some meat with their drinks. I'll be right back sweety." Lena took the bowl filled with pieces of baked turkey and almost rose to serve them in the living. Maggie held onto her arm and pulled her back into the seat.

"I'll go." She made her way to the living room with the bowl.

As Maggie got closer to the room and the male voices became audible, she realized the ostensible altercation, which was heard all the way in the dining, was actually an agreement between the four men who were strewn around half drunk and satiated, discussing the venal systems of the government with deep hostility.

She entered the room in a wordless fluidity, unruffled by the extreme expostulation which was a result of four opinionated mouths flaunting their knowledge about the nation's predicaments. But Martin and Dave were on the guarded end of that discourse. She silently sauntered to James, loading his plate with two pieces of turkey and a forkful of beans.

"The banks are scaring people away from an investment. That is a major problem propelling an economic downfall. I can't imagine how they intend to bring the economic structure back to life without common investments. Thank you, Maggie. I'm not even speaking about gains, just essential functioning of our economy."

"You got it." Maggie stepped further and Dave was served next.

"I'll agree with you on that. We are standing knee deep in debt. We owe most of our profits. The jobs are leaving our shores. Outsourcing is a growing concern all over the country and frankly, if this continues, there'll be a time when half of the people won't even have a home to return to. That's what's going to happen, mark my words. Every single sub-divisional and departmental service is being outsourced. Our manufacturers cannot put together a measuring tape without buying components from foreign suppliers. Of course, we'll see consequences. Communications, manufacturing, assembly, everything is leaving our land. The percentages are taking a hike, the interest rates are going up, the banks are reporting more and more delinquencies and they're almost forcing their customers to default on loans." Maggie came to Edward and just as she was about to refill his plate, Edward took the plate away and continued his reproachful grievance.

"These commercial banks, corporations are planning to capitalize on the situation. They're forgetting the more they push people into fear of investing, the more they lose."

"You don't want anything, honey?" Maggie interpolated.

"We're talking here, do you mind?" Edward rebuffed.

Maggie was mortified but swallowed her embarrassment and came to her father, leaning into the couch and putting her arm around his neck. Martin smiled and rubbed her forearm.

"People are facing mass layoffs like it was some kind of a flu everyone must go through once a year. There is nothing more humiliating than standing in front of your supervisor's desk and being handed your termination letter. You put your whole life on the line for these corporations, you put your time, your health and your sweat into their success and finally what do you get in the end? A boot to the rear. Why? Because the company cannot afford your cubicle anymore, they made millions off of your hard work, but when they lost some, you must be let go to compensate for that loss. Those degenerates, corrupt bastards--" Edward sealed his mouth before any more expletives were uttered. A long silence intervened.

"On top of that, the global warming. Half of the world believes we're right at the verge of extinction. The judgment day cometh, and we're being blamed the most." Dave disrupted that profound silence saving Edward from any more embarrassments. Maggie looked at him and grinned thankfully, he winked back.

"Now that's another one of those reasons the world hates us for. It's like false incrimination. When we're supplying goods to half of the world, we're inevitably going to have waste as well. There is no pretext for that. And if they're expecting us to go back to ice age and roast wild boars on bonfires for supper, they've lost their minds." Edward was fiercely indignant.

Maggie approached Dave and whispered into his ears. "Glad you brought it up?"

Dave had his brows raised in sweet surrender. Maggie tapped his shoulder and went on back to the dining.

As the children made another round of the dining table, Nancy parried their reckless scrambling and saved her phone from tumbling and splintering into fragments.

"God, would you watch yourself?" Nancy rolled her eyes and shook her head moving forward and searching for isolation.

Linda reached for her and grabbed her by the arm, removing her left earphone. "A little more participation would be very much appreciated." Linda's tone was reproving.

"Mom, please spare me this torture. I would rather die and rest in a coffin." Nancy was intractable.

"You know what, Nancy? You really amaze me." Linda was distraught with that reply.

"Do I now?" Nancy had a smirk across her face.

"You would spend hours talking to your friends over this phone with acronyms and words that aren't even comprehensible. And you haven't even an hour for your family, the people who love you? You don't get to see your grandparents every day, the least I can expect you to do is talk to them for a little while you're here."

"Little while? You call two weeks a little while? And not just any two weeks, the Christmas holidays. That's a cherry on the pie, mom, really. You knew I had plans with my friends, but no, no one cares about me, right? Great going, mom."

"This is your family, Nancy. You should be glad that you have one. There are people who spend their lives alone, and that is a terrifying thing. What's wrong with you?" Linda's voice choked with sadness.

"Is there a question in there somewhere I didn't get, or can I go and have my peace now?" Nancy sounded impervious.

"Please go away." Linda ceded.

"That's the intention." Nancy reapplied her headphone and strutted away.

Maggie returned to the dining and parted the blinds. "The weather is hurtful today. I wonder how Jeff's going to make it. Did he call you, ma?"

Lena joined her assessing the inclement snowfall. "I don't even know if he remembers the number. He said he'll be here on the fifteenth. He took the morning train. He should have been here by now. If he had called I would've advised him to skip the travel at least for two days. I'm worried for him in all this horrible snow."

"Nah, if he said he'll be here, he'll be here. Trust in my trust in him."

"Make a right here." Jeff guided the driver in navigating the snow-shrouded roads.

Jeff glanced around with jubilance glinting in his eyes to look upon the town and neighborhood that once housed his shenanigans. The streets and trees and houses all lined up were a blessing to see again.

"Coming home after a long time?" The driver spoke never disrupting his gaze from the dangerous road.

"Yeah, more than five years."

"Oh, that's harsh on your folks. I'm not going to say wife and kids because I don't see a ring on that finger." They both laughed.

"And you'd be right. Well, that's me right there. The second from the last."

The driver pulled over and parked the car. Jeff took out the promised fare and paid the guy with an extra hundred on top.

"Hey, the deal was for three. I'm not taking a dime over that." The driver objected.

"Outrageous favors call for outrageous compensations. What you have done today, only a few would do. And if those few were made into many, this whole world will be a different place. Besides, you have to drive back as well."

"I'm just a greedy man, that's all I am." The driver accepted the payment.

"Look at the roads, so am I," Jeff said plainly.

"Thank you, man." They both shook hands and Jeff exited the car.

He swiftly unloaded his luggage from the back. The passenger side window slid down once again.

"Hey, I got to know a lot about you but your name." The driver leaned and hollered.

Jeff returned. "Jeff, Jeff Saunderhurst."

"I'm Michael, here's my card. You ever need a driver, call me up."

Jeff accepted the business card. They nodded to each other and Jeff hastened over to the house. Michael slowly drove away.

Jeff reached under the shelter of the porch and brushed away the snow from his coat. His flicking hands came to a sudden stop when he remembered something. An illusion perchance, but his grandpa sat there in his favorite corner, on his favorite chair and smiled back at him. Jeff stepped toward it with yearning in his eyes, but it vanished. He breathed a beaming sigh, but just before he could know, a tap on the window riveted his attention.

Maggie stood on the other side of the window with breathless exhilaration surging within her. She went into the dining and informed the others. "Everyone, Jeff is here."

There was a sudden silence in the room, but they all got up in excitement and went down the hallway to the door.

The door was opened by Lena and Jeff stood there before her in his tacit felicity. They were speechless, both of them, and there was nothing but tearful gazes shared.

"Ma, it's Jeff." Maggie shook Lena out of her stillness.

Jeff placed his hand upon her cheek as tears escaped his eye. "How are you, ma?"

Lena's lips began to quiver as she took his head and kissed it frantically and burst into tears. Maggie and everyone behind her were equally moved and tears streamed. The mother and son embraced each other and Maggie ran a hand through his hair relishing that moment of togetherness.

"Five years. Five years and you never came once to see your mother? What did I do wrong? Do you know how I survived?" Lena parted from him but exuding interminable emotions.

"I'm back now, and I'm not leaving ever again. I promise." Jeff smiled and kissed her forehead.

"Let's close the door, there's a cold draft coming in. Let others meet the little brother." Dave exclaimed for the end of the queue that brought laughter to every teary face.

Jeff went on to embrace Maggie and Linda, then the men of the house.

"Edward, still mad at me?" Jeff questioned searching for an answer in his eyes.

"Nah." Edward smiled and hugged him.

James, Dave, and Gloria followed with all the children. Martin stayed behind in the living room doorway, waiting.

Jeff reached him, kept aside his luggage and a long stare ensued.

"Pa, not happy to see me?"

"Look what you did, made everyone cry!" They clung to each other never to let go. The family gathered, finally together again.

# Chapter Eleven

The house was teeming just as Martin was used to and yearned to see once again, treasuring the presence of all his children under one roof. The family was now settled as each was assigned their old rooms, the luggage was unpacked and strengths recovered after an hour-long respite. Jeff requested to be lodged in his grandfather's room and was granted the wish forthwith.

Entering the enclosure, he envisioned the pleasure of sharing the flank of that bed with his grandpa during the days of his infirmity, keeping a keen eye on the old soul while he rested. Or at some instances when their places were reversed and the misty eyes of an elder kept watch over him in his sickness. The times he lay on it convalescing after the injuries sustained from the bus accident and the whole family lavished their affection upon him. They loved him then, and they loved him now.

Jeff stepped out onto the porch, which was directly accessed from the room, and reflected on the memories of mischief he would commit during his recovery, like coming out in the open past midnight, when all were asleep, and watch the stars and nebular skies until they turned indigo with dawning rays. And the night he was caught red-handed sitting in the cold by Erica from across the grounds and the way he pleaded for her connivance afterward. That thought shifted his sight to the neighboring house and he began to wonder whether the residents still inhabited that rickety abode.

Then suddenly came the view of the elephantine oak tree that still endured and willed to last for decades more and along with it the memory of the days when life had returned to its immutable functioning and the image of three young souls hopping about its massive trunk in playful recreation.

Still ameliorating, Jeff was permitted some outside activity every day after complete bed-rest for three weeks. The tire swing that would cheer up Maggie and Erica as he pushed with all his might up until noon, and then all three of them would be out and about frolicking in the yard.

"Knock, knock." Erica approached Maggie with a game of words.

"Who's there?" Maggie asked excitedly.

"Can't you see, silly?" Erica tricked her this time. Jeff joined Erica in a playful laughter that intended to tease Maggie.

Maggie chased after them both down to the street.

But the bliss lasted only a short while as their companionship was about to be disbanded.

The death of nine young children had blazed the headlines for many subsequent weeks and the loss attached to this event was colossal. There were nine homes that were deprived of a child that doomed morning and countless lives were acutely affected by that irreversible tragedy, and being an inconsequential town, it wasn't able to bear the burden of those deaths. The lives of the surviving children went back to regularity, but there was a latent storm stirring that was about to blow away the hopes of many more homes.

Through the validations coming from an autopsy report, the bus driver was found with extreme levels of alcohol in his blood which would directly impede his cognition, and it was an irrefutable liability imposed upon the school. As such allegations rallied against the school management, the chances of its survival seemed tenuous. The supervising board sat in quiet discontent throughout the trials, occasionally contesting in favor of their continued operations and the cause for young ones to leastwise receive a basic education. But the wrath of vengeful parents and townsfolk easily crushed the plea for a just cause. The myriad lawsuits that amalgamated against the school, ranging from damages to compensations, accumulated one after another, inhibiting the school operations and eventually encumbered it into closure. It was an indefinite shut-down initially, which ingrained unfathomed delight across the world aged fifteen and under, but as days changed into weeks and weeks into months, that ennui of being home-ridden emerged to be slothfully dispiriting. The school was a privately operated educational institution and it simply couldn't endure the burden of such immense pecuniary losses that were paid in all sorts of recompense and restitution. It was never going to open again, the town had come to terms with that truth.

Just as the speculations about the school never reopening strengthened, a new era began for parents who were invaded by disconcerting thoughts that insinuated a possibility of divesting their children of an education. Daunted by such a situation to eventuate, the parents began an impetuous and anxious search for alternatives. A light shone for many as there was a Catholic school for girls in the vicinity and quite esteemed in its standing which proved to be a godsend for concerned parents. But that blessing was driven to delve deeper into the shallow pockets of those impecunious creatures of burden. The people had no other choice but to accept that option as the only resort, whether it was out of consent or reluctance, it hardly counted, but their compliance was obligatory.

The Catholic school proposed a daily bus convenience to all its distaff students which was a service dedicated to collect from and drop them all at their doorsteps. The paining afflictions of the town were partly resolved as the girls, including Maggie and Erica, were back to the quotidian practice of educational gain, while the boys were still wandering the streets in a restless lethargy. The town had always lacked communal ambition, as a result, a majority of the households contrived to get their young boys to work right after high school. The future of the male populace was simply conventional and a sudden shutdown of the school brought the boys closer to their objective sooner than they imagined. Those who were nearing completion of schooling, especially boys in high school, were ushered to seek employment which was inevitable in a few years, for some a few months.

The factory that employed Martin and Dave became a major contender and surfaced to assist the emerging youths of the town by barring all alien recruitments for two years and hiring just the local workforce from its hometown. The young hopefuls were further in luck as the minimum educational requi rement for employment at the cannery was eighth standard. If one graduated junior-high, one was welcomed with extended arms and a modest paycheck.

That same year the cannery hired seventy-nine new recruits in labor and management according to their proficiency and aptitude. The company was thriving and along with it, the young men it employed. There were some that were denied a job at the factory, but not all hope had been lost as they sought and seized employment with other businesses and towns that were accessible by cars to those who owned one.

But then developed the most compassionate act of altruism and benevolence when some of the young fellows who owned a car opted to leave their jobs in the town and travel in proximity to give work to those who didn't own a car and, consequentially, couldn't travel far. It was seen, remembered and cherished as a fraternal generosity that forged the foundations of the small town upon pillars of love, humanity, and empathy.

Even the myriad love could not solace eighty-four young men who cursed their languid strides of growth and age. Some families resolved to relocation but were few in numbers as there weren't many who had the capital to start their lives and careers anew. The families that stayed, found themselves in a deeper quandary as there were no schools, except the Catholic school for girls, within thirty miles of the town. Parents began to dispatch their boys to relatives in different towns, cities or states altogether. It was an emotional and unwilling separation as boys were seen in a storm of weeping when they departed their homes, but it was all done for the betterment of their upcoming lives and the boys, resentfully but gradually grasped their guardians' intentions.

There were yet a few boys that remained hopeless and Jeff was one of them. Not all families had relatives or kin they could avail to shelter their sons until they studied, as they were not deeply rooted in the country. The Saunderhurst family was one of the few. The possibility of Jeff being deprived of an education troubled Martin and Lena many a time, and their solicitous discussions would soon alter into heated disputes.

"The Smiths just shipped their boy to California last night. He's going to stay at his uncle's. They say it's a good school they have there, one of those most famous ones too." Martin lounged in a chair in the backyard and uncrowned a bottle of beer.

"I'm worried, Martin. Jeff needs a school or at least some kind of activity to engage in. That poor boy is wandering all day long. He doesn't have anywhere to go, anything to do. Most of his classmates have left the town, his best friends are leaving one by one. Maggie and Erica aren't here until three, he's going to feel deserted here if we don't sort this out." Lena wrinkled her forehead anxiously.

"Why don't you put him to something?" Martin eluded her stare.

"Put him to what? Cooking?"

"What do you want me to do? I didn't ask for that school to shut down. If there isn't one single school anywhere around us, that's not my fault. We don't have anyone we can send him to, no one." Martin inefficacy agitated him even more. "There is boarding school, but I don't think we can afford it."

"Can't afford it? This boy's life is at stake here, Martin!" Lena tapped the armrest of her chair.

"Linda is about to graduate and we have all her expenses to cover. Dave is putting in his life to support the family. We can't ask him to do more. I'm putting in overtime. Do you see any other option through which we can find a way out?"

"Then what is he going to do? Waste his life?"

"You want me to say it out loud, I will. I don't make enough money for my family. There, you're happy now?"

"I don't mean for you feel bad, Martin. I'm just thinking about our boy." She grew sullen.

"Well, so am I, Lena. Maggie's school is expensive and I've put in my efforts to get her in there." Martin eased on his vehemence.

"I'll take up a job. I'll work." Lena brightened with an idea.

"And earn what? Enough for us to move to another town? To buy a car? You think I haven't thought about all these things? But... The closest boarding school is about thirty miles from here. The school there is not agreeing to any transport because it's too far. Besides, even if I could afford to send him to a boarding school, would you agree?"

"I'm not sending him away from me." Lena became very cautious with Martin's proposal.

"I know that. If there wasn't a school for girls, Maggie would have stayed home too. I will find a way out of this, trust me." Martin searched her eyes but the answer was verbal.

"I trust you." Lena smiled thinly.

Jeff had listened to this and many similar conversations furtively behind doors, making sure no one discovered him eavesdropping. But these talks had made him aware of the grave situation his parents encountered that until now he treated with frivolity. In all seriousness, he started to comprehend the influence of this ramification and how it might impact his youth. But knowing that the adults couldn't find a solution, he doubted his callow intellect could.

Jeff had realized that his mother was correct about one thing in this trying misfortune; a wave of unfaltering solitude was propelling toward him to flood his young soul in its effect. Jeff counted his sluggish strides to the sealed playground of his deserted school and sneaked inside the fences along with a few friends, trespassing against the official notice bearing the law and its repercussions. But prosecution was hardly feared as there weren't any who guarded and enforced that law and could possibly report the transgression. The young boys were oppressed and aggrieved already, and the law had wronged them enough for one lifetime. They simply just sat in company of each other and their discourse ranged from recent movies and radio shows to their domestic bitterness that involved their education most of the time. After hours of rumination, they all would disperse, once again returning to their isolation. As weeks passed swiftly, that company of eight reduced to six, then five, and three, and the numbers kept declining as more arrangements triggered the boys in leaving the town.

Many of the town's abandoned locations and ruins were included in the desultory excursions of the remaining companions. The school-ground was one of them and the foremost spot where the gang met. Then their roving feet took them to the stream where Maggie was faced with a horrible misadventure, and then to the demolished shops at the far end of the town, and finally to the defunct railway route that hadn't felt the weight of a train in decades.

The three friends would totter on the rusted tracks for a mile until they reached the extent of their audacity to travel alone. Jeff would, at times, glimpse behind him as he excelled in light treading down the metal. A week later he discovered it was just the two of them, and with another glimpse the next day, his loneliness had caught up with him.

He refused to tiptoe any further and traced his steps back home. That night he stood on the porch and observed the ancient oak tree in his yard. It had endured years of strident environments that were ever-changing, never ceasing to its liking. It had survived storms and blizzards and yet given life and shelter to those who relied on it. It was alive and substantial still and through its rustling murmur, it gave away the secret behind its persistence.

It was the same tree he saw tonight after more than twenty years of perseverance. It had given him courage back then, it had given him courage tonight.

# Chapter Twelve

✵

Jeff was called in for supper and when he entered the populous dining room, he saw a food strewn table for six accommodating eight adults, three children and a teenager all clustered around, some in perfunctory disinterest and some with an illumined spirit. They added another chair to the huddle and Jeff joined the feast of thanksgiving which was made possible after five years. As each of them finished their dinner, they retired to the living once again with their nightcaps. Jeff tarried and helped Lena with the dishes, much to the dislike of other women, but they conceded just to allow him more time with his mother that they both longed for.

"I'm feeling younger again. The last time I saw you do dishes with me was when you couldn't even reach the counter. Oh, how beautiful were the days when you all were little."

"So, you're reminding me I haven't helped you around kitchen that much."

Lena nudged him.

"It didn't matter if you helped me in the kitchen or not, at least you were there somewhere outside when I searched for you. That was gratifying enough. These recent years haven't been so pleasing."

"I'm sorry ma, I wish I could change... everything. But what I've learned in these years is that everything has come together in changing me. And that's the most encouraging thing that matters."

"You left a boy. You've turned into a man now. That's the most encouraging thing."

After some time Jeff trailed after Linda into the living and both stumbled upon another one of Edward's tirades directed toward the government and its policies.

"We are working our asses off here, piling up our taxes in IRS receivables, and they can't find another charity than Social Security benefits, unemployment, public assistance, Welfare? I mean what the hell is wrong with these people? A common man works hard to make a living, grinding his health and age against time until it deteriorates to the last bit. And by the end of the day what do we get? A measly paycheck after I've spilled my blood and guts and sweat for people I don't even know? You're feeding off all those lazy, worthless bastards on my wages that I earned after a hard day's work listening to my lambasting bosses and their finger-wagging right at my face? And you expect me to be compassionate with these degenerates who are sucking my blood and money out of my life?" Edward was clearly liquor-sodden and manifested a wayward behavior.

"But wouldn't you want to consider this whole situation that you've controverted from the opposing perspective?" James leaned in curiously, trying to reason with him. "You are dissenting from the common opinion on the matter, let's not forget that."

"What common opinion? Who wrote the common opinion? People, who are too lazy to get off their couch and step out to look for work? I know what kind of people write these 'opinions' you call them, I know. Exactly those who benefit from these. You don't want to sleep hungry, get out that door and work for it. Don't expect people to pity you and put food on your table, you have to do that for your family. No one owes you anything. That's what it is, charity. I pity these people, so I allow the government to take out of my paycheck to give them food. I pity them, that's why. Out of my mercy are their families fed." Edward was contemptuous in his tone and sneered.

James shared a fleeting glimpse at Dave and Martin contritely.

"I believe everything would turn out to be just fine, we must have some patience. In time, our economy will improve, people will find more and better jobs and all of us are going to have food on our table." Dave assuaged the rancorous air that upset everyone in the room.

"Yeah, but their table will have more than ours, that's for sure. The American dream, right? Everything will be fine. It looks great on a campaign banner, Dave. Next time you find a republican walking down the street, give him the idea. They'll hire you campaign manager or something. If all of us had a little sense in our brains, which you clearly don't, we'd know how to deal with these 'opinions'." Edward had reeled the conversation to a derisive angle.

Dave took it silently and just smiled.

"Okay, I believe we're a little bit out of our reins here. It's been a long day, let's all go to sleep." James interrupted before things became unruly.

"What do you think we should do, Edward?" Jeff stepped in with a sharp voice. All eyes rose to his face.

Edward rose truculently and accosted him. "I'll tell you what I think."

James and Linda neared them both anticipating a fist-fight. Jeff folded his arms non-combatively. Maggie joined the spectators for an exhibition.

"You want to please them old fellows who'll be dead in a couple but can't die in peace without driving the young out of their last dollar? You better do it out of your own pocket, because my money belongs to me, to the last dime. You want to toss some leftovers to those crippled veterans and worthless deserters, you better invite them to your table, coz mine ain't free to join." He almost drawled in his drunk condition. "And if you want to feed those unemployed, lousy, little lowlifes, you better poison their next meal because they absolutely deserve it. The fewer the better." Edward's lip quivered with rage and contempt. Jeff was stoic in his stance, he hadn't backed-up an inch.

Edward acknowledged Jeff's silence as his own triumph and stalked back to his sofa haughtily.

"Your brother is still living in Watren, isn't he?" Jeff's words were composed and assured.

Edward stirred on his seat, "yes."

"He's found a job yet?" Jeff's stare was piercingly straight.

"No."

"How is he feeding his family?" Jeff's questions were rapid.

Edward was dumbstruck.

"Five years and he couldn't find a job. Maybe he's worked occasionally here and there, heck I don't know even know if that's true or not, but let's just fancy for argument's sake. Five years, maybe more, how did he manage to get along? Maybe the wife works?"

Edward's speechlessness was insulting his pride now.

"Yes, no?" Jeff demanded an answer. He received a shake of Edward's head. "No, great. How does he feed his family of three? He had a son, right? Must be six by now? He quit his job right after his birth, didn't he? I'm not even going to discuss under what circumstances he had to quit his job and if he could or couldn't find other work. This isn't about that, is it? You have a problem with giving your 'leftovers' to others, so let's talk precisely that. How do you think he put food on his table for the last five years?" Jeff's brows were dauntingly raised urging an answer.

"Disability--" Edward's voice cracked.

"What was that?" Jeff confirmed.

Edward cleared his throat. "Disability."

"Disability insurance. For all these years. Why? Because he broke his leg at the work-site. His child eats every night because of a program initiated by the government that protects people like your brother. So, next time you see an unemployed lowlife who isn't in the queue out of choice but compulsion, you better give him that poison yourself. And let's forget about him and talk about you for a moment. Your father was in the army, wasn't he? Why didn't any of you two follow him into the barracks? He could have gotten you in training in a flick. And if I can remember correctly he wanted you to be a soldier, but someone here wasn't up for it."

All eyes were fixated on Edward now. There was s silence in the room.

Jeff continued, "you could have made a captain by now, but you chose a different path. So, next time you see soldiers who have put their lives on the line for the safety of their people back in their country, throw them a piece of bread so they can relish it for a while. And as far as the old fellows are concerned, when their sons and daughters, for their own interests, leave them behind all alone to rot their old lives in an old house, they need someone to look up to. To feed themselves and not die of hunger. It's a shame it's n ot their children but the government they end up getting help from. The day you return home and spend your life caring for them, being there for them and it's never for eternity, they will leave sooner or later, that day you may go around and curse the hel l out of Social Security benefits. But until then, you better loosen up your pockets, because your old folks are still alive and doing well." Jeff concluded his argument and pungently glared at his adversary. There were a lot of parted mouths and wide eyes all across the room.

"Okay, who wants some ice cream?" Maggie disrupted the severity that engulfed the room. Everyone eased their shocked expressions.

"Nah, I'm done for the night. Heading up to the room for some sleep." Linda answered and exited the roo m. James winked at Jeff and followed his wife.

Edward rose in his mute state of mind and body and staggered out of the living, bumping into tables and rocking the picture frames on the walls.

Maggie pressed her lips in amusement and joined her brothers. "Glad you're home?"

"Yeah, out of touch with accepting different perspectives. Living alone does that to you. I'm sorry about that, Maggie. I couldn't help it when he spoke to Dave like that--" Jeff tried an explanation.

"I hate you so much for this." Maggie's face grew stern and hostile, eyes ever expanding.

Jeff dimmed with contrition.

Maggie's frown worsened, but it all suddenly exploded in a laugh. "Oh, I wanted to see your face like that so bad."

Maggie rolled along holding her aching stomach with all that laughter. "Oh God, don't even worry about it, it's not your fault. He deserved it. A man should drink only as much as his stomach can take. When liquor fills him up to his brains, that's what happens. And this is how you drain it." Maggie high-fived Jeff. "But really, that was one good scare I gave you, wasn't it?"

"You got me there... once." Jeff conceded.

"So, who wants ice cream?"

"It's the middle of December, Maggie. Ice cream, really?" Dave tried to dissuade her.

"So what?" Maggie was uninspired. "Let me tell you something big brother, ice cream is food for soul. It satisfies your belly just as much, but when you take a spoonful and the way it melts in your mouth, it's not just your taste buds that rejoice but your spirit. If angels ever landed on earth, this is going to be their fuel for survival. Mark my words."

Jeff chuckled, "you go get some ice cream, let's give angels a break for now. Don't starve yourself."

"Okay children, I'm off to bed as well." Martin helped himself up to his aching feet and headed off with Dave trailing him.

"Are we the only ones walking dead around the house like zombies?" Maggie went on to investigate.

Jeff rambled in the room looking at some old things that gave him pleasure of memory and nostalgia.

Maggie came back with a bowl of chocolate-chip cookies in vanilla. "Nope, we have a few more people alive over there."

They both took a seat next to each other on the couch as Jeff wrapped her legs in a coverlet.

"Haven't spoken to you in while," she gobbled a spoonful.

"Five years to be exact," Jeff smiled lightly.

"And counting." Maggie eyed him expectantly.

Ron and Helen ran across the hallway stomping the floor, riveting the adult siblings to peer inquiringly.

"Ron, Helen." Maggie called out.

Lena went after the little rascals. "Now who left this door open? There's a blizzard outside in case someone hasn't noticed."

"I should go after them," Maggie strained to get up.

"I'll go." Jeff stood up and went to the hallway. Before he could reach the door, he saw Lena ushering both her grandchildren inside and locking-up for the night.

"Oh, it's freezing out there." Lena rubbed her arms to warmth. Jeff embraced her tightly as the kids chuckled and went to their mother.

"Get to bed, you need it." Jeff kissed her mother and sent her away undoing her apron. "And Gloria, you too." He turned around and saw her sister-in-law outside the kitchen. "You both have worked too much for one day."

"And take this sugar-storm along with you, ma." Maggie cried from the living room softly spanking her boy.

The women smiled and went upstairs together with Ron scrambling ahead of them.

Jeff returned to the room and found Helen snuggling with her mother comfortably under the covers.

"I don't want to wake her up." Jeff shifted to a different couch.

"Wake her up? Once she's asleep, you couldn't get a wink out of her until seven in the morning even if you tied her to the back of a space shuttle. Come here." Maggie insisted he joined her on the same couch, he did deferentially.

He caressed his dreaming niece. "The kids just grow up so quickly."

"Quickly?" Maggie smirked, "you should try taking care of them for one day. Let's see how quick it goes by." They both laughed. "But she is my angel here, and he's the little devil. Guess the difference between boys and girls."

"I seriously feel offended, right now," Jeff admitted mournfully.

"I was always the angel," she teased.

"Yeah, you were. There's no doubt about that. How old is she?"

"Four."

"She looks exactly like you when you were four. The same eyes, same hair, tiny." Jeff reminisced Maggie's young little face.

"Tiny?" Maggie was doubtful about that.

"Yeah, you looked like a stick figure wearing human clothes."

Maggie punched him on the arm.

Jeff rubbed his aching injury. "People used to ask me why I didn't give you anything to eat."

"Really? Well, I never heard anyone worrying about my breakfast." She protested.

"Yeah, you ate plenty, but it never showed."

Her mouth filled with air of anger, but she quickly dismissed it sighting Jeff's sinister laughter intended to provoke her.

"You're lucky I have your niece in my arms right now. She just saved your life."

"Yeah, I'll thank her in the morning. Ron's what, six now?"

"Almost six."

"I remember I was there when he was born. But this one I didn't even see until today."

"We all missed you, Jeff. A lot of things happened since you left." There was a long moment of profound silence between them that articulated many feelings. Jeff held her ingenuous gaze which quickly became intrusive from her end.

"Why are you looking at me like that?" he questioned.

"Five years and you suddenly show up calling us all together at one place, there must be something you're hiding? I've tried all day long to see that one sign that will give away your secret, but you're smart, not as smart as me, but you are." Maggie suspected something.

"Didn't I fool everyone, you included?" Jeff enjoyed the raillery.

"I know there is something. I've searched your finger there, it doesn't have an impression of a removed ring either. But something is fishy here."

"A ring? So, that's what I've been hiding so far. Did you check my pockets for a love letter?" Jeff joked at the possibility.

"I'll check everywhere I need to get the truth out of you. But I will, that I'm sure about."

"You're taking up a challenge?"

"I'm going to win it and unmask you in front of the whole family."

"Oh, I can't imagine the stares."

"Just wait a while." Helen stirred in her arms moaning in protest against the verbiage. "I better take her to bed now, but I'm watching you."

"So am I," Jeff whispered and kissed them goodnight. "I'll close up."

Maggie went to her room and Jeff loafed around the living for a minute before heading to the front door and taking a cursory glimpse at the snowy conditions outside. He began locking the door.

Suddenly a hand rested on the glass and knocked in urgency. Jeff opened the door again and Nancy ran inside cowering from cold.

"What were you doing outside?" Jeff inquired worriedly.

"Nothing, just needed some fresh air," Nancy replied indifferently.

"For that long? You could have caught a cold out there."

"You don't need to be concerned about my health. I'm fine and I'm headed for bed. Thanks for opening the door." With that said, she stormed toward the stairs.

"You are too young to be smoking, Nancy. I shouldn't have to tell you that." Jeff had sniffed the stifling odor of a cigarette from her.

She stopped but didn't answer or dared to confront, then continued her ascend and faded from Jeff's view.

Jeff shook his head in disbelief and went back to securing the windows and doors before turning off the lights and saluting the night away.

# Chapter Thirteen

Jeff had awakened to a boisterous morning as the turbulent uproar from the dining and the hall was deafening in his room even across a couple of walls. He skittered to the bed-flank and removed himself from under the folds of a blanket, headed for the window and saw the snowstorm had diminished into light flurries now. Emerging from a bath and packing himself into his pants and a jacket, he went on to join this chaotic gathering.

Throughout his sixty-second trip to the living room, he saw a world of a cohesive family in a bustling rush about him. Women were busied around a stove complimenting each other on weight loss or gain, and alluring changes to their facial glory defying age which was a commendation they all idolized. And the men were back to being cross, sulking around the table devouring scrambled eggs, bacon, and croissants.

Jeff continued to the living, skipping all that mayhem for a moment's peace, and found himself staring at the mantelpiece that was topped with an array of pictures and memories. There was one that riveted Jeff's attention the most and he stood gazing back at a lovely, delightful couple right after their vows, in the middle of a reveling family. Jeff picked up the frame and examined the picture closely. Out of all the Saunderhurst family leaning joyously toward the newly married Maggie and Edward following the wedding, Jeff was nowhere to be found and his absence was perceived in Maggie's glum eyes, though, her face cozened her true inner feelings.

A few years had elapsed since the ordeal had bemused the town and its people, and forced a stinging separation of the young from their families. Jeff hadn't been subjected to this particular experience, but the experiences that befell him weren't any less trying. Time and circumstance had brought considerable, if not arrant, isolation into his life. But as the townsfolk and Saunderhurst family returned to their vapid diurnal commotions, it didn't take much time for them to reckon Jeff's reclusiveness as normal.

His existence was cryptic even to his own understanding, and in the shadow of this dejection, Jeff began to distance himself from everything, whether they were relations or life itself. The reasons behind his aloofness were justified when he'd begun to imagine whispering laughter, rumored talks, and mockery directed toward him, making him a freak in town lacking education which was the basis of human existence. It was true to some extent as he had become an example of an event and its aftermath, and in a small town where nothing was hidden from anyone, eluding those stares and pointed fingers, as the one who was affected the most by it, became quite impossible.

Though, the seasoned regard inclined towards empathy and consolation, the young distinctly regarded him with ridicule. The truth was far from the fact that everyone in that town was educated, some hadn't even seen the threshold of a classroom in their lives, but in his seething incertitude that inhibited self-belief, he somehow inflicted upon himself to suffer in a manner so believed.

Quite accustomed to seclusion, Jeff wasn't all alone; a cherished friendship and a sister's affection always arrived in time to deliver him from oblivion of self-hatred. All three of them had an unbreakable bond that continued to thrive for years that came next.

Following the school closure, he hadn't received any official education but spent his evenings with Maggie and Erica, giving them company in various assignments and home-work as their distress had escalated from studying in an institution administered by a faction of austere nuns. But seeing the two women of his life toiling industriously to educate themselves, he began to develop a love for books along with them.

Jeff saw Erica graduate with honors and Maggie followed right behind two years later with honors as well. His accomplishments were shone in the success of his friend and sister for which he was equally credited by both.

But then came to pass quite an amusing event that eventuated in reopening of the school in town. The mayor allied with the representatives and rallied together for a cause to reinstate a comprehensive school for the youths of their homeland. They had managed to receive all permissions to reopen but as a public school, after five years of endeavoring disputations to acquire state, federal and court ratifications.

It was a happy day for the population as the reason causing a feared separation from children was obliterated once and for all. But it could not avail Jeff in his purpose to attend a school. At twenty, he was quite reluctant to join a classroom setting with fifteen and sixteen-year-olds as his classmates.

The town had expunged that dark event from their memories and many of the boys had already returned home after schooling. But there was a sudden inexorable wave of young men driven to leave their hometowns in search of better and fulfilling employment in metropolitan areas and urban cities. Whether this compulsion kindled from the liberty they had assimilated at a very young age and were not frightened of a solitary life anymore, or just the education of a alien soil that suppressed and rendered the feeling of peace and solace that originates from living at home with families obsolete, was yet to be revealed to the parents left lonely and hopeless back home. But there were more than countable families that saw their young men leave the peripheries of the town and conduct their lives independently. The last time the separation took place it was painful for both ends, but this time it happened out of consent and alacrity from one.

Erica was one of many who left town for New Jersey to her aunt's and admitted herself into college for business studies. While Maggie wanted to accompany Erica to further her education, but she curbed her desire and refused to go as the expenses on Saunderhurst family were accumulating. Observing her heartbreak and bearing all culpability upon himself, Jeff began a desperate search for a job.

Initiating his hunt at the cannery where Dave and Martin had harnessed all their power to get him to a managerial position which was unlikely because of a long-enforced educational stipulation that wasn't met in this case, therefore, a strong rejection was imprinted across Jeff's application from which he had hoped greatly. However, a job offer did emerge from factory management in consideration of Martin's and Dave's tireless services. It wasn't a managerial but rather a floor custodian position which was the only available vacancy at the time. Martin had utterly refused that offer, denying his son to work as a custodian where he and his elder son managed. A couple more factories were tried but after their inquiries into Jeff's family history with the cannery, there weren't any willing to hire him fearing a competitor's trick to obtain rival insights.

This futile quest went on for months until, out of despair and anger, Jeff decided to rebel against Martin's decree and joined the cannery. Much to Martin's dislike, who had managed to maintain a reputed name amongst his acquaintances, Jeff dismissed any disgrace his ignominious night shift might bring upon the family to endorse his sister's wishes of attending college. But this was one domestic situation in which Linda and Dave came together to support Jeff's cause and expostulated their father with a new-age perspective, that none of the works are small or dishonorable and that adherence to traditional conventions was antiquated. It was much grueling for the siblings to dissuade their father from his ancestral opinions, but with unanimity teamed with Jeff's diligence at his job, Martin acceded. Maggie was permitted and sent to attend college along with Erica.

In all these asperities, there were some delights as well. Linda had completed her doctorate in mathematics and emerged to be the most educated person in the Saunderhurst lineage followed closely by her grandfather. Subsequent to her accomplishments, she had decided to settle for a married life and tied the knot with James, a psychology professor at City University who was seven years her senior. Their marriage was an exclusive affair, as urbane couples preferred to keep their ceremonies a silent and private family occasion, but the celebration was tremendous nonetheless. And shortly after Linda's permanent departure from home, Dave had gotten married to Gloria, a local town girl hailing from a well-acquainted family. They had soon mortgaged a home in a newly constructed development, not very far from town, and it was a steal as the prices were extremely low because of its infancy in the housing market. The Saunderhurst house had become hushed once more and the solitude of Jeff's existence was ever-increasing.

But a revelation diffused some hope into Jeff's despondency as James had researched and proposed for him to acquire an accredited high school diploma from a university that honored distance learning and was an esteemed connection of James' through various convocations and seminars. The people in town, Jeff being one of them, hadn't ever heard of such a service before and were quite astounded to learn its possibility and convenience. Linda was more than impetuous in compelling Jeff to join and begin his journey in education again.

With hard work both at job and home, everything seemed to be mending gradually with time for Jeff, and he persisted in anticipation of a better tomorrow. He had hoped of completing that program in two years at an accelerated pace to have some better employment opportunities and depart the shackles of his night shift at the factory. With such ambition, he mopped the floors, cleaned the equipment, and took the frivolity of fate with a broad smile. He would close the place around two at night after the clean-up, and walk back home believing himself to be the only living soul in town. He had the streets to himself all the way up to the skies. The world belonged to him, but it was his as long as no one else existed in it. It was empty as the night with just the sounds of darkness.

But then a startling event had occurred in Jeff's life when he was placed before a bookstore that was newly inaugurated in town marketplace, and its ownership was given in his hands. Jeff was speechless and remained agape, staring at the new awning along with Martin who had given him a surprise of a lifetime. He hadn't felt the love of his father to such an extent ever before, and he knew that Martin must have used up all his savings to the last penny to establish something like this. The whole family gathered that day to celebrate the new business, but some things did not go as planned.

The opening of this new business had hindered all possibilities of Jeff seeking a daytime job at the cannery or any other place with his new-found educational gain, as it would emerge to be impossible for him to manage both with his presence simultaneously. Hence, he continued his night shift at the factory and gave up the idea of a better job altogether. His focus now turned to the bookstore.

Jeff had doubted the success of this line of business in his hometown and his speculations were appearing to be true. There wasn't much to be learned about the venture as it was a simple trade which didn't frequently occur. This was the one and only bookstore in miles and the fact that Jeff loved to read books might have been the foremost reason for Martin to consider this particular business. But his supposition was incorrect pertaining to the reason why Jeff relished his books. It wasn't because he wanted to sell them, but because he desired to write them, to see his name inscribed behind a five hundred page manuscript one day. That desire was still latent, so was the talent.

Jeff had arrived home after closing the bookstore and before retiring to his night shift that began around eight. Martin had also returned from work. Lena waited for the men to unite for supper and served them some steaming stew as each joined the table.

"I met with Kelson today on my way here. He mentioned his son is coming home in three months, finishing his degree in about a year. He said he plans to get him married next time he comes and send him off on his own after that." Martin took a loaf of bread and passed the basket to Lena.

"Is that Edward, his name?" Lena cleared her doubts.

"That's the boy," Martin affirmed. "He's a-- I don't know what they call this degree exactly but-- info tech, I believe. Something about new things called computers. They say he's already working while he studies. I was interested in speaking to him about Maggie."

Jeff looked up at his father, solicitous to know more.

"Oh, wouldn't you think it is too soon?" Lena attempted a subtle protest.

"Soon? She's almost twenty-four, it is a good age to settle down. She isn't going to stay at the university forever. And I'd like her to get married in a family I know personally. Linda's matter was entirely different."

"I believe she has another two-three years before finishing her bachelors." Lena's eyes darted from Martin to Jeff.

"She's done her associates, I guess that's enough of education for her."

"Well, I don't see any harm in trying. We can have them meet each other and if it works out between them, we'll let them decide." Lena resolved the situation satisfactorily for both ends.

"I will call her tomorrow and have her come for the summer holidays," Martin declared.

"Shouldn't we wait just a little while for her to finish her college? It's just two more years?" Jeff spoke soberly.

Martin glared at him for a moment.

"The boy isn't very mature that he's in a rush to get married right away. I think he's my age. We can have them meet each other and let them develop their relationship for some time?"

"How do you suppose they will develop their relationship?" Martin's tone was piercingly direct.

"Spend time with each other, get to know each other better." Jeff tried to reason with him.

"I know what a development phase of a relationship consists of, and in our families we do not allow that. We should not forget about our traditions. We will give them time enough to determine if they are compatible, but it wouldn't be two years. It doesn't need that long. Dave had gotten married to a girl we knew since she was a child. Edward is someone we know equally well, and I believe he will be a better choice for Maggie than anyone else." Martin's eyes were lurid by the time he finished.

"Yes." Jeff yielded a nod.

Busied with supper, Martin spoke once again changing the subject. "Any sales at the store?"

"None."

"What is the matter? Is there something wrong with the place?"

"There's nothing wrong, it's just that this town is not meant for a business of that sort. We opened a wrong store in a wrong place."

His honesty wasn't well received by his father. "Jeff, your disrespect really amazes me. You know that?"

Jeff eyed him with concern. "I didn't mean any disrespect. I was just saying that this isn't a town where people read many books. If we had spoken about this before you went ahead—"

"Spoken to you? Perhaps, ask for your permission, that's what you meant to say, isn't it? I have put all my money into this business for what? Why do you think I spent my savings on something like this?" Martin threw his fork on the plate as it clattered. Jeff was holding his lips together. "You don't know? Well, let me tell you. Because I didn't want to see my son walk around with a mop and a bucket for the rest of his life, that's why."

Lena tapped the table tacitly indicating her husband to stop.

"No, Lena. This young man should know and learn what reality of life is. He should know how to respect his parents when they have put their own old age on the line for him. You know Jeff, we both have no funds in our accounts to cover the expenses of our remaining years. To the last cent, I have invested in you. And if I am to hear that I should have asked for permission before I deprived my old age of a moment's peace because I wanted to see you flourish and happy, then I must be the biggest failure of a man ever to walk this earth. Frankly, I did not expect my son to sit at my dining table and refuse to devote himself to the last hope we have left only because it seems to be underperforming a bit."

"All I'm saying is that it will never work in a town like ours."

"Businesses are not born in profits, my son. They are made to earn profits. If you would pay but a little attention to your bookstore, maybe it will work out for you. Look at Dave, he's taken every responsibility ever laid upon him with sincerity. Whether it was this house or his own, he's always stepped up. Learn something from him if you can. Your made-up dream world isn't the reality of life. It is a refuge for people who run away from every little burden. Take a few responsibilities for a change because when the time comes, you would not be able to feed your old folks or yourself on that six-hour shift you do at the cannery. Be thankful for what you have." Martin took a furious sigh at the end of his tirade.

Jeff refrained from articulating his fear of a failed business any further from that point on, as in a few months there was no need for a verbal expression. The register bruited loud enough.

# Chapter Fourteen

✵

The failure of the bookstore was often imputed to Jeff's apathy rather than its true cause, and his father had become so accustomed to this judgment that his reasoning was constantly clouded by his belief. There had been many altercations between them that originated from the time Jeff had joined the factory, to the days Maggie was sent away to college and had grown quite recurrent in the recent months about the business. But Jeff maintained his composure and silence throughout trying with utmost certainty to never wound his father's expectations.

He received some special instructions about his demeanor along with an invitation that came from the Kelson family. It was a gathering called to celebrate the retirement of Mr. Kelson which was mainly an opportunity for the families to introduce Maggie and Edward to each other. Both had arrived home for their summer break and were oblivious of their parents' intentions. It was a contained celebration with only a few families attending a small festive dinner at their home. But Maggie and Edward appeared well-pleased with each other's company, appreciating their presence with laughter and meaningful conversations that sometimes digressed toward a humorous end. Maggie's big brown eyes sparkled as she spoke, exchanging some common interests and sharing opinions on matters that were remotely relevant to them both. Edward, with his own pair of blue eyes, found her laughter to be mesmerizing as he'd just irrepressibly harness his wry wit to make her laugh. The families had succeeded in bringing them together, but the reason was yet to be divulged.

Jeff confined himself from most of the conversations and people except for casual greetings and responses, but surprisingly, he found himself to be a young girl's object of affection who was Edward's younger sister, Liliana. As the elders spoke in whispers around the table, she constantly glimpsed at him from the corner of her eye and quickly shied away as soon as Jeff caught her gaze. Liliana's little sister, who was in her early teens and the youngest of the three siblings, nudged her teasingly which made her cheeks erubescent. Liliana attempted ogling him again, but this time she was caught in the act which made Jeff laugh. She adjusted her raven black hair behind her ear and reciprocated a smile. She wore glasses that complimented her freckled face perfectly, but she took them off growing nervous every moment, presuming he might find them uninviting. Jeff sat in sublime silence praising her resplendence in his thoughts, but suddenly a realization dawned upon him which hinted toward the possible indications she might venture to interpret from his cordial gestures. He circumscribed his smile and regard toward her, prudently ensuring that it doesn't appear abrupt and rude.

Maggie was her mother's daughter. Her beauty, which wasn't just external but internal as well, was indistinguishable from her bearer. When she was told about the reason she was called home and introduced to Edward, she did not object to it. And to embellish her obedience to Lena, she did not oppose a proposal for an arranged marriage either. Well, it was now partially an arranged marriage, but she agreed to the traditional practice following her elder brother down that path as Dave never challenged that family tradition either. They even proposed for another union between Jeff and Liliana, but his repose rested in someone else's beauty and he refused, which became another one of the reasons for Martin to be cross with him again.

That antipathy was short-lived between father and son as they both united in preparation for Maggie's wedding following a year-long courting which was mutually fancied by the groom and bride. With a binding promise from her in-laws allowing her to finish her degree after marriage, she returned home and busied herself, quite excitably, with the onerous prelude to the dreadful ceremony.

The preparations weren't any less strenuous for the rest of the family as Martin had resolved to effectuate all the unfulfilled festivities he'd missed to execute at Linda's wedding. Truck-loads of red tulips and white gardenia were imported from the neighboring flowery. A marquee was set up with an open side that housed a temporary gazebo-like construction which was made to be an altar with festooned white satin adorning the peripheries and a massive motley of tulips and gardenia bordering the canvas in a semicircle. Rows of pews faced the altar, analogous to a church, over twenty in count. Beyond the ceremony seating was a distribution of thirty oval tables placed with eight chairs each for dinner purposes and a bar was established at the far end. It was all erected at the side of the house with a clear view of the street ahead where files of vehicles stood hovering for space. Carts and dollies scattered all around the grounds still in recovery.

Jeff had assumed all responsibility for the lighting arrangements as strands of twinkle bedecked the marquee, the house and the trees in the vicinity. The whole town was going to know about this event. He dangled precariously over a ladder pushing on one leg and propped up against the edge, nailing the last strand of lights to the roof tiles.

There approached a young lady who emerged from the neighboring house and walked gracefully down the pavement skipping cables and wires on her way, dodging a couple workers crossing before her, finally reaching the porch steps of the Saunderhurst house. Jeff gazed at this stranger coming to their home and creased his brows rummaging his memory for that face, he couldn't locate it. The auburn hair with streaks of amber that bounced off her shoulders, parted in the middle, framing an elegant face and brushing off her square jawline. Her green eyes observed the arrangements with a glimmer of serenity and she stood with a certain poise that demanded regard from those around her. She was attired in a floral summer dress which was a blend of yellow, white and purple and she tarried at the porch allowing Jeff to conclude his surmise. But just as she looked up at him and he held that gaze for a good minute or more, he needed no more evidence but her slight smile confirming that his childhood friend, now twenty-seven and a lady, had arrived for Maggie's wedding. It had been almost four years since he had seen Erica and she seldom visited as her father made the trip to Jersey occasionally to see her as well as his sister. But Maggie routinely passed on messages from both ends which were strictly platonic. That day Jeff had contemplated dashing up to her and wrapping her into his arms for a kiss like they were some freewheeling twelve-year-olds, but he permitted her the dignity of being a youthful female of class and abandoned his impulse. She rang the bell and waited while Jeff dismounted the ladder and stood cleaning his hands with a towel. Their lips emitted nothing, but eyes conveyed all they needed to.

When Erica went inside, Jeff saw his father collecting the mail from the mailbox and becoming transfixed by a specific envelope. Martin swiftly ripped the flap open and began reading the letter. His face was imbued with outrage and alarm simultaneously. He was livid as he stormed inside the house calling out to Jeff and summoning him inside.

It was a little while later that Maggie had put on her wedding gown for final adjustments and Linda, Lena and Erica were all in the room upstairs complimenting on her comeliness and charm in white.

"I really shouldn't have to say this little one, but you look like an enchantress from paradise right now." Linda took Maggie to a mirror and pressed her to praise that reflection.

"I don't know, I believe it's a bit too tight around the thighs." Maggie criticized the invisible foibles imitating a typical bride disposition. "These hips of mine are too big."

"You're kidding me right now, that's what makes boys do a one-eighty when women like you walk down the street. I wish I had a body like that." Linda countered as Lena and Erica chuckled. "Yeah, it's something wrong with the generation ten years older than theirs, we are so skinny and all of a sudden here comes the new epitome of beauty. Look at you and Erica over there, quintessential women of shape. I should've been born a lot later, mother."

Lena laughed, "I should have waited then, about ten years?"

"What can I say, you were in a hurry." Linda's comment triggered a loving, soft slap on her cheek from her mother.

But suddenly some disruptive sounds of an affray became audible.

"I'm asking for an answer, what is this?" Martin deep growling echoed in the living downstairs.

"I applied--" Jeff's voice cracked timidly.

"What's that?"

"I applied for admission, there aren't many colleges that would accept a GED or a distance learning diploma, they do. So, I went ahead and--" Jeff never lifted his face to look back at his father.

"And you applied? Without asking anyone in the house, without a single concern for others, you just went ahead and applied?" Martin was bellowing.

"I didn't even think they would accept me."

"Well, now that they have, what do you plan to do next?"

Jeff stood in servile silence.

"No please, go ahead. I want to know the thoughts in your head right now. You plan to leave home? Live in New York City by yourself?"

"If it--" Jeff searched for his words.

"Speak up, I cannot hear you."

"If it comes to that, then..." Jeff drifted from a concrete reply.

"Then you will? All right, go ahead. Go upstairs and pack your bags. Right now. You're leaving." Martin extended his arm to offer him the letter.

Jeff refused and stood motionless.

"If this is the time you think would be best for something like this to be done then let's get on with it. Whatever money I was saving for this wedding, I would give to you. Of course, you will need some, if not a lot, for your travel, for the place you stay until you find a permanent lodging, the college fees, your personal expenses. I will write down a check, how does that sound? Perhaps you would want a full account of the money you have earned from work so far and given to me for Maggie's college. How do you want to be paid that loan? I will need some time to gather all that wealth as I am in a financially tight situation right now."

"I'm not asking for any money. I will work and I will pay for college." Jeff answered innocently.

"Work? A similar job as this one I suppose? Paying for the college, maybe two shifts would cover that. You don't plan on sleeping for the next five years, do you? How about some student grants? Have you tried that?"

"I can look into it."

"You haven't even started with that. I don't suppose a job would be waiting for you when you land at Penn Station, so until then all your expenses are on me. Let me ask Maggie if she would like to cancel her trip to Florida and I'll direct that money to you. So, what are you waiting for? You didn't need permission when you applied at this college, you don't need permission to leave home, then what's the delay? Let's get your luggage down and buy you a ticket. Let's go." Martin was sternly serious about this.

Lena came down the stairs with Linda trailing her and joined the conflict.

"What is going on here?"

"Ask your son, what he did." Martin fell into the couch.

"Jeff?" Lena eyed him with concern.

"It's an acceptance from a college in New York City, creative writing. I never thought they would accept someone with a GED, but they are."

"You're going to leave us?" Lena's tone was full of worry than dissent.

"I gave him a business of his own, how many boys do you see in this town call themselves owners of a store? How many? Some? Well, you are one of them now. Instead of trying to grow that bookstore he's going to go away and waste four-five years of his life on writing?"

"It's not about the store, it's just that I want to do what I like. I wasn't meant to run a store all my life." Jeff defended himself.

"Meant? Do you understand what that word means? Meant? What have you done so far in life that forces you to believe that you were or weren't meant for something? Creative writing, that is a big fancy word, I'm sure. But how much do you know about it? You are meant to do it, right? Then there must be a reason that made you believe you were meant for it? And equally, there must be a reason why you think you are not meant for a bookstore? There must be some great capabilities you have that I am unaware of? Some hidden potentials that I don't know about? Maybe I'm meant to learn about them now? What is it? You are able to write a few words on a piece of paper that makes you an extraordinary writer because of which you're suddenly meant for greatness? And who else knows about this, does anyone know?" Martin glimpsed the faces of others who stood there speechless. "I don't think so. And if you believe you are such a good writer meant for much more than a bookstore, then you need not go anywhere but your room, lock yourself inside and come out after six months of working on what you think is meant to make you famous. Let us read a piece of your greatness as well. Maybe I'm meant to send you to New York myself if I see the ability in you."

"I don't have anything completed now." Jeff was shaken, with his voice leaving trails of veiled whimpering.

"He can learn. It is a good profession, father." Linda added to his defense.

"Profession? Do you know how many of these professionals you see out there every day, Linda? Too many to count? Now, how many of them have you seen make it into a profession that pays? A handful? You know what kinds of people exist out there, you've been in the open long enough? I shouldn't have to tell you this, but do you think he will be able to survive the world that exists outside? Do you think he can handle the rejections, the denials, the criminals that ambush and cheat young men like him? Do you think he can do this alone? Tell him the truth. There are way better writers, thinkers than him begging for jobs because this profession doesn't cover the costs of the food that feeds you by the end of the day. Jeff, right now you may think I'm just making up stories to keep you here, but I really want you to step outside this door and look at the world yourself. I would hate for you to go to bed empty stomach, but I hope that happens and teaches you a lesson of life. I have protected you so far, but I honestly wish that people cheat and trick you into situations that will make you realize what I've been hiding you from."

"Martin," Lena demanded an end to this rant.

"New York City, big place, big dreams, your good life awaits. My dear boy, you are in for a rude awakening." Martin took up the letter and tore it into pieces.

Jeff was indignant but swallowed his anger and bolted, slamming the door behind him.

James entered as Jeff exited and quickly grasped the hostile ambiance. "What happened?"

"This shouldn't have happened, father," Linda protested.

"I know what is right for him, Linda." Martin sustained his view.

"You will just push him away, that's what will happen." Linda went back up the stairs and found Maggie in tears next to a distraught Erica. She took them both inside the room and drove the door shut.

# Chapter Fifteen

✵

The orchestra was accommodated upon a dais to the side of the altar. The guests filled the pews along with both sides of the families attired in old tuxedos from their wardrobe and women in conservative evening gowns. Martin and Lena welcomed more people near the entrance of the house. Dave and James ran around the back fixing eleventh-hour troubles with catering. Erica stood in a group of young women, dressed analogously, engaged in trifling conversations, but her eyes searched for someone in particular who was nowhere in sight. Linda came and excused Erica from her acquaintances and whispered something to her. Erica nodded and instantly aimed for the orchestra. She went over to the announcer and had a brief talk with him. He nodded and approached the microphone tapping it to test and signaling his players to stop the music.

"May I have your attention, ladies and gentlemen? Would we please gather around the altar and give our warmest welcome to the beautiful bride headed our way."

The people stood up and huddled near the altar leaving a path in the center for the bride to walk upon with her father. Erica pantomimed Maggie's arrival to the orchestra as they picked up with the processional music. An eight-year-old Nancy was the flower girl who tossed rose petals down the path and positioned herself adultly at the side of the elevation. The tradition of having numerous bridesmaids was abandoned in the ceremony as Erica was the only who proceeded before Martin walked Maggie to the altar. Edward stood with his younger cousin as his best man and awaited the moment. The loquacious parish priest, father Thomas, stood in a cassock, stole and a bible in his hands. Martin delivered his daughter to Edward's care and stood back with Lena who was soaking in tears now. Linda comforted her mother stroking her arm tenderly.

"Let us all pray for this young couple. Lord, our heavenly Father, we thank you for giving us the fruit of life and the sense of humanity. We thank you for showing us your love and presence and alleviating our burdened lives. We ask for your blessings for these two beautiful individuals who are here to join hands for the journey of their lives."

Maggie was picturesque in her shimmering beaded gown that outlined her contours splendidly. Her eyes were fixated at Edward who smiled in return and looked appealing in his black tuxedo.

"May this journey be fruitful, rewarding, filled with joy and happiness for the both of them and be very, very long so they may look upon each other with withered skin and drooping eyes and remember this day, and still bear the same amount of love for each other as they bear tonight."

Laughter swept the assemblage.

"We ask for your grace through our loving Jesus Christ, our God, amen. Be seated. I have read many marriages in my life. And I must admit that I have excelled in this service. From the mayor's daughter to those who couldn't afford a priest, refusal has never come across my services. This is the greatest work of the Lord, to unite two people in matrimony. I care not for the money, I do not do this service for money. I am the worker of the Lord, and I shall do his will. Tonight, we have gathered here to join this young, loving couple in holy wedlock. Once joined in union by the holy spirit and the hand of God, they may never part as long as they draw breath.

It is a commitment you both shall make to never let go in sickness and illness, happiness and sorrow--"

Bored by the verbiage, Maggie scanned the crowd for one face that she needed to see the most.

Erica caught her drifting sight and slightly stepped up to whisper. "Behind you, the tree."

Maggie followed her lead and found Jeff leaning against the oak tree and listening to the garrulous holy man go on about his words. He waved to Maggie which kindled a jubilant smile across her face and gratified her to the core. She turned back to her husband and their imminent bonding.

"Do you Maggie Saunderhurst take Edward Kelson to be your lawfully wedded husband?"

"I do," Maggie said with no reserve.

"And do you Edward Kelson, take Maggie Saunderhurst as your lawfully wedded wife?"

"I do," Edward was equally eager.

"Let them exchange the rings."

They put the gold bands on each other's finger.

"Then by the power invested in me by the parish, the mayor of this town and its people, I pronounce you husband and wife. You may kiss the bride."

The entire crowd erupted in cheerful revelry and the couple kissed each other. The orchestra strengthened that dissonance, blowing the trumpet and sax, and the strings doing the rest. As the bride and groom passed down the aisle basking in the blessings of the spectators, they collected a lot more of rice and flowers thrown their way. It was a happy moment for all and Jeff, taking a large swig from his scotch, watched contentedly.

The wedding marquee was opened a little more to make space for the traditional dance of the couple and family members, the rest made pairs swaying to the music just below the altar in front of the orchestra. There were young and old, relatives and strangers, couples and lovers, all strewn around, some holding glasses of champagne and some bourbon.

Maggie and Edward held each other close and moved along the slow jazz. Martin and Lena smiled as they watched the lovebirds cherish each other.

"Thank you, dad, this is by far the most wonderful wedding I've been to. Luckily, it happens to be mine." The couples had inched closer when Maggie expressed her mind.

"I'm glad you're happy," Martin nodded. "It isn't much, but we tried out best."

"It's more than I could've asked for," Maggie smiled warmly.

"It's not the wedding that bothers me, but what follows next," the groom jumped in. "You know when you start off lavishly, especially the ceremony, a woman expects to be treated with similar luxury for the rest of her wedded life. You have put me in a lot of trouble with all this, father-in-law. I'm a poor man and your daughter right here is going to mock me for the rest of my life that I couldn't give her a lifestyle as rich as her wedding." There was an incisive jest intended with that remark which triggered concern over Lena's countenance.

"Oh really? How about we head over to our lawyers tomorrow morning if you're having second thoughts?" Maggie rejoined.

"Maggie!" Lena reprimanded.

"Speaking of second thoughts, I think I'm subjected to those right now. I should have waited to tie the knot, really." Edward continued to doubt his decision.

The creases of distress deepened on the parents' faces.

"Edward, I'm really sorry for what she just said, but this is no time to have such thoughts. We're a middle-class family and Maggie has been raised just like any of the girls in your family. She isn't accustomed to any extravagance." Lena became the arbitrator between them.

Maggie and Edward eyed each other and burst into laughter.

"That really did scare them off a little." Edward joked, much to Martin's dislike.

"It did." Maggie conceded him a point.

Lena sighed with a lot of relief. Sweat had almost beaded her forehead.

"No, but I'm not lying about having second thoughts. I should have waited. Maybe you would have agreed to give me your hand in matrimony instead." Edward attempted to charm Lena this time. "I hope you don't mind, Martin, but I just proposed to your wife."

"Well, then take her and I'll stay right here with dad."

They all changed partners as Maggie teamed with Martin and Edward wrapped his arms around Lena.

"You two are something, I'm telling you. But listen to me children, never lose this humor in your marriage, ever. Because the day your relationship turns dry, so will your lives." Lena poured some words of wisdom.

"See, you're tempting me with your intellect already." Edward joked again. Lena struck him on the shoulder gently.

"Jeff!" Maggie left her father and strode toward her brother who came across the dance floor and held her gloved hands, kissing them both. She embraced him and parted with eyes swimming in tears.

"You look beautiful. My little sister. Aren't you a little too young for this dress?" Jeff giggled at his own comment.

"I don't know, aren't you a little too late for that question?" They both laughed together. Erica eyed them both from the dance area, arm in arm with Dave.

"You take care of yourself and everyone around you. I don't even have to say this, you know how to care for people better than any one of us here. But in all of that, you forget about yourself. That is what I want to emphasize. Take care of yourself." Jeff read her eyes as he spoke.

"You'll be there to keep an eye on me. And you're a man of your word. More than me, I trust in you."

"I know, I... I will always be there. Maybe not around, but--"

"What do you mean? Where are you going?" Maggie grew attentive toward the content of this talk.

"Somewhere, I don't know where yet, but someplace far."

The joy abruptly diminished from her face. Jeff signaled her to stay quiet.

"No Jeff, not today. Please," her eyes were misty and glinting. "Please Jeff, I'm asking you."

"Do you really mean to ask me that?"

Maggie had no honest answer to his question.

"I must leave and I must--"

"You are not going anywhere like that." Edward leapt out of nowhere and took Jeff by his arm. "You just made my wife cry, bro, you're not going anywhere until you compensate with a few of your own tears." He took Jeff to the center of the dais and elevated his voice for the rest to hear. "I want a speech. A long winding, tearful, heartwarming speech from a brother who is just about to lose a sister to another man." He took the mike and announced, "speech, speech...."

The request was picked up by almost everyone in the crowd as they chanted in unison. Saunderhurst family was a bit anxious at this.

"No, no I can't do it." Jeff attempted to escape. There was none.

"You have to brother-in-law. There is no other way out." Edward insisted and placed the mike in his hand.

Martin approached irately, "get him down from there, Edward. He's drunk."

Jeff glowered at him and clutched the mike firmly in his hand.

"Don't make a fool out of yourself, get down." Martin uttered in hushed shouts.

Jeff hardened his jaws and began.

"There was a time when Maggie and I sat together under that tree right there. I was ten and she was um... eight. We didn't know what life was like any other kid our age, all we saw were mischiefs. Though, a majority of her shenanigans were aimed to annoy me most of the time, I still remember she had a small scrapbook kind of a thing and she used to cut pictures out of newspapers and magazines, famous people you know, celebrities and politicians, you know how ugly that could get."

A hearty laughter sounded from the listeners.

"She would jumble different parts of their different faces, and she'd look for a perfect face. She used to show me those pictures and I, of course, never paid any attention. But today it seems she's found that perfect face in Edward. But that was when she was still a child and a face was the most important thing to her in all. Today, she's a woman who believes a face is the last aspect of attractiveness and compatibility in a person. It's not because she's grown to be ugly, if I said that I'd be farthest from the truth and closest to a lie ever told. It's because she's grown to become a human; a loving, caring, honest, blameless, immaculately pure-hearted human. And the splendor of her soul reflects in her outer beauty, the peace and calm that she's able to provide others with a simple smile of hers." Jeff wiped his eyes with his sleeve.

"I've loved her since she was born. I held her up in my arms, just a baby she was, even I was just about two, but I knew, I knew she would be beautiful like an angel and a guardian who's always there for everybody like a pillar of rock. And that's exactly what she turned out to be. Edward, I'm giving you the most precious thing I've ever had in my life. She's a jewel. Keep her safe and keep her happy. Or I'll come for you. Let her be free, encourage her in whatever she desires to do. She loves to design clothes, open her a boutique if you may. But keep her happy, because I'm taller and heavier than you are."

The crowd was encouraged to laugh through their tears that Jeff's words had brought into their eyes. Maggie wiped under her eyes and sniveled along with many other women from the family, Erica was no exception. Martin turned away from Jeff's glare and stepped back.

"You wouldn't find me here tomorrow. I'll be gone forever."

People stirred in their motionless stance. Lena, the most of all.

"There was a man once in my life who said that I was free to be what I wanted to become. He's gone, but not forgotten. But I wish there was somebody else who'd tell me that today. That I can do what I feel like doing, go places where I'd find happiness, look for what I think is best for me. But I was never told that. I was held back, told I'm not good enough, I can't do this, I can't do that. No one understood me like Maggie did. She always pushed me forward. Just like that guy, back when we were ten. But after him, I expected it from that man, right there." Jeff pointed to Martin. "But he was never there. I wanted to do something for this little princess on her big wedding day. I wanted to give her something too, something she might remember me for, like everybody else, a present. But for that I needed money, to buy something I need money, right? My brother is a big man, he could afford a three-week vacation to Rome he gifted her. My sister, a rich lady, she bought her a new car. Even my father gave her a bedroom suite and another vacation to Florida. But I... if I wanted to give her something, I'll have to implore every person in my family, kneel down before them and beg, stretch out my arms and wait for them to pity me and put something here on my palm. Because all I make in a month is a few hundred dollars, still not enough to give a wedding present, right?"

Edward eyed the crowd. Mortified, Dave came up the dais and attempted the steal the microphone.

Jeff yanked away and continued. "I am suffocating inside, I wanted friends but what I got were walls and empty rooms. I wanted a nice paying career but what I got was a small bookstore that barely covers its own expenses. I wanted to be a writer but I was told there are too many out there, better than me."

Dave took the mike this time and faked a smile. "All right guys, I'm sorry for that. I guess drinking too much does that to you. Music please."

The perturbed orchestra started with a dim tune and picked up slowly.

"Let's go, Jeff." James took him by the arm and led him down the dais.

Martin approached seething with wrath. "I am so disappointed in you. You were trying to dishonor me in front of all these people?"

"Why? You never set your hopes on me. Why are you so disappointed? And dishonor you? You have to have some kind of repute in someone's regard before he could go ahead and shame you. You are nothing to me, Martin Saunderhurst." Jeff chuckled ridiculing his father.

Martin landed a slap across his face which agitated the whole situation even further. Jeff was fuming with crimson eyes and lunged at Martin belligerently holding him by the lapels of his jacket. Edward approached on their right and along with James tried to intervene before a fist-fight could ensue.

Jeff without a glimpse behind swung his arm backward and walloped Edward in the face with his strong elbow. Edward was stunned for a moment and backtracked a couple feet away, collapsing to the floor. His swollen and bleeding lower lip brought the rest of the family to his aid.

"I'm all right." Edward tried to keep things friendly. The bride crouched by his side.

"Jeff!" Maggie cried in rage. She stood up and accosted him. "Please go away, go away right now." She stormed inside the house wiping away the effusion of tears. Erica went after her.

Jeff was humiliated by those angered stares hurtled at him. He took off upon the dark street that went forward to an unknown destination. With a burden of guilt and remorse, and the heart-wrenching cry, that sounded his name but in the most unpleasant way he'd heard from Maggie's lips, was going to haunt him forever.

Edward tried calling him back to resolve, "Jeff! Jeff come back, Jeff." But he was too far gone to hear the voice.

"Jeff."

It awakened Jeff from another reverie as he still held on to the photo frame. Edward had just entered the living and looked at Jeff surprisedly.

"I kept calling you, but you didn't listen." He sank into a recliner positioning to relax a bit more.

"What?" Jeff was taken off guard.

"Just now. I called you a couple of times, but I see where you were lost. That's quite an old memory to be looking at this early in the morning. It's usually done at bedtime, when one has nothing better to do."

"Yeah, I haven't many photo frames to look at near bedtime, just the one I took with me." Jeff placed the frame back on the mantle.

"Right, I guess you know who's missing from that picture, in case you didn't notice."

"Thanks for reminding me," Jeff remarked wryly.

"Ah, so that's the reason you didn't take it with you because you weren't in it." Edward gave a smirk.

"The one I took didn't have me in the picture either." Jeff retorted with a grin.

"Do you remember why you're not in the picture?"

"I think I just did." Jeff nodded.

Edward grimaced complaining about his back pain tacitly to himself. "Weddings are supposed to be a lot of fun, especially for the bride and groom. Didn't think it would be that funny."

"I'm sorry for what happened last night-- I mean that night. I'm sorry I was just--"

"You still living too close to that incident, believing it was last night. I better patch up my lower lip then." Edward joked about his injury.

"I shouldn't have done that, I didn't know you were there." Jeff was as earnest as he could sound.

"I know and I'm sorry too for last night. Not a night before or a night long time ago. Exactly last night. I think I had one too many. Just went on lamenting every other thing that entered my mind. Didn't know I was speaking out loud."

"That's okay, Edward. You don't have to apologize. A drunk man is usually forgiven for his transgressions."

Edward rubbed his lower lip sardonically, "really?"

"I surely hope so."

They both laughed together.

"Still doesn't account for an elbow on the lower lip. I was hit hard, it hurt a lot." He grumbled.

"I guess we're even then?" Jeff words were pungent.

Edward smirked again, "that'd be a first. Getting punished for things years before committing them? When do I start?"

"What are we starting with now?" Maggie came into the room fearing another dispute between the two.

"Nothing much," Edward dragged himself out of the recliner. "Just a bit of nourishment for the stomach now. Had a lot for the mind already." He flew a kiss to his wife and headed out for the dining.

"Oh wow, who is that stranger?" Maggie was pleasantly surprised with his demeanor.

"The one you married!" Edward shouted from the hallway.

"What's wrong with him?" She wondered. "He slept fine last night."

"It's the holidays, I'm sure. Snow, Christmas, and family bring a lot of changes in people." Jeff shrugged in awe.

"Well, better keep him buried in all three before the older version takes over. Who's going Christmas shopping?" She wrapped her arm around her brother and took him to the kitchen.

"I surely am," Jeff responded in all high spirits.

"I need to get presents for the kids. I will come along Maggie." Lena joined in.

"What's the hurry? We have nine more days to go, a lot of time." Edward objected.

"Nine? That's a lot of time? We're putting up the tree tonight, what are you going to keep under it, books and empty boxes?"

"You remember how we used to wrap up old hardcovers and keep them under the tree just for show, making a pretense of how many gifts we had to open?" Linda spoke joyfully remembering old times.

"Poor kids, we didn't have much to gift back then," Lena admitted to their indigence.

"Every house used to do that, ma. Some still do." Jeff veiled their grief.

"Well, we're going to get real gifts this time. And all of us are going, especially you, husband." Maggie ordered everyone around her. Edward accepted the command.

"Aye captain, when do we set sail?" Jeff saluted her playfully.

# Chapter Sixteen

Maggie led her crew out of the house and into the transport as James stayed home and waved them goodbye.

"You sure you don't want to come?" Lena and Linda questioned him.

"Nah, I've finally found some time to spend within the four walls of a home instead of a classroom, I'm going to enjoy it while it lasts. Besides, you know what to gift everyone better than I do."

"All right, I'll bring you something for lunch." Linda went on waving back to him and accommodated Lena and Jeff in her Mercedes while Nancy took the front passenger seat. The Kelson family trailed in their minivan.

The trip was short to the mall via highway yet delayed due to snow-covered streets and a crawling traffic. But finding a spot to park was even more irksome in a commodious lot that appeared diminutive this time of the year.

"Now would you look at this wise guy, he's taking up two spots right there." Edward commented on every other car or person as he plodded the parking for an open spot.

Two elderly ladies took their time crossing the path in front of him.

"Get out of the way, grandma. This is a parking lot, not a nursing home." Edward yelled from his driver's seat.

The women glared at him as he flew past them.

"Buy yourself a wheelchair, will ya?"

A kid playing with a cart abandoned it right in the middle called by his mother.

"Just look at that piece of..." he slammed the steering in extreme vexation. He rolled down the window and screamed, "do you freaking think you have a hired maid back here who's going to take care of your mess? Move the cart, damn it. Teach your kid some manners."

"I'll do it." Maggie got out of the car and kicked the cart to the side.

"Let him find parking, come with us."

Maggie heard the words on her way back to the minivan and glanced behind. Linda and the rest of the gang were headed for the mall entrance.

"What, you've got to be kidding me right now. They got parking. I've been looking here for a month and they've got one already?" Edward screeched from his driver's window.

"Ron, Helen, come with me. We'll go with them. Your dad will find us." Maggie came to the passenger side window and peered in.

"No, I like this." Helen giggled buckled in on the rear seat.

"Do you want to come, Ron?" Maggie extended her hand and he grabbed it, swiftly sliding down his door to exit.

"We'll wait for you inside. And please watch your language, she's right behind you."

"Yeah, yeah." Edward dismissed her and charged forward slamming on the brakes at a stop sign.

Piqued at his driving skills, Maggie shook her head and went into the mall.

A multitude of consumers marched like legions coming together for a common purpose. Some were hasty with decisive strides and some sauntering from one store to the next. Some appeared unnerved by the very custom of gift-giving, while some seemed beguiled by the illumined shops, lighted garlands, and trees that were laden with trinkets and ornaments. Christmas carols played loudly over speakers on each floor. Children rushed ahead of their weary parents, couples traveled hand-in-hand, if they were free, that is, of the gift bags that dangled abundantly from each. Stores of clothing and accessories, electronics, toys and novelty, all inundated with kids from four to eighty-five. Credits cards being charged across a row of counters, bills of hundred and fifty stacked in the dinging registers along with store vouchers and gift cards preserved since last year for this specific day. High-value purchases bringing a smile across cashiers' faces, but some daunted by countless sale items heaped on their countertops with a special request from the buyer to bag each item individually and probably toss in some gift wraps and boxes along if free ones are available. And it was accompanied by a wide grin and a wink that almost seemed too ingratiating, bordering suspicious weirdness.

The Saunderhursts were roving the floors eventually joined by Maggie.

"So, where are we going first?" Maggie's brows were interlaced with restlessness.

"I don't know, give me a list of the things you need to buy and then we'll prioritize." Jeff proposed deceitfully. "I'm sure you made a list."

"I actually did," Maggie began to ransack her handbag, but suddenly ceased, discerning his artful trickery.

"Now wait just a minute." Maggie hid a smile. "I'm not going to tell you what I need to buy. You just had me there for a moment."

She hit him on the arm and Jeff parried.

"We're not ten anymore, Maggie. You don't need to scream surprise when I open my present."

"What makes you so sure I am going to give you one?"

"Tell me one family member who's not going to get one from you and I'll change my name to 'fudge' for the rest of my life."

"You better start thinking of a funnier one. That's not embarrassing enough," she countered.

"How about Maggie? Can't get more embarrassing or funnier than that."

Maggie lunged at him and Jeff dodged with a leap sideways.

"But I'm not going to need it," Jeff returned chortling.

"No? All right, you tell me what you're buying and I'll tell you what I bought," Maggie offered a deal.

"I'm not buying anything, me being here is enough of a gift for all of you," Jeff boasted.

"Oh, quite pretentious, aren't we? Okay, have it your way. Nobody gives you anything this Christmas." She erected her neck pompously.

"You already have." They both stopped and looked squarely at each other.

"Stop with your fighting both of you. Linda's headed to that store. I believe we should shop for her first before she returns." Lena intervened.

"We're right behind you." Maggie smiled without disrupting her gaze from Jeff.

They had moved inside a clothing store and roamed the sweater aisles, searching a perfect fit for Linda. Lena picked out a bluish ribbed, button-front cardigan from the collection and brandished it before her younger two for their approvals. Both nodded, impressed with the quality of the article.

"You go get this cashed ma, I see Linda coming over." Jeff pointed to the end of the aisle with an indication of his eyes.

Maggie and Lena took off instantly folding the sweater into a hide.

"I'll distract her." Jeff scampered to confront the approaching threat and obstructed her strides. But before he could utter the words of diversion, Linda took him to the side behind the column.

"Where are they?" Linda was murmuring and secretive like an undercover agent.

"Who?" Jeff enlisted for the covert operation.

"Mother and Maggie, who else?"

"Oh, they are-- they went for the restroom."

"Good, here take a look at this," she retrieved two velvet cases and opened them both to reveal a necklace in one and earrings in the other. Both items sparkled divinely.

"Wow, for me?"

"Yeah, get your ears pierced, you have eight days," Linda teased.

"Nah, too much of a hassle. They say it hurts a lot. I'd rather have you give these to the women."

"Good idea." Linda concealed the gifts back in the bag. "Got a similar one for Gloria too."

"Nice."

"Can we get over with this already? I'm famished. You don't plan on carrying my corpse back home, do you?" Nancy's long-expected participation finally arrived, though, in manner of a complaint.

"There's a reason breakfast was invented, buttercup." Linda rejoined.

"Well, there was nothing on that table I could consider healthy and put down my throat without feeling queasy, in case you failed to see." She continued her scathing remarks.

"There were a lot more people on that table besides you. I'm sorry if I couldn't arrange for an organic salad eight thirty in the morning madam."

"Then you shouldn't have brought me here with you if you weren't going to take care of me." She flicked her head disdainfully.

"You are getting on my nerves, Nancy. I actually should have left you all alone for Christmas, you would have enjoyed that a lot."

Jeff tried to alleviate the situation by holding Linda back.

"That would have been heaven for me." Nancy glared right back at her mother never yielding that eye contact.

"There's nothing good to buy here, I think we should try another store." Maggie came concealing the purchase they had just made oblivious of the bitter barter between a fuming mother and her rebellious daughter.

Linda gaited resentfully with the rest shuffling along. Nancy returned to her world of a CD player and headphones.

"What happened?" Maggie asked.

"We're going to the cellar for lunch, I think." Jeff whispered.

They raided a toy store on the way to the food court and while Ron ran across the aisles with an imprudent desire to own everything, her mother just chased after him trying her hardest to contain the little one.

Lena picked up a stuffed toy contemplating Helen's choice of characters. Jeff assisted her.

"Are you kidding me, who the hell gives stuffed toys for Christmas nowadays?" Nancy went past them both speaking on her Nokia cell phone.

Lena quickly placed the toy back. "Linda, can I ask you something?" She approached Linda further ahead. "What do you think should be a better gift for Nancy? I see she has everything. Is there something she needs?"

"Her? You are looking for a gift for your granddaughter?" Linda smirked. "You can please God with a few things from earth, not her. Forget about it." Linda shook her head and rambled ahead.

"But still, we need to give her something." Lena spoke to herself.

"Electronics, that's what kids are crazy after these days," Jeff answered.

"I hope I can find something that we can afford."

"Don't worry about the price, ma, just buy it." Jeff strengthened her.

"I'm glad Ron and Helen could still be pleased with a stuffed animal, right?" Lena solaced herself.

"Not in a few years," Linda replied.

"You know we used to get socks and handkerchiefs from our grandparents when we were little," Lena recollected.

"That was a time when families mattered, these days things play a greater part in life than mere people." Jeff darted and lifted Ron in his arms rescuing Maggie from a marathon she'd been subjected to for the past fifteen minutes.

"Oh God, I wish I was a teenager again. Free from these exhausting responsibilities," she came panting.

"I added a book to my library almost every Christmas morn, that's what we used to get." Jeff handed his nephew back to his sister.

"You used to get the books, I got some really nice dresses." Maggie teased him.

"Books and clothes, ew!" Ron interpolated.

"Times change too fast," Lena reviewed the changes in life.

"Hmm, or maybe we just live too long," Jeff indicated an action figure set as a possible gift for Ron.

Lena looked at Maggie who motioned a big okay. They had their first present.

"See, your dad is here." Maggie spotted Edward trudging into the store with Helen in his arms. "Go bother him a little while." Maggie breathed in some repose.

Ron rushed to him immediately and Helen ran to her mommy, both children exchanging guardians.

"That parking lot is a mess out there," Edward continued caviling. "I had to race an old man at forty-five over a distance of thirty feet to get my spot. Imagine that."

"Edward, Helen was in the back seat!" Maggie objected fretfully.

"Yeah, she was enjoying the high-speed run, right Hen?"

She gave her father a high-five. "It was really fun, mom." Helen exulted.

"The world's in a rush, ma. Peace has become a legend of the past, an object of longing." Jeff remarked after hearing their conversation. Lena pushed him and Maggie along to search for final two presents.

The family had descended into the cellar and located an empty table near the elevators. They brought platters of an assortment of edibles and sat around.

"She was hungry just a minute ago and now that we have food, she's gone missing." Linda eyed the entire hall scanning for Nancy. "Should I call her?" Linda tried her cell phone. "No range, no network."

"I still can't understand how you can dial a phone without a wire," Lena marveled.

"New technology, mother. New things are leaving old ones behind."

"I'll go and look for her," Maggie volunteered.

"No, I'll go. I need a bit of fresh air," Jeff insisted and left before she could devise a word on her lips.

Jeff strode into the parking lot and glanced about, finding long queues of cars from the street to the ramps and the entrances, dropping and loading passengers. He espied Nancy under a lamppost near a taxi stand where myriad people exchanged dollars for food items, crowding several neighboring vending machines.

"Let me have a quick puff at that," Jeff joined her casually.

She wasn't startled at his arrival, rather vexed.

"You already know I smoke, and you didn't tell my parents. So, I don't need to hide from you." Nancy offered him the cigarette.

"I haven't told your parents yet. I thought they already knew."

She smirked, "would I be alive if they did?"

"Yes," Jeff answered definitively. "Without any complications arising from this bad habit too."

"If it is so bad, why'd you ask for it?"

Jeff smoked and coughed instantaneously.

"If this was an attempt at befriending me, it didn't work." She frowned dryly.

"Would you want to try that for a change? I tried befriending you by smoking a cigarette, maybe you can try befriending me by not smoking a cigarette?"

"No thanks," she spurned the proposal and took her cigarette from him. "What is it with all of you guys, I'm almost sixteen. I can smoke a cigarette if I want to. It's not a big deal."

"I didn't come out here looking for you because you were smoking, I came out here because you went missing and your mother was searching for you."

"I wasn't gonna turn up dead. I was just coming back."

"Why didn't you tell her where you were going?"

"Tell her I was going out for a smoke? You freaking kidding me?" Nancy sounded bothered.

"Are you afraid to tell her?"

"I'm not afraid of anybody," she was nearing aggravation.

"Maybe I can help you when we go back in?"

"She doesn't need to know about any of this." She was utterly provoked.

"Why?"

"It isn't something someone would typically be proud of--" Nancy suddenly restrained her tongue and resented her statement. But it was in all honesty that she'd said it.

"Yes, it isn't." Jeff began to leave.

"You won't tell her, you promise? I know you're not a snitch." Her concern stopped him in his tracks.

He turned and looked into her eyes and through them, into her mortified soul. "She's waiting for you to come back. Don't make her wait too long."

# Chapter Seventeen

Jeff fueled the singeing fireplace with some split wood and bark. He approached the tightly shut window and perused the view of the neighboring house just as the hearth warmed. A few flurries had drafted along some gusts and through that white obscurity, he saw a single window lit with yellow luminance. The house was otherwise deserted. He rubbed his hands to friction some heat and turned to an invading tune of a Christmas music that had just been introduced to the muted air inside the living room.

Frank Sinatra's 'Silent Night' played on the stereo and Maggie was the culprit. She had now pried open a metal chest full of trinkets and ornaments of old and planned to adorn a tree that had already been erected just aside the mantle, between the windows. Half of the house had already retired to their sleep cabins after dinner and the remaining half, who had recently brandished their enthusiasm of putting up a tree quite ardently, were sprawled over couches and chairs in sheer exhaustion.

"I think we better leave, it's past eleven now." Dave coerced Gloria.

"Why don't you stay for the night, Dave, like yesterday? We have room upstairs and it's terrible outside." Lena insisted.

"No, mom. I haven't been to our place in two days since Jeff came home. Gotta go and see how things are doing there.

Hopefully, the place hasn't been ravaged by bears by now. Gloria was also telling me about a leakage in the basement. Have to fix that too. Besides, we're not twenty minutes away from here. We'll be back in the morning."

"Okay." Lena acceded and kissed a good night to all of them. "Be careful out there."

Gloria heaved a sleeping Charlie in her arms, which was a travail in itself, and headed out following Dave.

"Mom, why don't you go and take a rest. We'll handle the decorations here. I have my knights here with me." Maggie patted her children each on the back.

"You sure you don't need anything?"

"If we do, we'll get it. Stop worrying about us. And get yourself warmed up, your hands are freezing." Maggie pushed her along to the stairs.

Lena nodded and went up.

"I guess it's just us now." Maggie acknowledged coming back into the living.

"Yeah, seems familiar?" Jeff intimated an event from the past.

"Yup, how many Christmases? Let me count, eighteen? That I can remember in details."

"Actually more, but yeah around twenty that I can remember."

"Let's make this the twenty-first tree that we've put up together, bro and sis. A joint venture."

"Us too mom." Helen tagged in.

"Yes, and make that the fourth for the two of you." Maggie nipped her nose.

"But I only remember last Christmas, nothing before that." Helen doubted her recollection.

"Yeah, there'll be a couple more before you begin to remember more than one. Now, let's put these ornaments on the tree, all right?"

Ron and Helen jumped to their given task deferentially.

Jeff helped put up the trinkets on the top of the tree which was out of reach for the children. But his eyes and attention were transfixed by that lonely window in the next house that was cast with a shadow periodically. Suddenly the wood in the fireplace snapped and flared loudly. He was shaken out of his abstraction which brought a smile to Maggie's face.

"She's still in town. Lives with her father, caring for him. He doesn't have anyone but her and she seems to have no one but him to look after. I met her about three years ago when I was here last. She looked sad. I guess it was mainly because of his illness. He was diagnosed with Alzheimer's sometime after you left, I heard. She's been here ever since. But her sadness wasn't just out of misery from her father's condition; there was loneliness I saw in her that seemed to be the bigger part of her unhappiness." Maggie ended with a concerned tone of voice.

"The colors of sadness are different to each, but its shadow is nothing but black to all, isn't it?" Jeff answered despondently.

"Jeff, what is the matter, is there something you're hiding?"

"I thought you were going to find out yourself. You're giving up?"

"I don't know. You have never looked so cheerful in your life." Maggie remarked sarcastically.

"What are you talking about, I always look this cheerful." Jeff dismissed her intrusive attempt.

"Really? Then you better practice your sad face because you're going to need one in a few days."

Jeff was dismayed at the comment and stopped his efforts.

"Mom's going to flip out the day you so much as hint that you're going back to New York."

Jeff breathed deep, smiling thinly. "What if I said I'm not leaving?"

"Then I'd be the happiest sibling you have." Maggie tapped him on the forehead.

"But you're not the happiest sibling I have right now. Am I allowed to ask why?" Jeff continued placing stars and bells on the top of the tree.

"What makes you say that?" Maggie corrected the clustering of ornaments placed by Helen around the bottom.

"You've never looked so cheerful in your life either." Jeff returned the favor sardonically.

Maggie returned the wry smile. "Aren't you going to take the challenge? I did."

Jeff smiled again. "You're trying to find out something you don't know. I'm just trying to confirm it."

This effaced the cheer from Maggie's face as well as her soul. There was a transient glumness that shrouded her now.

"I don't want to make you uncomfortable, Maggie." Jeff alleviated the bleakness.

"What if I said the same thing to you?"

"There aren't many things that would make me uncomfortable, especially that which involves my kid sister."

Maggie retrieved a red star from the box and handed it to her brother and pointed to the topmost branch of the tree. He hung the star up there.

"Boston isn't what it used to be in terms of jobs and work and all the stuff that relates to a disgruntled employee. He'd worked for his company for nine years and when he thought he was going to be promoted chief engineer, he was actually demoted. Annual turnover, they said. There was already some recession in the business and on top of that his company faced some massive lawsuits. They were holding their own until last April when they announced a complete shut-down and all the employees were dismissed. He suffered a lot of stress and depression dealing with it and going back to the whole tiring process of job hunting wasn't easy to tackle. His search continued for over four months when he finally got work in a smaller company."

"Do you think it is crooked, mom?" Helen interjected, about the placement of her favorite Santa Claus ornament.

"No honey, it's fine." Maggie answered rapidly and returned to her narration of their affairs. "This place is new itself, only been in business for seven years. The pay is half of what he received at his previous job. The satisfaction isn't too major either. He's less of an engineer and more of a site manager. He fears this company is going into bankruptcy as well, or maybe an acquisition. There was a rumor of a merger, but that didn't go as planned. So, he works and lives in that constant anxiety of losing everything once more and starting from scratch. The four months that went by without a job were frightening, Jeff. We almost had to remove these kids from school; they both attend a private one. That's how bad it was. We're hardly saving for anything right now. I kept on telling him that I can find a job and start earning something at least, but that somehow wounded his pride. I started with a tailor shop as a seamstress just two months ago. It is a nice place, nice people, basic sewing works and alterations. The good thing is they close for Christmas holidays for about twenty days. I didn't have to ask for days off to come here."

"His company as well?"

"Oh, they love to give days off to their employees, unpaid. It is a private management, if they could run the whole business themselves, they would. Edward says there are more opportunities in New York and wishes to go there, but moving is not an option for us right now. He was recently looking for some affordable quarters in the city, couldn't find many."

"Maggie, if you wanted to try New York, why didn't you tell me? I live right there, I could've--"

"I didn't know where you lived, remember?"

Jeff recalled his failure to inform anyone of his whereabouts.

"I had a slight suspicion that you might be in New York, but I couldn't be sure. There was another issue with me asking for help from any of our family members. The manly pride again. Linda was just an hour away from us, but he refused and forbid me to call and ask. He didn't even call his own family for help. His own family, would you believe that?"

"Has he forgiven me for the wedding night incident?"

"Oh yes, he's forgotten that. It's just that his ego might get hurt if I ask for help. And I don't insist. Well, that finishes the last detail to the Christmas tree." Maggie closed the empty chest recovering a final ornament from it.

Jeff gazed at it and filled with profound joy. It was an ancient red ball with two names inscribed on it.

"Remember this?" Maggie flashed it before him. It still glittered after all these years.

"You kept it?" Jeff stood in awe.

"Couldn't part with it. Our self-customized favorite ornament to hang together. Shall we?"

Maggie and Jeff both did the honors of securing the string nicely around the edge of the tree. It dangled and glimmered. Jeff then plugged the twinkling bulbs around the tree and switched off every other light in the room. The room coruscated red and green with subtle flashes and shimmered golden from the flaring fireplace.

"This is beautiful." Maggie's eyes were misty with delight.

"Can we sleep here, mom, please... please... please, just for tonight?" Both kids were adamant about it.

"Here, but where?" Maggie glinted at the disorder around them.

"On the sofa!" Helen exclaimed.

"I'll sleep on the floor," Ron joined.

"Because of you guys, I'll have to sleep here somewhere too."

"Please mom, please," they implored their mother.

"I'll sleep here," Jeff proposed.

"Yeah, please mom." Their puppy faces were not to be refused.

"Oh, okay," she acquiesced.

The gang cleared the sofas from all the debris and clutter and placed some blankets upon them which they transported from their rooms.

"Mom, what's a beldam?" Helen's curiosity was kindled as she labored carrying the heavy comforter around her petty frame.

Maggie frowned setting up an indoor camp for them. "Beldam, or bedlam?"

"Beldam, daddy called an old lady that today when he was looking for parking." Helen substantiated.

"That isn't a word, sweetheart."

"It is." Jeff brought a comforter from his room and placed it on the floor and Ron jumped on it instantly snuggling by himself. "A rare one, but it is."

"You should ask uncle Jeff, he knows many words." Maggie pushed Helen to question Jeff.

"What does it mean, uncle Jeff?" Helen asked innocently.

"Beldam is an evil looking old woman who is sometimes believed to be a witch." Jeff cleared the dubiety.

"Now, don't you go around calling people that." Maggie brought them some more sheets and blankets and instructed the little one.

"Okay. I want a bedtime story too." Helen added jumping onto the sofa and hiding under the blankets somewhere.

"Okay now, you're going too far young lady. I'm too tired for that," Maggie protested.

Helen went dolorous and limp.

"I want to hear a story too, mom." Ron pressured her further.

"Ron, you're half asleep, darling," Maggie cried.

"No, I'm not."

"Maybe uncle Jeffrey would want to tell you a bedtime story." Maggie played a trick.

"What, me?" Jeff was stunned, "I don't know how to tell stories."

"Oh come on now, that's what you do and they're your niece and nephew. It's about time you took some responsibilities of family relationships. You've been away too long, you can't hide forever."

"Uncle Jeff, please." Helen jumped onto his laps and her big eyes sparkled.

"Right, Helen. I will start right away. Let me gather the main characters for a moment here," he scratched his chin in deep meditation.

Maggie quickly took a seat behind them wrapping herself in a blanket excitedly, "I want to hear this."

"What kind would you like to hear?" Jeff collected preferences.

"The one with a beldam, a witch," Helen shouted.

"No, a masked wizard with superpowers," Ron countered.

"All right, no fighting. I'll tell you one with both," Jeff swallowed some time to compose the first act. "There was once a castle that was built strangely out of magic. It stood upon water. No one knew how it was made, but they all wondered. That castle had power over a small kingdom, and the people that ruled the kingdom were brother and sister. The sister was a beautiful girl who had the power of turning into an evil witch by night, and the brother was a handsome man who had the power of saving the world from any harm after putting on his mask and cape."

Maggie laughed gaily, nodding her head and making for the stairs. But before she left, she took a final glimpse at the peaceful sight of an uncle telling a bedtime story to the children, a tree glittering in the background flashing the walls, a hearth that kept them warm, and the dulcet sound of carols made it all the more idyllic. Contented, she ambled down the hallway and up the stairs.

# Chapter Eighteen

✵

Helen toyed with her Barbie on the dining table, sitting on Jeff's lap, trying to feed it some scrambled eggs. As the doll refused the breakfast, it eventually went into Helen's mouth.

"Helen, stop doing that. She clearly doesn't want to eat." Maggie demanded some table etiquette from her daughter.

Helen laughed at her mischief and leapt into Jeff's arms.

"Look at that. She likes you better than she likes her mother now. Even he can't leave this room unless you finish your breakfast, young lady. If you think he's going to save you from these eggs, you're mistaken." Maggie teased sitting on the next chair compelling her to finish.

Jeff nodded affirmatively.

"In the presence of God, I have never asked anything of you, Jeff. This is one thing only you are capable of doing." Gloria sat on the other side of Jeff and leaned in establishing grounds for a serious talk. "You have been to a big city yourself. You know how people could flourish and develop in such places. Look at Charlie, if we don't think about his future today, tomorrow might just be too late." Gloria had that pellucid conviction in her eyes that forced Jeff to take part in her resolve.

"What does Dave have to say about this?" Jeff carried on distinctly.

"He is in love with this town." Gloria nodded in exasperation.

"Or maybe the people who live here?" Maggie added.

"Maggie, the people he loves he's been with all his life. If he loves his son, then he has to do more than just stay here and make another Dave out of him." Gloria countered.

"Maybe he plans to give Charlie an option in life, let him choose what seems a feasible path to him?" Jeff changed his perspective. "Have you spoken to him about this?"

"Many times. But it usually ends at Charlie being too young to be given a thought right now. In the presence of God, I have traveled the world's end trying to convince him about the privileges of being a part of big cities because they offer so much more in everything, but he is as hard as a brick wall about it. The amount of money he could earn with a regular job in the city is gold compared to what he earns here. Futures are built with money, and we owe that to Charlie."

"Privilege?" Maggie uttered thickly with a smirk.

"Big cities aren't always sunshine and happiness, Gloria. I say that out of experience." Jeff attempted to define the truth to her.

"I know that, but a man like your brother who is hard-working and persistent and focused on family and his job, I believe it wouldn't be very difficult for him to survive out there. Do you? Do you doubt your brother?" She had twisted the words a bit that trapped Jeff right under.

Maggie shot a fleeting glimpse at Jeff and waited for his response enthusiastically.

"Do you doubt he'd be able to give you and Charlie a good future here?" Jeff had retaliated with his own version of a distorted expression.

"I don't doubt my husband, Jeff. I just know that the best future he can give him in this town is an ordinary one in the city. It's the simple conversion of availability and utilization. I heard you say that to your father once before you left."

Jeff was wordless momentarily, then revived his speaking skill. "Would you want Charlie to leave you like I left my mother?"

"No, that is why I'm asking you to speak to Dave. I do not want that whole situation to repeat itself."

"Gloria," Maggie objected.

"No, it's all right, Maggie. It's just family talk and she is right, there shouldn't be anyone in our family who has to go through what I did. But Gloria, I will say this one last thing. If Charlie wouldn't have anywhere to return, he will just keep running all his life. In your blind search for a future, you might take away his childhood from him. I've seen countless children going through the same all their lives. Give him a strong foundation of values in love and family. Let him grow with it for a while. If he doesn't cherish his home, he wouldn't cherish anything. That's what brought me back."

Gloria shifted back on her chair yielding a bit, Maggie and Lena eyed Jeff proudly.

The town had awakened to a new dawn. It was an indolent place still and its businesses were shuttered even after nine except a few that met their heaviest trade traffic early in the morning including bakeries and breakfast diners. The bookstore was one of the many that enjoyed its lethargy. It could survive another hour or more of it, but it was used to being unshuttered around ten since last five years, since it came under management of a new, but aged steward.

Jeff and Maggie had arrived at a conclusion to surprise their father at the workplace today. Jeff encountered a strange feeling of nervousness and culpability to enter the doors of a store he'd abandoned years ago, but along with it a profound feeling of strength which arrived from the fact that if a house comprising twelve members could forgive him for his insolence, a store with four walls, a few shelves and cabinets and about eight hundred books would be little easier to please.

When they reached their destination, Jeff parked the car in an empty lot near the store and followed Maggie to the door. They stepped in to the chiming of the bells which elicited an excited glimpse from Martin who sat silent and forlorn behind the counter until now. He jumped from his chair and greeted his children like a welcome customer.

"Maggie, Jeff, I never thought you'd come." There was a delightful smile across his face.

"Why not dad, it has been a part of our lives too." Maggie answered kissing him on the cheek. "You left so early today. We thought we should give a nice surprise."

"It is a wonderful surprise. Jeff, I have tried to keep it as you left it." Martin gestured to the setup of the store.

"Yes, I see that." Jeff stepped forward and examined the place reviving many old memories. He perused the books lined up on the shelves and ran his fingers across so much text.

"This is where it all began, isn't it?" Maggie gazed at Jeff emotionally.

"I believe so. So many books and they hardly ever left this store." Jeff answered with deliberation.

"Do you remember this?" Maggie revealed a book she had hidden behind her back. A battered second edition of Gulliver's Travels. "It was a gift, wasn't it?"

Jeff took the book from her and turned the last page. At the bottom he saw a handwritten closing note --'May your life be as adventurous as his. - From Erica Johnson on your twenty-first birthday.'

"Where did you get this?" Jeff was surprised.

"Last time I came, I found it. I have kept it hidden in here since." Maggie winked at him. "Let's find the one who gave it to you."

Maggie led him out of the bookstore to the neighboring line of storefronts and came to a scant, modest grocery stop. Jeff staggered with uncertainty in his strides and numbness in his legs to see that face of a companion who meant the world to him. As they reached the shop, they saw a familiar face lounging on a wheelchair outside the entrance, relishing the warmth of the sunlit day. Mr. Johnson hadn't lost his grace even in his old age, but had surrendered his endurance quite extravagantly.

"Good morning, Mr. Johnson." Maggie leaned forward and announced kindly. "Do you remember me? Maggie Saunderhurst, your neighbor."

"Who's that? Maggie? Saunderhursts? Oh yes, yes, my neighbors. When did you come back from school?"

Maggie glimpsed Jeff momentarily creasing her eyes. "That was some time ago, Mr. Johnson. I just came over to say hello and ask if you were doing well."

"I'm fine, there's nothing to worry about." He had difficulty enunciating his words.

"You see here, it's Jeff. You remember him, right. My brother?"

"Hello, Mr. Johnson." Jeff extended his arm for a shake. Mr. Johnson couldn't raise his own, so he simply tapped his hand.

"Oh Jeff, I remember the boy. You have grown tall, Jeff. What have you been doing?"

"Growing up, sir. And how are you?"

"Just counting my days now."

"No, Mr. Johnson, you shouldn't say that. You look as fresh as the morning breeze to me." Maggie invigorated him.

He laughed at her remark which was a rare and pleasant sight.

"What's making you so happy dad--" Erica had just stepped out listening to her father's laughter. But her words were stuck in her throat and so was her breath to see the sight of a companion who meant more than the world to her.

"Look, Erica, the Saunderhursts are here. And they are all grown up now. I wonder why you haven't." Mr. Johnson introduced them all.

"Yeah, dad. I haven't, even a bit. I'm still your ten year old." Erica joked dolorously. "Hello, Maggie... Jeff."

Maggie and Erica embraced tightly and parted.

"Hello, Erica." Jeff gazed into her eyes and she allowed him that for as long as he wanted.

When her eyes became tearful with surging emotions within, she looked away and wiped them clear.

"I think this boy has been away for too long, is that right?" Mr. Johnson chewed his words one at a time.

"Yes, sir. Five years to be exact." Jeff was equally moved by now.

"Five years, that isn't too long."

"It is, sir. It is long indeed."

Erica's lips quivered and she returned inside the store. Maggie caught Jeff's poignantly impassioned countenance. She knew their union was brief initially, but it was to go a long way now. She might have turned her back to him at first, but her heart was paining to beat next to his.

It was well close to two in the afternoon and Jeff had observed the tragic despair on his father's face, while Maggie sat in ennui at the other end of the counter and toyed with the empty register, driving the cash tray in and out. They both waited. Waited for some miracle to happen to this hapless bookstore, a miracle that was anticipated for years, but it was nowhere in sight. The door chimed once more and all three pairs of eyes jolted to the threshold but dimmed upon seeing another one of the family members enter the store.

"Dave? You're early today." Maggie shattered her boredom with words.

"Half day, the boss wasn't too happy about it, but when you're worked twenty-three years, this is the least they can do. And I managed to get a full week's paid holiday from twenty-second to the twenty-eighth." Dave relieved himself of the heavy jacket walking to the counter.

"Wow, that's nice," Maggie spoke appreciatively.

"So, what do we have here? Any sales?"

Dave's inquiry met with no response, it was quite standard for him to hear that. Then a protracted silence followed.

"What time do we close here?" Jeff disrupted at length.

"Five, four most of the days. When we don't have a single sale. It angers us both and then we leave early." Dave chuckled.

"Why don't you guys go home?" Jeff proposed.

"Go home?" Dave glanced at Martin and Maggie with uncertainty.

"Yeah, I'll close the place at four. If this is how well it goes, I don't see the reason for four of us wasting our strength and time here. I'll put the shutters down and be home soon. All of you look so tired, deserve a day off."

The family shared a glimpse again.

"Okay, let's go then." Maggie became the first to agree, the two men followed suit. "All right, dad?"

Martin's eyes were filling and his lips trembled. He stood up and shuffled over to Jeff, kissing him on the cheek. "It's a tragedy for a family to lose a son, but it's a miracle for them to find one again."

It fortified Jeff in ways he had never imagined before to emanate from his father's end. Maggie and Dave were justly obliged by their father's heartfelt promulgation for his son.

"And just before you leave, Dave. Can I speak to you for a little while?"

"Yeah, sure," Dave nodded.

"We'll wait for you in the car." Maggie helped Martin out of the store and across the street.

"He has aged," Jeff went from jubilant to grievous. "In just five years, he's aged."

"He didn't take your leaving sportingly. Mom was even worse for a couple of months. Comforted each other a lot, finally coming out of it with time."

"But they had you."

"Yes, they had me, and I did my best to pull them out of their misery. But somehow it wasn't enough. You know separation intensifies longing and that in turn increases love. I never left this town so I'd never know if I was ever their favorite." Dave had a remote smile on his face.

"Everyone loves you, Dave. You're our pillar."

Dave acknowledged with a sigh. "But life went on, everything went back to regular. After retirement, he just had this store to look after and nothing else. And it was good that he decided to retire. He did have an offer to work part-time, but he refused to stay with mom. She could use all the company she could get, especially after Maggie and then you."

"And you Dave, how did you keep up?"

"Nah, I never loved you that much." The brothers snickered.

"That's a good one," Jeff praised.

"Isn't it? Yeah, same old routine here. Not a single change in years. I don't expect much out of this job. It is just to keep alive. Nothing extra for the luxuries, but enough."

"And this store? Is it always like this?"

"The town hasn't changed much in five years, Jeff." Dave illumined the truth Jeff already knew.

"Has it helped at all?"

"You were right about this store. There was a reason this town was missing a bookseller and the ones around it. There are no buyers, not many. We do sell in bulk if I hear a deal across towns for public libraries, school libraries, but that's hardly ever. Apart from that, maybe ten books would sell in a week, sometimes a month. It never prospered, the only good thing about it is that the store was bought on a leased land. We don't have much expenses. The only time I saw people continuously pouring in and out of this place was back when you had your story published. That was the only successful event this store saw. Only you can repeat that."

"That was a disaster."

"Not money-wise, that register was full for so many days after."

"That was some day," Jeff reminisced. "So, it has never altered from its snail pace since?" Jeff said in a tone that inclined toward a disappointed statement rather than a question. "The want to leave this town is justified still."

"People are leaving towns, now. It is a new wave of city fever. Families are left behind, homes are deserted, and they are right to do so. City makes a capable man out of an ordinary man. I have seen even the most dumbest of folks leave town and a make a living out there."

"Do you plan to leave town?" Jeff reverted to the main purpose of this conversation.

"Leave it? No, I can't do that. We're old townsfolk, we can never abandon our homes. It's the young ones who do that, not us. And even if we do, sooner or later we end up back here again. I see an example right in front of me."

Jeff shot a look at him.

"Somehow that perspective completely changed within ten years or so. We wouldn't think about leaving our homes, but kids nowadays are just too eager to step out of their thresholds with little or no concern for what they are leaving behind."

"I made the same mistake, didn't I?" Jeff acknowledged.

"It isn't a mistake, but the way you left was hard for many people. No, I cannot leave. One doesn't have to if you make a living satisfactory to your family. A little bit of savings doesn't hurt, but just enough to know that your children are going to be fine a few years after your death, that's what most of us need."

"You cannot force your viewpoint upon Charlie, Dave."

"No, I can't. You're right," Dave agreed.

"You don't want to repeat what happened five years ago."

"No, if he wants to leave I will let him leave with a pat on the back and whatever money I would've saved for him. I would even go with him and settle him there and stay as long as he needs me. But I wish I could afford that. I don't think I'll be able to make enough money in my lifetime to send him to a nice college. He's not as studious as Linda to get a scholarship, so that's out. Heck, I can't even afford to shift to a city unless I sell the house."

"You have a family you can count on."

"Yeah," Dave whispered thoughtfully. "Family that have their own families to take care of."

"What about me?"

"Yeah, I never thought of that. You're a rich man. I could easily swindle a couple thousand from you without any trouble." They giggled again, a hiatus followed.

"I will not stop him from becoming what he wants to become, but I will not allow him to leave before he's wise enough to understand what could become of him." Dave finished.

Jeff smiled thinly, "since when did you become so wise?"

That triggered a loud laughter from Dave. "Well, you were influenced by someone that you became a writer."

Jeff brayed uncontrollably.

"Here are the keys, I'll go with Maggie." Dave hurled the keys at Jeff which he caught. He waved to him but just in the doorway, he turned again, "did someone ask you to talk to me about this, Jeff?"

"Just my conscience," Jeff answered artfully.

Dave nodded and left.

# Chapter Nineteen

A lonesome storefront was lit in darkness and cast its luminance on the street and sidewalk. The burden of an inexcusable guilt crushed Jeff's soul as he sat in the bleak confines of his bookstore. If an accidental wallop to Edward's face wasn't enough, it was supplemented with Maggie's scream of disappointment, and the latter afflicted his conscience atrociously. He had concluded that night to leave the town and its people to their own fate and never return to face another humiliation. But somewhere in that wrath, he had a slight hope of seeing a carful of family members arriving to placate his anger and reconcile the lost amiability. As hours passed, his hopes of conciliation diminished and frustration began billowing from his livid countenance. He decisively rose and stormed out the bookstore, shuttering it to a close and heading back to where he began.

Jeff reached home as the air of celebration and revelry had long ended with the remains scattered in the front and backyard. The people had departed and the house was dark and quiescent except for some light in the dining room.

As he ascended the steps to the door, he glimpsed a moving specter under the porch of the neighboring house. In the faint lightbulb, he sighted Erica who sat waiting there, possibly all this time since the conclusion of the wedding ceremony. She arose with deepening concern knitted across her forehead, but Jeff discounted her from his roiling reasoning and continued inside.

He made no audible noises opening the front door and moving inside like an unknown shadow as he attempted to reach his room and collect his belongings for a journey that he sought to take him far away forever. Passing through the hall, he found Lena in the dining alone and carrying her suffering past midnight, immersed in tears. She was oblivious of his presence out there in her state of deep rumination while sitting forlorn and pacifying her grief herself.

Jeff had listened to those unspoken words that his mother cried out softly through her unchecked tears. He had discerned the silent yearning that streamed out of her eyes. He was lodged between the love of a mother and the way of a future, stuck between the expectations of a family and his anticipation of a tomorrow. And in that ambivalence, he plodded away into his room, shutting the door behind.

He alighted on the bed and pondered the declining fervor of a decision that he had pursued so zealously some minutes ago. The sight of his mother's tears had suddenly thrown him into a dire vacillation and his departure from home seemed a remote probability now. But that quickly changed into a definite impossibility when his mother opened the door after a soft knock and peered inside through the slight gap. Her fearful eyes searched the room for that one indication that would delineate her son's departure, a luggage perhaps, or an indignant expression that might be hurtled toward her anytime now, but she failed to grasp any of them.

That certain silence, though otherwise uninviting, welcomed her into the room and when her eyes met her son's, it was a moment when her timid heart was reaffirmed of Jeff's intentions. He did not speak to her or signaled any conciliation, but sat quietly and marveled at the reason that capriciously gave him the strength to endure what he'd despised for so long. That reason, no matter how long he labored and contemplated, would remain cryptic even to his own reckoning for the rest of his life.

"Want to race me to the falls? My bike's over there. Though, I think I might be too tall to ride it anymore."

Jeff had stayed under the shadow of the massive oak tree in their lawn for the majority of the day. It was a warm September noon and a charming face with green eyes and auburn hair leaned in demanding an answer. He simply looked up at Erica and refused to give her one.

"You really need to be disciplined, you know? A lady is trying to make a conversation with you and you haven't even a word to share?"

That elicited a smile reminding him of forgotten times from long ago. Deriving pleasure from his smile, Erica reciprocated and sat right next to him adjusting her summer dress to propriety. Jeff passed a glimpse at her, which was intended to be fugacious, but her lustrous elegance and beauty prolonged it into a stare which became quite uncomfortable at length. He averted.

"What are you doing there?" Erica rescued him from the awkwardness that had buried him in timorous discomfort.

Jeff put away his notepad in which he's scribbled all afternoon until some other oppressive thoughts had sneaked and dominated his mind. "Nothing important."

"You're off today?" she attempted to make a conversation.

"The store's closed on Sundays. It's too early to leave for my night shift."

"I don't remember congratulating you for it, so here it goes, congratulations on your bookstore."

Jeff simply shook his head in acknowledgment. "That's all right, it's nothing to be excited about. Besides, you have many things to remember, if it slipped your mind I can't blame you for it.

Congratulations to you, you're settled in New Jersey now." Jeff's tone had a contentious inkling.

"I am? See, I didn't even know that. How negligent of me." Erica's eyes sharpened.

"Well, aren't you? Aren't you going to go back, if not tomorrow, maybe next week or the week after? Isn't everyone too eager to leave this town?"

"If that's your way of asking them to stay, no wonder they are. And I don't know what people you're using as an example here, but there are some of us who never enjoyed leaving home at all."

"Well, it surely doesn't feel like it. You've been away for quite some time."

"If my aunt didn't mention of a college that happened to be literally a block away from her house, I wouldn't have left."

"Five years, Erica. Five. Somehow the amount of time you spent there tells me you didn't want to come back."

"Yeah exactly five years, Jeff. I was loving my life over there. You didn't hear the rumors?" Erica spoke derisively.

"Then what made you come back? There's nothing left here. Your best friend is married and gone. You'll take after her soon enough and bring your dad along when you go back."

"Thanks for your suggestions. I will consider them one at a time."

"You finished your college more than a year ago, Erica. In all that time you could have at least visited once?"

"You're actually mistaken, Jeff. I haven't been to a classroom in two years. And you want to know the truth? I never finished college. How's that for a surprise?"

"What difference does that make?" Jeff smirked.

"It does. Taking care of a sick person makes it even better, won't you say? To care for someone who was diagnosed with tuberculosis, how would you grade that?"

"Your aunt?"

"Yes."

"Maggie never told me about this."

"Maggie was living in a dormitory. I was living in the same house. If she knew she would have told you. No one knew about this until recently. I wasn't there reveling if that's what you're implying."

A silence swept between them until Jeff spoke again.

"How is she?"

"I had her son take her to Houston after her recovery. He and his family are going to take care of her now."

Jeff clenched his jaws and swallowed his mortification. "I'm sorry. If I knew, I wouldn't have said it like that."

Her indignation mollified. "I know I wasn't able to come here to see you and the rest very often since I went there, especially after this ordeal, but I could never forget home."

"Tell me you're not going to leave again?" There was a glint of honest fear in his eyes.

Erica smiled, "I'm not going anywhere now. I'm here and I'm back."

A gleeful smile spread across him. "Maggie would be glad to hear about it."

"How about you?" Erica searched his face for an answer but she found it in his eyes instead of his lips.

"You are missing her, aren't you?" She was tired of circumventing.

"That house doesn't seem like it without her. When she was around, it was somehow so peaceful even with all her chattering and laughter, and that booming music she used to listen to."

Erica smiled at Jeff's observance of Maggie's inclination.

"Even when she was away with you in college, I'd look forward to her call every evening before I left for work. And those fifteen minutes were the most beautiful sounds I'd hear the whole day. No, I don't miss her. Now that she's left, why should I?"

"Jeff, if there is anything on your mind right now it's her and that night. I know it. I know what you're battling inside, but if you don't allow yourself to forget, you won't be able to forgive."

"I was wrong, what I did is unforgivable. Even if I apologized to the whole town, it still wouldn't be enough."

"Yes, what happened that night was wrong. But if there's anyone who deserves your apology, it is your family. You do not owe anyone else anything. Besides, it wasn't entirely your fault that you vented your anger. Maggie told me everything that you've been through. I probably would have reacted the same way you did." She took his hand in hers. "She can still call every evening and speak to you if that's what makes you happy. She can visit on weekends and holidays to spend time with all of us."

"Please go away, go away right now. Those were the last words I heard from her, Erica. I can't expect her to--"

"People say things they don't mean when they are upset, Jeff. Sometimes to show their anger and sometimes to show disappointment. But there's always some hidden emotion behind their words and it's never meant to be hurtful."

"That's not true."

"You just did."

It stunned him for a moment.

"Do you think she said that to make you leave, so that you may never come back? No. She said it to save you from any more harm, any more humiliation in front of all those people."

Jeff's frown began to unwind.

"These rifts," Erica continued, "never last long between siblings. You should know because you have three of them. Imagine hearing this from someone who doesn't even have one. Maggie has loved you all her life, your little sister, and if you have to be convinced about it then I'd say she wasted her life on a man who really doesn't deserve any of it."

"I ruined her wedding day."

"Yes, and that's probably why her disappointment has lasted a bit longer than usual. But the last minute before leaving this house she spoke to me about you. She wanted to see you and you were nowhere around. Do you need any more proof of her love?"

"She hasn't spoken to me since then."

"Yes, I know. She called two days ago and asked me to tell you that she wouldn't talk to you unless you start listening to her. And she said to look for her old scrapbook to find out where to begin."

Jeff glimpsed Erica in bewilderment.

Erica shrugged, "even I don't know what that means."

Jeff staggered up to his feet and hastened inside the house. He entered Maggie's room upstairs and ransacked the place for the old keepsake of their childhood. He found it resting under her pillow. Flipping through the pages riddled with faces, he found nothing riveting or unusual. Just as he reached the final page, he discovered a picture of Erica's taped to it and a handwritten note on the top and bottom of the photo.

It read-- 'You're next. And I didn't have to search long to find the perfect face for someone as ugly as you.'

Jeff laughed at the humor imbued in truth behind the mischief as he walked to the window and peered outside at Erica, who sat under the tree, waiting for something to happen just like him that might animate their dull lives a little.

Erica had been right about many things since her return, but out of all those the most important prophecy was the treasured relationship that Jeff hoped to reconcile. It happened soon enough when the following week Maggie had called from Boston and asked to speak to Jeff. They stayed on the phone for about twenty minutes whimpering and crying their hearts out to each other. It was in that moment he had realized that Maggie wasn't just a sister he had, but a blessing that would never be estranged from him. And there was another boon for which he had to be thankful; a companion who had pledged never to leave him or the town again.

As time accelerated, their bond strengthened. Jeff assumed his responsibilities of the house and became the son his father always wanted him to be and the idea of leaving the town gradually crept from his reasoning and vanished like a transient storm. With that difference out of the way, the Saunderhursts were encountering blessed tidings every once in a while and the latest was the birth of Maggie's son. It was a grand family event when the grandchild of two families was born and a greater celebration when he was named Ronald at his baptism. There was a rumor swirling in the air of another ceremony soon to be conducted at the church that would legalize the companionship of two young souls into wedlock. The proximity between Jeff and Erica wasn't hidden from their families, and upon some serious urging and advocacy from Maggie's end, they were about to be brought into a lasting relationship. But the ambition of fate isn't always perspicuous.

# Chapter Twenty

✵

"You wrote this?" Erica was in sublime shock as she read through some dingy pages of a manuscript.

Jeff sat in silence. His eyes squinted to read her appraisal. "Yes," he answered.

"It's incomplete though," she pointed.

"Yeah, I just couldn't think of anything to complete a story like that. Maybe I'm not good enough to write an end to it."

"This isn't possible. There is no way you could have wri tten all of this." She was awestruck.

"So you doubt my ability as well?"

"Doubt it? I can't seriously believe someone could write something of this magnitude and be stuck in this town. What are you doing with it? Have you tried sending it around?"

"Send it? Where?"

"The city, try any for a change. Complete or incomplete, this will be accepted right off the first page. It is terrible."

"Okay, you've got to stop this. I don't know it you like it or hate it." Jeff was concerned by now.

Erica stepped closer to him and held his gaze. "This is amazing. It needs to be published." She spoke with such admiration and certainty as if instilling her words into him.

"Published? Give it back to me. I'm not making this public. I let you read it because you found it, that's all. There's nothing more to it, so let's not get excited."

"You're not going to let it go to waste here, Jeff. What is wrong with you?"

"I can't publish this, Erica." He attempted to reason with her. "I don't know what to do, how to do. I--"

"You don't have to do anything. They take care of everything, you just make a couple of trips up and down and you're set for life. This is something you can achieve on your own."

"This was just once that I tried, I never wrote after that. My priorities are changed. I cannot leave, not even for a while."

She importuned, "what happened in the past is forgotten. If there's anyone who's doubted you, this is how you make them believe."

"I'd be the most unfortunate man if I had to ask my family to believe in me."

"I believe in you. I have always believed in you, and your family loves you."

"And I love them equally. It's out of that love that I can't leave them now. They both are all alone here. If I try to do this, I might have that urge to leave if it becomes a success. It will happen all over again. Last time I was a fool enough not to understand what both of them tried to say through their silence and their words, but now I do. They are alone and cannot look after themselves, they need me."

"What if I took care of them for you?"

"You already have a responsibility of your own." He was unknowingly hurtful.

"My own?" Erica was paining to repeat it. "Then you must be a stranger?"

"I'm sorry, Erica. But please, don't force me down the same path that almost ruined my life a year ago. I can't bear to go through it again."

"So, you will plainly forgo the possibility of doing wonders with this? Would you be happy with that, Jeff?"

"Happiness didn't carry me for months when I was unable to walk. Happiness didn't nurture me when I couldn't care for myself. It didn't educate me, which made me the man I am today. It didn't feed me to keep me alive. My parents did. I owe that to my parents, not my happiness. I know this town doesn't give away more than mere survival, but you decided to stay, didn't you? And your father became the reason behind that."

Erica smirked obscurely at Jeff's conviction which was only half true from her end.

"I stay for the same reason," Jeff concluded.

Erica nodded after a long rumination and approached him. While in an embrace, her tears just streamed her cheeks but her eyes glinted with a plan.

It was a cold March morning which was the first day of spring and Jeff had enjoyed the crisp breeze on his way to the shop. Just as he made the turn, he espied a considerable multitude outside the bookstore which was actually a terrifying sight as he instantly feared a calamity. He quickly parked the car and exited, making his way into the crowd, jostling through apprehensively and coming at the door against a queue of people that extended from the cashier's counter to the pool of customers that clustered outside. He saw many familiar faces in the throng and realized it was some kind of a spectacle in which they all wanted to participate.

He entered the door and found Erica at the register with a towering pile of papers right beside her that pitched dangerously to one side, about to topple. As customers suspiciously bought one book each with no relevance to their preference, they ended up receiving a sheaf of xerox, bound together with a string, bearing a handwritten title on each reading 'And Life... Goes On.'

Jeff was shaken to learn that Erica had just self-published his unfinished work to the entire town and possibly the neighboring ones too. His senses were permeated with dreadful nervousness and he scuffled backwards effacing into the shadow of a bookshelf. The line of buyers was unending and Erica continued to ring the register with one sale after next. The strategy she had managed to engage and tempt such a large gathering into making a purchase was partially enigmatic. But Jeff had presumed it might have something to do with her influence as being a native of the town, a child most of them had watched grow into a lady, and the fact that she knew almost each one of them, hence, extracting an inexpensive purchase of a book wasn't a feat that couldn't be attained. Jeff observed from his concealed vantage point and found himself beguiled at the number of people who showed up interested in a thing like that.

"Ladies and gentlemen, if you would just pay attention here for a moment. We have the writer of this beautiful work amongst us, Jeff Saunderhurst. So, let's give him a warm welcome first of all." Erica applauded followed by a thunderous approval from the crowd.

Jeff emerged unnerved at being the center of all attention and smiled anxiously.

"And in case if any of you need your copies signed by the author, all you need is a pen. Please feel free to approach our author."

People left the queue and hovered around Jeff presenting their purchased copies for him to sign. Jeff was overwhelmed and flustered, to begin with, sweating profusely at the sudden assault, but eventually eased into it as he eyed Erica, beyond all those faces, smiling back at him. There was exuberance that filled the air and Jeff breathed in all he could, relishing the moment that was built for him. But he never forgot the artist who painted him with content and fulfillment.

"Thank you," he whispered to her.

Though, that voice never reached Erica's ears, the message and intention were thoroughly conveyed. Erica looked away, quickly wiping under her eyes, hoping no one saw the emotional side of her.

The doorbell brought Lena out of her kitchen to answer and just as she sighted Erica at the door, she welcomed her inside amicably.

"Good evening, Mrs. Saunderhurst. How are you?" Erica greeted as she entered.

"Erica, this is a wonderful surprise. The last time I saw you come inside this house was Maggie's wedding day. You always run back to your place after seeing Jeff under that tree or the bookstore, but never in here."

"I'm sorry, Mrs. Saunderhurst. Next time I will make sure I come inside and stay for a while until you are bored with me."

"That would be a welcome change. That tree almost seems like Jeff's second home, doesn't it? You'll find him living there more than in this house. Why don't just give me a second and I'll be right back with two warm cups of coffee," Lena proposed.

"That is all right, I don't want to trouble you about it."

"Trouble? You'd be a beautiful excuse for me to leave that kitchen for a while. And I could use a cup myself." Lena insisted.

"Then I'll be glad to join." Erica agreed warmly.

Lena nodded and headed into the kitchen, Erica rambled after her.

"Is Mr. Saunderhurst home yet?"

"He will be arriving shortly. Is there something you needed of him?"

"I wanted to speak to both of you together."

"Oh, if it's important I can give him a call to hurry home. Is Mr. Johnson okay?"

"No, nothing like that. He's doing well, just a bit tired these days. But no need to rush, it can wait until he's settled for a talk.

"He'll be here soon." Lena handed her a steaming cup of coffee. "Erica, I want to thank you for what you did for Jeff some days ago. Dave was telling me about it and how you schemed to sell his work with townspeople. It was really thoughtful of you."

"I was more excited about it than him, Mrs. Saunderhurst. He is a brilliant writer. This was the least I could do."

"If you won't mind, even I would like to speak to you about something. But my matter of discussion is quite important and doesn't require Jeff's father to be present either."

"What is it?" Erica turned solicitous.

"I know you two have accompanied each other since the beginning of your lives. You both probably didn't even know how to speak but were able to form a companionship. It has lasted for such a long time. If I suggested transforming that companionship into a… um... relationship, would you object to that?"

Erica fell into silence which was driven by her reserve rather than refusal. Lena waited for her response with glimmering eyes.

"I... I have no objection, Mrs. Saunderhurst, but we have never spoken about it." Erica answered coyly.

Lena laughed at this, "well, there always a start to a new beginning. He's been inexpressive since infancy, but you are a wise woman now. I can only entrust his responsibility to you. Not yours to him, but his to you. And from now on, you call me Lena."

The doorbell rang again.

"That must be Martin."

Erica tarried in the kitchen until she heard the door being opened and closed, and someone entering the house relieving himself of his keys and sinking into a couch with a deep sigh. She slowly came out of her hiding and appeared before Martin who was slightly surprised to see her there.

"Erica?"

"Evening, Mr. Saunderhurst."

"Good evening, how are you? How's Eric?"

"Daddy is doing well. Thank you."

"So, what brings you here? It's nice to see a young visitor in this house. It's usually the old ones, our age, who can't find a better cup of coffee anywhere else." Martin jested as he received coffee from Lena.

Erica smiled, "I have promised Lena, I will visit her every once in a while."

"Well, you two are getting along then. The formal Mrs. Saunderhurst to the informal first name Lena, that's a start." Martin sharply noted.

"Have a seat. Jeff won't be here until six, but--"

"Erica has come to speak to us." Lena joined.

"Oh, is that so? Go ahead then young lady, we're all ears."

Erica hesitantly came to the sofa and sat down, placing an original copy of Jeff's manuscript, that she carried all along, on the table before his parents.

Martin was perplexed at the sight of it first, then glimpsed Erica. "And this is?"

"His life, his dreams, his future. This is what Jeff is made for." Erica gained assurance with every word she spoke.

Martin picked up the manuscript and flipped through the pages. Lena shared his amazement.

"It came to me as a surprise as well. I never thought he could write so wonderfully." Erica expressed her adulation.

Lena lighted up hearing the praise and interposed. "He never told anyone about this. I remember he did wanted to go to college to learn writing, but--"

"It is an amazing craft, sir. And he's capable of doing it splendidly. You should read it yourself."

"I'm sure he's pretty good at it. But what does this exactly mean?" Martin concealed his intuition of where this conversation was headed behind a sophistry.

"I have tried to convince him to begin writing again, but he refuses." Erica cleared the ambiguity.

"He thinks he's not good enough?" Martin confirmed.

"It's exactly that what he lacks, right now. Self-belief, to trust his own ability."

"It might take some time for him to discover that trust, Erica. He isn't a professional, he will need a lot of practice at this to determine whether he's a good writer or not."

"He is a brilliant writer, Mr. Saunderhurst. I can attest to that."

"Erica, somehow your opinion isn't sufficient to give him a rank of a writer. You aren't the only reader."

"The people have responded to his skill. I have discussed with so many of them since they received a copy and not one disliked his work." Erica pressed on.

"Is this what's been going on at the bookstore?" Martin questioned bitterly. "I did come to know about you doing some sales at the store, this was given for free along with the books? You had asked them for a favor and they gave it to you. It was nothing more than that." Martin was pungently hostile.

"That is not true, sir. I have spoken to them." Erica defended.

"Spoken to them about what? Would you ever find a person who'd criticize a work in front of its seller, knowing how close of a relationship you share with Jeff? They gave you those words of praise because that's what you wanted to listen. Besides, where are we heading with this argument? He writes, that's good, he's talented. That is the end of it then." Martin slapped the manuscript down on the table.

"I want you to support him in this. If he receives encouragement from you, it'll be the greatest gift for him at this moment. He needs to come out of this anonymity and his distrust in himself which is burying him in deep darkness and he's using you as an excuse to stay there."

"Us? You are mistaken, young lady. I have never stopped him from doing anything. I have never spoken to him about this in my life."

"That is exactly what has kept him back so far. He says that he needs to stay here because both of you are alone. He says he cannot write anymore because he has other priorities."

"He is not wrong to acknowledge them. He does," Martin declared.

"If he continues to think like that, he will never return to writing again. But if he manages to gain your trust, he will."

"I don't know what to say here, you're accusing me of something I'm not guilty."

"We have never stopped him from writing, Erica. We didn't even know he did," Lena interjected.

"Now you do. You have not stopped him from writing, but you have stopped him from pursuing it. This town will never make a writer out of him. For that he will have to travel to the city. I have a cousin who works as a journalist in Houston. I spoke to him about this and he said he has contacts in Jersey and New York he can talk with and probably get his book onto some desks for consideration. I want you to convince him to take this opportunity. It might not come his way again."

"Did he ask you to come here and speak in his favor? He always wanted to leave. We even had quite a display of his intentions more than a year ago at the wedding. Now he's using you, isn't it?" Martin incriminated both of complicity.

"If your perception of him doesn't change, you will be responsible for ruining a deeply talented man," she expostulated.

"Are you implying that a father has no regard for his son's talents?" Martin was incensed.

"You have kept him here for too long, Mr. Saunderhurst. If he is able to do such a thing, it will be a shame for parents to simply let it go to waste. And he doesn't even have to leave, he can do this from right here. But he will need your support to get where he wants to be."

"He is where he deserves to be. He owns a business and he has a job. That's about all a man needs."

"But he doesn't have an identity."

"I have given him everything."

Lena held Martin by his arms trying to abate his anger.

"Except what he really needed, your understanding and your love."

"You need not tell me how to love my son, Erica. What do you know about it? I have loved him for years. I have protected him--"

"And who shall protect him when you are no more with him?"

"Erica," Lena objected.

"Please, Mrs. Saunderhurst. Let him answer that for me. He believes he's protected him so far, assuming that a man of twenty-seven needs protection from his father, who is going to do that once you're dead? You say that you loved him and cared for him, then how come he feels trapped in a house that was supposed to construct a man out of him instead of a dependent. Love is not just protecting people from life, love is also preparing them for it. I might not know what love truly is, but at least I know that I have loved somebody and it grew to be sacred knowing that he might not love me back as much. You're bound to love your family which you receive in life. It isn't out of choice, but you do. But when two strangers come together, it becomes sacred. Love is an invisible feeling, but having faith in it is divine."

"Do you love my son?" Martin was terse in his query.

"I love him." Erica was arrantly trenchant with her response.

"And you're still willing to let him leave?"

"My love is not that which would hold him here, it would release him instead. He will come back and I will wait until he does. He will not leave forever."

There was a long pause between that heated, irate discourse.

"We should get these two married soon." Martin disrupted that pause with a surprising comment.

Erica almost trembled with anger, but it began to subside. Lena was equally stunned.

"Don't you think so?" Martin nodded to his wife. "I don't think he'll find a girl like this ever in life who'd stand up to his parents for him the way she did. This is what I wanted, young lady. To see where you two stand with each other. I have found out, quite hotly, but it was a marvelous discovery."

"Oh goodness, Martin, you almost gave us a heart attack."

Martin chortled, "I am not a bad father, Erica. The only reason I held him back so far was to make sure that he has a reason to return home. If he had left a year earlier, these two old souls wouldn't be much of a bait to bring him back, and the kind of relationship we've shared and the times I've been absent on him because of work and other things, he wouldn't be too excited to come back either. Now we could speak to him and beg him to come and see us, but a true sentiment is never asked of someone. Well, even after your marriage you both might want to settle in the city and we wouldn't be able to dissuade you for the same reasons, but at least I would have the satisfaction of knowing that there is someone out there to care for him, to look out for him. And that I'm sure you'll be able to accomplish gloriously." Martin finished with hopeful eyes.

"Thank you, Mr. Saunderhurst." Erica smiled through her tears.

"Oh, so she's Lena and I'm still Mr. Saunderhurst?" Martin raised his brows.

"I'm sorry."

"That's all right, it sounds respectful. You may call me exactly that."

A genial laughter followed from all three.

"Let's surprise him a little. Give me a week. I might even shock you with my plans." Martin prepared for something unprecedented.

# Chapter Twenty-One

The bells at the door chimed once again disrupting Jeff's reminiscent gaze from a wall clock that ticked close to 3:30. He was awakened from his thoughtful rumination. A man had stepped inside and through his all-black attire, a banded collar clergy shirt was the most salient feature delineating his obvious role in a Church. He was in his early 40s, balding but bearded, and crisp blue eyes that skimmed across the counter and the shelves, skipping Jeff, as if searching for someone specific. When his sight failed to grasp anyone else but Jeff, he approached him.

"Is Martin here?" he asked affably.

"I'm afraid not. He went home early today." Jeff smiled back.

"Oh, I missed him then. I was hoping to find him today, but I suppose I'll have to give him a personal visit now." He weighed the possibility of that unplanned excursion in his binding schedule.

Jeff contemplated revealing his identity to him but resisted.

"If there's a message I can convey? I'd be glad to oblige." Jeff proposed.

He shook his head, "hardly an imperative message, but he's well aware of the reason I'm here, or any other business down the block for that matter. We haven't met before, so a formal introduction would be most essential. I'm the appointed deacon under the apprenticeship of Pastor Riley. Last year we had devised a

Christmas Gathering at the church and entreated all congregation to participate in it. The time's here yet again and fortunately, all our patrons have generously contributed this year as well. Mr. Saunderhurst had assisted the church with a considerable donation last year, so I couldn't help but knock at this door once again." He paused for a moment, "are you new here? If I can shuffle my memory well, I haven't had the pleasure of seeing your face amongst the others."

"I'm quite antique to be exact, but you wouldn't have seen me at the church in the past five years."

"Oh, so you are his son?"

"I see I'm not a stranger, after all."

"People who are well remembered even in their absence are never strangers to those they never met. There's always someone, somewhere talking about them. And your folks confide in me quite trustingly." He eyed Jeff steadily. Somehow, his part in Jeff's parents' lives, especially Lena, was enlightened.

"I lost my certainty of being remembered somewhere down that trip to the bus stop after hurting a lot of people here."

"Well, there's always room for returning members of the congregation and what better time than Christmas to rebuild the lost faith and family ties."

"I plan to be a part of it."

"I must get going now. If you see your father before I do, tell him I'll come to meet him around dusk."

"If you wouldn't mind, I'd like to take care of that myself, that you're here now. I don't want to inconvenience you with the trip."

"No inconvenience incurred. I love visiting your mother for a delicious cup of coffee."

"Then I'd see you later."

"But, because I'm quite short on time as a lot of doors need to be knocked, some are opened some are not, I would actually favor your offer and prefer to save the trip just this once."

"I don't want you to think I prevented you from relishing that cup of coffee."

He laughed, "not at all, I'll have many more instances to visit and enjoy that coffee. Here is a small flyer which tells you the place and time of our arrangement and the check goes to the official --"

"Is cash a possibility?"

"It is even better for imminent expenses, but unfortunately I wouldn't be able to give you a receipt as I don't have my receipt-book with me right now. Didn't think any businesses would empty their cash registers tonight."

"I don't need a receipt from you, sir."

They both shared an amicable glimpse.

"All right, I will take that payment out of your trust in my faith."

"But you've got to help me out here. I don't want to disappoint you when you open that envelope. Usually, how big are the donations?" Jeff searched his wallet.

"Very big."

Jeff shot a glimpse at him.

"They contain a lot of love, empathy, brotherhood, understanding, and finally trust in each other. Out of these, one you have just openly exhibited to a stranger. I will not give you an amount that you are compelled to pay for the church never invoices its congregation. Though, much to my dislike, the priests have become quite involved in book of numbers, and I'm not referring to the fourth book of the old testament, since the introduction of tax-deductible offerings. There was a time when offerings were anonymous and all people of the church were catered with honor and respect regardless of their Sunday mass budgets. But it has changed somewhat in the recent past. All are equal in the eyes of God, only their faith ranks them wealthy to poor. You may give whatever you wish out of your goodwill."

Jeff listened to him intently. He was stirred by his sagacious perspective. Jeff, without a second glance, emptied his wallet and inserted the money into the envelope without counting. The deacon accepted it without looking.

"What is your name, sir? Jeff asked extending his arm for a shake.

"Solomon, Solomon Conroy." He clasped Jeff's hand amiably.

"Nice to meet you, Solomon."

"Likewise, Jeff." He smiled thinly. "Yes, I know your name. We had discussed your return many a time. Your folks needed all the prayers and support they could get. Take care of them, and yourself. I will see you on the twenty-fourth. Don't forget, you paid for it."

Jeff laughed and waved to the priest-in-training as he left the store.

When silence prevailed again, a thought pervaded Jeff's mind and he promptly sought around himself for something he couldn't locate.

"We don't have a phone here. Great." He whispered to himself and hastened out of the store.

Jeff scrambled toward a pay phone at the end of the block almost slipping at one instance on frozen ice. He regained composure and picked up the receiver dialing a number after the appropriate fueling. He waited as the ring went on thrice. Someone answered on the other end.

"Golden Diamond Publishing, how may I help you?"

"Anne?" Jeff spoke excitedly.

"Yes?" The answer came in uncertainty.

"Don't tell me you don't recognize this voice."

"I don't suppose this is Morgan Freeman calling from the Shawshank prison, is it?" A slight laughter sounded following the remark.

"Not that famous. But I'm inclined to believe he's not your type."

"Oh baby, that voice is anybody's type."

"Then let me give you a call thirty years later with a sore throat and I'll head over for a date."

Anne cackled hysterically, "what can I do for you Jeff Saunderhurst?"

"Ahh, so my voice is distinguishable."

"No, but your manners are, with me."

"What can I do? I keep asking you out, you never have time."

"The day a young man like you asks a fifty-seven year old woman out on a date would be a catalyst for change in this deteriorating world."

"You can't say that Anne, I did ask you out."

"That I can't deny. I'll give you that. Well, I'm free tomorrow."

"Oh, quite a late pick-up call, I'm already in my hometown. Hours away from you."

"You are? I thought you were taking me along to meet your parents?"

"I will. I'm just waiting to mortgage the next oceanfront, eight bedroom mansion to bring you in."

"Oh, now I'm not that expensive to flaunt around."

"But you do agree you are a bit expensive?"

"Maybe just a little. Hold on, let me connect you to Angela. I know you're calling for her. I have these phones ringing off the hook today. Talking to you was a warm dash of sunlight in a thunderstorm."

"Thanks! Take care, Anne." Jeff waited on hold. "Angela, how are you?"

"I'm doing well and you?" Another heavier voice returned.

"That's nice to hear. Okay, not taking much of your time, I've got to ask you for something. Consider this the first and the last of the favors, ever."

"What are you thinking this time?"

The sun had sunk behind the horizon and with its dying ambition, it painted the sky indigo and crimson. Jeff wrestled with the metal door that was ostensibly displaced a bit from its squealing hinges as he sought to close the store.

"You've got to lift them up to get them in their right place. Lift it and then push it in."

Jeff glanced at the origin of the guidance and saw Erica standing staidly behind him, folding her arms. Jeff obeyed the instructions and accomplished the desired task.

"Thanks." Jeff stepped back and waited for just another word out of her to which he would have adhered a much desired, prolonged conversation. But he was disappointed.

"It is an old door now." He took a chance himself.

"A lot of things are old and worn here, bent out of place with time and burden." Erica spoke stoically, didn't wait for an answer and went across the street.

Jeff saw her enter a ramshackle pick-up truck and give ignition an aggressive resuscitation. The engines refused at first, but gave in to her badgering attempts. She eyed Jeff sternly as he still maintained his immobility outside the bookstore, contemplating how to right the wrongs. The truck rumbled past him and down the road emitting a could of black smoke from the exhausts.

Jeff ambled down the sidewalk with a low face and spirit and searched for the vehicle Dave had left him to drive back. He clicked the remote and a car sounded a beep. He'd found his transport for the night.

Driving down the unfrequented streets of the town, he made a turn to another local road and espied a familiar truck pulled over and smoking profusely, out of order. Erica leaned under the hood trying to scrutinize the source of malfunction. Jeff stopped a bit ahead of her and came to her aid.

"It is old and worn. Time to change it." His comment stirred Erica.

"I don't like to abandon things that have helped me get by for years." Erica slammed the bonnet back onto the inoperative vehicle and collected her belongings from the passenger side and galloped down the road in solitude.

As she stormed past Jeff's car, he sounded the beep again which didn't inhibit her strides.

"Erica, wait!" he ran after her.

She halted.

"I'm sorry," he came close behind her.

She didn't turn for a look into his contrite eyes, but stayed.

"I know I don't deserve your forgiveness, but I --"

"You're absolutely right, you do not deserve even a speck of it." She finally turned to face him. "Forget about apologies, you don't even deserve to look into my eyes and say anything that would come close to justifying what you did. What do you think this is? A game? You're the star player, free to come and go whenever you want? That was the case twenty years ago, Jeff Saunderhurst, not anymore. You play that game with a bat and ball, not life and people. You expect us all to gather around you carrying smiles on our faces, look impressed hearing stories of your accomplishments in the big New York City and pretend that nothing ever happened? The successful guy comes back to his humble town, his humble beginnings? Well, you might have the rest swooning over your pretentious lifestyle, but not me. So, forget about apologizing and get on with your life and let others live their own. We're just as good as strangers right now and I intend to keep it like that, so there are no more heartaches." She stomped the gravel again.

"I'm not all the things you think I am?"

She turned yet again. "You still don't get it, do you? I don't care what you are or aren't. You being someone or being no one never mattered to me. I loved the man who...." she choked the next set of words in her throat, forbidding them to be given voice. She sniveled and concealed her emotions behind the veil of her auburn hair. "You just don't get up and leave like that." She finally uttered ingenuously the grievance that had lingered in her thoughts for so long.

"I was a failure then and I'm a failure now."

"Shut up, don't you dare say that in front of me. You might want to go ahead and disparage yourself all you want when you're alone, but I won't hear a word of it. You think this is your way out? You condemning yourself, I'll suddenly be empathetic towards you and it'll all be okay? That's quite an option, but it doesn't work here."

"Then tell me what does and I'll do precisely that. There are two of us here who agree with everything you've said so far. I was wrong and I'm guilty of it, but don't make such a man out of me you won't even share a ride with. I can live with being a stranger to you, but not your culprit."

Erica distanced herself with a couple more steps, but turned back a third time and lunged at him, kissing him hard, almost strangling him in an embrace.

She parted with an evident fulfillment seeping into her visage that curved her lips with satisfaction. "This is what you should do to make a woman shut up."

A pause followed.

"I will make notes for next time. Now, would you get in the car, please?" He opened the passenger side door for her.

She accepted the chivalry and boarded the vehicle. Jeff came around, got behind the wheel and began gliding down the road.

Erica bore a perpetual wisp of smile across her lips as they had driven more than a minute in silence.

"This town isn't changed in one aspect. Hardly any people out and about after dark." Jeff commented noticing the local inanition.

"Yeah, we like our supper early. I'm sure you're used to noises around the clock." She leaned in enthusiastically.

"It is the city that never sleeps. It's quite right, it doesn't. Even if the people have managed to doze off somehow, there are the sounds of the city itself that give you company late at night."

"Extremely late at night," she added.

"Yes."

"Well, here it's just the crickets and an occasional draft of breeze. Sometimes dogs too, you remember the deserted train tracks where we used to play? Some strays down there, they won't let anyone near the place, scaring them off even past midnight, especially after midnight. I'll tell you a funny thing; on calm nights the breeze here is so predictable you could time it with the clock. It blows every seven minutes in winters and during summers the interval is a bit longer, whiffs about every twelve minutes. The rest of the night it's just silence."

Jeff didn't respond promptly, but waited a good thousand feet to rush past. "I know. I've had a lot of practice at that too. Timing the sounds of silence."

They eyed each other, the gaze was prolonged to a point when Jeff was fearful of a collision if he didn't avert.

"Since when did you start timing the breeze?" Jeff asked grievously.

"Some years ago. Five to be exact." Erica rejoined sharply.

"I'm glad it wasn't more."

Erica shot another gaze at him, but this instance, she was partly rapturous and partly wistful. A droplet of pensive emotion slipped her eye and she hid it away somewhere between her palm and the folds of her sweater sleeve, feigning a cough.

"Let me guess, you have an apartment there, don't you?" she eased the mounting severity of the conversation.

"Did someone tell you that?"

"No," laughing, she shook her head. "Apartments are usually the preference for people who spend their childhood in a house. And it's the other way around for those who're stuck in an apartment. Opposites attract, you know."

"I'd rather call it a matter of convenience. But yeah, I bought one about two years ago. Nothing fancy, it's in a central area, but a modest building and a small place."

"What else is needed? A small home is a happy home."

"It must be quite unhappy right now, that I left it for the holidays."

"What else did you leave behind?" she asked skillfully.

"I never took anything else with me. I left everything right here." He responded prudently.

"I can say one thing for sure about you. You haven't changed in one aspect."

"You're wrong. I haven't changed in any."

Jeff pulled the vehicle to the side and parked it outside the garage. They had reached their destination, but both implored their fate to make the journey longer. They kept inside the car, never sharing a glimpse at each other but panting with questions and feelings and answers to both.

"Can I walk you home?" Jeff pleaded.

"It isn't a long walk."

"Sometimes the smallest of distances become the longest of journeys."

Erica appeared rapt and was urging to kiss him again only if he had given her another slightest of intimation, but he resisted. She waited for it, but failing to elicit out of him what she searched vehemently, she exited the car without a word. Jeff followed her out and led her to the Johnson residence. Their strides were slow and measured.

"The cold doesn't bother you much, does it?" Jeff disrupted the silence.

"Outside? No."

Her answer riveted him again.

"I'd like to take you for a walk sometime. I know it's usually summertime people prefer their evening strolls, but... the sooner the better."

Erica just nodded, ringing with an entirely different reflection. "I'm sorry, I shouldn't have done that."

"Done what?" Jeff imploded with surprise.

"The way I--"

Jeff barked before she could finish, "hold on a minute, did you just apologize? I wish I had a tape recorder or something to have everlasting evidence of this. Okay, let's hear it." Jeff rubbed his hands together in excitement.

"That's about all you're going to get." Erica flicked her hair.

"Short and meaningful works, but I wish your earlier tirade was similar."

"I wasn't apologizing for that, it was exactly what you deserved. I was apologizing for kissing you, I should have asked first. I just assumed that you were..." her voice trailed off.

Jeff's thrill vanished. "If people asked permission before exhibiting their emotions and feelings, there wouldn't be anything called truth in this world."

"That isn't what I meant. You um... you might have a girlfriend or a fiancee, and this is one emotion inappropriate in such a case."

Jeff brayed at the suggestion. "You didn't know any other way to ask whether I was still single or not?"

"No." Erica joined with some tittering of her own.

"Quite a thing to apologize for." Jeff controlled his laughter.

"But you're wrong about one thing." Erica turned solemn.

Jeff waited for the rest of the allegation to come along.

"This isn't the first time I've apologized to you. Though, the circumstances were quite different back then."

"That is one instance I prefer not to remember." Jeff cut in gravely.

"I wish I could say the same. It was one event that changed my life forever." Erica pressed her lips and took the remainder of the trip to her porch all alone.

Jeff was impaled at the sidewalk. He quickly retracted himself out of a recollection and went after her. "Erica!" he approached her on the steps and took her hand in his.

Erica radiated with delight in clear night moon.

Jeff kissed her gently and parted. "It is a trick used not only to make women shut up, but to make them talk as well." Jeff backtracked, "will I see you tomorrow?"

"Yes." She answered in a tearful glee, "will you?"

"I'm willing to see you every day of my life until the day I die." Jeff extended his arms sideways and promulgated.

"Don't make promises you can't keep."

"I'm willing to keep this one. Good night." Jeff ran back to his place while Erica waved in exhilaration and went inside her home with a sense of joy in her formerly aching heart.

# Chapter Twenty-Two

A perfect bank shot deposited an object ball into the called pocket. Jeff curved his brows impressed by the prowess. Erica stood up lauding her own dexterity as she chalked the cue tip.

"That's not a bad pocket considering..." the remark was left incomplete.

"Considering?" Erica erupted with playful indignation, "I'm not even going to try to finish it for you. I never expected something so disrespect--"

"Considering that you've been out of touch for some time." Jeff cut right back in. "That's all I was saying before you made a villain out of me."

"Is that so?" Erica grinned moving around the table. "Let's make things a little more competitive here. I call the ball, I call the pocket and I call the shot. Twenty bucks. How about it?" she escalated the stakes.

"You've made my life miserable already, wasn't it enough now that you want to bankrupt me as well?"

"When did I have that pleasure?"

"I can't go anywhere in our town without people asking me how it ends."

"Oh, that," she admitted.

"Yes, that! You and I both know why you brought me all the way here to play a silly game of pool. Back home we wouldn't have survived a minute in a place full of people."

"You gave them a story without an end, what else did you expect?" Erica teased.

"I gave them the story? I heard tales of some shrewd people and how they escape blame and responsibility for their evil actions. I witness one tonight."

"Well, you're the one who's tardy, not me. If they want an end, give it to them."

"Isn't that the reason why you did it, to make me write again?" Jeff creased his forehead.

"Hey, I didn't do any of this, remember?" She artfully parried.

"There's no winning an argument when you're at the other end. I simply give up." Jeff raised his arms aloft in surrender. "Now pack your bags, it's past ten. Ride home is another thirty minutes."

"Left corner pocket, red, bank shot." She stood with a wry smirk. "What if I said there was another surprise waiting for you when we get back?"

Jeff, taking it to be the last one, examined the bet skimming around the table. "I think it is possible." He scrunched and viewed the cue ball beyond the cushion intently, transfixed as his articulation became slow and limited.

"Is it?" Erica commented with fake derision.

"What surprise?" Jeff tipped forward making preliminary estimates for the shot warily.

"If I told you it wouldn't be one." She joined the meticulous consideration and propped herself against the edge of the table.

"Is that the reason we're here?"

"Partly."

"Is this table taken?" A man had approached and disrupted their game.

Jeff and Erica erected themselves and found a man leaning in close against her denying her the space of stranger's comfort.

She stepped back. "I guess so."

The man parted his mouth in a mocking simper and called in two of his friends to the table. All three were unkempt and shabby, and ogled Erica from head to toe obscenely.

She felt uncomfortable in her red, knee-length sweater-dress that outlined her figure exceptionally. She switched sides and went to the other end of the table.

"Let's give them balls a jiggle," one of the three croaked.

The other two flouted at the reprehensible remark and commenced their game.

Jeff glared at them. Erica approached and rested her hand on his shoulders signaling indifference toward them.

"So, you up for it?" She abated the situation with her genial voice.

"I bet you twenty he won't shoot right." The man interrupted again.

"Well, we're not playing the game with you, are we?" Erica retorted.

"Nah, I'm just sayin'." He stepped away, turning back to his company, giggling. "I like 'em vocal." The men snickered.

"Come'on Jeff. Let's get back to the game." Erica precluded hostility.

One of them headed for the cue rack and got himself a new stick. He walked past Erica's table rubbing against her back as she leaned forward trying to eschew any physicality. She flipped instantly reeking of repugnance and pushed him away.

"Stay away from me, you asshole," she was wrathful.

Jeff came around the table, but before that confrontation could eventuate in a fist-fight, she intervened again.

"Let's go, let's go. We don't need to stay here." She held Jeff back.

"Hey, it's a tight space back here. She need to lean forward a little for me to fit in there, no harm done." The man high-fived his cohorts as they abetted him in his odious demeanor.

Erica tossed her cue on the table and directed Jeff away from the loathsome group of goons.

"Feisty bitch," the men laughed detestably and grew louder as they walked out. "Give us that ass for one night, that's all we're askin'," vile remarks followed.

Erica and Jeff stormed out of the tavern and towards her pick-up truck which was quite workable some years ago. Jeff took the wheel and they went off sailing into the night.

The drive was fast and silent at both ends as neither spoke of or palliated the repulsive act. Erica gazed out of the window at the passing trees that framed the road while Jeff glowered at the dark, unfrequented path ahead that led back to their town.

"We shouldn't have come here. It was my fault. I'm sorry." Erica trembled with anger and disgust as she uttered the apology.

"Don't apologize for something that's not your fault." Jeff's sounded a categorical rebuttal.

"It is, I asked you to come along--"

Just before she could finish, some strident noises emanated from a distance, muffled at first but gradually gaining in volume. Jeff and Erica stirred in their seats and examined the rear-view mirrors.

The cacophony originated from another pick-up truck that was gaining ground behind them and two pairs of arms flailed, clasping beer bottles, extending outward from the windows and a familiar face emerged from the passenger side that screamed imprecations. The group from the tavern was chasing after them.

"It's them!" Erica was alarmed.

Jeff pressed the acceleration and the pedal was thrust all the way, but the old truck had endured its share of sprints. It had lost its practice now after many years of senility.

"This goddamn truck won't go any faster." Jeff walloped the steering wheel in helplessness.

The rowdies approached and sped past them hurtling empty beer bottles that detonated into fragments as they struck the hood and the windshield of Erica's truck. A strand of expletives was slung along.

Erica rolled up the window and cowered apprehensively. Jeff was shaken to the core. He quickly switched on the wipers for a clearer view of the road ahead. Just as the windshield cleared, Jeff slammed on the brakes and the tires squealed to a stop.

Their way was barricaded by a truck and three ruffians wielding a metal rod and a baseball bat stood unyielding before the obstruction.

All three moved forward brandishing their weapons and one of them swung a bat at the truck, denting the metal in the front.

"Get the fuck out of there. You, what the hell did you call me? Asshole? Huh? I knew you wanted it, babe. You just told me where!" He lunged at the passenger side door and ripped it open, pulling Erica out of the truck.

She screamed and thrashed about, but he wrapped his arms around her not giving her an inch to squirm.

Jeff jumped out of the driver's side. "Let her go!"

"Or what, you dumb fuck?" The second man whipped right across Jeff's abdomen with his metal rod.

Jeff instantly collapsed to the ground emitting a painful groan. Erica struggled, horrified at the fatal blow. She kneed her assailant between the legs and just as he released his arms to tend the hurting groin, she bolted to Jeff's aid. She crouched by his side as he wiggled in pain.

"Jeff, are you all right? Jeff?" Her voice quivered dreadfully, she lifted his shirt and discovered a crimson bruise about a foot long right across his stomach.

The two drunken men laughed at all of this.

"Get her in those trees," their chieftain commanded, recovered from a low blow.

The two deferentially trammeled Erica before she could react to escape.

They both pounced on her and grabbed her by the legs and arms, carrying her into the trees as she cried and writhed to be freed. It was futile and her screams became distant.

The third man kicked Jeff violently before going after his friends into the woods.

They found a glade with a perfect cover of trees around and threw Erica on the ground. She landed with a thud hurting her back.

"Hold her down." The man ordered unbuckling his belt.

Erica, in her state of trauma, began to whimper. "Please... let me go, please. Jeff! Jeff!" she shouted at the pinnacle of her breath.

The leader leaned into her and slipped her dress above her thighs. Erica thrashed her legs, the other man held her down firmly.

Suddenly he was shoved away. Jeff had come to her rescue.

"I'm going to kill this piece of shit. You, don't you let her go." The chief ordered again.

The man who was pushed aside gained his ground and joined his leader in smashing their fists into Jeff's weakened body that couldn't defend itself anymore and clobbered him to the ground yet again. Jeff rolled in the dirt in excruciating pain.

"Stay there, you shit." They returned to their act of crime as Erica wailed and resisted.

"Jeff… Jeff, help me. Jeff…" Erica yelled for his aid.

Jeff, rallied by her cries, rose up again but suddenly floundered away, leaving the woods and back to the pick-up truck.

He had escaped his doom, leaving Erica all alone to face hers.

"Jeff... no, come back... come back." Erica screamed and begged for him to return, but he was too far gone to hear her plea. She winced, evidently traumatized with eyes and mouth agape.

The men surrounded her once again and inched closer like a beast preparing to feast on its prey and they held her by the thighs parting her legs.

She kicked the approaching offenders and endeavored to wring herself free from cumbersome restraints that were upon her, but failing at every attempt.

One of them positioned himself between her legs, while she resisted, and cuffed her couple of times across the face which attenuated her shrill shrieks and flailing limbs considerably.

"You get the fuck off of her, you filthy cowards."

The three miscreants turned to the source of the new threat and saw two hulking jacketed bikers frowning back at them.

"Get out of here before we break your faces in," the second said.

The prodigious adversaries were demonstrably too immense for them to counter. The three scrambled for their lives and vanished into the woods.

Jeff rushed to Erica's aid and helped her to her feet. She adjusted her dress as tears streamed down her face. She rubbed her aching arms and tended her abraded wrists and inner thighs.

"Thank you." Jeff expressed his gratitude to the two saviors.

"You've got to man up, you hear me?" One of the large men spoke. They both left the clearing and headed back to the road.

"Are you all right?" Jeff denoted his concern.

"I'm all right. Don't touch me." Erica spurned him.

Jeff distanced himself a couple of steps.

Erica brushed the filth of the ground from her dress and trudged away from him.

"Erica?" Jeff called in utter disbelief.

She refused to answer and plodded further. Jeff, shielding his torso with his arm, darted after and blockaded her path.

"Let me go, Jeff," Erica said sternly.

"What's wrong?" Jeff requested.

"What's wrong? In case you didn't notice, I was almost raped by three filthy thugs, that's what's wrong." She flicked her arms away that Jeff attempted to grasp.

"They're gone now."

"I know they are, and so were you." She was infuriated as she spun and scowled at him.

"I just went to get some help." Jeff advocated his cause.

"Help? You were my help, Jeff. I was counting on you to save me, and you needed others to help you protect me? I trusted you so much, all my life I did. But tonight you proved me wrong. You being by my side, I used to feel the safest of them all, but I'm suddenly afraid to trust you anymore. The moment you left me, I felt like I've lost my life, like there was no air left for me to breathe. All my hope disappeared in those moments that I faced alone. Do you know how that feels?"

"I'm sorry, Erica, I couldn't think of anything else."

"Stay away from me," she screamed. "Stay away. You know what, I confronted everyone who spoke badly about you since we were children, I always did. And tonight, for the first time in my life, I needed you and you ran away? What if they killed me back here, what if you never found anyone to help you? What if you ran just a little late and they had done what they wanted to? If any one of them so much as touched me, I would have killed myself. I wasn't going to live with that disgrace. And if you really were the man I believed you to be, you would have stayed and stopped them."

"I was really hurt, Erica. They were three, I couldn't--"

"Then you should have died. At least I would know there was someone who loved me enough to die for me. Who could take any harm to save my life. I just realized I was wrong. Thanks for giving me that opportunity to know."

They had reached the truck and a light drizzle had commenced. Erica accosted him once again.

"You just go around blaming others for the miseries of your life, don't you? Why do you do it? To gain sympathy, so all could commiserate with you and say what a pitiable man you are? But you know what? You deserve it. It is no one's fault but yours that you are so inept at everything. Now that I'm here and I see the truth in front of me and I'm not afraid to say it to your face. Your incompetence and your fear are the reason why you're still here in this town. You're not man enough to take a stand for yourself, I was a fool to expect you to take a stand for me. You've almost ruined all lives around you, but you're not going to ruin mine. Out of all the weaknesses I knew you had and I embraced them, I never figured you for a coward. But that's exactly what you are."

Now completely drenched, Erica entered the vehicle and started the engines. The vehicle dashed forward burying Jeff in a dreary smoke of suffering on a lonesome road.

She noted his flaws one by one right before him and like everyone else who'd ever been a part of his life, she abandoned him as well.

Martin lounged on a couch inside the living room drinking from a cup of nightcap while Lena stood next to a window eagerly awaiting Jeff's arrival. She held onto a ticket at which she had glanced the fortieth time in the last hour.

"He'll be home soon enough. Your standing there isn't going to bring him any sooner." Martin abated her excitement.

"I can't wait to tell him." Lena lit with joy as she returned to the couch.

"None of us can. Sit down, drink your coffee." He passed her the cup.

After a moment of silence, the door swung open and Jeff barged inside. Lena and Martin shared a gleeful gaze and endeavored to stand and greet him with the news. But Jeff headed for the stairs stomping the creaking wood floor and darted up the steps. He was dripping wet.

Their countenance altered a bit toward incertitude.

"He probably wants to change before he gets the carpet all wet." Lena proposed a possibility.

Martin nodded incredulously.

"I'll go and check up on him." She went up the stairs searching for an answer.

Lena stood outside Jeff's bedroom and heard some hostile strides and tapping of furniture caused by rigorous opening and shutting of them. She parted the door ajar and saw Jeff collecting his belongings into a luggage. Lena entered to intervene.

"Jeff, what is going on?" she questioned trepidatiously. "Jeff? Why are you doing this?"

"I don't want to talk, ma. Please, no more talks." Jeff answered tempestuously.

"Okay, we won't talk, but I need to know what you're doing with your clothes and your things." Her trembling voice surfaced her deepest fears.

"I'm leaving, that's what I'm doing. I'm sick and tired of staying in these walls like an inmate. I cannot take it anymore."

"You can't leave us like this," Lena pleaded.

"Yes, I can. I know all of you think I'm a coward, I can't deal with life on my own, I can't handle things. Ma, you're going to be surprised with what you see now. I begged you, but no one ever listened. Well, this is how it ends."

Martin had arrived by now and stood at the doorway.

Jeff eyed him furiously. "I've been a fool all this time to believe the lies you've told me, but not anymore. You're my father, right? I really doubt that at times!"

"Jeff!" Lena objected.

"No ma, let me speak just this once. For all these years you've tried to convince me that you did all this to protect me, to save me from the people out there? But I have lifted off the false veil of love and generosity that you used to hide your true intentions. I'll tell you why because now I know. You did that so I could be your s lave for the rest of my life, so there'd be no one who would trust me and want to be with me. Have I pleased you enough, dad? Are twenty-seven years enough for your hunger to destroy a life, your son's life? Wasn't that a gratifying experience to watch me crumble day by day? Are you happy or you need more? That's what you ultimately want, don't you? A normal life, I wanted just a little part of it, I deserved it. But you chose me to suffer. How'd you decide that? Did you play a game and my name appeared in the magic ball? This is the person we want to torture. Well, congratulations dad, you did and I suffered. So, thanks for everything you've done for me. And most of all, thanks for making a coward out of me. I'm leaving." Jeff snapped away at his luggage and stormed out the door slamming it behind.

"Oh Martin, stop him. He's leaving." Lena whimpered.

"It's no use anymore. It is over." Martin's soul was rattled and aghast.

Jeff had loaded the back of the car with his luggage and entered the driver's end swiftly in the downpour.

Lena had come out of the house trailing him into the open. She was instantly soaked in rain.

"Jeff... come back inside." She added a bit of severity in her voice, but it was no more than a supplication.

"Go back, ma. Go back." Jeff raced the acceleration and sped down the road.

Lena wiped her tears and headed for the neighboring house and struck their door helplessly.

Erica answered and marveled at her deplorable condition. "Lena, what is the matter?"

"Erica, Jeff had just left us. He took his clothes and he went that way. Do you know what happened?" Lena appealed.

Erica was unnerved and thrown into myriad thoughts of culpability.

Lena shook her out of it. "Erica? Do you? Oh, I've lost my son today, I've lost him."

"You stay here, I will bring him back." Erica snatched at her topcoat and headed off to her pick-up, driving off after Jeff into the dark.

Erica had pursued two specks of red tail lights in heavy pelting rain for fifteen minutes until it came to a stop in a parking lot of a local bus station. She drove up to the car and found Jeff unloading his luggage from the trunk. She got out and blocked his way.

"Tell them the car is here. I'm leaving the keys inside." Jeff dismissed her presence for its true cause.

"They are not concerned about the car."

"There's nothing else that's theirs anymore." Jeff circumvented.

"Jeff, why are you doing this?" Erica demanded.

"Out of all the people, you should know."

"This doesn't prove anything. You can't leave your family like this."

"That's enough," he screamed. "I don't need anyone to tell me what I can and can't do. Not you or anyone else. You don't exist for me. I will forget you like a bad memory. And as far as my family is concerned, they never needed me. Whether I'm there or not, it doesn't make much of a difference."

"You're wrong. You make the biggest of difference."

"It's over." Jeff cantered towards the station.

Erica followed, "I'm sorry. I said things I shouldn't have. If you must punish someone, punish me for my words, not them. People say things they don't mean when they are upset."

"Yes, they do. To show their anger or disappointment. I don't want to disappoint anyone anymore, Erica. Goodbye." Jeff strode into the station entrance.

Erica entreated him to return. "I'm sorry, Jeff. I apologize. Don't leave us." She began to yell as he grew distant. "I'm sorry. Please..." Erica wept, but her tears diminished in the raindrops.

Jeff had left the town and his people behind.

# Chapter Twenty-Three

"Please mom, I'll be back before you know it." Nancy tried reasoning with Linda who had surpassed the eleventh stage of her tolerance.

"How is this event so imperative that you must leave all your family in the middle of a vacation and attend so passionately?" Linda cried dismissively.

"It's my friend's place. Everybody is going to be there. I don't want to miss out on it."

Jeff had entered the hallway into another vociferous ruckus, only this time the components of this altercation were just two.

He stepped into the living eyeing the arguing women and claimed a cup of coffee Maggie had poured for herself and sipped a couple from. She surrendered it without a frown.

"What's going on?" Jeff whispered.

"She wants to go to a friend's place. Mama won't let her." Maggie explained and took the cup back from him sipping the remains.

"Everybody is not going to be there. You know it and I know that too. It isn't just you who's out on a vacation, many families do that." Linda expostulated.

"Vacation, vacation, I'm tired of hearing that word over and over again. An old broken-down house where I don't even have a proper bed to sleep in and nothing but snow and cold in sight, that's not a vacation, mom. So, stop calling it that." Nancy screamed insensibly.

Jeff left the room and entered the kitchen finding Lena at the stove manning a couple of pans.

"They're still arguing?" she queried.

Jeff nodded and grabbed a toast for himself.

"They've been going at it for the past thirty minutes. I'd rather have Linda give her permission to go if she doesn't want to stay." Lena ceded in subtle words.

"No, she shouldn't. If everyone in a family was given permission to leave like that, a home would be nothing but a lodge with a complimentary chef who asks nothing but their time and love in return." He landed a kiss on her cheek.

Lena glimpsed him with a tender smile. "I'm glad you're back."

"So am I. I needed to tell you something similar but--"

The debate moved into the kitchen now as Linda had entered and Nancy was in hot pursuit.

"I didn't expect that to come from you, Nancy. I thought I raised you better." Linda reprimanded the words she's heard.

"That doesn't mean I'm not supposed to have a life. I have friends and I intend to keep them." Nancy was adamant still.

"You did not come here for the house or its walls or the weather outside. We're here to see our family. People. If you don't know how to differentiate people from things, then I have failed as a mother."

"Linda, please. This doesn't have to be needless." Lena allayed the confrontation.

"No mother, she had tested my patience today."

"What is it, Nancy?" Jeff interposed.

"All I'm asking is to go there for a couple of hours and come back," Nancy pleaded.

"And who's going to drive you? I'm definitely not. Your father isn't going to either." Linda proposed another plight.

Nancy was wordless in response. She articulated at length, "I hate you for this. You can't even do that for me, can you? You know I don't have a license yet and you're taking advantage of that?"

Linda's eyes were wide after hearing the expression from her daughter. Lena was equally displeased. Nancy averted from six pairs of disappointed eyes and darted in frustration out the kitchen and up the stairs. Silence prevailed for a long instance until Maggie entered.

"She'll be all right, don't worry Linda. We all went through this." Maggie reassured her sister.

"I think we did, but never so eloquently expressive of our feelings in front of parents." Linda's murmuring voice had a tinge of emotion and dismay.

Jeff was pensive at the remark, but also resolute in an unknown determination.

"Jeff, you were saying something?" Lena directed all attention toward him.

He spoke with careful consideration, "I need to go to New York."

"What!?" the women yelled in unison.

"So it's not just a fifteen year old who's tired of a family gathering, huh?" Linda remarked.

"No, I'm coming back. It is something extremely important that I need to do there. I'll be back in a day. If it weren't such a long drive, I would be back in a couple of hours." Jeff tried to justify.

"You're leaving again?" Lena was emotionally moved as she questioned. "Please Jeff, I'm begging you this time."

"No ma, I'm not leaving. I'm not running away. It's just some stuff, some work that needs to be done. It's vital that I do it right now. I'll be back before you guys miss me."

"Why do you even have to go then?" Maggie joined in.

"Don't make it look like I'm not coming back. All right, I'll make a promise. I'll be here by midnight, if you let me leave right now."

"You promise?" Lena gazed into his eyes searching for any evasiveness.

"I give you my word. I'll need a car, though. Where are the men?"

"Sweet dreaming, I guess," Maggie joked.

"Here, you can have mine." Linda tossed him the keys. "It's best if the car is absent for today. I fear she might try to sneak away. In fact, keep the keys with you tomorrow as well and hide the car somewhere. Take her mind off of it."

"Thanks, I'll get my things." Jeff left the kitchen.

Jeff entered the Mercedes keeping a pack of things on the rear seat and turning the ignition. But before he could roll the wheels to embark on the trip, the passenger side door opened and Erica boarded the vehicle adjusting the seat to her liking, along with the heat vents and finally buckling for safety, all performed in such obvious certainty as if she was a part of this excursion since its inception.

Jeff gazed at her questionably. "If I am permitted to ask, what are you trying to do?"

"Taking a morning walk! Don't you love fresh heat on your face this early? I adore it, especially when I'm out for a stroll and my legs don't move an inch." She answered sardonically.

There was silence from his end, still anticipating a straight answer.

"People usually get into cars so they can drive to their destination." She responded.

"Which I will."

"I know. I'm just going with you. In case you get tired of driving." She was insistent.

"Do you know where I'm going?"

"I don't need to," she returned.

Their eyes met.

"I'm going to the city for some important work. You don't need to be bothered--"

"I won't be bothered at all, neither would you. Look mister, no matter how much you try to dissuade or talk me out of this, I'm not leaving this car until it finds its way into New York. If you wish to abandon me there, you may, which I highly doubt. I will not let you go alone. Five years ago I gave your mother my word that I couldn't keep, but now I'll make sure you stay here as long as she likes. I failed to bring you back then, but this time, I intend to fulfill my promise to her. So, it is better that you put the vehicle in gear and start the trip, or we're going to be late."

"You never used to speak that much. All of a sudden you're a chatterbox."

"I was always a chatterbox," she confirmed.

"Yeah, you're right," Jeff agreed.

"Don't take that 'leaving me in New York' thing seriously. I just went with the flow." She said innocently.

"No. Yeah, I wasn't thinking about it." Jeff pushed the accelerator and the car flew down the street.

After an exhausting drive lasting about five hours, Jeff navigated the streets of downtown and a familiar milieu once again. He entered the cellar parking of a seventy-floor commercial building and went up on the fortieth, while Erica stayed in the car napping.

Jeff stepped into a small reception area and was greeted heartily by a woman who sat behind the desk.

"Anne."

"You handsome devil, what are you doing back in the city?"

Anne was a woman in her late fifties. The grace of age and experience glimmered right across her face, and the elegance of her wardrobe rendered her an ineffable resplendence. Her blonde hair jumped upon her shoulders as she walked to give Jeff a hug revealing a gray pantsuit that fitted her yet alluring figure perfectly.

"All right, I admit we've procrastinated enough and it's about time we finalize the particulars of our date." They parted. "Tell me the day and the venue, and pick me up at seven."

"Oh, you stingy little penny pincher. I was hoping for a limousine to roll up my neighborhood, so I could flaunt it in front of my envious friends and make them jealous."

"You have your hopes set on a poor man. I couldn't afford it even if I tried."

"Oh please, honey. You could afford a ride to the moon if you wanted. Don't you go around hiding your bank figures from me," Anne teased.

"Let me work a little more then, I want to impress you with seven figure statements. How about twenty more years in and out of this office?"

"So, now I realize it's actually not our date that brings you back. Something much more important that you drove all the way here?"

"You say the word right now and I won't see Angela at all, but take you out." He said ingenuously.

"I'm working, remember? Besides, if you really wanted to take me out, you could've come tomorrow. The last day of work, finally getting two weeks off." She rejoined dryly.

"Only if I knew, but here's what I'm going to do. I'll put up a blanket right outside that elevator and wait for tomorrow night."

"No need to spoil your holidays, we'll have plenty of time for that in the coming millennium."

"Yeah, I hope so." He spoke thickly with a vanishing smile.

"Hey, what happened to you all of a sudden? I have a surprise for you. You're the last appointment she has today, and boy is she in a good mood. Go right in, she's waiting."

"Thank you, Anne." Jeff took her hand and kissed it.

She tilted her head and smiled back. Jeff went inside the office.

He entered, after a knock, into the office that reeked of nothing but affluence. Teak furniture all over the floor, plush carpeting, a view of the city from all glass right-side wall, a separate conference area with white executive chairs and table, paneled walls and a large desk in the center that accommodated a computer and a spectacled woman who worked the keyboard with some evident difficulty.

"I hate these new systems. All of the things are going digital they say. Can't do without them. Heck, I can't even remember half of the things these technicians have been teaching me. I am getting old now." Angela removed her glasses, rubbed her nose-bridge and welcomed Jeff inside with a handshake.

She was about forty-five, astute, subtle in her appearance but success had adorned her with an indescribable charm.

"Have a seat, Jeff. And allow me to get to the point right away because I couldn't wait to ask you this question since the time we spoke on the phone. Do you realize what you're asking me to do?" Her brows arched.

"Okay, let me make it clearer."

"Here we go again." She folded her arms and waited.

"Think of one situation, any of your choosing, that you want to get rid of forever. Right? Now, think about that compulsion that has kept you from getting rid of it so far. Take courtesy for example. All of a sudden, if you were given that one chance to break free the chains, how far would you go to kick it down the drain once and for all?"

"This sounds like my marriage. But why is it so important, whatever you're trying to do?"

"It's a recompense for something terrible."

"You doing something terrible is hard to believe. But do you know how much I would have to plead for him to agree to something like this?"

"If I were close enough to him, I would take your place."

"But why, Jeff? You know how much you could lose? I mean he'll take a lot of money to do this appearance. And on top of that the bills, the venue."

"And the advertisement. I will cover that with my savings."

Angela seemed to give up. "All right, it's your money you may destroy it the way you please. I will get him there."

"Thank you so much, Angela. This means the world to me."

"But remember, Drake's a pontificating, fastidious, pretentious smart ass who likes his wine cellars and shoe shines on command. And there's a reason I don't say request. He wants his lodging replete with all amenities possible. It's a small town you say, making available the provisions he needs would be most imperative. I don't want to discomfort or aggrieve a lucrative client for another one. He'll arrive a day earlier and leave a day later. He'll also need an assistant. You'll pay for everything?"

"I will take care of it." Jeff assured her.

"Get the place ready, I'll get him there. Now get out."

"Thank you, Angela. You don't know what you've done for me by saying yes."

"Leave before I shed tears," she answered sternly.

Jeff laughed and waved a goodbye exiting the office.

"You crazy genius." Angela shook her head in disbelief and got back to the onerous set of a machine before her.

Jeff returned to the Mercedes and found Erica stirring by the sounds of his ingress into the vehicle.

"Mornin' sunshine." Jeff tapped her forehead gently.

Erica wiped below her the creases of her mouth. "What time is it?"

"Almost four."

"That was a long nap." She took a mouthful of water. "It's almost nighttime."

"Yeah. One down, one more to go. Ready?" Jeff drove out of the underground parking.

Jeff sat inside another one of those costly, opulent attorney offices on a top floor of a building being attended by a young, urbane, individual who was dressed to impress and carried a blend of amiability and acumen simultaneously across his visage.

"Just before I proceed with the requested revisions, Mr. Saunderhurst, you are certain you wish to make the changes that you have proposed?" The man questioned gravely reviewing the paperwork before him on the desk.

"I'm certain, Mr. Bradburry," Jeff nodded in approval.

"Being your counselor for the past three years it is my obligation to convince you to reconsider and also that you are fully aware of the consequences if these changes are brought in effect. I hope you understand, sir, you are essentially writing off your entire life to others. You are not under any external pressure or compulsion of any sort, are you?"

"I really appreciate you taking that time to discuss this with me and for your concern as well, I really do. But there will be no consequences. That I'm sure."

"These are your investments, you may do as you please with them. I have completed my responsibility."

"I appreciate it a lot."

"When would you require all these documents?" Bradbury removed his glasses and shifted back on his tufted chair.

"I'm not trying to inconvenience you, but before Christmas." Jeff appealed.

"Day after tomorrow is the last day of our office? I can have these completed by then. It will be no inconvenience at all, Mr. Saunderhurst. I'll even have them delivered to you express."

"I couldn't be any more grateful."

"You need not be. Thank you for your business."

"Thank you, and I would like to take care of any pending fees that are due."

"Don't worry, Mr. Saunderhurst. We'll send you an invoice. You may satisfy it when you return." Bradbury smiled thinly.

"No, Mr. Bradbury. I'd rather take care of it now," Jeff insisted.

The counselor deferred to his persuasion. "Very well, you may check with the office on your way out." He arose and shook hands firmly with Jeff.

Jeff returned to his car which was parked on the street and found Erica exploring the gray facades and summits of surrounding skyscrapers with eyes that were nothing but reverential.

"Hey, it's cold outside." Jeff noted the overcast skies and fading daylight.

"This is beautiful!" Erica exclaimed in awe.

"You never came to New York City?"

"Not once. Being so close, I never came here."

Jeff lit with a thought of surprise for her. "Get in the car, I want to take you somewhere."

Jeff brought her across the bridge into Queens and took her to Long Island City Pier.

When Erica sighted the tremendous view of Manhattan across the river, she paced down the pier and stood at the brink against the rails, thrilled at the picturesque vista. Jeff joined her side and relished the splendor of the bliss he found in her eyes.

"Wow. This is so beautiful. Look at the lights. The Christmas trees, see over there? There's another one." She noted excitedly the illumined city skyline in twilight, and flashing lights and ornaments of Christmas decorations that were visible through some windows.

"I knew you'd like it." Jeff went to one of the benches and perched.

"I love it." Erica turned around toward him with glinting delight, but it dwindled. "I'm sorry I came here."

"Sorry?" Jeff asked nervously.

"I should have asked for permission before I just jumped into the car with you. You might have come to..." she refrained from ending that sentence.

"Come for what?" Jeff was anxious.

"To see someone, to bring someone home with you. Because of me, you might not have met her." Erica uttered innocently.

"Her? Who's her?"

"I don't know, you tell me."

"There is no her, Erica. If I had to bring someone home, I would've brought her the first day I came."

"Are you telling the truth?"

"I don't know, look into my eyes and you tell me?" Jeff came to her and gazed without blinking.

"The world is such a beautiful place." Erica submerged herself into the depths of his eyes and found him honest.

"It's that way." Jeff pointed to the view of the city behind her.

"Uh-uh, it's all here. All that *I* need." She clung to him and buried her face into the folds of his jacket feeling his heart and the affection it gushed with each pulsation.

He enveloped her with all the warmth he could afford.

# Chapter Twenty-Four

It was past midnight when Jeff pulled into the driveway, parked the Mercedes and walked Erica to her porch.

"I almost forgot, what about your father? He must be famished by now." Jeff was extremely solicitous.

"No, I asked Maggie to check up on him every hour or so." She smiled, his concern subsided. "I see she did her job well. The lights are off. He never turns off the lights until he's put to bed. Besides, your mother is a better cook than me. He would have enjoyed that change of flavor."

"He must have missed you, at least."

"It doesn't really matter to him now. Maggie or Erica. He hardly recognizes people. I wonder how he remembered you?" she shrugged.

"Probably an old, unforgettable memory that caused too much pain to someone he loves the most."

Erica stepped up to him and pecked on his lips. "Good night. You're tired, go to sleep right away. Don't stay up."

Jeff nodded deferentially and headed back to his place. Erica watched him leave, then stepped into the dark and lonely interior of the house.

After about an hour of restlessness on the bed, Jeff decided to inhale some cold, exterior air and came out on the porch. He espied a parked BMW right on the street which was lit internally. He squinted for a better view of the people inside and discovered, to his disbelief, Nancy kissing a boy her own age.

The couple made-out as the boy leaned into her sneaking his hand under her shirt and reaching up to her breasts. Nancy allowed it for a moment, but just as it became a tad uncomfortable, she shoved him back into his driver's seat.

"What're you doing?" Nancy protested.

"Hey babe, it's just a little fun stuff, nothing to worry about." The boy assured her.

"Hey, I'm not a retard. Don't treat me like one."

"You want me to leave then?" the boy bluffed.

"No, I want... I don't know."

"Come here, babe." The boy stretched out again and kissed her unbuttoning her denims.

She pushed him back again. "Not this, Randy. Are you serious about what you said?"

"What?"

"That you love me?"

"You know it, babe. Do you think I'd be here if I didn't? I love you, love you like my breath. I couldn't survive without you. Let's run away, let's elope. We'll go somewhere no one would know us, and we'll have our own place and have children together."

"Okay, let's not get too far with our futures now." Nancy rolled her eyes.

"How long are you going to stay here? I can't live without you."

"I hate it here. But these guys aren't planning on coming back until next year."

"Next year?" Randy sounded perturbed.

"I mean early January, on the fourth. I can't wait to get back."

"Me neither, babe. Let's go tonight. They won't know where you went. We'll go up in the mountain and start a new life. Make a kid ourselves."

"Why do you always talk about having children?" she objected in all uneasiness.

"Because I want you to be the mother of my child. I want a kid with you."

"You don't want a kid, Randy. We're too young. I don't want to talk about this anymore."

"Okay, we won't. Can I get a kiss now?"

Nancy nodded and they kissed again.

"Let's do it tonight. You and me."

"No, not in a car. Not like this."

"Come'on." Randy attempted to remove her shirt.

She elbowed him away and stepped out of the car slamming the door behind.

"Bitch," Randy was furious but went after her. "Hey, I'm sorry. Aren't you going to come tomorrow to my house?"

"No, I can't make it."

"I needed you to come so bad."

"I wanted to, but I just can't... I have no one to drive me."

"I'll drive you."

"No, my mom can't know you were here. She'll be ecstatic if she does."

"You sure you're not coming, right?"

"I will see you when I return."

"Do you love me? Give me a kiss."

Nancy obeyed and stayed in a liplock for a minute until pushing him away and walking back toward the house.

"Call me."

Randy waved to her and scurried to his car driving away.

Nancy came back inside and closed the door with extreme caution not to produce any sound to awaken the house.

As she passed the living room surreptitiously, a lamp faintly lit up. She stopped and flipped, horrified.

"Do you ever sleep?"

Jeff stood in the corner watching her tiptoeing down the hallway.

"Who was that, Nancy?" Jeff questioned grimly.

"A friend."

"It's past midnight, do you know that?"

"I do have a watch, thank you."

"What kind of behavior is this? If your parents' anxieties do not trouble you, at least have some concern for your safety."

"I haven't seen him carry a colter. When I do I'll let you know."

"I saw what happened in the car and outside. You're openly kissing each other, you're only fifteen."

"Sixteen in two months. You were making out with that neighbor of yours. I didn't say anything." Nancy crossed the line triggering wrath in Jeff's eyes.

Jeff took a moment to rejoin. "Only if you knew what you were talking about, you would have some sense to curb your impertinence."

"You're not my father, Jeff. So, stop trying to act like him."

Nancy darted up the stairs leaving Jeff all alone in the hallway.

The next morning was a quieter one as most of the family was gathered around the dining for breakfast, except for one carping voice that sounded peevishly objecting to the food served on the table.

"I don't see a single thing here that isn't saturated in oil or butter. Calories, fats and unhealthy written all over these bowls," Nancy said fractiously. "I can't believe you can put that in your belly, dad."

"Someone woke up in a good mood today," Linda grumbled leaning into Maggie, avoiding eye contact with Nancy.

"It's a nice break from grazing grass. Now stop caviling, Nancy, and eat something," James retorted.

"Finally someone from the city who doesn't defend cattle food for humans," Edward commented dryly.

"Hey, I'm from Texas. Though, I've lived in almost every northern state in the past forty years, I still like my grits and chicken fried steak." James admitted with a shrug and a laugh.

"There's my man, right there." Edward fist-bumped him to which James had no idea how to respond.

"I can't believe I'm hearing this. You've just rattled my creed by saying that, dad." Nancy was incessant in her trivial dissent.

"No, the food we eat at home is healthy without a doubt. But the food we eat with family, no matter how deleterious, it satiates you pretty well."

Linda shot James a look of affection when he completed, he nodded back. The whole table was replete with harmony to what he had said.

Jeff emerged from the hallway and patted James' back in adulation. "A true family man we have here."

"Well, I can't eat any of this." Nancy rolled her eyes.

"Nancy, I'm sorry we ran out of cereal. Let me fetch a box right now. I just couldn't remember yesterday when I went for groceries." Lena grew with concern.

"No, mother," Linda protested. "You don't have to run to the store to please anyone in this house."

"Anyone?" Nancy shot back.

"That's all right. I got it," Jeff interpolated before the situation could transmute into another dispute. "But I'd like Nancy to come along and choose the box of her liking."

"Me?" Nancy uttered.

"I insist. I might want to buy a pack of--." Jeff's unyielding stare implied a possible disclosure of some concealed incidents.

It was well inferred by Nancy, "okay, I'll go!"

"A pack of gum myself," Jeff finished.

Nancy conjured a fake smile and followed him out of the house.

A small family diner catered a handful of customers about an hour before noon initiating their lunch menu but still serving breakfast leftovers.

Jeff met with a couple of nods as he took Nancy to the last table near the window.

"What are we here for?" Nancy demanded before even taking a seat.

"Sit down." Jeff ordered and received a menu from an attendant.

"Hey Jeff, good to have you back! When'd you come home?" the middle-aged waitress was an old acquaintance and very benign.

"Hey Renee, just five days ago. Couldn't miss the breakfast here."

"Oh they just put the breakfast stove to sleep, but I have some saved specialty just for you."

"I appreciate that. No need for a menu then." Jeff handed the menu card back to her. "Renee, meet Nancy. My niece."

"Oh," Renee was surprised, "you're the cute little flower girl at Maggie's wedding, aren't you?"

"I don't remember," Nancy dismissed her with a forced, derisive smile.

"You have a sharp memory," Jeff affirmed her suspicion.

"Oh, children grow up so quick. I'll be right back with your order." Renee smiled and left.

"So, what are we here for?" Nancy reverted to her concern.

"To those you leave behind, a mere smile from a memory is enough for you to be remembered through time," Jeff whispered distantly.

"What?"

Jeff poured himself a glass of water and gazed at it keenly. He spoke after a long consideration. "Do you think anyone can survive with just water alone for life?"

"I don't know, what you're saying?"

"Water is as essential as breathing to our survival, isn't it? But can you live your entire life drinking water only?"

"No one can."

"Well, what do you think we need along with it? That's where food comes in, right?"

"Duh!" Nancy mocked him.

"Good, now if we consider our existence as one life. Water, the most needed of all things which could be the love of a companion, you still need to feed yourself something to stay alive, don't you? Maybe just a little bit of it, but you do?"

Nancy opted for silence.

"That food is the love of a family. And for those who are not born into one, sooner or later create it for themselves. You cannot just survive with the love of one person all your life. You need to have the love of a few more. Children, parents, grandparents, distant relatives. Water alone cannot sustain life, you need food, like your box of cereal."

Renee brought a platter for both with burgers and fries and a shake for Nancy.

"Thank you, Renee."

"You got it. Give me a wave if you need anything else."

Jeff waited to pour some tomato ketchup over his fries. Nancy was transfixed by the words she had just heard, didn't move an inch.

Jeff noted her trance and smiled. "A person, who loves one, loves all. A person, who hates all others, would come to hate the one too. It is the truth of human nature. You or me or anyone else, we can't change that. Hatred drives many insane, I know that. Love is what brings them back, I know that extremely well."

"I love him," Nancy declared.

"More than you love your mother and your father?"

Nancy's lower lip trembled. Her eyes were filled. "No... I don't know."

"Even if you love them all equally, why have you shown your love to him more than you've given your parents in the past few days?"

Nancy gave into tears and hid her face inside a parapet of forearms.

"Hey, don't cry. That is a realization of truth. And I don't need to hear whom you love more, because I know." Jeff ruffled her hair. "I'm going to make a mess up here if you don't look at me."

Nancy wiped her tears and looked up with red, swollen eyes. She sniveled.

"You love your parents, Nancy. One fight with your mother is not enough to distance you from them, and one trip to nana's house is definitely no reason at all. And these small differences will continue all your life. But never stop showing them your affection. Fight one minute and forget the other. Because when anger carries on for long, it alters into hatred, which could tear you apart for a very long time. Perhaps, five years."

Nancy took a moment to reconsider and wiped below her eyes.

"I like him, that's all."

"Yes, I know. He's in your school?"

"He's a senior."

"How many days a year do you see him?"

Nancy was riveted by that inquiry.

"Almost eight to nine months?" Jeff gave her an option.

"More, we meet during summer break too," Nancy admitted.

"How many days a year do we get to meet you? Me, your grandmother, your grandfather, Dave, Maggie, your little cousins?"

"They don't care about me."

Jeff waited quietly this time and allowed her to acknowledge the erroneous belief.

"I'm sorry," she submitted an apology. "I didn't mean that."

"I know what you're thinking, Nancy. I am not your father. I don't know what I'm talking about. And even if I do, who am I to give advice, right? Let me ask you something, have you ever given advice to someone younger than you?"

"Yes, a lot of times."

"Why?"

"Because they didn't know what they were--," she paused, gazing up at her uncle. "They didn't know what they were doing."

"Right. Have you ever thought that you knew of a situation better than them because of their age? Let's say they were five years your junior?"

"That's usually why."

"What would you say to someone who tries to make his niece understand things when she's almost twenty years younger?"

"I just like to spend time with him… and my other friends." She rephrased herself.

"Yes, we all need friends. That's the reason he was here last night? To spend time with you?"

"He came to invite me to his place. He begged me to come. His parents are in Hawaii for the holidays. He has the whole place to himself. He was going to call in all the friends together. We were supposed to have a lot of fun. But now I'm going to miss it because I'm here."

"What did you tell him?"

"I told him I can't come because my mom won't let me. He said he'll cancel everything. He won't like anything without me."

"So, he really thinks you're not going?"

"Yes."

Jeff shifted back on the couch and gave a wordless smile.

Jeff conducted another expedition only this time with a different companion on the passenger end of the Mercedes. Nancy sat in subtle excitement for the duration of the trip as she was well conversant with the road to their destination. After a drive lasting more than four hours, he pulled into a rather luxurious neighborhood of the city and navigated the roads slowly.

They found a long driveway leading to a grand estate to which Nancy pointed as Randy's residence. Jeff veered into the open gates and drove past the extensive landscaped lawns as large as a football field. They reached a baronial mansion which was reflective of a grandeur only a few can afford. He parked the car along with many others and followed Nancy out to the courtyard which was home to a deafening ruckus only the young could induce.

The marble fountain was a pool for many drunken youths and the surrounding garden, riddled with trees, a mating ground for many couples, though they had just initiated with French kisses. The DJ dissonance was blatant and the beats rumbled for yards, and there were laser lights projecting in the sky.

Nancy plodded further very much startled at the lack of festivity which was promised upon her absence. She also wondered and feared the magnitude of this conclave if she had agreed to be present.

They came inside the mansion and found the capacious hall filled with young men and women parading half drunk and half dressed. Nancy stormed through the multitude searching for Randy in the wayward horde. The music was thumping and so were the cohesive bodies everywhere. Jeff bolted himself by the foyer and waited.

"Hey, you are a stranger?"

Jeff was approached by a pair of twins, who were quite skimpy with their Santa's helper attire to get employed at the North Pole. "You're not from class, are you?"

"Not your class ladies."

"A gentleman? Wow. Look at his shoulders, fills up a jacket pretty good." Said one of the beautiful blondes reeking of beer.

"I'm sure he fills up everything else pretty good too." The other said nudging her suggestively. They both laughed and drank more of the liquor in their plastic cups. "Would you like to try one of us?"

"Or both maybe?" The other one was naughtier.

"I'm looking for my niece."

"We can be your nieces, uncle. Spank us, we've been naughty this year." Both of them joked alluringly.

"You both are drunk, go home." Jeff turned serious.

"If you'll take us with you," the taller one teased.

"This is our home, we live here." The second added.

"You live here? Do you know Randy?" Jeff inquired

"Of course, we do. Our brother, but he's younger though."

"Where is he?" Jeff attempted to elicit information this time.

"In the pool. You want to go to the pool? I have a jacuzzi in my room upstairs."

Nancy reappeared jostling through the swaying crowd. "I can't believe I'm doing this."

"Hey Nancy, we didn't know you were into older guys." The shorter one blurted.

"Alison, this is my uncle," Nancy objected.

"Not mine." The taller one inched closer to Jeff and tried to strip him of his jacket.

"You're so gross, get away from him." Nancy dragged Jeff out of there and out into the courtyard.

"He's by the pool," Jeff straightened his jacket.

Nancy stopped and looked back with a deep, indignant sigh.

They walked around the construction to the rear and found countless bodies splashing and jumping into the steaming pool. Nancy scanned for that one face she desired to see. Her search stopped at the hot tub.

Randy was in an embrace of a brunette who was embedded on him exploring his tonsils with her tongue.

"Randy!" Nancy screamed in arrant disgust. Her breaths grew shallow and rapid.

All eyes turned toward her which triggered Randy's attention as well. There was an awkward silence except for the music booming inside. Nancy was enraged, but humiliated with all those stares hurtled at her. She eluded them all and escaped from there. Randy emerged from the tub and trailed after her right behind Jeff.

They were in the courtyard when Randy accosted her, taking her hand and ceasing her furious strides. "Nancy, listen to me."

Nancy was tearful as she turned around.

"Nancy, I'm sorry. I didn't know you were going to come." He presented his flawed defense.

"You didn't know, right? That's why you started kissing her? Beth? Because she plays volleyball, that's why? She has a better mouth or a better ass?" Nancy was incensed.

"I'm sorry, if I knew--"

"I wasn't coming, so I wouldn't know right?"

"It's not like that, baby."

Nancy swung a slap right across his face. "I'm not your baby, never call me that again. You fuc..."

Jeff contained her animosity by placing a hand on her mouth and taking her along back to the car as she flailed in his arms trying to get her fists closer to her transgressor.

"Nancy," Randy called out to her.

"Stay away," Jeff warned him after which Randy retraced his steps.

Jeff brought Nancy to the car and released her.

Nancy thrashed about, "let go of me. Don't you ever put your hands on me again."

Jeff lifted his arms aloft in surrender. Nancy kicked at the cobblestone pavement in rage and screamed, some weeping followed. Jeff waited in silence and gave her the time she needed to recuperate.

"I was supposed to be there with him, it's all my fault. Mom and dad forced me to go to see the family." Her voice cracked and dwindled into sobs. "If I'd never left he wouldn't have cheated. It's all their fault," she began imputing blame.

Jeff stood wordless.

"If I wasn't away, he wouldn't even look at Beth. She's nothing but acne and arm hairs. She's... she's the team captain, they all look great in shorts. I never played any sport, that's why I'm so skinny. If I did, he wouldn't cheat on me. It's all my fault."

Jeff, hoping she had ended her grievances, opened the passenger side door for her.

"He's a pig. I did everything for him. I even took cooking classes because he likes pies. He doesn't know what he's going to lose if I walk out of his life. Boys like him don't deserve someone like me. I'm never returning to him, not in this lifetime. It's his fault." She was resolute this time. "Isn't it?" she looked to Jeff for assurance.

"Nancy, I am not going to say whether he deserves you or not, or what he's done is right or wrong. I've already heard I'm not your father, so I'd leave all of that to James. But I will say just one thing being someone who loves you. That guy, Randy, is having the best time of his life right now. Are you? And if you aren't, why and for what? When you answer these two little questions for me. It'll be over."

Nancy assimilated the purpose of his words for a while, then stepped into the car. Jeff closed the door for her and joined her on the driver's side.

Their drive back home was muted. Nancy's head was propped against the glass of her window and was churned with many pensive thoughts. Jeff occasionally found her eyes dripping some tears as she brooded endlessly. After a beeping indication from the system, the vehicle was pulled into a gas station to refuel.

While Jeff performed the task, Nancy found herself staring at a neighboring car that was parked with a similar purpose. But on the passenger side, she found a young woman with a newborn and both were exuberant to be in each other's presence. Their bliss was eternal as the woman played with her baby caressing and rocking it at times, and bussing in between.

She eyed Nancy across the pumps and caused her baby to wave at her, helping it with the motion. Nancy smiled and waved back.

"All set?" Jeff had entered the car.

"Yeah. How much longer to get back home?"

Jeff looked at her, "sooner than you think."

The Saunderhurst family was in a frenzy as everyone was fidgeting in the living, rendering support to Linda and James who were disconcerted at the absence of their daughter. When the door opened and the noises of people entering disrupted the silence, they all clustered in the hallway.

Jeff came in with Nancy and they both took off their coats.

"That was quite a prolonged grocery shopping, what is wrong with both of you?" Linda erupted. "You had us worried. It's almost eleven, you've been gone the whole day. She's a teenager, she can be excused. But Jeff you should assume some responsibility, you have a fifteen-year-old with you."

"Where have you been? We were going to call the police." James was equally agitated.

"I'm sorry everyone, it is my fault. I just drove and she tagged along. We just lost the track of time." Jeff accepted the blame.

"Are you all right, honey?" Linda perused her daughter.

"I'm fine."

"Where's your phone, Nancy?" James queried.

"I left it here."

Linda aimed her anger at her brother. "Jeff, you should have called at least. This is no way to act when a young girl is with you. Do you even realize the kinds of thoughts that have entered our mind for the past five hours? You're the adult, have some sense to--"

"Please, stop it," Nancy interrupted. "You say one more word to him and I'll never speak to any of you again. Not a single word." She glowered at everybody before running up the stairs.

"What did you do to her?" Linda rushed after her.

Maggie approached Jeff with perplexity. "What's the matter?"

Jeff addressed everyone there. "It's better if we don't speak about it until she does. I'll get some things from the car."

Jeff returned to the car and took out some bags of eatables from the rear. Coming back to the house, he saw a stationary shadow at

Erica's porch, faintly lit by an exterior lamp. He went to investigate firsthand.

Erica sat on the steps, covered in a thick blanket, her head cushioned against the railings. Her auburn hair veiled her face. Jeff gingerly leaned forward and tucked her hair behind her ear. Her immaculate beauty became apparent in the moonlight.

"Hey," Erica, still with eyes closed, whispered with a smile.

"Hey, what're you doing?" Jeff doubted her reasoning.

"Waiting for you."

"Out here? You could be an icicle in a few more minutes."

She laughed widely, "at least I'd keep my end of the promise."

Jeff rubbed his temples, "oh my goodness, I forgot about it."

"I know you did. I just wanted to remind you."

"I suppose you are aware of the fact that there are better ways to remind people which do not involve a thermometer and a pharmacy on your bedside table."

"I'm not too fond of the two, but I'd love to see you as my aide until I recover."

"Like you did a long time ago?" Jeff became nostalgic.

"Kind of."

"Maybe I'd just call a nurse," he teased.

"Nah, you won't do that. I know you well enough."

"Come'on, get up from there. You need to warm yourself. And I need you completely rested tomorrow. It's a very long day. Go to bed."

"What are you up to now?"

"You'll know, just a bit of surprise, for the whole town in fact."

"And now you expect me to go to sleep?"

"Butterflies in your stomach inspire a better slumber."

"No, it doesn't."

"I know," they both laughed together. "Tomorrow morning, I'll see you."

"I hope it won't be one of those 'I forgot' moments again."

"Not a chance. Good night."

"Good night." Erica stepped back inside her house and saw Jeff leave from the mesh screen door. She nodded to his gaiety and impishness that reminded her of a time twenty-five years ago that she still treasured.

# Chapter Twenty-Five

"I believe there is something worth a mention going on between the two." Lena pulled the oven shut and approached the younger women around the counter.

The distaff members of the Saunderhurst family had convoked in the kitchen and a motley of scrumptious delicacies were being prepared. Surprisingly, Nancy was a part of this huddle with her fingertips drenched in a chocolate mixture.

"Erica and Jeff?" Linda asked incredulously.

"Yes," Lena confirmed.

"They've known each other since genesis, of course it's going to spark a little after five years of separation." Maggie had a concrete view of their intimacy.

"I saw them together last night." Lena assisted Nancy in blending the mixture the correct way with hands.

"Where?" Maggie got excited.

"Outside her home. It wasn't anything unusual, just a simple talk. But I know when my son is delighted. There have been only a few such instances." She instructed Nancy to pour the mixture onto a baking tray.

"They've been in love since they didn't even know the true meaning of the word, ma. I can't believe you're surprised at this." Maggie commented tasting the mixture off of Nancy's finger.

"Well, if you were so certain of their affection, why didn't you tell anyone?" Linda prompted.

"I was aware of their relationship, daughters. I even spoke to Erica about their marriage once. But soon after, Jeff went away. Since then it has been a thing of the past. Erica kept her silence on the matter, so did I. No one knew where he was or when he'll come back."

"I would suggest that they move to New York after their marriage. This town has nothing for them." All eyes turned toward Gloria who stood wiping her hands on her apron. She shrugged embarrassedly.

"If they love each other so much, we should be the ones bringing them closer." Nancy disrupted that silence consciously.

The women seemed impressed by that suggestion as they nodded in unison.

"Welcome to the family, Nancy," Linda remarked gleefully.

Nancy beamed.

Jeff hurried into the kitchen, "Maggie, I need you for a moment."

There was no verbal reply but all five pairs of eyes were fixated on him.

"How was last night?" Maggie teased him to speak.

"Last night? I guess it was all right. Nothing to be concerned about. Went to sleep okay and woke up to a staring contest that seems quite suspicious early in the morning. You didn't see me howling up on a cliff last night, did you?" Jeff answered in wonderment. "Clothes torn in the backyard, blood smeared on my pillow?"

"We don't have a cliff in or around town for miles." Maggie joked.

"Oh boy, you just saved me there. An overnight trip to one would be exhausting even when you could leap across trees and dash a mile in a minute." Jeff added to the tease.

"No, we're just checking." The women giggled with Maggie. "If you have nothing to say, we have nothing to ask."

"I have a lot to say, but I need you to come outside with me."

"I'm working here, Jeff. Go find some idle men in the other room." Maggie said uninterested.

"Can I come?" Nancy raised her arm, reminiscent of a classroom.

"Sure, I'd like that." Jeff agreed, which drove Nancy to sanitize her hands under the faucet and quickly put on a coat.

Jeff took off his woolen hat and placed it on Maggie's head, pulling it down to her brows. Then removed his jacket and forced her into it which could have wrapped her twice. Maggie enjoyed that instance of being garmented without moving a finger in the process.

"Aren't you going to carry me now?" she requested innocently.

Jeff shook her head and dragged her down the hallway and out the door with Nancy trailing behind.

Erica was already waiting expectantly under the oak tree drawing figures in the snow with her boot. Jeff brought the women out of the house and flocked them together.

"Okay, now I want you all to promise me something," Jeff ordered, "this stays between us. No one should know in the family what we're up to."

"What are we up to?" Nancy queried.

"I know what you two are up to," Maggie suggested naughtily.

"Us two?" Erica questioned.

"I know your little secret, Jeff."

"You do?" Jeff ached. "But how, I haven't even told anyone. Not even Erica."

"Yeah." Erica substantiated.

"Well, then you two are the only ones who don't know that we know." Maggie nudged Nancy impishly.

"What do you know? I just told you even she doesn't know what I'm about to say." Jeff was baffled.

"What are you talking about?" Erica added in her own state of perplexity.

"You and Erica, it's no mystery. We all know about it."

"What? Maggie, I didn't pull you out of the house in twenty-degree temperature to discuss our 'secret' relationship. I have something different to say here. Let me do the talking for a minute," he pleaded.

"Okay, I was just saying--" Maggie shrugged.

"Zip it up, one minute. That's all I need."

Maggie folded her arms and looked away.

"Now would you look back here, please? Be a part of this group?"

Maggie turned, but still distantly.

"I'm going to bring Drake Jarick for a book signing event at our store." Jeff announced.

"What?!" A look of downright shock diffused with excitement brightened their eyes and all three women barked in disbelief. "The Drake Jarick?"

"Yes."

"Oh God, he's the biggest mystery writer of all time!" Nancy was explicit with her praise.

"And he is so good looking!" Maggie drifted to a nebulous world of dreams.

"Why didn't you have your own event, Jeff?" Erica inquired.

"Me? I'm not that famous. You see these faces right here? I couldn't evoke such expressions on people's faces." Jeff pointed to the two women in reverie before him. "So, I need you guys to set up the store for tomorrow. Christmas decorations, get everything you need. A nice desk and an executive chair and we'll make some space in the store as well."

"But who is going to come if no one is told?" Maggie was confused again.

"Oh, people know about this all right. My publisher has advertised in newspapers, reader's journals and magazines all across major cities and towns in the vicinity for the past three days. She told me Drake's never been so far up north for an event and it is a good initiative to see his following in the northern states. She's also managed some media coverage. We're looking at Vermont, New Hampshire and Maine to name a few. People are likely to pour into our town tomorrow. I've also brought in some mailmen, with the help of a friend, to undertake distribution of our flyers. They'r e delivering more than just mail to houses in ten neighboring towns as we speak."

"Henry?" Erica surmised.

"Yes. The only place that's left is our own hometown. And that responsibility is best given to Erica here, because she has some experience drawing the crowds to our bookstore for an event.

"Aye sir, I'm ready for it." Erica volunteered.

"Good. Drake's a nationally renowned author, wherever he goes, the crowd follows. The publisher assured me it will be a success. I'm inclined to believe her. So, are we ready to do this?"

"Yes! Let's get some lights up." The women answered in ardent liveliness.

"It'll be the best day of our lives." Jeff concluded avidly.

The snow had begun to transpire, as a clear exterior view from the terminal manifested. Jeff's petrified stance apparently grew gloomier with desertion of the weather in the essential hard times. He espied someone amidst the plodding passengers and erected himself preparing a graceful reception at the arrival stands.

Drake Jarick appeared aloof from the rest of the crowd and his long strides were almost a pretentious gait. He was a tall man, dusky in complexion, lean and chiseled, groomed with a light beard, a two thousand dollar tweed suit honored itself by receiving a coveted fortune to attire such a prominent personality, and an even more extravagant herringbone topcoat took it as a blessing to be neatly folded around his forearm. He was meticulous with his demeanor, as he paused and allowed people walking across to pass before he could continue, but he was pompous enough to hurl a hostile glare when they did commit such a felony. Jeff had conjectured his age to be around the golden number fifty through the aura of intellectual supremacy that reflected upon his visage.

"Afternoon, sir. My name is Jeff and I'm here to receive you. Did you have any troubles during the flight? I hope the trip was satisfactory. I'm going to conduct you to your hotel." The introduction was wooden, nervous and hasty.

"Conduct yourself to my luggage first. And if you're not planning on carrying me to my transport, you better make your strides longer and quicker and bid the driver come to the gate as I'm not in the habit of fraying my soles against concrete for too long." Jarick spoke in the clearest of American accents Jeff had ever heard delineating British roots.

"No, sir. I have your transportation ready just outside. If you would follow me?" Jeff collected his luggage and wheeled it toward the exit.

They had come out into blaring winds and billowing snow. Thankfully the limousine waited just a few steps from the automatic doors, much to the dislike of the famous writer.

"This is completely unbearable. I despise these conditions. Is this the reason for which you pleaded me to come? To be ravaged by inclement weather?"

"I'm sorry sir, I prayed all the way here for a nice pleasant day. I'm not a religious man." Jeff was artfully caustic.

"Hopeless." Drake stepped into the limo.

Jeff loaded the luggage in the trunk with Michael, the driver, and boarded the luxury car.

Drake brushed off the flakes from his coat. "I believe your other arrangements would not be as troublesome as this."

"Not at all, sir. I will personally make sure of it. Your transportation would be ready on command for the duration of your stay along with me. Your hotel suite is specifically designed to suit your needs and penchants. I will be at your disposal at all times."

"Where are we going to stay?"

"It is a very small town, some miles from here. We can't even consider it the outskirts, that's how remote it is. I'm sure you haven't heard of it."

"I'm certain of that. Angela could've might as well sent me to the moon for this book signing event." Drake muttered. "I have to inform you of a slight change in our itinerary."

"What's that, sir?"

"I am to attend the event tomorrow? I will be leaving for New York right after my work is finished."

"I thought you'd be returning a day later."

"I have no desire to spend my time in this torturous, forsaken, ruin of a hamlet any longer than I'm obligated to. I will leave tomorrow evening. I believe facilitating this slight adjustment wouldn't be much of a hassle for you?"

"I will love to be of service, sir." Jeff conjured a fake smile.

Drake picked up his satellite phone and began dialing a number.

The car suddenly lurched upon a pothole on the uneven road and the impact bounced the riders in the back. The phone slipped Drake's grasp and dropped to the matted floor. His aggravation amplified and cascaded his livid countenance. Jeff quickly retrieved the phone handing it back to him.

"These venal miscreants, they gormandize our money in taxes like leeches and can't even patch-up a pit like that which costs no more than a hundred dollars at the most?" Drake grumbled violently.

"It is a sad and greedy world, sir."

"It's not the world I'm complaining about. It's these miserable towns that have no grit to rouse their dissent for a cause."

Jeff refrained from riposting.

"I can't wait to get out of this harrowing little place." Drake expressed his displeasure blatantly.

"Neither can I," Jeff grumbled soundlessly.

"Did you say something?"

"No, sir. Just making verbal reminders in my mind."

"Good." Drake noted his impudence but stayed quiet on the matter.

It was quite late a dawn to commence the challenging engagement of clarioning the word, but all welcomed in great spirits. Erica had started her work by posting the flyers at the populous junctions of the town and slipping it in hands of many old acquaintances she came across. She also entreated other store owners to solicit their customers with a flyer each to hone the promotion. Henry, the mailman, came into the picture to draw in the reclusive crowds who, for some reason, skipped a day out in the open or preferred their coffee and readings within the walls of their fortresses. He had to be extra prudent not being carried away and delivering the Saunderhurst home with one of the pamphlets and wrecking the pleasant surprise. But fortunately, not a single envelope compelled him to digress from his path as he went straight through skipping the house.

The days were short and seemed minuscule when such travail was attempted. Erica returned to the bookstore well after six and found Maggie and Nancy excavating the boxes of trinkets halfway down their assignment.

"Hey ladies!" Erica sprawled on a chair.

"Oh poor thing, you look exhausted." Maggie retrieved a pack of confetti from the box.

"That was a marathon."

"I'm sure. Give your wheels some rest." Maggie went to the counter and poured a steaming cup of coffee right from a thermos. "Get a taste of this. It'll keep you up another four-five hours."

Erica tasted it, at the very collision of the liquid against her mouth, her eyes and temples crumpled. "Wow, these are some strong beans. What is it?"

"It's a secret recipe, keeps me alive around the kids." Maggie sat by her side.

Erica smiled and meditated an abstract reality of time, "kids. I could still remember the time when we were kids, now you have two of your own."

"Yeah, that's the loop of life. The only thing that changes is your part in it. Oh, how much I adored those days of our togetherness, our freedom. We just went by like birds, day by day, hour by hour. Things I'd give up to see that time again. It was so short, but sweet."

"It isn't that short, Maggie. Believe me." Nancy interposed.

"You have no idea, little one. You only understand the true value of something when it's gone and you know it will never come back," Maggie countered. "Time is a merciless teacher of the lesson of longing."

"Everything was so different back then," Erica added. "Without a single care in the world, our lives went on like nothing mattered, like nothing else existed."

"The whole world was different and the best part about it, we had it all to ourselves. Our little bikes took us everywhere we wanted to go, didn't care for cars, didn't care for anything. Long hours of playing out in the open, running around like crazies all day long, looking forward to weekends to stay home and do some fun stuff, or maybe just get together in the front yard and sweat our guts out, unlike you guys with all these computers and video games, and all the worries of the world. What we had in our minds were the falls, the bridge... the accident."

"The accident?" Nancy got excited and joined the discussion.

Erica quickly interrupted, "now let's just hold our reins there. We don't want to go too far, Maggie."

"No one actually ever spoke about it since. It was like the evil you never talk about."

"It had to be forgotten. It wanted to be forgotten." Erica suggested.

"Don't make me a stranger to family tales, come'on I want to know. Please?" Nancy begged to be included.

"It can't harm me anymore, talking about it." Maggie shrugged it away. "I almost drowned once," faced Nancy. "I was about seven?"

"Almost eight." Erica corrected her. "She was trying a trick too close to the edge of a bridge. It didn't have any rails and she was on wheels. That coveted red, little bike she rode, took her right into a stream."

"That was a head-first fall, wasn't it?"

"You did hit your head, but not right away. You took your time, screaming out for help, calling your brother."

"See, it's too foggy in my memory," Maggie acknowledged.

"Uncle Jeff saved you?" Nancy was abuzz with excitement.

"He did. I don't know how, but he did. Tell me, Erica, was he frightened?" Maggie searched Erica's eyes for an answer.

"He was frightened. He might have given up too. But when he saw you lying there, not breathing and white as snow, there must've been something that made him run, that gave him courage. Nothing else mattered to him at that moment but you. And when he took you up in his arms and ran those two and a half miles to the infirmary, I saw that rage of love in his eyes, not loss, but love. It might have been the fear of losing you, but the want to save you overcame that fear easily."

Maggie was stirred to tears with that.

"Wow!" Nancy spoke in amazement.

"Many people suffer accidents in life, but not all of them are lucky enough to be saved. Uncle Jeff saved aunt Maggie's life that day." Maggie reflected.

A silence lingered amidst them.

"The bridge is still there? What about the falls?" Nancy queried.

"It's all there." Erica nodded. "But they have some construction going on across the woods now. They cleared a path right through the forest. I'll take you there along with Ron and Helen to see it someday. The place that caused a lot of suffering to their mother."

"Yeah, they would love to tease me about it for many years until they forget." Maggie turned toward Nancy, "we'll tell you about another incident that almost killed us all, but some other time."

"Another one? What's going on here? What's up with these run-ins with life and death situations?" Nancy marveled.

"Yeah, we've been the fate favorites for a long time. Let me do some adult talk here, Nancy, excuse us for a minute, will you?"

Nancy got up and trudged back to her arduous task.

Maggie took a pause to review her next words. "Can I ask something of you, Erica? As a friend to another, who've known each other for years, possibly as more than friends?"

"I like the latter better." Erica smiled thinly.

"There are relationships that are sometimes not given a name and are simply called a bond. But when such a bond goes beyond the limits of any relationship, it's called eternal love. It is not commonly seen around us. In fact, I haven't seen it in my life so far and I'm married. But I have seen it between the two of you. It's been there for a long time, and it is meant to stay forever. I ask you to take his hand and hold him through. Please." Maggie besought her by joining her hands together.

"Maggie, what are you doing?" Erica entreated her to stop.

"He needs you. I see it in his eyes every day. Forgive him for anything wrong that he's done, I know you will. He needs the woman who gave him the courage to save a life. I know it was you. He needs your strength, your love, your presence. It is in you where he will find his peace. Hold him through."

Erica took her time to respond. "It is not my forgiveness, but his that I seek."

Maggie leaned in closer to her and whispered. "He's loved you all along. There is no wrong you can do to him. If you doubt me, ask him yourself." Maggie tapped her right leg and abruptly arose with a greeting. "Do we have the pleasure of meeting our first customer of the evening?"

Erica turned and saw Jeff entering the store.

"I have no money. I was thinking if I could help out with the dishes to cover the expense of my purchase?" Jeff rejoined teasingly.

"We have no dishes, but a lot of work needs to be done around here." Maggie gestured towards the walls.

"You may use me as you like."

Nancy had just put in a Christmas rock songs CD and the atmosphere of the whole bookstore went wayward. The four reveled having the merriest of time without a care or concern, embellishing the store for the event with tinsel & trinkets and lights & holly. Each of them reached for their cups of insipid coffee and savored its bitterness, as the profound ecstasy of happiness vanquished any acridity of the world.

A Christmas tree was put up in the corner near the storefront adorned with twinkling lights and ornaments. Banners were hung between aisles and the entrance welcoming the esteemed author. Garlands pinned against walls and cabinets, confetti and streamers taped to the ceiling. And it was all conducted with sublime conviviality which coerced Maggie to bring the ladies to the dance floor and tap a performance on the beat to the best of their dancing ability. Jeff refrained from gyrating along, but tagged in randomly with a couple of steps of his own. All of them wrapped in garlands and strands of lights, and showered each other with confetti, encompassed by festive joy. That was all that mattered that night.

Maggie's prolonged yawning brought her weariness to Jeff's attention.

"Tired?" he looked up still setting the desk for Drake.

"Way too much to be said." Maggie slouched on a chair.

"I think we did a good job. The store looks nice, doesn't it?" Nancy looked at her elders earnestly.

"You all did a wonderful job," Jeff reassured her.

"Wherever there are a few with an aim, the outcomes are always satisfactory." Erica joined.

Jeff approached Nancy and clenched her by the shoulders. "Thank you for all this, thanks for being here."

"No, thank you for that drive back home. I only met my family just yesterday. Thanks for making me a part of it." Her eyes were swimming in tears.

"You are always going to be a part of the family, always. Nothing can change that." He gave her a bracing smile. "Why don't you take your drained aunt along and wait in the car, I'll finish this and close up. All of you."

"I'll close here with you." Erica insisted.

"Well, I'm going then. Nancy, come'on." Maggie propelled her out of the store. But before exiting she leaned back in. "Where's your car, Erica?"

"Oh no, mine's at home. It's not a truck anymore, it's a wreck. Henry dropped me here. I was going to come along with you guys."

"Oh, that's fantastic. We'll wait." Maggie gave a wry smirk and left.

Erica inched closer to the cassette player and put on a song. 'I'll be home for Christmas' by Frank Sinatra came up.

She came close behind Jeff and touched him on the shoulders as he completed the desk placing a nice ink pen next to a framed picture of Drake Jarick and a couple of his previously published books.

He looked back at her and his eyes filled with her radiant smile.

"May I?" she asked.

Jeff turned to her and she helped him get into a swaying stance by guiding his hand on her waist and holding the other. In certain vacillation, they began to move gently in affinity with the composure and serenity of the song itself. Their diffidence soon became rhythmic and their slow movements became uniform as the strength of their clasp fortified.

She placed her head on him and there was nothing among or around them but peace. The peace of the night. The peace of their companionship that was converged from individual loneliness. The peace of the holidays and the bliss that emanated from it. The peace of the tranquil weather that had just subdued and stifled its rage. And the peace of intimacy that drove them closer inch by inch, moment by moment. And in that peace, they found each other.

# Chapter Twenty-Six

The lights were turned off as the splendor went dark inside the store. Jeff yanked the metal door shut and turned the lock in while Erica waited. They both turned toward the street and searched for the lonesome car that was parked across only ten minutes ago. Now, it was nowhere in sight.

"Where is Maggie?" Erica scanned the entire block confoundedly.

"Did she just leave us back here?" Jeff spoke at length.

"She was tired," Erica defended.

"They could have just waited, I asked them to." Annoyance had just trickled across his face.

"Well, you want to walk me home? We can't find a taxi here at this time."

"Are you cold or anything? We can find an extra sweater inside."

Erica stepped near him and took his arm in hers. "I'm perfectly fine." She led him down the street in the calm and cold of the night.

They had plodded the street, for about half a mile which had a thick cover of snow, still closely entwined.

"The amount of times I've walked these streets. Every night I used to come this way, making sure the stores were fine. No burglars or trespassers taking away books or some bananas from next door." Jeff reminisced while Erica chuckled at the comment.

"Yeah, it's all over again. But with an exception this time." Their eyes met tenderly, but his nostalgia soon turned into an objection. "You aren't cold, are you? This is really unacceptable, they shouldn't have done that."

"That's all right, we can forgive them for being a little considerate." Erica hinted on something, enjoying the stroll.

"It's not about that. I still remember that prolonged throat infection you suffered when we were little after I challenged you to three ice creams in a row, who gobbles it faster. I was an idiot back then knowing that you were forbidden from trying even a cold sandwich in winters, I forced ice cream down your throat. You couldn't speak for eight months. I still remember, from November to June you lost your voice. Every day I saw your dad wrap you up in a scarf all throughout winters. Those months were the most quiet and gloomy times of my childhood. I don't what that to happen again."

"Hey, it's all right. I haven't worn a scarf in years. Remember? It was just a precaution and maybe that illness cured me in a way. I love my cold sandwiches in winters now, with a lemonade and ice cream for dessert. You helped me get over it." Her grip tightened around his arm as he reasoned with her belief.

They walked in complete silence after that until Jeff spoke again.

"But what about your dad? He must be all alone. He hasn't seen you today at all."

"Oh god, here we go again. He did. I went home twice, once for lunch as well. He was all right. Somehow, I believe Maggie might have put him to bed, again."

"I'm going to get her when I get home."

She flicked his nose tenderly, "you are so cute when you're angry."

Jeff dismissed her remark with an embarrassed smile. They hushed for another minute.

"Remember when you were angry with me thinking that I would leave when I returned from Jersey?" It was Erica's turn down memory lane.

Jeff nodded, "remember when you got angry telling me you won't?"

"Yes. I kept my word. I never crossed the boundaries of this town since. I couldn't afford you to come back and not find me. Didn't know when you would return, so I took my precautions and stayed, doesn't matter the season or the scarf. I did end up with a couple of seasonal sore throats in the past five years, but they stopped bothering me somehow. Probably because I had a greater pain to deal with. I stopped acknowledging them and then they left me alone. One ill is enough for one human, I suppose. Every time I'd hear your parents greet someone at the door, I'd rush to the window. Christmas, Easter, changing years, Linda would show up at times, Maggie maybe once or twice, but you didn't. I waited and I kept my word." She laughed concealing her aches. "It almost feels like it was just yesterday, you leaving me back here. Doesn't it to you?"

"Yesterday? I'm not as forgiving as you are. It seems like a lifetime to me. These five years have not been so swift for me. I've counted months, days, hours go by. I left my life here, Erica. I didn't take it with me. All I took along were memories and time. And time without life is as frightening as life without time. When life is taken out of time, five years to be exact, it becomes the longest phase of your existence to get through."

"Then why didn't you come back, Jeff?"

"As much as I wanted to, I didn't have the courage to face all of you. I just couldn't show up like that."

"Everyone here waited."

"So did I." Jeff gazed up at the sky, tears brimming.

Erica cupped his face and pierced his gaze with her tearful eyes. "You are not going to cry anymore," she wiped her own tears away with her sleeve. "And answer me once, I promise I won't be angry at all. You are not going to leave us again, are you?" Erica had an impression of a plea in her trembling voice.

Jeff answered with decisiveness. "I will not go back to New York."

Erica smiled and threw her arms around drawing closer into him. They stayed in an embrace for a moment. They parted, drying their tears and regaining their equanimity.

"Tell me, what happened in the past five years. What have you done all this time?" Jeff queried pleasantly changing the subject of discussion.

"Nothing's been too exciting. This is a simple place, you know it as well as I do. People spend their simple lives in this simple town and simply pass on. The only thing extraordinary is that everything that happens here is simply ordinary. I'm just a part of that simplicity. I knew I was going to be here for the rest of my life, then why bother doing anything special?"

"There's nothing ordinary about you. You were an ambitious girl. If I can remember correctly, I think you were the first out of our class to go to college?"

"I was back then. If time had been faithful, maybe I would have done something with me. But that which never stops changes everything. I couldn't keep up with the pace of the world around me and with some storming responsibilities that came all of a sudden, I was done. I did think about going back to college once you left, but then daddy was diagnosed with Alzheimer's and... our lives just stopped. I became his mirror. A family is made up of two parents, but since I was little he never let me feel our family was incomplete. He played the other part really well. He was and is my family, the only one that I have. I couldn't just run away now when he needed me the most. The treatment is underway but... there is no cure for it. With his age now, they say it's just a matter of time. But you can't just sew your eyes close even when you plan on sleeping for the rest of your life, can you?"

"No," Jeff replied.

A small hiatus followed.

"You know when you're away from a place," Erica continued, "and you don't get to live it every day, you begin to forget about it. But when you come back to it, there is something strange that keeps you from leaving again. That's exactly what happened."

"It's not the place that keeps you from leaving, it's the things that happen and the people who live there. Like a relationship as profound as father and daughter, or sometimes a promise made to someone."

Erica gazed into his face, not moving an inch. There was a divine exchange between them which glinted in silence.

Jeff stole away his eyes before their affection could escalate beyond contain. "You shouldn't have waited, Erica. You didn't know I was going to come back."

"I placed my bets on fate just this once. Yes, it lasted a bit longer than I expected, but I never lost my faith in you."

"I'm sorry for what I caused." He failed to hold that gaze any longer.

"Don't apologize for things you're not at fault. I caused all of this, I should be the one apologizing for your forgiveness. But I'm happy all of this happened. You're a changed man now. You've changed your life and given everyone who thought you couldn't do anything a lot to regret."

Jeff jeered at the remark, "changed? The things you all have presumed about me and my work are the farthest from truth. I was a weak man then, and I'm just the same now. There isn't much that I have accomplished in New York, it's all lies." Jeff had an intimation of honesty in his cracking voice.

Erica listened intently.

"I've been blaming this town all my life for keeping me here. Not giving anybody any opportunity to become someone, but now I wish I had never left. It is not the town or family that chains a man, it is his own capabilities that cage him. I was a coward to blame others all along and I get that now. It wasn't easy to survive out there." Jeff began trembling with rage and diffidence. A darker shade of hysteria began crawling into him.

"The people there are so skilled at everything and I kept falling behind against that rapid pace of city living at every level. It seemed that I had no place being there. People gallop in their given professions there and I lost every race I tried to run. It took so much away from me until I had just my soul to sell. And I did that too. I sold my dreams to survive. To put bread on my table by night and shelter over my head, I gave away my dreams for money.

"What?" she showed her earnest concern.

"I sold my stories. The publishers, much to my disappointment or yours, were not waiting with a contract unfolded on their desks and a pen in their hands when I visited their offices one after another. Almost fifty to give you an approximate of how many doors I knocked. Took up odd jobs seven days a week, two shifts a day, construction mostly, but it wasn't the hard work that broke me down. It was pure rejection. The work that you loved and this town adored, returned back into my hands. Everywhere I went, I was simply incompetent. I didn't have a degree in writing, unlike other prospects, or much education and lacked presentable pitching skills, all of which somehow foreshadowed the flaws in my work without having them to turn a single page of the manuscript."

"You worked so hard to write them."

"I worked even harder to sell them. I found a buyer who was willing to give me a good amount in exchange for many of my works. I believe he had better reading skills than the publishers, so I agreed. The deal gave me a nice balance in the bank account, and I was asked to become a stranger to my own works, my own words. It became an addiction and I continued to bury myself deep in it until that same person referred me to a publisher. The funny thing was that most of the novels they had published in the past were my works, but bore a different name. Now I work with them, but with my own identity." Jeff took a sigh.

"I know I've ruined your expectations. The reality of the world outside is not what it seems from the window right next to your front door. I was warned, but not prepared. Dad was right, I wasn't meant for it. It proved to be too much for me. All I ever knew was family, parents and siblings and you. They never competed, you never criticized. I couldn't adjust in that world outside of my hometown and I hated myself for that. I hated myself. I felt my father winning over me, day by day, strangulating me with the truth of his words.

"It was not your fault."

Jeff rambled without heeding her voice. "I failed and everyone was right about me. I am a coward. I wasn't meant for anything. I would've been better if I just stuck a blade through--"

"Hey, look at me," Erica demanded, holding his face in her hands. "Stop, stop saying that. You are not a coward. It was my fault that I put that in your head. I said things that I shouldn't have. But you are not a coward."

He was shaken out of his hysteria.

"All that time we spent together, I thought I knew you the most. But it was in that moment before you left that I betrayed my own faith. You didn't fail, I did. It didn't occur to me until we parted and being away from you these five years, I couldn't stop thinking what went wrong. And then I realized..."

"Realized what?" Jeff acquired courage bit by bit.

"That you were the bravest man I've ever met. The kind of life you've lived could have stifled anyone to death, but you survived it. The way you went to a city you've never been before and you established yourself as a writer there, doesn't matter how long it took or how hard it was, you did. That city out there could break the strongest and the most powerful of people, but you persisted. You endured for more than five years all by yourself, without any single help from anyone. You came out to be a success in the end. You were ready to give up on your dreams for the ones you loved, just because they'd be left alone and you didn't want to leave them. That's not what failures or selfish do. I have no regret admitting that I was completely wrong in saying you were frightened. I know because I have that responsibility now. I know what it means. You were never a coward, not then and not now."

Jeff resisted an impulse to kiss her with great difficulty as she had expunged his self-doubts from his conscience.

She looked at him fervently, "I love you."

There was silence from his end. It became uncomfortable for Erica to wait for his answer and she grew restive.

"Jeff, I can't help it. I might not be the woman you want and this might not be what you're looking for in life, but you are all I can think about. And if this isn't what it's meant to be between us, then what kind of a relationship are we supposed to have? Why are we standing here together holding each other like nothing else matters to us anymore? Are you in love with someone else?" She implored for honesty.

"I do not love anyone else." Jeff answered most limpidly that made his intentions concrete.

"Then what's wrong? You said you're not leaving again, you don't love another woman. Then what is it? I have apologized for my mistakes, you want me to beg you for forgiveness again, I will. You want me to go down on my knees, I will. You need me to plead in front of other people, your family, my family, I'll do everything. But just once say that you love me." Tears coursed her cheeks.

"Erica, don't fall in love with me, please," he begged.

"I don't need your permission to love you." She was adamant as ever.

"I'm sorry, I can't do this." Jeff escaped her lurid glare.

"You're sorry? You're asking me to forgive you for something that I'm asking you to do. Forget about asking, I'm pleading you to love me. It's not that I haven't tried to forget you, but you are in my mind and my imagination like a bad memory that no matter what you do, you cannot erase. I love you, I love your heart, your spirit, your mind and everything about you. I don't know if you realize this, Jeff, but this is my life. As small as it seems, this is it. All I've inherited is that store and this is where I'm going to be until the end. The one thought, that you will come back, is what kept me alive so far. And because of that let me make one thing clear as crystal, my life and love began with you and it will end at you. I have never begged anyone for anything, but I am now. I can't talk about my life without the mention of you somewhere in the same line. It's you who must make a choice. I have been alone so far, am I going to be alone forever?" Erica stayed with a fiery, poignant stare that pierced his soul. "Five years I stayed away. But I came back, I made a promise and I kept it. Five years now you've been away, let's see what promises you make and let's see how you keep them." She shuffled away from him wiping her eyes with the back of her hand.

She had gotten about half a block ahead of Jeff on the deserted street when a pick-up truck rolled by and a man leaned out of the window.

"Hey, a wrong night and weather to be out and about, don't you think so?" he revealed a strand of grotesque teeth behind crooked lips.

Erica shot a glimpse at the sordid drunkard and quickened her steps. Jeff lagged close behind.

"Hey, listen. It's just three of us here. I'm sure it's nothing to fret about. Tell us how much you need, we have plenty." He brandished a wad of bills.

"Go away." She spurned the flagrant proposal with a shriek.

"Oh, come on now. We'll double it."

"See, looking at that bod in this dark, snowy night, I know you're looking for clients. What's wrong with us?" the second from the driver's end commented.

"Leave me alone, all of you."

"Yeah? What do you think you are, a princess? We'll treat you like one." The odious remarks were ceaseless.

"Hey! Get away from her!" Jeff finally intervened approaching the truck.

Erica was in tears by now as she rummaged her handbag for a tissue. Jeff arrived to her aid. She jerked his hand away.

The truck stopped and the three drunken men emerged from it. Two of them were prodigious and bearded, a stench of alcohol perceptible a mile away. The third one, a bit inferior in size, reached for a baseball bat from the truck and took a pugnacious stance.

"You talking to me, you punk?" the one with the bat threatened.

"Jeff, let's go." Erica recommended a retreat. Jeff was too enraged to listen.

The trio pounced at him and Jeff accepted the unfair challenge valiantly. One of the big guys charged at him with furled fists and a menacing intent. His veins just bulged under his skin and he was imbued in a hue of red caused by wild frenzy.

Jeff lunged at him and slammed a massive blow, crushing the side of his head, which was deadly enough to render him unconscious but saving him from a concussion. Shoved off his feet, he landed about eight feet away with a thud against snow-capped concrete. He never rose again for the duration of the battle.

The one with the bat quivered with reluctance. He coerced his next troop to combat. Jeff brought the duel to him and hurtled at the big man, smashing him against the metal of the truck.

The bat swung out of concealment at Jeff from behind in a surprise, unjust assault by the third. Jeff deftly parried. The bat landed a hard whack on the shoulder of the big man who was already on his knees, eventuating in another unconsciousness. The second guy collapsed, but before he could hit the ground, Jeff hoisted him up on his shoulders and loaded him in the trunk of the pick-up.

The man with the bat watched in a crippling trauma.

Jeff hauled the first giant from the sidewalk and piled him upon his twin in the truck. He now stood against the remainder of the company who in turn was lonesome, beaded with sweat and regret.

"They'd need a driver to take them home," Jeff grumbled.

He simply shook his head, abandoned his bat in servility and stumbled to the truck, clambered into the driver's seat and sped off.

Jeff wiped his brow of some sweat and brushed off the snow on his shoulders. He coughed acutely but as it abated, he turned and looked at Erica who stood motionless in awe, impressed by the obtrusive display of strength but also with a little painful concern for the grave sounds she had heard from his enfeebled or rather restricted respiration.

"We're already drawing in crowds from the city," Jeff commented restoring strength into his breaths and his stature again.

"That wasn't very wise. You might want to impress me with your brute strength some other day. What if they had a gun?" Erica was indignant again.

"I'm sorry."

"Next time you breathe, you might want to apologize for that too."

"If it makes you upset, I won't breathe."

"Ahh, it is a disaster talking to you." Erica stormed ahead shaking her head in vexation. "Please don't come after me."

"We live twenty feet apart, I have to."

"God..." Erica stomped her way down the street.

Jeff smiled roguishly and followed.

Jeff entered the house and found Nancy and Maggie braying at some funny talk in the living room. Their laughter waned as Jeff stood in the doorway.

"Hey, we were waiting here since ten, what took you so long? Everyone went to bed except us." Maggie said casually.

"I think we were supposed to drive together? Ring a bell?" Jeff was incensed.

"Oh, someone seems to be in a ringing mood tonight. Out of all the different kinds of bells, which ones are we supposed to hear?" Maggie jested.

"I'll take a wild guess; wedding bells?" Nancy joined the fun.

"Is that so?"

Jeff opened his mouth to speak a few angry words, but their gesture had eased his anger a bit. "We had to walk for three miles in the middle of the night in the snow."

"You made it home just fine. Besides, a nice evening walk is always recommended for good health."

"How about an evening brawl?"

"A brawl? Did you get hurt?"

"Nah, I'm fine. Nothing to fret about. Just a passing draft of insolence."

"I'm really sorry, Jeff. But I knew you couldn't blame me for leaving seeing how exhausted I was. My back is still minced meat from all that work you made me do."

"Maggie, this was the only car we had."

"I know." Maggie left the couch and made for the kitchen, Nancy followed suit.

"And I precisely remember Erica telling you that her truck broke down."

"I absolutely remember that too."

"Then what happened?" Jeff demanded.

"What more could I ask for?" Maggie winked at Nancy and she responded identically. Both laughed and filled their plates with some dinner.

Jeff stood nodding in disbelief.

# Chapter Twenty-Seven

It was a dawn to a day that was eagerly yet secretly awaited by a handful of Saunderhurst family members, but immensely anticipated by the rest of the town. Maggie had forced the family out of their beds and slumber, from the elders to the youngest, and urged them into their winter covers to board the transport. Jeff and Nancy had already departed the house and were missing this chaotic disarray. The family had dissented at first, but the intimidation was too great from the tyrant who was designated the duty of bringing the whole family to the bookstore and the most remarkable surprise of their lives.

"But Maggie, I have to get things in line for the feast. I have to go for groceries, have to gather so much stuff for supper." Lena implored to be left out of this excursion.

"We can do all of that when we return, mom. I'm not taking you out for the whole day. It's just a couple of hours, maybe less."

"But where are we going?" Martin quested for an answer.

"That is a surprise. Now go and get yourselves in your jackets. Now."

The parents had no protest against the command. They swiftly wrapped their cloaks and headed after her out to the cars.

"Do I have to come, really? I can't think of one thing I'm useful for." Edward had yet to be convinced.

"It is a family thing, Edward. I want you to be a part of it." Maggie requested.

"I hope I'm not getting into something tedious here."

"You're not. It's never boring with the family. Now get in there."

Maggie had compelled everyone out of the house and the three cars were packed. The convoy departed.

The bookstore had caused mayhem in the marketplace as the streets were teeming with people that poured in from all ends of the town. Vehicles congested the roads and parking spaces to a point where enthusiasts simply parked wherever they found an opening. It was an arrant disorder in sight and the sheriff with his deputies just watched in silence and smiles.

Thousands of spectators had arrived to meet their favorite author and cluttered outside the store in queue waiting their chance to shake hands with him. The natives of the town just watched in profound bewilderment, some discontented to witness such a multitude of strangers in their conservative town.

"You sure we needn't be worried about this, sheriff?" an old man had approached the law for encouragement. "It sure looks a lot like a rebellion."

"Everything is under control. You just go home and take your sleeping pills." The sheriff answered coolly.

"I just want to make sure." The old man was unhappy with the response.

"The man requested permission for this event, don't be too worried."

"Oh, I hope I find my roof in place when I wake up tomorrow."

"You don't worry about your roof, grandpa. Just lock your wig safely." The young deputy mocked the old man with a chuckle, much to the displeasure of his senior.

"I'm sorry," the deputy quickly apologized.

The Saunderhurst convoy arrived and had to park about a block away due to unavailability of space any further. The family exited the cars and observed the horde with a hint of shock and a lot of perplexity.

"What is going on here?" Martin was astonished.

"You'll see, let's get in. Hold hands. Helen, Ron come with me." Maggie led them jostling into the crowd.

Drake Jarick sat behind the desk with a welcoming smile, quite incongruous to his face, signing the copies for the customers one by one. Jeff stood next to him like a submissive assistant holding the book Drake was there to sign, called 'All I want for Christmas is Christmas.' Nancy manned the counter and the register and perfected her counting skills with ceaseless transactions.

"Morning, how's the little one?" Drake greeted a mother and her young daughter who handed the book to him.

"Good mornin', Mr. Jarick. It is an honor to meet you." The mother was delighted.

"The honor has to be mine as I believe she is the youngest reader I've signed for so far." Drake smiled and autographed the book. "What's her name?"

"Juliana." The mother answered.

Drake indited a cute message addressed to Juliana -- Dear Juliana, a reader in the making. Love, Drake Jarick.

"Thank you, sir, I appreciate it so much." The mother took her daughter along.

"Don't forget to check out the collection back there. They have some first editions of many great fairy tales. Not a bad start to get her into reading." Drake advertised the store a little.

"Yes, Mr. Jarick. Thank you." The woman took her little one to the back of the store and scanned for an appropriate beginning for her.

Jeff glimpsed Drake with striking gratitude in his eyes. Drake was quick to grasp the tacit gesture and nodded.

"What's your name, sir?" Drake started with another fan.

"Howard Kallis."

"Mr. Kallis," Drake began signing the book for him.

"I'm a big fan of yours. I have read every book you've ever written. From the times you wrote the journals to the latest one. I even have a collection of your first editions." Howard was hysterical.

"It is an honor to have a reader like you, sir. I mean it. Run your fingers around some other first editions back there. You'll find some more nice reads. Good day."

Howard saluted the writer and went off further inside the store shuffling the shelves.

Martin and Dave had finally reached the threshold and peered inside. Jeff signaled them to enter and just when they did, he went over and brought them to the desk.

"Mr. Jarick. These are the owners of the store. Martin Saunderhurst and Dave Saunderhurst."

Drake arose and shook their hands. "It's a pleasure to meet you both."

"The pleasure is ours, sir." Dave greeted him cordially.

A photographer jostled through and clicked the moment capturing it in a flash.

"Is this really our store?" Martin wondered.

"It sure is, sir." Drake spoke with utmost geniality. "It's just been resuscitated. And let me tell you one thing, this renaissance will be remembered for a long time."

"Come'on dad, we should allow him to continue." Jeff took Martin behind the counter and gave him a chair.

Drake took his seat again and welcomed another young reader. "Hey, pretty lady, what's your name?"

"Rebecca. I'm such a big fan. I read your last book six times."

"Six? Well, then you've read it more than I have. I believe you will not be disappointed with this one either."

"You are amazing, Mr. Jarick," Rebecca added.

"Thanks, Rebecca. I will keep trying to entertain you and the rest of my readers. Check out the store, it's really vast." Drake shook hands with her and sent her off.

After almost four hours of grating a pen on the first page of his hardcover, Drake had finally completed the event and stretched his dulled limbs devouring the seventh cup of coffee. The crowd had lessened outside the store as the shadows slanted preparing to greet the twilight, but some avid followers, indifferent to their fatigue and hunger, still lingered to fill their sight with his presence. The store had been locked while Drake prepared for another enervating journey on which he was about to embark.

"I'd rather suggest you stay the night, sir." Jeff approached with Jarick's topcoat helping him into it. "It's been a demanding day so far."

"That demanding day will soon transmute into a daunting night if I don't make it back to my wife and kids in time." Drake hinted on his necessity at home.

"The tickets are right here, sir. The flight departs at six thirty."

"We have enough time to make it to the airport. Shall we leave?"

"Whenever you're ready, sir."

Drake led the way sauntering out of the store and waving to his cheering fans and boarding the limousine. Jeff followed inside the vehicle and they drove off.

The crowd began to disperse while Martin marveled at the hours of insanity he had just witnessed. Dave wrapped his arm around his father and delighted in his joy.

"You see that, dad? That's our boy in a couple of years. Jeff's going to be this famous very soon."

"He already is. He has done the unthinkable. I'm beyond proud of him." Martin displayed tears of elation.

"We all are." Dave pacified his whimpering father by rubbing his arms.

"I'm so proud of my son." Martin promulgated overcome by emotions.

Maggie, Dave, Lena and Linda all came together in abating his surging emotions.

"And look at this amount of dough we have here." Nancy held up two thick bundles of cash that elicited immense laughter from everyone.

"It's been a successful day, planned by a successful man." Maggie commented ingenuously.

Jeff tipped an usher who assisted with the luggage and presented Drake's passport along with the ticket at the checkpoint to the attendant.

"Well, Jeff Saunderhurst, it is done and dusted. I believe my services were to your expectations." Drake alighted from the limousine and joined him by the departure gate.

"Well beyond expectations, sir. And it isn't a service, it's a favor."

"Stop calling me sir. We are men of the same profession. The matter of renown is merely ephemeral. This celebrity was someone else's yesterday, it's mine now, and it could be yours tomorrow. We just await its moment of betrayal."

"Mr. Jarick, you are most kind." Jeff offered him an envelope.

Drake took it with a frown and without opening it, he tore it to pieces.

"That was the payment, Mr. Jarick." Jeff was startled.

"Payments are for services, favors require gratitude. Doesn't it please you to find people living in humble towns, diminutive dreams and modest homes, and yet so content with their lives? And we work our hair off our heads, day and night and still remain in such contest to finish first just to return home with no satisfaction in our mind." He contemplated as if recollecting some fond memo ries from his past. "My beginnings were no different. I once lived in a small town. My father was a florist, we had a store, mother was a seamstress. The event that people despised, we used to look forward to it. Funerals. Used to be our profitable days, apart from that there weren't many customers. People grew their own gardens in that age. Impoverished for a majority of my early years, but when I reached the stage where I could make my own decisions, I resolved to transform my family's living forever. Seventeen years later I did, only I had a new family by then, the old folks were.... You have attained the greatest success by showing you parents this day. And somehow I believe by making some old strangers happy, I've somehow managed to please my folks as well. Thank you for doing me that favor."

Jeff clasped his hand for a shake. "Thank you... sir."

After a reminiscent smile and a final farewell, Drake strode into the stream of travelers with the same conceited pride with which he arrived. The only change was a subtle smile that replaced the once implacable scowl.

Jeff headed back to the limousine and got into the passenger side. "Hello, Michael."

Michael, now a good acquaintance of Jeff, motioned him to buckle up. "You're supposed to be in the back, you know? It's a hired vehicle still."

"The vehicle is the only thing that's hired." Jeff retorted incisively.

"Man, it's so difficult to beat you with words, ain't it?" Michael gently slammed the steering wheel.

"It's not the words, but the meaning behind them. Try it next time." Jeff reclined on the seat, then sat up again. "Tell me how much do I owe you?"

"I'm not giving you a number again because I know you'll double it. So, whatever they quoted you at the car place. That's all I'm takin'."

"No, you're not. You spent two days here, you put in your time and effort, you're not leaving without a pay." Jeff had objected to another free service.

"I can walk empty-handed from here and still not be disappointed."

Jeff spoke after an interval. "There, I just lost."

Mr. Johnson lay quietly amidst a clutter of modern medical equipment as the cardiac monitors beeped intermittently in a white, dreadful room. A nurse had just visited to examine the readings and the patient executing a routine, periodic check-up. Erica waited by the doorway as the task was carried out. She had an obvious sense of foreboding descending into her with every passing hour, but there was certain fortitude in her as well that guided her mind away from perturbation.

In five years of Jeff's absence, the town had only improved in one aspect and that was the transformation of the small infirmary to an upgraded medical facility which was almost as imposing and enhanced as any hospital of the city. The edifice was renovated and developed into a five-floor facility that was complete with an ICU ward, emergency ward, three floors for patient wards and a waiting room.

The nurse had left after a commiserating look at Erica who now stepped back to her father's bed and sat down on a stool. She flattened the creased sheet to an impeccable smooth.

"Erica?" Maggie had entered the ward with Jeff right behind her.

Both were increasingly solicitous, but their fear subdued as they watched the monitors showing graphs of hope. Erica looked behind and arose. Maggie came over and embraced her, but Erica's frown was aimed at Jeff.

"What happened?" Maggie questioned with deepening concern.

They had come into the waiting room and Jeff brought the women a drink of water each from the water fountain.

"When I got home last night, he was well asleep. He likes his spot on the couch, so I let him stay there. It was very early in the morning when I heard him coughing. I came straight down, it was about six. He was on the floor and was having difficulty breathing. I tried asking him the problem, but he couldn't properly speak. So, I brought him here." She wiped the corners of her mouth after taking a swig from the paper cup.

"What did the doctors say?" Maggie queried.

"Severe tracheal inflammation to start with, but that's now what they are concerned about. He's recovered from tracheitis before. They have found traces of flu virus in his blood. If it is not detained it could cause some serious problems for him. Viral pneumonia is what they fear. It could be... fatal. He's going to stay here for a while now. There must be something wrong with the way I took care of him. I mean I tried to keep him warm all the time, feed him right and regularly."

"There is nothing wrong with your care, Erica." Maggie emboldened her.

"I just don't want him to leave me, he's all I have." Her eyes were swimming in tears.

Jeff and Maggie brooded over her tribulations wordlessly.

"But we don't have to reach our conclusions. He might get well this once for me." Erica sniveled and illumined with a smile. "How did you guys know?"

"We went to your house just an hour ago. It was locked which is hardly the case with Mr. Johnson always being there. Jeff felt there was something wrong. We came right to the hospital."

"You felt?" Erica arched her tone contemptuously. "Good to know you have some feelings left."

There was a prolonged stare between the two, while Erica glared lividly, Jeff tried to mollify her wrath with some warmth exuding from his gaze. Maggie retreated from interference.

"How was the event, Maggie? We worked hard for it, I'd like to know." Erica averted her glare from Jeff.

"It was wonderful. I wish you met or even saw Drake. He is a really nice man. There were so many people there, like a thousand. Half of our books were sold, more than half actually. We missed you."

"I'm sure *you* did." Erica rejoined, a trenchant remark directed toward Jeff again.

"Why didn't you call us?" Jeff finally spoke. "It doesn't matter how early it was, you knew one of us would come. All you needed to do was make a phone call, or just yell."

"I don't think you would have heard me, Jeff. Sometimes our voices are lost traveling the shortest distances."

"Any one of us would have come."

"Any one of you? I'm sorry I forgot. Next time I need that favor I'll ring the bell." Erica said derisively.

"Maggie, why don't you go and wait in the car?" Jeff asked her to leave.

Maggie swiftly traced her steps to the door while Erica sat sulking in the chair.

"Why don't you leave with her, I don't need anyone here. I can take care of my father myself. Thanks for your concern and visiting. I'm sure he'll love to hear that you visited once he's conscious again." Erica stormed away from him.

Jeff clasped her wrist and drew her back toward him. He gazed into her seething eyes and attempted to alleviate her frustrations.

She allowed him a moment, but realizing this tacit exchange was headed nowhere close to her desired destination, she flipped.

"Stay away from me. You think I'm going to forget about everything and romp around no matter how badly you treat me? You've been away for quite a long time, haven't you? You're essentially a stranger to me, so go back, or I don't care where you stay. You're just as good as gone to me. I hate you. I hate you like I've hated no one else in my life. I thought my loathing had peaked when you were gone all these years and I cursed you for leaving me. But that comes nowhere close to the hatred you've burned inside of me now. So, the next time you try to touch me or so much as come close to me, you'll find your name in the police records for the first time and I'll derive immense pleasure from corroborating that act of crime."

Erica wrenched her arm away and darted out of the waiting room. Jeff stood in grievous silence mingled with helplessness and remorse.

# Chapter Twenty-Eight

The church bells sounded at a rather odd hour of the evening and resonated throughout the town, mild at distance but deafening in vicinity, faint in some ears while shrill in others, but welcome nonetheless. The townsfolk sat prepared to answer the calling an hour after the drowning of daylight, to gather in the commodious church grounds at the behest of their deacon.

Crowds poured from all ends and assembled around a monolithic bonfire that could keep the farthest circle of attendees warm. The Saunderhurst family was a part of that assemblage as Father Thomas, who had aged in his appearance since last Jeff had a dealing with him, and his esteemed deacon, Solomon, welcomed the congregation gleefully, handing them each a wrapped, homemade sandwich and a cup of coffee.

All the neighbors greeted each other cordially as there was hardly a family that didn't recognize one another. Conversations ensued that ranged from weather forecasts to the worldly issues and the discussions were bilateral. There was a sonorous hum in the air that only grew as more people added to the gathering.

Erica joined the convocation and moved to the front warming herself with some heat blazing from the bonfire. Jeff shared a glimpse, which was made cursory as she averted her incensed eyes to a more pleasant sight. Maggie and Lena approached her with a comforting chat which brought a diminutive smile to her face. Jeff couldn't surmise what was said because of the incessant rumbling of muffled conversations, but he delighted in the fact that she had smiled.

"Jeff?" a voice called out to him and Jeff flipped to see a friendly man sauntering toward him.

"Henry!" Jeff hugged him and parted with roiling appreciation for his assistance. "You don't know how thankful I am for what you did. That was an immense favor. I couldn't repay even if I tried."

"There are no favors in friendship. What am I here for if I can't even take care of a little business once in a while? Here," Henry introduced his companion who was holding a one-year-old in her arms, "my wife. I'm sure you remember her."

"Jessica?" Jeff was surprised to find Henry labeling her his spouse. "When did you two get married?"

Jessica stood a little above five feet with her petite frame but a genial smile and striking blue eyes.

"Been four years. I dropped you an invite personally, but found out you were..." Henry refrained from bringing up the past.

"Oh, look at this little one here, a girl?" Jeff grazed the baby's cheek with his thumb.

"Yes," Jessica said softly. "The older one is at home with her nana."

"Wow. I can understand this wonder right here, but what the hell did you see in this chump to marry him?" Jeff nudged Henry teasingly.

"Everything." Jessica's answer was absolute as the couple shared an intimate glimpse.

"Most importantly a heart of gold," Jeff remarked and patted his friend's shoulder. "What's her name?"

"Sarah."

Jeff leaned and pecked her forehead. "God bless you, Sarah."

The church bells repeated again and the audience reverted their attention toward their parish leaders. Father Thomas initiated the service with a short prayer and an expression of gratitude.

"Thirty-seven years I have given to the service of this church and its people. Thirty-seven Christmases, Easters and New Years, I have celebrated amongst you as a part of your family and rejoiced in those celebrations. But there comes a time in all our lives when we must delegate the duties, the responsibilities we've managed so far, to our next generation that waits to establish itself in the society just as once we were handed the obligation of service to people and God. I see that Mr. Riley has created for himself quite a following amongst us, which is a commendable endeavor. It somehow reflects in my reckoning that my congregation is in altruistic and compassionate hands after my retirement."

A sigh was released in unison with some suppressed words of heartache.

The pastor persisted, "yes, it's been quite long and my decrepit days are imminent." He took a meditative pause. "Youth answers youth. I believe that's what has driven most of the young ones out here tonight. They have found in him the religious vanguard of which they would become a part and follow. It is a fact quite evident to all of us. So, I would like to welcome Solomon Riley to administer this gathering to a promising future and extract such benevolence out of this youth that it may become a legacy to be passed on to our coming generations."

The crowd invited Solomon and this introduction with a cheering applause. Father Thomas nodded to all of them and allowed his deacon to assume his rank.

"Thank you, pastor. It is an honor to be a pupil of such a steadfast minister, and I say that with utmost sincerity. And thank you all for your presence here. I must appreciate it or I wouldn't find many next year."

A wave of laughter surged across the gathering.

"That was an honest jest, but I really do appreciate all of you taking that time out of your busy Christmas schedule and coming out here. If it were a simple work day, I wouldn't have valued it so much. But we all know how grueling Christmas Eve can be and how unremitting the tasks hours before the big day. This town is a small town. I have seen that for the past years I've been here. I tried this last time and managed about fifty people to answer my humble request to gather here. I see many people renewing that oath of fellowship this year again, and almost double that number of new faces. I am glad to observe and bring that change. Pastor has brought quite a demanding or rather daunting issue to my attention that has now, after his introduction, transformed into a challenge, and I am willing to accept it. The youth of our world has drifted away from religion, from faith, from a fundamental thing known as trust. Whether it is a demerit of the church, or their upbringing stemming from incapacitated families or perhaps the educational system, that is one debatable discourse I'm inclined to avoid at the moment, but there must be a problem. To have no faith is to have no life. And I do not mean to insinuate that faith in Christ is the only way of life, but faith in good, in good deeds, in good love, in good companionship, that will lead to eternal life through the promise of Christ. I want to tell you all something." Solomon took a swig from his coffee to warm his throat.

The congregation rejuvenated with a bite and a sip as well.

"It was a silent night, yet a holy night. Tonight is a silent night. The winds are calm, the temperature is alarmingly cold, a mild nip of frost on our cheeks and noses. But the peace of that night was not in its silence or the cold, it was in the holiness that descended from heaven. Nature has made tonight a silent night again, but just as that night was made holy by the presence of Christ, can this night be made holy with his presence once again? The question we must ask ourselves is whether it is necessary for Him to be amidst us in a physical form? Isn't His Spirit ample that dwells within all of us? Peace be with you, he said and showered his grace upon many of his followers. Isn't holiness in that heavenly peace that makes this world a habitable place? The nature's running its course, but we as humans are falling behind. It is a silent night already, but to make it a holy night, we need to act. To make this a holy night, we must forget our differences, our grudges, our curses, our vengeance, our hatred-"

Jeff glinted at Erica and she held his gaze for a long moment with lambent flame in her eyes.

Solomon continued, "to make it holy like it once was, we must feel the presence of His word within us and fulfill our promise to him. That shall bring us the heavenly peace in which we all shall sleep tonight. The greatest commandment ever given by Him, love one another. And that love will redeem us. So, all our fears, our worries, our dilemmas, our loneliness, we shall shun from our lives tonight and celebrate a new birth tomorrow. With the coming millennium, let's abandon the loneliness of one and strengthen it with another one of its kind into a unity of two. It arrives in a week, one nine nine eight, one nine nine nine, two thousand. Even time multiplies itself that is why it never ceases to exist. Come together in love with your parents, your siblings, your spouse, your children, your friends and your community. Learn to love, and in that love, you shall know forgiveness, humility, kindness, and compassion. Silent night, holy night. Let us sleep tonight in that heavenly peace by performing our promised deeds."

The choir of twenty young singers started to hum the mellisonant hymn slowly and sweetly.

"Our town consists just two hundred and seventy souls out of which some are not with us because of their old, or in some cases, their young age. Both requiring an aid of a youth. So, my plea is to the able adults among us. We must come forward to take care of both, the young and the old. And not just our families but our neighbors, our friends. I would request the youth of our congregation to come forward and light their candles as an oath to make this night a holy night and all nights and days that follow such. And in that vow of love, we shall march to the hospital and vitalize our afflicted members with zeal and empathy. I would yet again ask for those too frail to make this ten block journey to stay behind with our pastor and treat our young ones with a small incentive from the church to keep them coming, gifts from Santa Claus which were just delivered an hour ago for all who have been extremely nice to their classmates all year."

Children leapt ebulliently at the mention of presents.

Solomon lighted his candle and passed the flame to the gathering behind. He led the group of approximately seventy people down the street with flickering wick of hope and peace in their grasp.

Erica was in the front of the horde as Maggie matched her strides to provide her the essential courage she needed. Nancy and Jeff trailed in the rear.

The crowd hummed the hymn incessantly as they marched forward, while some who had recently dealt with or expected an impending loss, pressed their eyes close for a miracle and murmured a prayer. Erica had just added herself to that tally of precants.

# Chapter Twenty-Nine

There was a crackle of step ladders around the Saunderhurst residence as the men of the house were nearing completion of the task commonly known as the lighting on Christmas Eve. There were snapping sounds of heavy duty staplers and nail guns as countless strands with infinite light bulbs were hung securely across the roof and the porch, even the hedges and the oak tree were wrapped in luminance. Jeff, Edward, Dave and James all participated in the family event while Martin and Lena watched the work in progress. Maggie and Gloria emerged with a platter filled with steaming cups of hot chocolate and distributed the much needed warmth in the cold night. Nancy had carried on humming the tune of the hymn she had incorporated into her soul from the earlier occurrence that had moved and awakened her immensely. She snuggled close against Linda and rested her head on her shoulder while she jo ined in buzzing the tune with her giving it the words.

"I'm sorry, mom." Nancy whispered an apology that was audible only to Linda's ears.

"Sorry for what?" Linda clenched her tighter.

"That's exactly what I want to learn how to do, the way you do it."

"What? Holding you like this?" Linda glimpsed into her eyes with a smile.

"No, forgiveness. You forget things like they never happened." Nancy was in awe of her mother's ability.

"It's one of the perks of being a parent. You'll learn it well enough when your time comes."

"Even when I hurt you?"

"Did you? When was that?"

They both laughed as Nancy nodded in amazement. Linda rubbed her arm and kissed her forehead.

Edward went on around once and confirmed the setup of the lights. The group of laboring men gathered and concluded their toil.

"All right, everyone we're ready with the lights." Edward went to the final connection of the extension cords and stepped up to plug it in.

The family convened in the front of their house and waited. The cord was attached the house lit up like a Christmas tree. The family applauded.

"Now that's a work well done." James commented at the glimmering house.

Linda inched closer to Jeff and held his hand. "Thank you, Jeff."

Jeff creased his brows with incertitude, "for this?"

"You are very well aware of what I mean."

Jeff smiled, "probably."

"And I'm sorry as well. Both of us said things that night that were unwarranted. Nancy told us everything. Thank you for bringing her back to us."

"All of us." Jeff corrected her.

"Yes, all of us."

Jeff squeezed her hand in return and glanced at the house.

"It is so beautiful." Lena approached hugging Jeff and Linda. "Call everyone in for dinner. I'll prepare the table."

It was a quick dinner for the young ones as all three were determined to hear a Christmas story before the night was over and were fidgeting from the living to the dining, compelling the adults to shorten their prosaic conversations around the table and carry on to the essential part of Christmas Eve. But the tedious adult conversations were far from being encapsulated. Finally, as the supper was completed and the children got their one true wish for the night.

Martin was dragged into the living room and placed on a couch with a children's storybook forced into his hands and was cemented in that position by three ardent listeners who banked around with a single intention. The rest of the family came and went with their nightcaps, but the story somehow awakened the six-year-old in all of them and Martin found all of the Saunderhurst family in the room listening intently after a while of wandering.

"And then came the night of Christmas Eve, the boy had yet, in his aching heart, to believe. That Father Christmas was a truth and not a myth, a lie for many years he'd slept with. It was dark and stormy, the rain poured outside. The boy cringed in his bed, in his misery, he cried. In his sobs and an endless stream of sorrow, he paved a gloomy path for a faithless tomorrow. But out of the dark appeared a hand of hope. It was gloved in white, guiding him to cope."

Martin's proficiency at rhyming beguiled even the sturdiest hearts to melt. Maggie and Edward stood by the fireplace watching their children engrossed by the storytelling. Dave smiled at Charlie who was equally enthralled.

"A bearded man emerged and found some trails of tears, realizing his mistake, the boy had been missed for years. And when the soft voice cried asking him the reason. Why he never visited until this stormy season? The man took the boy in his cold hands and showed him a glimpse of all his plans. My name is Santa Claus, he said, and tonight I take a vow, I may have forgotten you, but I shall never leave you now. I ask you for forgiveness, permit me a gift of Christmas. For I have given gifts yet never received any, but this forgiveness shall mean, for me more than many. The child smiled, kissed him the night goodbye, and went to sleep again with no more tears in his eye. For until he became a man, he found a gift by his bed. Every Christmas Eve, to which he looked ahead. A visit from the bearded man was never then skipped, and his heart, of the faith he gained, was never ever stripped. End of the story." Martin finished to an applause from everyone in the room, the children were exhilarated.

"That was truly wonderful, dad." Maggie kissed her father.

"Thank you, everyone. I guess we shall all get to our own beds for Santa Claus to leave some gifts under the tree? We don't want to stay awake and make him skip the house, do we?"

The children acquiesced to their grandfather's proposal and darted upstairs to their beds. The family dispersed along with that fading into their rooms.

Jeff stayed at the window gazing at the neighboring house and the dark dolor that engulfed it entirely.

"How is her father?" Lena whispered following his line of sight.

"He's doing well. Probably a few more days in the hospital." Jeff answered without disrupting his contemplation.

"It is sad to see her all alone like that on Christmas."

Jeff looked into his mother's eyes and gasped the bidding.

Erica nestled silently between the folds of her blanket, right upon the couch in the living room with a flaring hearth that coruscated a blend of crimson and gold across her face as well as the walls. She ruminated in her plaintiveness, eyes wide with trepidation and stationary at the flames. A doorbell riveted her out of a trance and propelled her to answer after the fourth ring. She went and unlocked the door finding Jeff at the threshold.

"Yes?" she asked impassively.

"Hey." Jeff took a moment to read her eyes and her sorrow beyond them. "I brought some food."

"I ate," she was concise this time.

"I knew you were not going to stop by or have time to prepare something, so I decided to drop--."

"I did prepare something that was suitable enough for this festive eve. I have my supper once and I prefer not to overburden myself with excess at night."

Jeff's eyes implored her to forgive him. "Can I come in?"

Erica remained wordless and after a long consideration, opened the door fully. Jeff entered.

He found himself in the warm living room as Erica collected the bag from his hand and took it inside the kitchen. He warmed himself by the fireplace and observed the pictures upon the mantle. He found himself about ten years of age in one of them with Maggie and Erica all hustled in a playful exchange of water balloons. A smile coursed his face.

"Thanks for your concern, but you don't have to stay. There hasn't been a loss in this family… yet." Erica returned from the kitchen and wrapped herself in the blanket again, staring into the fire.

Jeff turned to the couch and their eyes met. "Please don't say that." He alighted slowly and warily. "How is he?"

"Same as yesterday."

A long pause ensued after the phlegmatic response.

"That picture there, your dad took it, didn't he? If I can remember correctly, he had the first camera in the entire town. People used to gather out there for him to take their pictures once in a while. We were too little back then." Jeff chuckled softly, "I haven't been to your house in years. I can't even remember the last time I was here." Jeff tried to manipulate the conversation toward a more genial junction.

"Nine years, I precisely remember. You never liked it in here."

"I never said that."

"You didn't need to. Nine years are enough to indicate that."

"I love this place! It's warm, it's large and spacious, and it's next to my own house. I could never dislike it."

Jeff gestured toward the dearth of furnishing in the room. It was widely capacious with just a couch, a recliner, a coffee table, and a cabinet in the corner.

"You forgot one splendid feature about it. It's at a dead end. I guess that's the reason you never peeked in here. People who accidentally reach here make a u-turn and go back." Her caustic rejoinder sparked a bit of vehemence in Jeff, but he contained it.

He knelt by her and attempted to take her hand in his. She flicked her hand away into a fist and then unfurled in dismissal.

"Stop doing this, Erica. Please, I'm begging you."

"You are? Now you know how it feels to beg someone for something? I genuinely wish you knew what it feels like to wait for someone and years later realize that he was never yours to begin with. The way that emotion crushes you within, I just hope you get to live it some day. The day someone breaks your heart, you will understand how it could rattle your soul, your very existence."

"It's happening to me right now."

"Oh no, this is nothing. You don't get the true feelings unless it's someone you really love. I thought you did, but now I know you don't."

Jeff closed his eyes in utter despair and couldn't conjure the words to counter her belief.

"If there's nothing more to be delivered, you may leave. I guess the pain and the food are enough for tonight."

Jeff tarried in the room just another moment and then plodded to the door.

"And Jeff, it's better that we don't see each other anymore. The more we meet the more I'll hate. So please, help me forget this."

Jeff opened the door and left the house. Erica was lurid with rage and exploded into tears burying herself in the blanket and trying to weep herself to sleep.

A moment passed and a sudden burst of flashing lights penetrated through the thick draperies on the front window. The red and green intermittent flickers illumined the living room, compelling Erica out of her woe to investigate the source.

The main door opened ajar. Erica peered and tardily stepped out on the porch sighting a couple of strands wrapped around the columns and handrails of her front porch. Jeff still lingered, reaching for the beam in the center of the roof and securing a star with strings at the entrance. He plugged the star into the strand of lights on the left and the star lit up in white luminance that glimmered from afar in the misty night.

Ending his task, he stepped down the stairs and glimpsed once again at Erica. She was apathetic. Jeff continued shuffling back to his place, defeated and abject.

It was that one morning out of three hundred and sixty-five days in a calendar year when children defeated their parents quite soundly in waking up earlier and quite inspirited.

The impatient trio sounded their fervor, masked in a Christmas greeting, hurtling down the stairs awakening the neighborhood to the sudden cacophony. Ron, Helen, and Charlie raced into the living room and found mounds of glistering presents under the tree. They dove into the wrapped boxes and ripped apart those that were named to them.

The adults began dripping into the room one after another, diffusing throughout, some rubbing their itchy eyes and some their aching temples, but all covering their yawning mouths.

The gifts were unwrapped and appreciation and gratitude pervaded all across. Linda and James claimed their supremacy with the most expensive gifts of all, while the elderly hosts of the house relished the adoration of the young who animatedly treasured the load of toys. A lot of embraces and expressions of joy and acknowledgment were shared. A drink of coffee was distributed to all who toiled in the room, picking up after the kids as the pile of crumpled wrapping paper and discarded boxes was even greater.

The doorbell had been ringing for a while, but, in the dissonance of children chasing each other with their new toys and the tape player bruiting the day of revelry with carols and hymns, it was discounted. Lena finally answered the door and espied a welcome face at the threshold.

"Erica, what a nice surprise. Come in." Lena allowed her inside.

She kissed Lena and wished her a Happy Christmas.

"How is your father, Erica?"

"He gained consciousness today. I thought I should let you know." Erica was seen with a resplendent smile once again that was missing from her countenance since a very long time.

"That is wonderful news," Lena caressed her hair.

Maggie came and embraced Erica, both greeting each other.

"So, prayers have worked!" Maggie rejoiced.

"Yes, they have." Erica nodded gazing into her eyes. "Is Jeff here, I should tell him."

"He's in his room. Go, give him the news. I'm sure he'll be glad to hear about it." Maggie coerced her forward.

Erica waved to the rest of the family and reached the bedroom door. After two knocks and no answer, she went in.

Just as she entered, she caught a glimpse of Jeff swiftly turning away from her and the door, and scrambling back toward the bathroom.

"Oh, I didn't mean to startle you."

"Just a... just give me a minute," came a muffled answer from Jeff through his back. Never allowing her a glimpse of his face, he faded behind the squeaking bathroom door.

She scanned the grim room, which once belonged to Jeff's grandfather, as she had been inside it only a few times. The space that was still maintained with emptiness and just needful things in sight. The walls were old and reeked of a certain smell that was neither an odor nor an aroma, but rather human.

She waited for a moment before retrieving a small velvet case and stepped up to Jeff's bed, placing it under the pillow. A Christmas gift perhaps, that Santa furtively delivered last night. It probably encased a ring or a small ornament of some sort, but

Erica's brows converged in discontent and it was clearly not arising from the thought of Jeff's unacceptance of the gift.

She descried a blotch of dried stain on the pillow cover. It was still fresh but only recent. Just before she could scrutinize it further, the bathroom door opened and Jeff stepped out changing into a new shirt.

"I'm sorry I forgot to..." he had detected her sight fixated on the red spots on the pillow, "lock the door."

Their eyes met. Jeff stood flustered for a moment, then dissembled his disarray with a laughter.

"That was just a nosebleed. I'm all right now." Jeff wiped his face with a towel. "It happens sometimes."

"A nosebleed?" Erica was unsure whether to believe his lies or accept it as the truth, "since when?"

"It's a Christmas present from New York City. The weather there does this to many people."

She dismissed his words incredulously and began searching his eyes for the answers she sought.

"I haven't heard a sneeze out of you in winters in twenty-seven years. You expect me to believe this?"

"I've had my share."

"Don't make a stranger out of me, Jeff."

"What do you mean? I'm all right, this is quite common in some people, you know." Jeff banished her suspicion again.

"You know you can't see what's written in your eyes unless you're standing in front of a mirror because your heart reads your mind like no one else can. You are standing in front of that mirror right now."

"I'm… there's nothing to be told."

Erica raced into the bathroom and searched for the recently exchanged white shirt he had on when she entered. She rummaged a wastebasket and found it buried into concealment right at the bottom. She took it out and discovered those red, moist spots marking the whole front.

She went back into the room conveying it to him. "I came here first thing in the morning to forget everything and cut short our distances. I didn't know we would start off so far apart. What is this?" Erica's voice intimated her fear.

Jeff looked squarely into her face and deeply sighed. He gave up, "sit down."

She took the edge of the bed and waited restively.

Jeff reached for his luggage on the side and unzipped the pocket to retrieve a thick clasp envelope. He handed it to her.

Erica removed the contents from inside and recovered a medical report reading it from the top to bottom.

She drew in a breath that refused to be anywhere but stuck in her throat for a prolonged minute.

Jeff knelt by her side and brushed her arm in commiseration.

Erica cupped her mouth with her hands and in a grimace of loss, darted to the window.

"Oh God... oh God...." she was traumatized. Her eyes squeezed and tears streamed. She gasped and tried to reassemble her composure, but failed at every attempt. She began to sob.

Jeff filed the reports back in the envelope, hiding it in the luggage and dispatched the cover from his pillow taking it inside the bathroom. He came back and embraced Erica, alleviating her misery and shock.

"It's okay, all right. All right... easy." Jeff abated her fears.

Erica was too hysterical to be controlled and it took about ten minutes for her to be mollified of her intense emotions. Jeff took her out on the porch and away from the house toward the stalwart oak tree.

"The family cannot be told, not right now." Jeff held Erica's face in his hands and wiped the tears upon her cheeks.

She sniveled and curbed her whimpering, gaining her strength to speak through her shallow breaths, "no one knows?"

"Nope, and I intend to keep it that way at least until the end of the day. It's Christmas, I don't want to ruin it telling them about my... my departure. If I have to hide it, I will. It's just that it has started getting worse."

"It will be all right, I promise. We'll do everything we can." Erica tried reassuring him.

"It's quite too late for false hopes. But it doesn't hurt, right?"

"Don't talk like that, please." Erica helplessly reprimanded him.

"Listen to me, Erica. You have to stop crying, for me and the rest of the family. I don't want them to see you like this."

Erica tried containing her tears, but failed. "I hate you so much." She articulated her grievance.

"Even now?" Jeff pleaded.

"More now. You lied to me."

"I didn't lie to you. I would have told you, but I never had a chance. I'm sorry."

"You said you didn't love me." Her tearful eyes pierced his soul.

Jeff gazed right back, "and you believed it?"

"Never," Erica stated concretely and kissed him passionately, he allowed her to.

She pecked his face all over and they both chortled at the puerility of their love. "How could you do this to me? Did you think I would leave you if you had told me?"

"No Erica, that's not it. The reason was the exact opposite. If I had told you, you'd never leave. And that was a terrible thought."

"Did it work, the way you thought you could get rid of me?"

"Unfortunately, no."

"Then listen. With or without your troubles, I am not going anywhere. I am not leaving forever."

"That is what I feared. I guess the only thing that could separate us is my death."

She slapped him across the face, then regretted. "Don't talk to me about death, never in life. Not yours or anyone else's."

"Yes, warden Johnson," Jeff jested.

"We can still do something? We'll go to the best hospitals. There's enough time."

"I have been to the best hospitals. There's nothing that can be done."

"Don't you say that," Erica clung to him ardently. "Please don't say that. I won't let you go. Not again." She wept.

"I'm done here, it's almost time. But listen, I can't afford you to give up on me like this. I need you by my side to give me courage. I cannot face the remaining days of my life on my own. I... I am frightened. I'm just another human, I get scared too. Please, I need you. I need you to work with me until I tell the rest, okay? It'll be our little secret."

She simply nodded without looking up at him.

"Good girl." Jeff closed his eyes shut and the light of heaven filled the darkness.

The church bells sounded up to the peripheries of the town and the congregation assembled inside the chapel filling the pews from the first to the last. Erica had wheeled her father in and anchored him in the aisle by the space designated for the handicapped and took a seat nearby. Mr. Johnson had his oxygen supply clipped to his wheelchair as he slouched with infirmity but acknowledged the greetings directed at him with a blink of his eyes.

The Saunderhurst family had arrived and took up the entire pew in the center. Jeff perched with a clear view of Erica up ahead and they shared a glimpse. He appealed yet again for her to maintain her courage and not give away the news to his family out of ungoverned emotion. She had somehow agreed to it.

Solomon took the altar in profound silence and waited another minute to begin his sermon.

"Another year has just darted past. The millennium stands at the doorstep. Let's pick a resolution for the coming year. I shall strive to fare well this whole year and be financially stable by the end of it? Manage a savings of perhaps ten thousand, if I'm lucky, maybe more? Nah, the dependence is too external. How about something I have more control over? Lose some weight? Yeah, that's a good one. The flabby arms need to go, how about the love handles? Hmm, take about thirty minutes off from my busy schedule and I might just achieve the body goals. Well, some of us are more inclined towards something more concrete and tangible. Perhaps a material possession? Let's buy a car, a nice sports car that growls and rattles the old church windows when racing past?"

The people grinned.

"Move into a new home? A mortgage is feasible, we could afford it. Or maybe just remodel the old house, new furniture, kitchen appliances. The wives are always up for that, aren't they?"

The husbands chuckled this time.

"Aren't we forgetting something? I have spoken for about three minutes now, I am definitely forgetting something? I've forgotten the reason we're here today. Simple as that. More importantly, I've forgotten to mention someone whose birth we've gathered to celebrate. Where is Christ in all of the above-mentioned resolutions? Where is the son of God? Christmas is the time of celebrations, which is true. For some, it is a day away from that tiring, quotidian bustle we go through each day of the week. It is actually more than just one day if we can flatter a couple of holidays from our bosses. For some, it is the time of receiving long lost desires wrapped as a gift. I'm sure all of us here had something to look for under our trees this morning. We revel by the night with feasts and champagne and expensive gifts to our families and that is a wonderful thing. That's what festivity is. But what amazes the most is the forgetfulness of the fact that Christ never wanted us to celebrate his birth the way we do. Never in his life did he say that you shall feast or drink and rejoice the night of Christmas. Or you shall buy yourself new clothes or cars or homes for my birth. These are the worldly things that humans have somehow associated with Christmas and New Years and Religion. Wealth was never our salvation, it is the word. And the word is God. God is love and love is the feat of goodness and virtue. The eleventh commandment I give unto you, which is the greatest of all; love one another. There has never been a word greater than this, my friends."

People nodded and introspected where they'd fallen behind.

"Things change our lives, but deeds transmute our souls. Body shall perish, the soul is eternal. Let's enrich our souls, with love, peace and wisdom. Let's make ourselves worthy. Christ didn't resurrect for us to change our living, he arose to change our lives, to bring the change in us. How many of us have had their houses painted in the past?"

Some hands were raised in the congregation.

"Excellent, then the experience of watching the work is still fresh in your memories. We have seen the chipped paint being removed with a scraper or a putty knife, haven't we? Why do you think the painters do that? I'll tell you why, because if you roll your brush on the area that's peeling, the paint will never reach the wall underneath. It will stay colorless and soon after some time, it shall peel away again and show unwanted cracks on your wall. We must scratch and scrape that old paint from the walls for the new color to apply itself. We shall scratch and scrape that old evil that has deposited on our conscience since ages for truth and righteousness to take over our hearts and minds again. So, just like we paint our houses anew, we might just want to paint ourselves as well, in love. Let's bow in prayer."

The congregation began streaming out of the entrance greeting and shaking hands with Solomon and Pastor Riley. The Saunderhurst family followed as the crowd aggregated into the open, Jeff being the last one of them took his time congratulating the new parish leader.

"Thanks for showing us the way, pastor." Their hands met.

"The way has always been there, I just cast a bit of light where the path becomes narrower. It's a deep fall down that bridge, and no curb to hold on to."

"I will remember that." Jeff smiled and continued shuffling forward.

"Merry Christmas, Jeff."

"Merry Christmas to you, sir."

Solomon busied himself with the queued members behind as Jeff eyed Erica rolling her father's wheelchair down the ramp onto the sidewalk and entering a circle of acquaintances who showed their commiseration as well as regard toward her ill father. She then moved toward the Saunderhurst family and joined in for some more discussions.

Jeff waited for a while then found Erica taking leave and continuing with the wheelchair down the street.

"You could have asked for a ride." Jeff startled her from behind and tagged along.

"I'm parked at the end of the block. No need for a ride."

Going up the slope, Jeff took the handles of the wheelchair relieving her of some travail.

"Merry Christmas, Mr. Johnson. We didn't get a chance to see each other." Jeff addressed the man they both pushed forward.

There was silence from the other end. Jeff nodded in response.

"He hasn't spoken much except asking me to bring him to church this morning," Erica elucidated. "The doctors weren't too happy about it, but he was adamant as ever and I simply couldn't refuse. He just gained consciousness last night. I received a phone call after you left."

"Well, we have him. That's enough of a Christmas present."

They ambled a little more approaching Erica's dilapidated truck.

"Thanks for putting up those lights. I really needed them. The place had been cloaked in dark for a couple of years. I had gotten so used to it that I didn't see a reason to light it up anymore, couldn't ask anyone either. This year, I didn't have to."

"I wish I had more of them to make it even brighter. But those were the only strands I was left with."

"It's bright enough out there. Enough to cast a light inside as well."

"I hope Mr. Johnson isn't bothered by the flashes."

"No, he used to sleep even better in them. I was the one living in pitch black."

Jeff gazed into her eyes.

"You're going to take him back to the hospital?"

"Not right away, I thought I'll take him home for just a bit. Then I'll take him back. The house is so empty without him. The doctor said it'll be another week or more depending on how soon he recovers before he could come home."

"He'll recover, I'm sure."

They had reached the truck, as Jeff hauled Mr. Johnson up in his arms and placed him cautiously on the passenger seat. He shut the vehicle door and folded the wheelchair, loading it in the back. Erica watched him perform all the tasks. He came around the truck and neared her once again.

"Jeff, I wanted to apologize for the things I said--"

"Everything that you said was deservedly right. I wasn't hurt by any of it, not even for a moment."

"I treated you so harshly--" streaks of remorse coursed her face.

"You treated me like you should have. I was the one who took you for a stranger and kept secrets from you. I would have done the same if I were in your place."

"That's not true."

"It is true. Do you really believe with those words at the hospital or last night you were trying to distance me from you? Or rather I took it that way? Expressions of love aren't always paraded through smiles and kisses. They're sometimes hidden in disappointments as well."

He wiped away her tears with his hands.

"Now look alive, we have a dinner date tonight. With about ten more people."

She laughed at the wry remark.

"Don't try to haul him out alone if you get home earlier. Wait for me, I'll be right behind. And there's a setting on the lights which could turn off the flashes and give a steady glow. If you want it, I'll change it."

"Don't change anything. I like it the way you put it up, just as it is." Erica got inside the truck and turned the ignition. "I'll see you in a bit."

Jeff stepped back from the cloud of black smoke emitted through the tailpipe and waved.

# Chapter Thirty

✵

The dining table was all adorned with several platters of home-cooked delicacies and traditional recipes. Salad being the final of all preparations was being embellished with cucumbers as they were sliced with great precision and arranged in a cosmetic appearance atop the rest by Maggie. The women around commended her dexterity. The candles were lit on the table. The kids stole a bite or two from the platters much to the annoyance of their mothers.

"Stop doing that kids," Gloria reproached.

The children responded with laughter and scuttled off and away. The banquet was set, awaiting the family.

"Shall we call everyone in?" Linda exclaimed excitedly.

The table was populated as everyone was given a seat around and they all adjusted snugly to make space. The champagne was popped open and the flutes were filled with bubbling spirit. A clinking of glass followed and a short grace from the youngest member of the family, Helen. Amen sounded in unison and then commenced the haphazard juggling of plates and platters.

It was a tumultuous task filling every plate with its owners' preferences, but finally the swirling settled and all came to order. Therefore, feasting began.

As the dinner reached its conclusion, Martin raised a glass to the unity of the family and attracted all attention toward him.

"To give thanks for this time and this celebration is a basic thing, and we all have done that quite a few times today. I raise this glass tonight to thank someone else. This is my seventy-third Christmas feast. I do not remember a couple of them at the beginning of my life when I was little, but to determine the number of Christmases I've seen, it is customary to refer to one's age. When I was young, my grandmother used to conduct the festivities around our small home and mother used to help her. They had their differences when preparing things. You know when you put two women in one kitchen, pans are bound to rattle."

"Five in this case," Maggie toasted.

Martin smiled and continued. "When she passed away, my mother took over the responsibility, much to her relief. But when she passed on, I found your mother replacing my mother. And without a frown or a glare, she has worked to the end of her strength every Christmas for forty-five years that we've been together. I couldn't go on anymore without thanking her for everything she's done for this family and this house. Her family and her house. Lena, we all love you."

Lena gazed at her husband and allowed some tears to slip down her eyes. Linda embraced her and subdued her emotional effusion.

"There is just a bit more I want to say tonight. And this goes toward someone equally important to our family. Let's bring a little past into our discussion, there isn't a life without the talk of the past. You kids used to play in the woods and there was a small stream there that went through the forest? I'm sure you saw it."

Maggie, Jeff and Erica all nodded in confirmation.

Martin continued, "I had seen that stream only twice in my life and that was ages ago. It wasn't there to begin with, but due to some constructions near the river, that stream found its way into the woods. The first time I saw it, I found that it had made itself a path going right through the trees and I don't know where."

The trio glimpsed each other impishly. A whispering "we do" was heard somewhere in the room.

"But then about a decade ago when I saw it again, I saw a huge rock detached from somewhere, blocking it entirely. It did not stop the water from going forward, but it had parted the flow into two smaller streams that went separate ways. And the path, the water coursed before, dried up. Now it's not even deep enough to drown the heel of a shoe. The strength of that stream has perished. When the roots of a stream start to dry, the water begins to recede and it looks to find new sources, be it rain or a river. But when something as heavy as a rock falls in between and separates the water, it's as good as dead. A family needs to sustain itself in a similar way. This table had been incomplete for many years. Your mother and I watched from these chairs every Christmas that some of you were always missing. It would be Edward or James skipping at times, sometimes Gloria would go to her folks, a few occasions even Linda and Maggie couldn't come. And then Jeff for the past five years. But tonight the table is complete, the family is complete. The rock removed. In our flow together, we will find our strength of unity. I want to thank Jeff for bringing us all together once more."

The family applauded, Jeff acknowledged their appreciation.

"And Erica, when Johnson is feeling better, I wish to speak to him. To make sure the stream continues." Martin interpolated which triggered more of an upheaval in an already convivial atmosphere.

Jeff had caught Erica gazing at him throughout the duration of supper as she stole her eyes away, but this instance both held that stare.

"I wish to speak to all of you." Jeff disrupted the jovial conversations around him. The dining room went silent. Erica implored him tacitly to delay the announcement, but he disregarded the supplication. "In the living room."

The dessert was relished a minute ago as everyone nodded and began leaving the table while the women emptied the tabletop of the leftovers filling the refrigerator with them.

Erica had approached Jeff in the hallway and her eyes swam in tears. "Does it have to be now? Please, Jeff, it can wait."

"There is no use giving them false hope. It's time." Jeff held her hand and took her to the living as the family gathered around on couches and chairs, all seated.

Jeff stood by the window holding a couple of envelopes in his hand. He searched for the strength to declare what he must and took about a minute to garner all of it, finally speaking to them.

"Doubt produces fear in almost all of us. Uncertainty about situations, people, family, and then you start worrying about things that don't even exist. I had a similar fear. To tell you honestly, I feared how this will actually turn out to be. Writing those letters to four different households, especially the people you've caused so much suffering and pain and don't know how they would respond to your request, that was one terrifying task. Inviting all of you here to celebrate Christmas together, I didn't know what to expect. And believe me, if you came here with a baseball bat swinging at me, I wouldn't fault you."

A wave of suppressed laughter was transient.

"After the things I had said and done, the sorrow and the tears shed on my account, I feared. But when faith replaces doubt, a strange, undying strength suddenly becomes a companion. That faith is the love of a family. There are only handful days in a life that are worth so much, but when my family answered my letters, my calling, if someone had asked me for all the riches of my lifetime, the few that I have, I would happily give them away. Ten days ago I gained my faith, and defeated my doubt. Children are afraid in the night, we're all aware of that. We outgrew that phase in life. But when they grab on an arm that guides them to the light, they suddenly feel safer, that nothing can harm them anymore. A family is that firm grasp in the dark that gets you into light every time you're afraid. I love you all for being exactly that for me."

The women flicked a drop of tears that had just escaped their eyes.

"Thank you for this wonderful time. The laughter, the happiness, the warmth of being together, thank you, all of you. Five years and nothing changed between us. You all welcomed me back with forgiveness and I'm grateful for that. But staying away all this time, it made me understand something substantially. I'd always thought that I'd become a writer, have a lavish lifestyle, become someone important, but I realized being important is not being rich or famous or a celebrity. This is what's made me important. The fact that I'm still forgiven and loved by all of you is what's made me important. There could be the richest man in all of the world, but if that person dines alone tonight, what good has his money brought him?"

Jeff coughed harshly. Erica arose to help him, but he gestured her to stay seated. He took a drink of water and recovered.

"Living here in this small town had kept me alive and I had the best of childhoods with Maggie and Erica, but somehow I never lived. I never felt the wave of true happiness of life inside me. And leaving this town, when I thought I would live with freedom and satisfaction, all I could do was survive. Life was a stranger to me. I never knew it, I never enjoyed it. But today, I can scream out loud with a content smile on my face that I have lived. All the days of my life have been compensated by these ten days, and I have lived to the fullest. But in all the excitement I cannot forget to thank the place that gave me all of this. If I never left, I wouldn't be the person I am today. If I stayed I would have nothing to give. I'm glad that I left and came after five years to find so much love for me in all of you. To know the value of water, one must thirst. To know the measure of love, one must hate. I was overwhelmed with hatred before, now I'm overwhelmed with love. And this was the kind of love I was always given by one member of this family. Maggie, I couldn't ask for a better sister, my favorite sister. I love you, and I hope I'm still your favorite too?"

"You are." Maggie managed a hoarse response through her tears.

"Oh, so this is what's been going on behind our backs. Dave, you see that?" Linda sided with Dave in this matter.

"Hey you were always the older siblings, we're the young ones." Jeff teased with laughter.

The family was well amused at this. Jeff took out an envelope from the bunch and held it.

"I still cannot forgive myself for what happened at your wedding. I'd like to apologize for that, to you also, Edward."

"It's all over, Jeff. Forgotten." Edward dismissed the matter instantly.

"Then I would like to give this to both of you. Please accept it." Jeff handed the envelope to them.

Edward accepted it and checked the contents. He unfolded the agreement and went through it.

"Jeff?" Edward's voice was ringing with perplexity and surprise. "This is a property deed, transfer of your apartment?"

"Yes, it belongs to you now. We just have to complete the necessary paperwork. It's been paid off and it's good to go. Just some maintenance, that's all."

"What? What are you doing, Jeff? Where are you going to live?" Maggie was slenderly incensed.

"I'm going to live here, with ma and dad. I'm not going back, so it must go to the family, right?"

"But Jeff, we can't--"

"It's a good neighborhood, nice space. Enough for the four of you. You'll love it there."

"This is insane, we cannot just take this!" Maggie objected fervently.

"Please Maggie, don't say no. You wanted to move to New York, now you have a home there. And it doesn't even have to be yours or mine. It was never like that between us, right? I'll visit for holidays, maybe next Christmas... please, take it."

Maggie wiped her tears away and embraced her brother almost strangulating him. Edward came for a hug as well.

"Thank you, Jeff. This means a lot. I really won't forget this." Edward patted his shoulders and went back to the chair.

Jeff continued, "there's always that one person in a family who essentially assumes the responsibility of a father when he's not around. Who teases you a lot more but beats you a little less, and that's a big brother, those who are lucky enough to have one. I am. Dave, I always found you when I needed you the most. When my bicycle needed to be fixed, when I had to run an errand but wanted to play and you took the trouble instead. When I needed that extra dollar for ice cream. There are hardly any moments of affection between brothers, right? That's not common."

Dave shook his head with a big no and ratified his supposition.

"Yeah, we all know that. But on the contrary we never fought each other either. Possibly you showed a bit of mercy being eight years older, you could have mangled me to pulp and I wouldn't make a scratch on you, but you never took advantage of that. But I hated you, whenever you got those big boy things from dad and I didn't, I cursed you to hell. But I did that within, didn't give it a voice ever."

Gloria squeezed Dave's arm smiling to the revelations.

Jeff smiled, "but today I will give voice to one feeling that I have toward you. I love you." Jeff took another envelope and handed it to Dave.

Dave went through the papers and inserted them back in the envelope offering it back to Jeff. "Now this is going too far, Jeff. I will not accept this under any circumstances."

"What is it?" Lena asked.

"He's giving away his partnership in the store and a check of two hundred thousand dollars," Dave answered irately.

"Even if it means that I must leave? Dave, I'm not doing this because I'm forced to or that I want you to sing praises for me, please. It will only make me happier."

"But Jeff, why are you doing this?" Martin was confounded.

"It's nothing, dad. Everything stays in the family. It's not that I'm a stranger doing charity. If I need anything I will ask for it. Please,

Dave, this is for Charlie. If you think my love for him is honest, you will not refuse."

Dave sank back into his chair coerced by his wife.

"You are so nice, Jeff. Thank you." Gloria acknowledged.

"You are nice, Gloria, to spend time in this house and doing things for ma and dad like their daughter would do. Thank *you*."

Jeff turned toward the couple on his left. "Linda, James, there is hardly anything I can do for you. Both of you have been like a rock to this family and I know you will continue to be."

"Jeff, the most precious gift of all are your children. You reunited us with our estranged daughter whom we'd lost some time ago somewhere between work, money and technology. There is nothing more we can ask." Linda glimpsed at Nancy who sat by her side and then back at her brother appreciatively.

"Then it's all good. Ma, dad, I know I have done many bad things to both of you. Leaving was the biggest mistake I'd ever made, and I can only imagine the amount of suffering you would have gone through for the past five years. But that mistake changed my life, my perspective on life. I don't know if I should feel regret or relief, but I wouldn't be here if I didn't go."

"You are my son. You may be anywhere, but we will always love you." Lena's voice trembled and Maggie sat by to strengthen her.

"And I will always love you. From the depth of my heart, I'm truly sorry for any pain I've caused." Jeff reached for his parents and embraced them both.

"Jeff, you are the son every father wishes for." Martin spoke with utmost authority.

"All right, let's take a moment here," Jeff wiped his tears. "There is just one more person that I must speak about now." He took a pause. "Whether it was inspiration, encouragement or simply just the words I wanted to hear, she fortified me all throughout. And somehow she knew what kind of consolation I needed at that exact moment as if... as if she knew me inside and out, as if she were a mirror looking back at me. She's not old, her experience with life is just as limited as mine, yet she knows everything. Yet, she loves everyone. Since I have known the world, I have known her. And all these years have been a blessing to find her by my side, no matter what the trouble, no matter who was at fault, she was there. I am what I am because of her. She is the necessity of my life--"

"Stop, just stop." Erica came close to him, sank her face into his shoulder and wept.

Jeff caressed her hair, "and when emotions run so deep between two souls, even death seems like a minor pause."

She held onto his hand.

"I knew this will happen." Maggie jumped rapturously along with the rest who envisaged another marriage in the family.

"It's time for me to leave, Maggie." Jeff ceased all such celebration.

"What?" Maggie was confused.

"There is something else I want to tell all of you." Jeff took the medical reports and handed the envelope to James.

James didn't waste a second and hurriedly read the reports.

"I'm ill. Though, I expected myself to be the last pers on to fall for it, but it has roped me in. Cancer, and the love's so intense, it can't help but take me along."

All the astonished faces in the room exhibited profound disbelief and held on to each other for strength and fortitude. All eyes turned toward James who had just concluded reading the footnotes and he nodded helplessly to fortify their doubts.

Maggie arose and snatched the reports from James and went through with the esoteric jargon in utter daze. "This is a joke, right? Jeff if this is a prank, I'm really upset right now."

"Only if it was." Jeff gazed into her eyes. "The way I used to startle you in the basement and switch off the lights to frighten you even more. You got so scared. I wish you could beat this illness out of me like you chased me down and struck me with your little hands. I wish we could cry this disease away like we cried away our injuries, a scratch here and a scrape there. But this has bribed my own life to abandon me."

That poignant stare brought streams of tears into her eyes and she simply gave up collapsed to her knees and imploded along with Lena, Linda and Nancy. The men tried commiserating and subsiding their emotions, but failed miserably as they were traumatized themselves. The air in the room dimmed with sorrow, grief and whimpering souls.

Jeff reached for Maggie on the floor and lifted her up, disapproving of her reaction. "This isn't how you're supposed to act, Maggie. You're making me weak crying like this."

"But this is not fair," Maggie complained.

"Ma, you have to make her understand. This isn't the way you deal with sickness."

Lena was hardly capable of abating her own tears let alone her daughters'.

"You can't do this to us, Jeff. Please." Linda added.

"Linda, you're supposed to be the strongest one out of all of us."

"But there must be something that could be done?" Martin inquired expectantly.

"It's the advanced stage. I'm afraid not much is left to be done." James corroborated.

"How did this happen?" Nancy joined the weeping family holding her mother and father taut and close to herself.

"A year ago. It started with some symptoms that were minor at first, and as frightened as I am of hospitals and doctors, I neglected them all. I thought they were just some infections and carried on until the day I couldn't breathe anymore. They took me to the hospital and the diagnosis showed advanced stage lung cancer. The doctors forced me to go into treatment, but the outcome would still be uncertain. All they could do was prolong my suffering. So, I refused. I wanted to wait a little longer until New Year, but my condition is worsening now. It didn't happen that frequently before, but I have coughed blood many times in the past week. They gave me eight to twelve weeks. This is possibly my last Christmas, and all I wanted to do was make it the best I've ever had. We all did."

"Oh God..." Lena leapt for an embrace as did Maggie, Linda, Nancy and Martin, encircling him.

"I never expected to see all of your crying like this." Jeff gathered his family within his arms and wept with them. "I had thought of never coming back and dying there alone. But then I realized something; death might have to be faced alone, but life doesn't. As long as I'm alive, even death can't take me away from my family." Jeff squeezed them together and grasped Erica. She pecked his hand.

That evening, a great performer had just completed his act of farewell and the audiences roared with applause and adulation at his final moments on stage. The fall of the curtains was impending and that last bow instilled lasting memories across. He was prepared to fade behind the curtain now.

# Chapter Thirty-One

Three weeks had passed since the new millennium had unfurled its wings of ambition and unprecedented possibilities upon the world, but the town that housed the Saunderhursts saw the new dawn as just another year of wonted toil and labor, and subtle conventional delights that diffused through a vapid life. Though, the amenities of the new world began to knock at the threshold, it still lay in its unstilted languor. Jeff had delivered on his word by never mentioning the thought of leaving his home again which was one fair blessing to the people who loved him, but the gratitude for that boon was evenly overcome with grief as the truth of his departure imbued their thoughts.

The family refrained from speaking of that harsh reality or even a slight intimation of it, but they all carried that cumbersome gloom within their hearts.

Jeff began to habituate himself to his home again as he meandered the old rooms and the hallways noting the sublime silence that he once felt after the passing of his grandfather. But back then it wasn't observed to be so dreadful or protracted as it was now. The family had dispersed to their own homes and the house was empty and devoid of laughter or happiness of any sort. The three souls that remained were old and weary and burdened. As hard as it was to part for everyone who left, life was meant to go on and after some continuous insistence from Jeff, they decided to leave but only with a promise of returning periodically on weekends and whenever a day off could be availed.

Jeff would find himself navigating the forgotten attic and the stored memories inside that stifling enclosure as he would unbox ancient photographs and relish them for hours. Clothes that belonged to his grandfather and were quite too big for him back in the day, but now fitted him perfectly as he had taken a liking to a particular plaid shirt that he exchanged with the one he was wearing. A sudden cover of nostalgia clouded his memory and it was a pleasant one as there weren't many that brought a thin smile to his face that swiftly.

He would then shuffle down the stairs and find his mother in the kitchen still laboring before the stove as she had for the past forty-five years even more perhaps. She would stand there oblivious of his presence in the doorway, calmly brooding about the impending loss that might as well claim her life, and her abstraction would only be disrupted by a steaming pan that had been scorched in fire long enough to emit odorous vapors.

Jeff would efface himself slyly before embarrassing his mother with a realization of being watched in her condition of dejection.

"That was a quiet walk down the stairs." But a mother's perception of her son's presence is not a slave to sight.

Jeff leaned into the doorway silently admiring his mother's ability to grasp his presence without a single sound.

"The wheezing has stopped." Lena turned to look squarely into his eyes.

"It'll come back." Jeff took a chair near the counter.

"Your medications seem to be working well." She lightened the room with a sullen smile.

"Miracles are a work of prayers not prescriptions."

Lena sat down with him and clenched his shivering hands.

"Well, then our prayers seem to be working. Just one miracle, that's all we need."

"Maybe this is too great a miracle to ask for. Sometimes even miracles look for a prayer to come true."

"Then there are plenty of those. I'm sure at least one would find its way."

"But your eyes speak differently."

Lena lowered her eyes that were enfolded in melancholy. Then wiped them clear. "Is that all you see?"

Jeff shook his head with a smile and embraced her, "no. A lot more than that. A drop of dreams, a measure of hope, and a world of love."

He contemplated Lena's heartache for a long time under the shelter of the porch, absorbing warmth from bright daylight, sitting on the rocking chair that once unwound his grandfather.

After a while of such troubling rumination, he found his repose in a personable laughter that imbued an approaching face.

Erica would visit him recurrently switching between the two houses as her father had returned from the hospital convalescing after his severe affliction. She would quickly arrive and search for a blanket to cover Jeff and ward the cold of late January breeze from giving him another ailment to deal with. But she was considerate enough to let him stay out for a while knowing how much he loved the touch of cold air on his skin.

"It is not the kind of weather you should be out enjoying." Erica came up the steps of the porch and took off her own cardigan wrapping Jeff in it.

"That's exactly what I'm trying to tell you. If I catch a cold, it'll be hardly more than a sneeze here and there. But if you do, that'll be a disaster." Jeff commented ambiguously.

Erica frowned, "how's that?"

"I'm sick already. I'm not leaving this chair or that bed inside, the only two places where I belong. But if you get sick with as little as a sniff, there are two other people who'd get even worse without the care and love they've been getting from you for so long."

"Oh, so that's the science behind it?" Erica nodded impressed with the concept.

"You know why a concierge is the most important and indispensable employee of a building?" Jeff leaned in excitedly staring into her eyes.

"No."

"Because that person opens doors making it easier for everyone else to pass."

Erica crouched by his chair and took his hand kissing it gently.

"How is he?" Jeff inquired in a deep voice.

"He's feeling all right." She pulled herself a chair and sat down. "He was feeling much better after that breathing tactic you taught him that night. He says it somehow makes him feel refreshed."

"Does it? Well, I'm glad it's working for somebody."

Erica's smile vanished. He looked away in all seriousness toward her hidden grief.

"Have you told him yet?"

Erica just shook her head without venturing to gaze back at him.

"You should, Erica, for his sake and yours."

"Mine?"

"I'll explain it to you, but promise me you won't be upset. I don't want to lose my lunch, you know."

Erica beamed at the humor and listened intently.

"It doesn't matter how far we try to run away from the truth, it'll catch up with us eventually. I'm not here for long, and keeping your father in mind, he would have always thought that you see your future with me and that may be the reason he never forced you to consider it or think about it. But if that hope has faded for him, he deserves to know the-- change, if you will, that has somehow altered things. And there is another harsh truth in this situation, I'm sorry to say it, Erica, but your father wouldn't be here forever. If he wishes to see your happiness before he leaves, I will not dare blame him for it. And my own desire wouldn't be any different."

Jeff's protracted plea had incensed Erica in a way but she kept it latent with a piercing glare fixed at him.

"Can I ask you something, Jeff?" Erica spoke sharply.

He allowed it with a blink of his eyes.

"If I were going to die, would you have married someone else?"

Jeff took a moment to reply then clenched his jaws, "yes." He said viciously.

Erica had intuited the spurious intention behind the response. "Then why didn't you? You had all the reasons to. You could have saved a lot as well, two weddings at once. Liliana is a beautiful girl."

"That was a different time, Erica. You were not going to... you were going to come back."

"You didn't know that. I could have come back a bride."

"The circumstances back then were different."

"Women get married out of love, not circumstances. It's about time you understand that."

A long silence intervened.

"You hear that?"

There was not even a faint noise to be discerned. Erica shook her head.

"Exactly. Nothing, right? Silence. That's what I'm leaving behind for you. I haven't been able to give you anything and this silence could drain your soul out of you. I have been through it and this is what I've received. I can't see you go through the same."

"If you don't like to see me or want me to leave, you can say it out loud. I'll take it and go." Erica stood up but Jeff grasped her wrist.

"I don't want you to leave."

"Then why are you trying so hard to make me?" Erica knelt by him with tearful eyes.

He held her face and kissed her forehead. "I cannot see you sad and lonely ever again. These past five years were enough for you. No more."

"Have you ever seen love? But people spend their lifetimes in it. It is not necessary for you to see what you feel, and when you really feel loved, how could you be sad ever? How could you be lonely when everything around you reminds you of someone all the time?"

"You don't understand how hard this life could be for you, Erica." Jeff averted his swimming eyes from her gaze.

"No, *you* don't understand how hard that life could be for me, Jeff. If I can spend five years without a single hope of seeing you ever again, I can definitely spend a lot more in faith of finding you again someday. Please, don't send me away like that. Because if I get married to anyone else, and even if I learn to love him, I will always love him less and love you more. And that would be unfair to anyone. Besides, you're wrong about one thing, you've given me more than enough memories to outlast a lifetime. You like to sit out in the cold and feel that air against your skin, don't you? Well, that's me all around like the air caressing you all the time. I won't leave you in peace. No matter where you go, you can't escape me. I'm a small town girl and my aspirations are not as vast as some people you might know. All I want is a small home with you filling every corner of it and an old age to treasure all the years that passed in such joy."

"A want I can't fulfill." Jeff added woefully.

"Maybe you have, you just don't know it." She gazed back at him without a shade of doubt in her eyes.

Jeff filled his arms with her whimpering body and warmed her soul. At length, he spoke, "okay, get me inside. I'm freezing out here."

Erica parted chuckling, "you monstrous liar. You're not the one who's cold, I am."

"I don't care about you, take me in. You can stay out if you want."

Erica nodded incredulously and helped him to his feet.

"Lead the way, I'm right behind you." Jeff pushed her forward and inside the cozy interior of a home.

# Chapter Thirty-Two

✵

Jeff had taken a couple of trips to the town hospital in the past two weeks as his condition exacerbated and suffering magnified. His breathing had reached a point of suspension quite a few times and the traces of blood in his cough had augmented to a dribbling effusion upon a gurgling exhalation. Maggie had arrived with Helen as the news of his declining health reached the family and added to the number of caregivers that were aiding Jeff in his final days.

Jeff was content to see the crowd of his loved ones around all day long which was reminiscent of a time about twenty years ago when a similar perilous threat lingered upon him. The only difference was that he had recuperated from that previous illness, which seemed unviable this time. He relished his nostalgic conversations with whoever took the shift of observing him in his room, as they laughed and recollected the lost memories of the past. A stifling streak of sorrow still endured in the hearts of those who watched him diminish and wither day by day, but they still managed a fallacious smile to conceal their grief.

It was Jeff's long-awaited plan to tour the sites forgotten ages ago in the company of his sister, while Erica guided the excursion. Upon his persistent requests, the three boarded Erica's rickety pick-up truck that had miraculously started at the first attempt. The exhaust emitted a cloud of black smoke as the truck went jouncing down the street much to their pleasure like children enjoying a fair ride.

They had journeyed the abandoned train tracks and the length of the single freight car that had rusted there for decades, almost forgetting the reason for which it was created. Jeff had begun to use a cane for ambulation due to weakness in his legs after a certain amount of exertion which was directly related to his respiration and a stringent recommendation of normality forbidding any stimulation or activity that might excite his breathing.

He plodded upon the tracks and along with the freight car tapping his cane on the metal, attempting to tiptoe on the corroding bars. Erica and Maggie followed keeping a keen eye on his balancing, waiting to assist if he stumbles. They sat on one of the large wheels that were strewn across the grounds and saw a view of the woods far away and a narrowing end of a tenuous stream that altered into a swamp. The winds were murmuring, the place was hushed, the duration of their stay was silent as well. Jeff refrained from disrupting the peace of the quiet, so did the two companions with him.

Their next stop was the bookstore which was manned by Martin for the day and his delight was immeasurable when he saw his son coming into the store. All three entered and made space for Jeff to sit behind the counter. Martin quickly poured him a cup of coffee from a thermos.

Jeff spoke after a moment of intrusive stares that made him uncomfortable. "It's all right, I'm okay."

The three took away their eyes from him and glimpsed the store in a desultory manner.

"Did you get to speak to Edward? He called in the morning before leaving for work. I told your mother to pass on the message." Martin sat down near the entrance on a small wooden chair.

"Yeah, I did, just before coming here. He was curious about things here," Maggie kept it pleasant, "about Jeff and the rest. I told him everything was fine and going great."

"He must be missing you there, Maggie. It becomes exceedingly difficult for a man who works to take care of a six-year-old son. I believe you should go back. See, I have all these people to take care of me. You have a family back there." Jeff suggested while playing with the register, opening and closing the cash drawer intermittently.

"I have a brother here who needs me too. Besides, he'll be fine. His sister is there to take care of them both. Liliana got married last year and is living in Boston, you know that." Maggie countered.

"What about Helen? She would miss her father."

"Oh, don't even start with her about leaving. She loves it here. No school. She couldn't wait to get into the car and drive here. They can do without me for a few days--" Maggie choked with the words she had uttered that were pungent to all who heard them.

"So, how is the store going, dad?" Jeff breached the wounding silence.

"It has been good since that day. We've gained many customers from neighboring towns. I believe it will help us a lot." Martin sounded pleased with the outcome.

"That's great." Jeff still toyed with the cash register.

Erica had noted his ambivalence to glance at the cash collection in the drawer, but also his urge to find out if the store had made any money today.

She went over to him and placed her hand on his shoulder and whispered, "go ahead, look. Open it."

Jeff pulled the cash drawer out completely and looked at it. He found three bills of twenty and a ten. He was elated to see that.

"It's not the same anymore." Erica smiled back at him.

They had driven to the bridge that led to the falls and the journey ahead was required to be completed on foot. They all alighted from the pick-up and just as Jeff was about to retrieve his cane, he reconsidered and left it inside closing the door shut.

He took the hands of the two women with him and crossed the beam bridge with their aid. All three traveled through the woods and arrived at the falls shortly. They found the place arid and somewhat desolated. The pool had dried, and where a stream of water amply coursed giving life to the trees now barely dripped a runnel and the old, parched leaves buried the rocks and the clearing. The devastation of the falls disconcerted them deeply but they refrained from articulating their despondency.

"It has dried up," Jeff remarked sadly.

"They have blockaded the stream about half a mile north. They're building something. It's the new age development, old places have to diminish." Erica commiserated with him.

"We used to sit on those rocks there," Maggie sprang forward pointing out the elevation.

"Yeah, you with your scrapbook and Erica brought those magazines for you." Jeff joined in the dulcet recollections.

"Right after school, wasn't it?" Erica added. "The way we used to ride our bicycles frantically, like that was the only minute we had to get here. Might be lost otherwise."

"And then once here we would just throw away our bikes, our clothes, jump into the water and remember nothing of the world back there." Maggie was a tad emotional.

"How much time did we usually spend here?" Erica wondered.

"I think more than an hour," Maggie answered.

"I think more than two hours," Jeff countered.

Erica dwelt upon a memory that brought laughter to her face. "Knock, knock."

"Who's there?" Maggie answered excitedly.

All three spoke together, "can't you see, silly?" They treasured that old, arcane exchange intended to be a tease years ago.

"Who came up with that? I can't remember." Maggie inquired.

"She did," Jeff tipped his head toward Erica.

"Yes," Erica confirmed, "it was actually to wake him up out of boredom in the classroom. I'd always find him daydreaming right behind me, sometimes buried on his desk off to sleep. It was better than being hit by a chalk right on the head."

"Which I did, a couple of times," Jeff admitted.

The two shared a glimpse.

"Oh, I still remember when it rained," Erica ventured upon one of the rocks still intact. "The whole place looked so beautiful. The pool filled up to the brim, the sound of rain hitting the leaves and the ground dampened. We played in the mud and when soiled, we jumped into the water and cleansed ourselves. It was like a massive shower, the way rain dribbled from trees."

Maggie reached a vantage point and tried searching for something. "That tree there where you climbed and jumped from, splashing water all over the place. Where is it? It's missing?"

Their laughter faded. The branch was reduced to remnants.

"It's broken now, gone." Jeff ended the evanescent exhilaration.

They trudged back to the pick-up after a few more moments of reminiscing at the falls and boarded the transport for the journey back home.

"Did you have a good time seeing the old places?" Lena sat down at the dining table delivering the final bowl of baked potatoes to the cluster of bowls filled with eatables.

"The most delightful time, ma." Jeff took the bowl of beans and stuffed his plate then passed it on to Maggie.

"Which places did you go to?" Lena filled Martin's plate with roast turkey leftovers and then managed her own with the remainder.

"We went to the falls, the train tracks--"

"The deserted lot?" Martin questioned taking a bite.

"Yeah," Jeff confirmed.

"Don't forget the bookstore." Maggie reminded, feeding Helen and then herself.

"Yeah, the store too." Jeff coughed and a sudden silence swept the table. He emerged unscathed after a couple of rasping exhales. "I'm all right."

The family went back to wordless nibbling for a while.

"Jeff, can I ask something of you?" Lena disrupted. "Promise me you won't refuse."

"Sure, what is it?" Jeff nodded with complaisance.

"Your father and I were speaking about it this morning and we included Maggie in our discussion as well. We want you to undergo treatment." Lena had forgotten all about her supper and her eyes were fixated in a plea.

"Ma, I think we spoke about this before."

"It is nothing to be afraid of, Jeff. We have heard of so many people who have recovered from cancer after successful treatments."

"Afraid? I'm not afraid of it, ma." Jeff clarified.

"Your sisters are living in big cities, you have a house in New York. We'll go to whichever place you feel most comfortable in. Linda is willing to assist us throughout and James will be a great help in all this. If you want to go to Boston, Maggie and Edward are there."

Jeff glimpsed his sister remembering the financial hardships she mentioned not too long ago.

Lena continued, "and if it's New York, you have an apartment there. They have some big cancer hospitals there with able doctors, there wouldn't be any problems at all."

"Ma, do you think I haven't tried? Do you think I just simply gave up on my wish to live and decided to die? I have been to these hospitals and research centers several times. I consulted a team of doctors who had nothing more to say to me than their sympathies and their uncertainty."

"They could be wrong. There is no harm in trying again." Lena implored.

"It was already too late when I was diagnosed and they told me I didn't have much time. I made a mistake of ignoring it at first, I admit that. We can't go back in time and change it. Six months that's what they gave me, and out of that I already took half in gathering the strength to come back here and see all of you. Probably, they could keep me alive another two months maybe, even that's just a probability riding on a fluke. I don't want to spend the last days of my life in a hospital. I wanted to spend them with you."

"You don't understand, Jeff. You're not losing a son, we are." Lena began weeping, Maggie sent Helen away to the living room and went around the table holding her mother with empathy.

"I won't give up even on a splinter of hope I have to keep you. Surviving this loss will take my life. I'll be just as good as dead if you are no more with us."

Jeff went over and crouched by her side taking her into his arms and abating her pains.

"If I can have you for a month more, a week more or even just a day, I will give up anything in life to have it. Every moment I can spend with you, I'll exchange that for a lifetime of happiness. Even my own." She spoke unintelligibly through her sobs.

Jeff embraced her which subsided her hysteria and trepidation gradually.

"Okay, ma. Now stop crying like this or I will too." Jeff was already tearful. "If that's what you want, then it will be done. But I need your word on something too. If this doesn't work, no more running around. What I need is peace of having all of you by my side. Nothing else matters to me now."

"So, you will not say no, right?" Lena effaced her tears.

"I'll go wherever you want me to go. I will lie on a bed of coal s if that makes me better."

They all smiled and breathed in a bit of relief with a fragile ray of hope that might remove the bitterness of loss from their lives.

# Chapter Thirty-Three

✵

Jeff was back in New York, but this time the only sensation of the city that pleasured his sight was through a glass wall of his private patient room which gave him a view of the illustrious skyline. It had been five weeks since he had arrived at the hospital in special cancer care unit and was treated in an accelerated medical program that induced the physical effects of chemotherapy eventuating in a sudden bodily change in him. He was beginning to lose hair which he concealed behind a woolen hat at all times, and his diminished strength engendered weakened limbs which forced him to seek the aid of a wheelchair to travel. Jeff had despised these conditions of living, but he was deferential to the entreaty that emitted from the person he loved the most, his mother. And he was in no position to deny her last request of him before he passed on.

In this short duration of five weeks, he had acquainted himself with many fellow patients that lodged on the floor temporarily. His days were spent in the company of his new friends which ranged from five to seventy and the vivid experiences and conversations that he was subjected to brought about a lot of appreciation as well as courage in him.

Sporadic between these convivial days were episodes of his augmenting affliction that constrained him into the solitude of his room. He suffered the ailment of restricted breathing with excruciating difficulty, which at times was reduced to suffocation and near death symptoms.

Jeff was wrathful and misanthropic upon contemplating his misdeeds that merited this boon, but those transitory instances of animosity soon dwindled when he saw the faces of his loved ones in the doorway called by the hospital staff to be present in case the unthinkable happens.

It was just another morning when Jeff sat in his bed quietly reading a book when Maggie entered with a fruit basket.

"Well, someone looks refreshed this morning." Maggie kept the basket on the side and took a seat near him.

"It's a new dawn, a new day. Besides, I'm hardly doing anything. These are the easiest days of my life, ever. Either I' m in bed, resting, enjoying, and when I'm out of it, am on a chair that has wheels. My legs are at a complete rest, they almost don't exist." Jeff smiled softly.

Maggie checked his forehead for any signs of a temperature.

"Ma went home late last night?" Jeff inquired, remembering another painful incident of breathlessness.

"Hmm, around three. She said she couldn't find a taxi outside so she came back to the front and asked them to call her one. I wish I could be here, but I was busy sleeping." Maggie tapped her temples.

"After spending ten hours here in this depression, I'd be sleeping for the rest of my life. You needed it."

"She was in bed when I left. I left her a message in case she wakes up." Maggie reassured him.

"I'm troubling all of you so much. The two of your here and dad back home. Then there's your family, and--"

"This is my family too, Jeff."

Jeff kissed her hand. "I'm sorry."

"And don't worry about dad at home. He has Erica and Gloria taking care of his meals and Dave taking care of the rest. Edward is there for both Ron and Helen and his sister is staying with them. Thank god she doesn't have kids."

"One life and so much hassle." Jeff imprecated his existence.

"A valuable life. And you're calling it a hassle? I get to live in New York City in such a nice apartment. I get a bite of the big apple, and believe you me, I love your room with the balcony overlooking the avenue that is so much alive with people and sounds of all sorts."

"Especially at night. Don't you love them when they keep you awake?" Jeff commented corrosively.

"That's the part of the experience. You have a beautiful home."

"*You* have a beautiful home." He reminded her who owns it.

"Yes, my home. Our home."

"So, when are you shifting here?" Jeff took a bite off an apple.

"Edward and I were talking just last night. He suggested he wants to stay and spend a little time here alone first. If he secures a good job, we're coming over right after."

"What's the delay then? That could be arranged right now."

"He's just thinking of quitting his present job or taking some weeks off."

"Hmm, that's a tough decision."

"That's the delay."

"Yeah, I hope I'm alive to see what happens." Jeff had uttered insensitively, triggering a loss of gaiety from his sister's countenance.

A nurse knocked on the door and let herself inside. "There are a few people to see you."

"Yes, please." Jeff straightened his creased coverlet in anticipation while Maggie withdrew in a corner partially due the abrupt gloom effectuated by the words.

As Jeff watched the threshold, he found three familiar faces ambling into the room with delightful smiles. Angela, Anne, and Drake, three formidable personalities came over jovially greeting a startled patient.

"Hey, boyfriend," Anne leaned in for a kiss.

Jeff allowed her to steal one, still speechless. "I can't believe it." He said incredulously.

"Neither can we, what do you think you're doing on that bed, in this room, inside this hospital?" Angela demanded in a daunting tone.

"Which one do I answer first?" Jeff's response infused laughter in all of them.

"I'm not done dealing with your pestering phone calls every other day with changes as little as quotation marks and commas. So, you better pull yourself out of there and start working on something new, because somehow I've grown accustomed to those calls after all these years of you feasting on my patience."

"What can I say, you had terrible editors." Jeff was flippant this time. "But I'll try to call you long distance. Hope they have phones up there. Stay ready for some collect charges."

"The only thing I'm collecting right now is another manuscript from you. I don't care how long you take to finish it, I want it on my desk by next month and here comes the big surprise. You're going to read your name right next to it this time. No more selling your work."

"I'm sorry to break your heart, Angela, but I think this time it'll have to go on the shelves."

"You think you can plan your exit so easily, Jeff?" Anne joined the conversation. "There are a lot more blank pages left to be scrawled over in your book."

"I guess they put in too many pages. It's the words I'm running out of."

"A writer is never deprived of words. Especially someone who has written many successful lives with them."

"Mr. Jarick, it's a profound pleasure to see you here."

"Don't make it formal, Saunderhurst. I just came to see a friend." Drake managed a smile through his hurting eyes.

"And you're most welcome. Taking time out of your taxing schedules, all three of you, it really makes me feel special."

"Especially on a weekday," Anne joked.

"That is true indeed. You guys don't get paid hourly, do you?" Jeff acknowledged.

"I do!" Anne confessed. "But in all seriousness, we need to take care of our little arrangement once you've recovered and discharged from here."

"We don't even have to wait that long. They have a cafeteria in here. I can ask a nurse to be a sport and serve us tonight, they have very nice pizzas, and I can transport myself anywhere on that wheelchair right there. The only thing we're missing for this date is a violinist playing 'when somebody loves you' by Frank Sinatra."

"Nah, that's no trouble at all. I know the tune, I can hum it for you." Anne abetted the idea.

"We can sing it together. I think I can manage. Why don't you start with meeting my sister who just stepped out in the hallway? You will have to mingle with the family some time. Now's a good start."

"Oh, don't worry. We'll have a lot of time for that."

"Time? Time is something that I don't have."

The faces hardened with misery.

"You know, that's the tragedy of death. No matter how soon or late it comes, you're always out of time. There's always something left behind that needed to be done." Jeff finished with a subtle, conceding smile.

Drake took in a deep sigh and stormed out of the room never looking back.

"Mr. Jarick?" Jeff was stirred to have discomfited him.

"That's all right, Jeff. He is a bit sensitive to this facet of life," Angela explained. "He's suffered the loss of his mother to cancer. It was a few years ago but some memories are indelible. I'll see to him. And you, better get yourself out and about or I'm rescinding the contract."

"We have a contract?" Jeff was stunned.

"Anne, give him the details." Angela went after Drake in the hallway.

"Your works are exclusive to our company now. It doesn't matter how many you have, complete or incomplete. They will be published." Anne placed a file with an official agreement before him awaiting his signatures.

Jeff looked up at her with swimming eyes and found a pen shoved into his face. "In case if it ever makes any money, will it go to my folks?"

"All of it."

Jeff took the pen and posed his signatures. "It pays to have friends, doesn't it?"

Drake leaned into a column wiping under his eyes which was an arresting sight to many of the nurses and doctors who watched him from a distance.

Maggie maintained a good distance as well, approaching him solicitously. "Is everything all right, sir?"

Angela had arrived with a drink of water for him. "Here, take a sip."

Drake took the water and gulped from the paper cup. "You're his sister, right?"

Maggie nodded in response.

"Is there nothing that can be done?" Drake's pleading voice was replete with hope and despair simultaneously.

Maggie had an answer to his inquiry, but not the heart to tell him. And as much as she wanted to falsely believe in the lie that she and Drake wished for, it was nowhere near the truth.

The vacant apartment had a faint lamp illumining the dark room which Maggie had just entered after a long day at the hospital. She closed the door shut behind her and reached for the balcony, permitting some fresh air inside along with the city sounds and liveliness.

She trudged into the adjoining bedroom and found Lena fast asleep on the single bed that occupied the otherwise empty room. She came over to the flank and sat down quietly, eschewing any possible noise that might awaken her.

She gingerly caressed her mother's head gazing at her in her peaceful slumber. Then traced her steps back into the living and sank into a lonesome chair in the corner, opening a box of cold pizza and nibbling on a slice.

An abrupt blare of a phone ring shattered the tranquility of the house. Maggie reached for it on the second ring. A sudden veil of alarm accompanied by deepening creases on her forehead delineated the nature of the dreaded phone call.

Maggie and Lena had taken a taxi to the hospital and hastened in a headlong gait through the atrium and into the elevators, reaching the hallway and finally the room with ceaseless thoughts of fearful expectations.

They turned into the room and found a crowd of nurses and doctors hovering around Jeff's bed while he lay restrained to the bed rails with an oxygen mask clouding his shrieks.

Jeff was relentlessly convulsing, hurtling up and down, struggling to attain the most common of necessities; breathing. He coughed and heaved, inflating and deflating his chest with utmost conflict as if a burden of the heaviest kind mounted upon him. His limbs shuddered and his neck strained in strangulation.

His mother and sister watched his suffering escalate which debilitated their strength. Tears streamed their faces as they stood defenseless witnessing the impending death that shall rattle them both to the core. They both embraced each other to garner courage to at least retain consciousness in this trying moment.

Jeff attempted to speak something. His lips quivered to form words with grave difficulty, but muffled behind the mask, and his eyes dead-set at his unnerved family.

Transfixed by the heinous view of death, Maggie couldn't react at first, but as she grew more observant of his floundering brother through the moving cluster, she stepped forward to listen intently.

Maggie cringed and inched closer, holding her hands together in supplication. "I cannot hear him! He's trying to say some thing!" She beseeched the medical professionals. "Let me hear him!"

The doctors were engaged in determining the right dosage to sedate him, and Maggie's entreaty was unheeded.

Lena emerged with a louder and more demanding voice. "Remove that mask just once, please."

It brought the room to a standstill.

"I'm begging you, please." Lena implored reaching out for her son. Both the women neared the bedrails, clasping Jeff's forearm delicately which placated his restiveness. Still, his throat protruded in aching distress.

The nurse removed the oxygen mask from Jeff's mouth.

Jeff battling the stifling encumbrance, managed to speak audible words. "Take me back. Take me home. Not here, please, not here." A teardrop slipped his eyes and marked his right temple.

"We cannot deprive him of oxygen. Please, step out of the room." The doctor ordered and gestured a nurse to lead them out.

The mask was replaced and the nurse took the whimpering women out of the harrowing enclosure.

# Chapter Thirty-Four

Jeff awakened to a feeble shaft of early daylight that penetrated the cleft between the draperies on the window and directly illumined his face. He sat up and watched the day unfold before his eyes. He staggered up to his feet upon his emaciated legs and approached to undo the drapes seeking aid down his path, leaning and pitching his body weight upon furniture, bracing his infant strides. He parted the drapes and revealed a bright morning and the everlasting oak tree beyond the view of the porch.

It was just another one of the days, since his return from New York two weeks ago, when he planned to have breakfast in bed, a movie in the living room by afternoon, an evening stroll and supper, in company of his parents and younger sister, who still persisted in her adamance to stay for a little while longer which in fact became a prolonged stay away from her husband and children.

Jeff had spent his day according to his unvarying schedule until the hours of late afternoon which brought a capricious consideration to his mind engendering an unwonted change in his routine.

He had managed a trip to his room with the help of his walking cane and prepared a banker's box with all of his manuscripts which he had retrieved from a luggage. The box was filled up to the brim and was topped with a copy of his unfinished manuscript that Erica had once read and raved. He placed the lid over the box and dragged it to the corner of the bed, pushing it underneath with his foot. But then remembering something, he reached for it again and removed the top manuscript from the pile and buried the rest in their place. He gazed at that bundle of papers and then glanced at the clock. It was nearing six and he waited.

After a while, he discerned a knock on the door and Erica entered giving him an extreme sense of satisfaction. It was customary for them both to spend an hour together out on the porch, since his return from New York, and relish each other's company before returning to their homes for supper. And so, in a moment of her arrival, Jeff found himself lounging on the same rocking chair and Erica took another in front of him and conversed about the peaks and valleys of the recently exhausted hours. But Erica surprisingly found Jeff to be scrabbling his coat for something he had concealed close to his heart all this time. He retrieved a manuscript and offered it to Erica.

"What is this?" Erica accepted it in perplexity at first then realized it was a work long forgotten by both. "Your first manuscript?"

"You wanted me to end it, didn't you? I have ended it." Jeff observed the quick changed of expressions of Erica's face as she flipped through the pages searching for its conclusion.

"I can't believe it."

"Do you remember where we left off?"

Erica lifted her eyes to meet his gaze. "I could never forget." Erica found the last couple of pages and read through them.

She excelled with a quick read excitedly. Then, her darting eyes slackened. Her countenance mellowed and she began reading out loud.

"To you I must forever return, no more the world I sought I seek, for love is the flame that yearns to burn, all else apart from love is weak. Your touch I remember, your tender embrace, your kiss, your laughs, could never erase. Ached I have, for such times are gone, you'd be in my arms, to the light of dawn. Restore the days of intimate blaze, the sun, the moon, the stars agaze. The frigid nights of cold we felt, the winds were strong, the snow would pelt. But in your arms of warm repose, all ice would melt, my strength compose. The warm of scorching summer afternoons, the breeze, the falls, the hidden lagoons. The morning rays caressed your face, the evening gold made your beauty unfold. Your eyes would glow at the full moon glimmer. The blistering sun and your skin would shimmer. Oh, so I regret the time I left, your touch of which my soul bereft. I curse the day I thought to depart, a bane, a blunder, it pierces my heart. In the wake of separation, my wisdom arose, was it not the path I took, not the road I chose? The truth arrived in its dark attire, a calamity at door in wait to transpire. But life appeared, in your thoughts I revered, and all my doubts, my fears were cleared. I ran back here from all I had gained, to you my love like a prisoner unchained. For I seek forgiveness and nothing in return, but you gave me it, and more in turn."

Erica's wiped her face with her sleeve and continued.

"Your grace unremitting and your beauty still breathless, you met me like a dream or rather life that's endless. Your hair in waves like knolls in the night, your eyes in a trance like mist in moonlight. A visage of a goddess who blushed like a rose, tears like drops of dew they wore like clothes. Delicate yet so strong, a woman complete, in forgiveness and love her spirit replete. It is you I shall cherish and want no more, the ways of love we together explore. In your hands I give my life that remain, you are my wealth and all my gain."

A long silence intervened between the two.

"He gives her this as an apology?" Erica finally spoke.

"He sort of doesn't have the words or heart to apologize himself."

"Oh, he has a lot of words." Erica chortled.

"Or rather the will." Jeff acceded to the truth.

Erica finished the last page of the manuscript. "And then they get married?!" she uttered wistfully

"And they lived happily ever after?" Jeff questioned his own reasoning.

"Yes, that's what you have written," Erica confirmed.

"How silly of me."

That expunged the sublime contentment off her face.

"Would you take me for a walk, Erica? Just down that way up until the dead-end?"

Erica nodded and swiftly tucked the manuscript away on the chair and helped the decrepit companion down the porch steps and onto the sidewalk.

Plodding to some distance, Jeff stopped and immersed himself in an arduous endeavor.

He went down on his one knee and proposed his right hand to Erica, with the other holding the cane.

"Would you, Erica Johnson, hold my hand and walk with me to the end of this road?"

Erica's eyes were soaked in tears and she accepted the proposal scrambling for words. "Yes, I will."

Jeff rose up to his feet with a torturous effort and smiled in return. She hungrily kissed him on the lips. Taking his hand, she led him on down the street, past her house and towards the dead-end.

At the end of the journey, they came across the crooked bench that had aged with time but yet persisted in its place. Jeff sat down upon it, serenely recollecting a familiar memory almost twenty-five years old, when he, in company of a long lost friend, had decided to take an evening stroll just before the day ended and its light vanished.

He caressed Erica's hand and began to speak.

"I love you, Erica. I have loved you since the moment I found out what love is. I know you have searched for these words out of me for years, and I couldn't be any dumber that I never said them out loud. Before, out of circumstance and now out of illness. But I reared these three words and the meaning attached to them inside of me, never allowing them to come out. And if I've ever loved someone truly, it's you. I'm not afraid to say it now, though, it might be too late. We have reached the end of our journey together. It doesn't go any further for you. You must turn back from here. But remember one thing, whenever you need me, find me in my words. In all the works I have written, if I have written of love, it's because of you. You taught me everything about it. You once asked how I started writing and I avoided that question back then, but I'll answer you now. That first manuscript, I wrote it to express my feelings for you. I couldn't say it directly, so I used my words as a disguise. I completed it hoping that our future might be just like its ending, happily ever after. I wrote it, so our love could grow as vast as theirs in the story. But in that aspect, I think we've outmatched them. If you ever feel that you miss me, all you need to do is turn a page, any page. I'll be somewhere close. This is the dead-end where we must part, but you have always been a dead-end for me. There was nothing beyond you. I hope you will forgive me for leaving you like this, but I tell you truly; if I could stay to live until eternity with just you by my side, I would. I love you."

Erica embraced him and wept irrepressibly on his shoulder.

"Erica, please. If you cry like that, where shall I find my strength?" Jeff caressed her hair but she was uncontrollable. "Want to race me to the falls?"

He received no answer.

"You really need to be disciplined, you know? A gentleman is trying to make a conversation with you and you haven't even a word to share?"

That brought a nostalgic laughter to her face and she chuckled through her sobs.

"There, that's what I like to see. Your beautiful smile." Jeff kissed her forehead.

"Knock, knock." Jeff tapped her forehead.

"Who's... who's there?" she sniveled.

"Can't you see, silly?"

"I haven't opened the door yet." Erica laughed through her tears.

"Oh, so that's how I was supposed to get back at you?"

"Yeah, you were too silly to figure that out."

"Oh god, how silly of me." Jeff took her face in his hands and searched her eyes for a moment, then spoke again. "Don't make me wait outside too long when I come knocking. I'm sure you'll open the door."

They returned home about fifteen minutes after, and Jeff found a delightful surprise right at the porch. Linda, James, and Nancy had arrived and they all rushed to him with torrents of greetings, hugs and questions about his health. Dave and Gloria had also arrived along with Edward and the children.

"What is going on here?" Jeff cheered jubilantly.

"It's the weekend. We all wanted to surprise you." Linda shared her ebullience.

"And guess what, we're not going anywhere until Sunday," Edward added.

"This is a surprise of a lifetime," Jeff rejoiced. "It's Christmas all over again."

They all took Jeff inside for a joyous celebration to start off the weekend.

That night the Saunderhurst home saw another one of those convivial gatherings around the dining which was quite reminiscent of Christmas Eve. The family rejoiced their reunion and credited Jeff for bringing them together once again while he simply sat and cherished the laughing faces of his loved ones.

Upon completion of the feast, he was assisted back to his room and tucked into his bed after some hugs and embraces from the visiting members and a wish to meet again in the morning.

Jeff adjusted himself with his back propped against the pillows under him. Maggie sat at the edge of the bed stroking his forehead, and Erica lingered in the shadows at the far end holding the bedpost.

"It's not there whatever you're looking for." Jeff teased, tipping his eyes with a smile.

"Yeah, what do you think I'm looking for?" Maggie rejoined softly.

"Temperature. Well, maybe a bit."

"Do you need any pill for fever?" Maggie inquired.

"Nah, I'm all right. It's been there permanently. Do you remember how grandpa used to tell temperature with just a single peck on your forehead? I mean right to the exact digits, even the decimal."

"Ancient people did have ancient gifts."

Jeff laughed then coughed running out of breath. He recovered from it quickly. "Come here, both of you." He extended his arm to hold Erica's hand.

She quickly came to the other side of the bed and clasped his hand.

"Promise me when I die--"

"Don't say that," both women protested.

"Listen, I need your word on it. When I die, you will bury me next to grandpa. Promise me," Jeff pleaded.

"Yes, I promise," Maggie assured him.

"There, now I can sleep in peace tonight."

"It's not fair you talking about such things at night," Maggie objected.

"We have yet so much to do," Erica added.

"Yes, you do, with or without me. I'm glad I've established just enough memories that may last a while in your thoughts. Who knows if I should venture this side of life ever again." He emitted a sullen sigh and kissed both their hands. "Good night. I'll see you the next morning."

They softly responded and gently went towards the door. Maggie stepped out first, but just before Erica could exit she heard a voice calling out her name.

"Yes?" Erica turned toward the bed and saw Jeff in a peculiar stillness inside his covers.

"Jeff? Did you say something?" she stepped inside the doorway. "Jeff?"

She rushed back into the room and Maggie followed. Erica felt his face as it had begun relinquishing its warmth of life. His breathing had halted.

"Maggie!" Erica screamed.

Maggie hastened to the bed and kneeling by his motionless body she held him by the arms and shook him trying to revive the defunct remains. It was to no avail.

"Mom... mom, dad." Maggie wailed summoning the house into the room. She slowly released him back onto his bed.

Erica staggered back into the corner of the room, stifling her cries that would otherwise be unbearable shrieks.

The family was stunned as tears began streaming down all faces. Nancy whimpered holding the bedposts while Linda and Lena approached to look. Both exploded with emotion and collapsed upon Jeff's corpse. The men stood back mourning. There was a burden of loss levied on each soul.

The chapter had ended and the book closed. Jeff had passed on.

# Chapter Thirty-Five

It was a bright, pleasant day in early May and Jeff's funeral was an event for which most of the town had summoned. The circle forming around his grave was vast and abundant with people. His casket rested in the center and Solomon stepped up to commence the burial ceremony.

He flipped through his Bible and attempted to read a verse, then gently closed it shut after a short, but unfathomed introspection.

"To grieve a loss, as if death were the end, is quite common amongst those who survive the departed. But if death brings itself to become a beginning, it is a welcome dawn. I will not speak out of the bible today. I will not serve you a sermon that I've instructed myself to employ in allaying the mourning family members and loved ones. Because it's not death we've gathered here to grieve, but a birth that we've come together to celebrate; the birth of a man's legacy that brings about a change in countless lives. This legacy has not bequeathed a material wealth upon us, but rather something that makes us all dreadfully rich. And I say dreadfully because something has to fear it such. The legacy of love. And if a handful of people decide to pass on that same legacy to the person next to them, it shall only multiply. Multiply to an abundance where no one is deprived of love and affection. Such a monumental amount of people possessing the power of love could prove to be dreadful for something. I surmise all of us here are aware of what that something is? Hatred, lies, envy, the sins of evil. We have turned to the Holy Scriptures to enlighten the path of righteousness many times in our lives, but this was a man whose righteousness enlightened our path to the Holy Scriptures. And that is a rarity."

Lena, emitting tears incessantly, was held on both sides by her daughters. Martin stood with the men of the family, and Erica anchored herself behind her father who sat in a wheelchair.

"I personally did not have the pleasure of meeting this man every Sunday at church or having him as a part of the congregation to visit and converse with every now and then. You might even seem to doubt my opinion of him due to the brevity of our acquaintance. But believe me when I say this, that transient period of time was all I needed to know him." Solomon cleared his throat. "I usually do not praise people for their monetary contributions to the church as it is against the word I have personally pledged. But now that he is gone I will break that promise once. I went to see Mr. Saunderhurst that night before Christmas and found him instead at the bookstore. I did not know the man at first, but after a pleasant conversation and the mention of a donation for the event, he simply reached into his pocket and without looking at how much he had extracted, he offered it to the church. I did not have the strength to count it even until the day that money was spent. I simply couldn't, because his deed was beyond numbers. And in his life throughout, such magnanimous works were pervasive. Whether they were for the benefit of his family or this town and its people, we have all profited from his deeds. I'm certain my fellow faithful would agree with me when I say that our businesses have thrived since the spectacle at the bookstore. We have suddenly found our place on the map. Great works of those who depart reap wondrous rewards for those left behind. Our reward is his legacy of love. Whether you live to be forty or a hundred, a life well remembered is a life well lived. Your kindness, your wisdom, your benevolence, may be passed on to others so they may do the same. Life is too precious to be denied, too vast to be selfish, make a memory out of it. Jeff Saunderhurst has given us a beginning, let us carry it forward."

Erica looked away wiping below her eyes.

"Let's not disappoint him." He took a deep sigh.

Following the prayers, people progressed in a single file to pay their final respects with a stick of gladiolus or a fistful of dust cast onto the casket. It took over fifteen minutes for the assemblage around the burial site to diminish and disperse and ultimately the last goodbye from the members of the family which was an excruciating sight to behold as there were seething emotions strewn when Lena stumbled in soft earth around the excavation and cried for her son. Lamenting women held on to their husbands and the men, equally unsettled, had no one to look up to.

Erica had done well throughout this ordeal to contain her tears and feelings by being inviolable to such tempest of emotions around her but rather helping the rest to attain composure and fortitude. But she held on to the last piece of Jeff's memory firmly in her arms against the warmth of her heart, his manuscript.

They shuffled back to their cars with each face bearing the burden of loss. Erica went through the arduous travail of boarding her father into her truck and then folding his wheelchair and loading it in the back.

"Our son is dead." Martin uttered the words of his aching heart that had long been kept hidden. He tarried along with Lena before entering the car.

"Father, please." Linda tried to alleviate his pain.

"I killed him, didn't I?" Martin incriminated himself.

Erica noticed this torrent of grief in Martin and gradually motioned toward them.

"Dad, what are you saying?" Maggie swiftly approached, taking him by the arms before he could inflict any more harm upon his senescent conscience.

"I had strangulated him with my stubbornness. He was dead a long time ago, just breathing. Even that didn't last too long for him."

"No one killed him, dad. He died of an illness." Maggie tried to reason with him.

"Illness was just a cover, the truth was different." Martin persisted in his supposition.

"He could never die, Mr. Saunderhurst." All eyes turned toward the origin of the words.

It was Erica's lips. "That's the thing about him. He could never die. There isn't a corner in your house that doesn't echo with his laughter, not a room that doesn't reek of him, not a person who doesn't remember. He lives in everything... and in here," she tapped the manuscript handing it to him. "He's alive in there. And as long as the last one of these survives out there anywhere, he'll be somewhere making someone laugh, making someone cry. You never read any of his works. Now is a good start to find him again."

So, the life of Jeff Saunderhurst had come to its end. Four months had passed since the departure of a well-beloved person from many lives, but as the law of nature requires all humans to yield, so did the Saunderhursts and Erica. Their lives went on.

Maggie had returned to Boston with her children while Edward had gone job hunting in the Big Apple, and it was just a week ago that Lena had received a call from her and splendid news of their relocation to New York in their new apartment.

With Maggie in New York, Dave found it feasible to have Charlie leave the town and initiate an education there which could possibly transmute into a profession. Gloria was thrilled at that consideration and thanked God, in his own presence, knowing that they would have no troubles executing that plan financially. But that was an eventuality far, far away.

Nancy had recently learned how to bake Christmas cakes with the help of her mother and plotted to feed the whole family with dessert come Christmas Eve.

Lena and Martin found themselves to be lonely at times, though, Dave and Gloria's frequent visits kept them busy with life. For the days that somehow deprived them of a company were assuaged by Erica who visited her neighbors regularly with a casserole and was invited cordially into the warmth of her second home. They shared their table as well as mentions of diurnal occurrences since last they had met through which Erica fulfilled her promise to Jeff of caring for both the houses and the old souls that lived in them. There was placidity in all their minds and hearts as their lips spoke, but most imperative of all, their eyes did not convey differently either.

Fall had descended all around Erica with traces of autumn air enveloping her in an early October haze and the trees had shaken off their green covers to adorn earth with abandoned gold. She would spend her weekends under the pleasant shadow of the oak tree in sunlit afternoons while waiting for winters to approach. There rested the box filled with Jeff's manuscripts beside her with its cover removed. She sat in tranquility reading from it with just chirping of birds up in the branches and a murmur of winds that sometimes caressed her face suddenly reminding her of an intimate touch she'd felt not too long ago.

"The day will come as ever before, the sun shall shine on field and shore. The night will streak the skies in black, and race the stars to moon and back. But that which would be gone forever, to bring them back is a lost endeavor. A mark is left and an empty space, those words, those smiles, and a warm embrace. Nothing is changed, the world's the same. But someone is lost, who was more than a name. In the rush of time, between living and wishing, look closely around, perhaps, I am missing." She read the words softly to herself.

She finished the last page of the manuscript and embraced it against her breast. Her eyes shimmered and her face beamed. She had found him in his words yet again. She collected the box and headed inside her home.

Entering the living room and reaching for the telephone, she dialed a number. After waiting for two rings someone picked up at the other end.

"Hello, Anne? This is Erica. Yes. I have a message for Angela. Tell her, I have another one ready. This will be even better than the last. Thanks, I will wait for her call. I know. All right... Jeff says hi," she laughed. "Bye."

Erica kept the receiver down and in her ecstasy, she almost sprang joyously. Then retained her sobriety and took a seat on the couch, waiting.

In that profound silence, she heard a knock on the door. She calmly went to answer. As she opened it ajar, she found no sign of a stranger or an acquaintance, for that matter, on the porch. A hallucination, perhaps?

She searched the whole frontage but failed to grasp a sight of any living soul.

Then a riveting thought pervaded her mind and she smiled contently upon remembering it. She stepped back inside the house and gently closed the door shut. That smile lingered on her lips.

Winter had withered the lush greens and shrouded the ends of the town with its rustling remains. The graveyard was a perfect venue to witness the views of post-autumn foliage and with the day being pleasant and sunny with soft random gusts, not all tombstones were buried under gilded leaves.

Erica made her way across passing graves and arid trees. She needed no guide to find what she sought.

She stopped near a tombstone and brushed away the rusted veil. She had brought a bunch of tulips and roses and held firmly on to them.

A moment of silence ensued, which brought a serene smile on her face. There was a tinge of grief somewhere in it, an intimation of despondency, but it was her inner peace that was reflected greatly.

She rested the flowers upon the headstone and tucked a note card right next to it making sure it doesn't drift away. She kissed the stone and slowly sauntered back down the uneven ground and finally onto a smooth surface of the paved path.

The card fluttered in a gust of wind and lay open, still pinned under the flowers. It read -- 'Until we meet again.'

Right next to Jeff's grave was an adjacent headstone with a name etched on it. It read Anthony Saunderhurst.

It was an end to Jeff Saunderhurst's existence in life, but his existence in death was bound to be eternal. Some things that we know of, like the skies of earth, without knowing when they came into being, without knowing when they shall die, never come to an end. Such things simply go on forever.

Love is a perfect example of that.

# Novels by Enosh S. Lazarus

www.ingramcontent.com/pod-product-compliance
Lightning Source LLC
Chambersburg PA
CBHW020243200626
46816CB00001BA/104

* 9 7 8 0 9 9 9 6 1 8 2 0 2 *